THE WANING

THE WANING

Age of Realignment I

Wunmi Aramiji

ISBN: 979-8-9904709-1-0 (Paperback)

ISBN: 979-8-9904709-2-7 (Hardcover)

ISBN: 979-8-9904709-0-3 (Ebook)

Library of Congress Control Number: 2024906691

First Printing: July 2024

Aramiji Publishing

Acknowledgements

T hank you to everyone who supported me throughout this process: my two amazing sisters, Kuse and Blessing, my friends, and the wonderful community of authors and writers in my six a.m. writing group.

A special thank you to Christian Giadolor, who held my feet to the fire and demanded that I finish writing and editing the book in front of you. I am so grateful for his love, support, and even his aggressive encouragement.

Last but not least, thank you to all of you who've dared to give my debut novel a chance. I hope this book becomes as special to you as it is for me.

Author's Note

While I was in the process of writing this book, I learned that I am a survivor of female genital mutilation. It was perhaps the most shocking thing I'd learned about myself up until then, but, in retrospect, it made perfect sense.

I grew up in an environment where being male was venerated. It meant that you were inherently valuable and that there was nothing—no misdeed, no crime, no transgression—that could lessen that value as long as you were not queer.

Being female and/or queer, on the other hand, was inherently offensive. It was now your obligation to placate people's disdain for your very being. You could hope to do so by being pleasant, obedient, and, most of all, by fitting into their narrow definition of "woman." Nothing else you could ever hope to be or do mattered. And if some harm should come to you, that was right, as it meant that you had failed to placate.

So really, considering the environment I was raised in, my FGM diagnosis should not have come as a surprise, and yet, I found myself trying to make sense of the diagnosis anyway. I transformed that understanding into the book you hold in your hand now.

Many of you might be surprised that, given my earlier characterization, women are highly regarded in traditional Yoruba culture. That is because I presented the dynamics of a family heavily influenced by Western colonial thought. Traditionally, the Yoruba Goddess Odùduwà birthed the entire universe. She is the sacred womb of all creation and her blessing to women is Àjẹ́. Àjẹ́ is both witch and witchcraft, and when pronounced slightly differently, wealth and prosperity. It is both creative and destructive. Àjẹ́ are secretive by their very nature, yet their powers, which rival those of the Gods, are necessary for maintaining the functioning of society.

The clitoris is seen as symbolic of Àjẹ́ and their powers. In Yoruba art, it's sometimes displayed prominently, a reference to its disproportionate power considering its small and hidden nature—much like the Àjẹ́.

So, what does it mean to rob a woman of her pleasure? Many indigenous cultures liken the Earth to a woman's body—Mother Earth. They know instinctively that violence against women is violence against the Earth itself. The hope of FGM is to control women by dimming their pleasure. And in some Yoruba communities specifically, FGM may be practiced to dim women's spiritual powers in addition to the aforementioned.

So, we violate the Earth with the goal of "taming" it, only to find that our actions backfire, leading to hostility in the form of extreme environmental backlash as the planet dies before our eyes. Then we violate women and queer people, only to find that we dim their inherent spiritual power and are paralyzed in our efforts to placate the increasingly angered Earth or, otherwise, heal it.

The Yoruba believe that the world is like a marketplace where ideas are traded and "fight" for dominance. The name Ile-Oja can roughly be translated to "land of markets." It's undeniable that in our modern era, Western colonial ideals have had an outsized impact on societies far and near. I take the power of literature seriously. I believe we have an obligation as storytellers and artists to shift the dominant cultural narratives that have led us to this point and will eventually lead to the destruction of our societies and planet if we do not counteract them.

In every piece I produce henceforth, that is my central aim.

Contents

1. Prologue   1

2. Chapter 1   3

3. Chapter 2   17

4. Chapter 3   37

5. Chapter 4   53

6. Chapter 5   71

7. Chapter 6   85

8. Chapter 7   99

9. Chapter 8   113

10. Chapter 9   123

11. Chapter 10   137

12. Chapter 11   153

13. Chapter 12   163

14. Chapter 13   179

15. Chapter 14   193

16. Chapter 15   205

17. Chapter 16   225

18. Chapter 17   239

19. Chapter 18   251

20. Chapter 19   259

21. Chapter 20   269

22. Chapter 21   283

23. Chapter 22   295

24. Chapter 23   315

25. Chapter 24   327

26. Chapter 25   339

27. Chapter 26   357

28. Chapter 27   359

29. Chapter 28   373

30. Chapter 29   391

31. Chapter 30   405

32. Epilogue   411

33. About the Author   413

Prologue

E very person in Ile-Oja knows the story.

In the beginning, there was nothing, and so it was until Rah shone his light upon the world. The Sun God created all things, but his most worthy creations were the titans, sixteen immortal beings that resembled their creator in every way. Rah and his creations lived in perfect harmony. They knew no suffering, they knew no hunger, and they knew no thirst. They needed and wanted for nothing, feeding only on the light of their god.

All things were as they should be until Adara, Goddess of Death and Chaos, descended from the heavens and destroyed the balance. Her touch infected the Earth, turning magma into stone and stone into soil. With her came a great flood, which saw barren land become sea. The infection spread to the very titans Rah cherished, transforming them into the first human beings. These ancestors were the first to drink her waters, they were the first to know suffering, and they were the first to understand death.

The Sun God wept when he saw this. He turned his back on the very beings he created, returning to the heavens and vowing never to walk the surface of the Earth again. Though Rah turned his back on his people, the people did not turn their back on Rah. They worshipped him, sacrificed in his name, and prayed for his return. Their prayers were in vain until that fateful day five hundred years ago.

The Goddess, Adara, wrought a new plague on the planet, possessing the weak of mind and spurring rebellion against the monarchs who had been so faithful to Rah. Rah descended from the heavens and, his touch saved the people. It cast Adara's poison out of their hearts and minds and siphoned it from the land. He bound her essence in the first of five women forever-more known as the Galed.

But the battle between the two gods scarred the planet. When Rah left the Earth once again, the land had already begun its transformation from rich, fertile forest to desert wasteland. The rain fell no more and the waters coalesced into a singular body. The peoples of the world had no choice but to migrate to be near it, unwittingly forming the last surviving kingdom in the world.

That is the beginning of Ile-Oja. At least, that is the history the scholars and monarchy want us to believe.

Chapter 1

We walked over ten thousand paces from the palace to the Midzone, watching as the densely vegetated lands and opulent villas gave way to sparse cacti and more humble dwellings. Occasions such as these require the Galed to honor the departed by keeping our feet on the ground regardless of the distance to our destination. It's a symbolic gesture to show our respect to those who've served the king tirelessly.

The sun sits low on the horizon. Its rays cast a faint orange glow on the sand-brick houses dotting the path to the commissioner's house. In the Midzone, the buildings tower perpetually higher and higher, and the buildings seem to draw closer to each other. The design is meant to maximize space and give the people below some reprieve from the desert heat.

The Midzoners of Ile-Oja meander about on either side of us. We hear the sounds of chattering women bartering in the marketplace, the cry of playing children, and the bolstering of pompous men who rant about this or that. As we get closer to the people, the commotion fades. The children stop in their tracks, the men grow quiet, and the women avert their gaze.

At the time of Rah's second ascension, they used to say of the Galed: winds, and laughter follow them—a euphemism describing those the people thought insane. In reality, we leave nothing but a trail of weary quiet behind us.

Our sandals clack in unison as we walk towards our destination, as if we've taken special care to rehearse the timing of our footsteps. The hamel leather wicks the moisture off our feet, and the flap at the heel of our shoes claps to scare off the scorpions hiding in the desert sand.

Annabeth walks in the middle of our pack, slightly in front of everyone else. Her cowrie shell headdress sits atop her crimson veil. It's intricately woven, forming triangles near her crown before swooping down in front of her face. The headdress and veil cover Annabeth's face completely. Both flow to the floor, leaving a trail as they sweep the sand behind her. Annabeth is our mysterious mother. The one who rises at dawn and returns under the cloak of midnight. Her whereabouts remain hidden even from the rest of the Galed but I get the sense that her quests are both grand and devastating. She's already survived the Waning twice, making her the most experience and our high priestess, the rightful leader of our group.

Iyanu and Torrin follow behind Annabeth, one to her left and the other to her right. Sade and I trail behind them.

4

The palace guards surround us on either side, sitting atop their hamels. They are clothed in dark leather from head to toe, donning black masks that hide their faces except for the small slits at their eyes.

The moon is just starting to show itself by the time we reach the commissioner's house. The piers at the top of the capitol jot out from some distance behind the humble dwelling.

There was a time when the capitol was not *sunken*. It once sat right on the shores of Lake Sarran. It's hard to imagine that the lake ever spread so far, but the capitol building and the records it holds are proof that it did. The capitol collapsed about a hundred years after Rah's second ascension. As the water in the lake evaporated, the vegetation that made up its foundation withered to sand, leaving the building to crumble. Sarran has only sped up its retreat since then. Nothing can be done about the lake and the water it provides. It will vanish, and we will vanish with it.

The commissioner's house is not much bigger than four servant quarters at the palace, but unlike the rest of the tall, lanky buildings in the Midzone, which house families one atop the other, the commissioner's house stands on its own, a feat only the wealthiest Midzone families can boast of. The house is decorated with spiral arches and flowers carved into the lowest layers of its sand-brick exterior. Glass holders adorned with glass flowers are affixed on either side of the palm wood door. The palm wood must be courtesy of King Ryland.

5

The palace guards take their positions, lining up on either side of the door. Annabeth slides her left hand across her right forearm, bunching her sleeve into the fold of her elbow. She reaches one slender hand towards the door and knocks gently. Her blue veins are purple in this lighting. They branch out and press against the pale skin of her forearm like the roots of the ever palms pressing down through the earth. She knocks once again, more faintly than the first time. The door glides open before the sound tapers out.

The woman standing at the doorway looks like a ghost of one past. Her short, amber hair hangs limp by her cheek. Her lips are chalky and peeling, more likely a sign of grief than a lack of water. While the Endzoners of Ile-Oja often die of thirst, Midzoners rarely suffer the same fate, and indeed, the commissioner and his family could never want for water.

"It smells delicious in here," Sade says pleasantly. The savory scent of cactus pecker fowl emanates from the sun oven in the kitchen. Sade turns towards our host expectantly.

"Jordan," the woman says, "pleasure to make your acquaintances, Your... Holinesses." Her words come out clinched and forced, but her smooth, melodic voice mellows out any of the hostility that might have been contained within them.

Sade snickers. "Holinesses..." She brings the tip of her index finger to her cheek. "That's a new one," she says. "I like the sound of it."

6

Jordan leads us towards the back of the house and into the commissioner's bedroom. Annabeth removes her headpiece and veil, revealing the red gown she wears beneath them. She drapes them over the edge of the bed frame neatly. Our veils and headpieces follow on top of hers. All of them are identical to Annabeth's except our veils and gowns are bright white.

Annabeth takes her seat at the edge of the bed, beside the commissioner. His cheek is pressed against the bed, his mouth agape, and his body still. His skin is riddled with deep wrinkles but taut against his cheekbones. His unblinking eyes bulge as if they were in the process of falling out of his eye sockets. Part of the bed is damp with saliva where his mouth hovers. Annabeth lifts his head gently and places it on her lap. Jordan, who has kept her gaze fixed on the floor until now, glances at the commissioner and gasps when she makes eye contact with Annabeth. The blue of Annabeth's veins doesn't end beneath her skin. They snake out and envelop her eyeballs, stopping right before they meet her iris.

Annabeth laughs a ringing cackle that would give most children nightmares. "What, girl? You've never seen eyes like mine," she asks.

This is not the first time someone has remarked on the strangeness of Annabeth's eyes, and by now, she's learned to get some pleasure from the reactions her looks garner.

Jordan fixes her gaze downward again. Her hands tremble by her sides. "Witch..." she mutters under her breath.

Sade smirks. "That's more like it."

In truth, Annabeth is nothing to be afraid of. That honor belongs squarely to Sade.

Torrin, Iyanu, Sade, and I sit on the mat at the foot of the bed.

"We're deeply sorry for your loss," says Torrin, aiming to elevate the mood. "But we're here now to make your father's transition as peaceful as possible."

Her voice feels like silk against my eardrums. Torrin has always been like that. Every word she speaks, every action she takes seems like it was designed to put you at ease.

Annabeth presses her thumbs against the commissioner's forehead and rests her palms against his cheeks. Jordan's right arm jerks suddenly. Her discomfort permeates the air. The others feel only pity, but I know something isn't right. It can't be easy for her to watch her father's death, and while we've been sent here as an honor to her father, our presence certainly doesn't make it easier.

"You seem really nervous," I start, but before I can continue, Annabeth begins the ritual.

Guide this soul with your calming winds

Our bodies go slack. Heat rises from the earth into the soles of our feet before settling in our chests. The death ritual feels like a mother's embrace. We are all trapped in it. Tears blur my eyesight, but I can make out Jordan's figure moving in the shadows. My brain refuses to hold on to any thoughts. My fears and anger fade until I am nothing but warmth.

So he may be as effortless as the breeze
Blessed are those who sing your na—

Annabeth shrieks while our necks erupt in agony. The walls of our throats feel like they're closing in. We try to exhale, but something thick and ferrous travels up our windpipe. We manage to let out one word.

"Choke." We hear something drop to the floor.

The world feels too cold, and our skin feels too clammy. We are afraid, and we are confused. Annabeth releases her hold on us. My posture straightens as a shock runs up my spine. Suddenly, every bit of our skin is hypersensitive, and we are painfully aware of how our gowns rub against us. The insides of our foreheads feel like they're on fire. The feeling can only be described as a mixing of our spirits and our feelings. Only Annabeth can make this happen. It's a consequence of her pulling the part of Adara within us out, so she can use it for her own means.

When I come to, I can tell Torrin is screaming; she's squeezing her head between her hands, her eyes squinted, and her mouth opened wider than I've ever seen. All I can hear is a high-pitched ringing in my ears.

Annabeth lies dead atop the bed. Her body is slumped over the commissioner, and a bone knife sticks out of her neck. Her blood drips across the commissioner's torso, dyeing the white bedsheets red. Stained like that, the bedsheets seem like an extension of her crimson veil, one blending into the other. Jordan lies motionlessly with her cheek pressed against the floor by Annabeth's feet. She's not outwardly wounded, but a trail of blood drips out from her mouth onto the floor, and her eyes stay open in some twisted mimicry of her father's. Suddenly, Torrin's screams become loud and painfully clear, piercing my eardrum.

"Annabeth," I say. I can barely raise my voice above a whisper. My throat burns with the threat of tears. Torrin rushes over to Annabeth's side. She grabs her forearms and shakes her violently, but Annabeth's body remains limp. Torrin pushes Annabeth back towards the bed in horror when she doesn't respond. Annabeth's skin starts to turn blue where Torrin's grabbed her. Torrin manages to look even more horrified, sending a sharp pang to my chest.

She stares down at the bruise her touch has left and hiccups. "I didn't mean to," she says, looking at the corpse on the ground.

"Torrin, she's dead!" Sade screams. Then, sighing, she adds, "She can't hear you."

Iyanu hasn't moved an inch from where she's standing. Her face is expressionless, her form motionless, until the guards come rushing in. The sudden action jolts Iyanu out of her state of shock and sends her rushing towards Torrin.

The captain, Braun, makes a scene of kicking the door in, even though it's unlocked. A middle-aged man with speckles of gray in his trimmed beard, a shining head, and stomach folds above his waist, Braun was promoted to captain shortly after the last Waning.

"What in Rah's name is going on here?" he says. He surveys the room before bleating, "Fucking hell!"

Iyanu clenches her hands into fists before releasing them. She does it again. And then once more. Torrin doesn't even look up to acknowledge the guards pouring into the room. Her gaze remains fixed on Annabeth's corpse.

"I was just trying to help her. I didn't mean to hurt her more." Torrin covers her eyes with her hands.

Annabeth is dead. How is the most powerful woman I've ever known dead at the hands of a girl holding nothing but a bird bone in her hand? Fuck. Something catches in my throat, but I refuse to let the tears building in my eyelids spill down my face. Keep it together, Meera. Annabeth would expect more. My people would expect more.

Braun grows nervous at the silence, his eyelids twitching as he meets my gaze. I want to explain what happened, but I struggle to understand it. Still, I speak in hopes that Braun doesn't take Torrin's last statement as an admission of guilt.

"The commissioner's daughter..." I turn to glance at Jordan, but staring into her stale, stagnant eyes turns my stomach. This is the first time I've killed. It's the first time *we've* killed. Jordan's death stirs up the exact opposite of the emotions that Annabeth's brings. I tamp down the euphoria threatening to reveal itself in my voice. Two years. It's been two years since the last

Waning that saw Iyanu, Sade, Torrin, and I become Galed. In all that time, this is only the second time I've truly felt deadly.

"She stabbed Annabeth in the middle of the blessing. Then she died," I tell Braun. I don't mention that we asked her to choke, nor do I mention that in her last moments, Annabeth used us to kill the girl who killed her. *How did she do it? What would it take to do the same to the man who sits on the throne?*

A guard steps up beside Braun and puts his hand over his shoulder. "King Ryland won't let this go unpunished," he says matter-of-factly. "If I were you, I'd be going home to spend my last moments with my family."

"Don't be daft. They're just pets," Braun says plainly. "He'll get over it."

"How could you say that?" Torrin's voice drops an octave.

Braun sneers at her, but he retreats instinctively.

"How could you say that?" Torrin asks again.

The entire room shakes. Annabeth slides off of the bed and onto the floor. Braun and his guards pull out their swords.

"Torrin, please," says Iyanu. "You need to calm down,"

But the house refuses to stop shaking. Glass flowers affixed outside the doors and windows come tumbling down with a smash. Adara's power is multiplied in each of us now that we are four. Annabeth isn't here to funnel or channel it.

Iyanu walks towards Torrin with her hands in the air, signaling to the guards that she is no threat. She pulls Torrin up from the bed and spins her around so that Torrin's back presses up against her chest. Iyanu hugs Torrin from behind and rests her chin on Torrin's head before whispering something in her ear. I don't miss the way her lips graze Torrin's ear when she pulls away. I start to walk towards them, but I stop myself at the sight of Bruan's quivering eyes. I silently will his heart to explode, thrusting myself into the state we fall into when Annabeth pulls from each of us. But, Braun remains standing, and while I can feel Torrin's heartbreak and Iyanu's tumult, I know the connection goes one way only.

"You two," he says, pointing toward me and Sade. "Go join your friends over there."

The other guards' swords remain drawn as they circle the room's perimeter. They lead us out the door, beckoning us to mount the hamels. One of the guards appears with Annabeth's corpse, which is wrapped in the bedsheets she died on. They throw her over Braun's lap after he mounts his hamel. The commissioner's daughter is left uncovered and made to ride on the hamel of another guard. The rest of the guards maneuver their hamels around us as we return to the palace grounds.

The moon is high in the sky now, and the golden rays of dusk have transformed into the silvery beams of night. Faces dart behind the windows of the houses near us. The neighbors attach their sun blockers to their windows all at once despite there being no sun in the sky. People have been crucified for lesser crimes than witnessing official palace business without invitation.

13

Annabeth's body bounces without resistance as Braun's hamel prods along. Torrin rides in front of me and a little to my left. I can tell she hasn't stopped crying since we left the commissioner's house because of the way her shoulders bounce periodically. Iyanu is as still as a statue. Sade, the only Galed whose face I see, stares into the distance. Her body is here, but her mind is thousands of paces away. Braun leads us, riding his hamel in front of Iyanu and Torrin. I know that Braun has not purposefully put his hamel in this position to honor Annabeth, so I wonder if Adara's will bends him into doing so.

As we walk the path towards the palace, Endzoners crop up one by one in the distance. They've begun their ten-mile journey back to the Endzone. Their clothes hang tattered across their shoulders. Adults and children alike walk barefoot across the desert sand. Even those at the innermost levels of the End-zone can't afford shoes. The thought brings my attention to my sandals, which slide against the smooth skin of my soles. All of the calluses I once had are long gone. I've been in the palace too long, and I have nothing to show for it. At least the sands have cooled enough by now to not scorch their feet. But the comforting chill of the early dessert night will give way to a biting cold in just a few short hours. Those Endzoners who are caught in the tundra will endure a different form of suffering.

Soon, my entire field of view is flooded with their forms.

"Swimming through a sea of rats," Braun spits to his left. His saliva hits a man right in the middle of his cheek. The Endzone man fixes his gaze forward, not bothering to wipe the fluid from his face. One man leaves a trail of milky red with each step he takes. Even in the dark, I can see that his feet and ankles are swollen, leaking blood and water from the center of each swelling. The man collapses just five paces in front of the guards near the front.

"Get up," one of them says without so much as an inflection in his voice. "Have it your way," he continues when the man remains sprawled on the floor.

I brace myself to hear the piercing screams the man will make as the hooves of a thousand-pound hamel come crashing down on his body, but all I hear is the whisper of parting sand as the man's body is dragged away. Between the hamels and the bodies of the guards, I make out a sharp Black face, pulling the man away. His skin is so dark that it appears like a void against the backdrop of the night sky. His buzzed hair shines a metallic bronze under the moonlight. He's tall for someone from the Endzone, maybe even as tall as five-ten. That's as tall as any Endzoner I've ever seen.

"Endzone maggots," Braun hisses. "What horrors they must have committed against Rah to be a part of that lot." Rah, the supreme god, delivers absolute justice. Everyone deserves their lot.

"You're going to be joining their rank soon enough with this latest fuck up." The guard who cautioned Braun before taunts him again.

"Shut it, Nicholas," Braun counters.

Sade snickers audibly, earning a sharp stare from me.

"You got something to say?" Braun reigns his hamel to the side to stop the troop.

Sade stops laughing, but she keeps the smirk on her face, baring her teeth. Torrin, Iyanu, and I continue looking forward. Men like Braun are more likely to act out when they feel like there's an audience for them to entertain.

"I'd close those pretty lips if I were you. You wouldn't want something going between them now, would you?" Braun says, his voice slick as oil.

"Don't make this worse than it already is, Braun," says Nicholas. "You know they're all as good as dead anyways," he continues. "Already the second Waning of Ryland's reign," he says with a shake of his head. He turns to look at Sade. "I wonder which of the four will survive."

Chapter 2

The maids meander through the palace gardens, throwing buckets of water over fields of lush flowers that spread as far as the eye can see. I watch as they walk the garden paths one by one, each person working with purpose and efficiency, executing their tasks as one small part of a larger hive mind. The gardens are organized in plots of hexagons and six-sided stars as an homage to the sun god. The motif is seen throughout the palace grounds and in the homes of the nobility. Even well-to-do Midzoners decorate their homes with intricate displays of complex geometric patterning, blending and weaving together. Many of the plots are filled with laverers, plants so demanding of water that they are now found nowhere else in Ile-Oja besides the palace grounds. Yellow Solitites, green Marshas, and white Cardows glow in the light of the morning sun. There are probably over a hundred types here. Most have never been seen by those outside of the fertile halo the nobility live in.

On the other side of the palace, out of view, is a field of dense vegetation. Beyond them, a sand-brick wall rising higher than any Midzone dwelling separates the land belonging to the king and nobility from that which the Midzoners are allowed to inhabit.

Though my bedroom window is one of many on the palace grounds that oversees the gardens, I count myself lucky to have such a view. Just two years ago, all I had was a small pit dug into the ground by my father's hands. Sleeping pits, they're called. Makeshift structures that could collapse at any time should the sands composing their walls shift with the wind. Too many Endzoners have been buried alive in those things, never to see the light of day again. I wept the first time I saw my room in the palace, with its small bed, desk, and chair. I wept, and I swore vengeance all in the same breath.

My father once told me that the palace was moved in his grandfather's time, only about a hundred years ago. Already, its walls sit relatively far from the retreating lake. Yet the gardens thrive, thanks to the servants who siphon water away from the lake in buckets and trek back to the gardens.

The king has summoned us to his throne room, but I find myself glued to my windowsill. Before the Oguni go on a mission, the warriors still themselves on the way to their destination, so I do the same for the battle I know is ahead. If I sit here for long enough, the stillness will take hold of me, and my body will become part of the stone or dissipate into the air surrounding it. The Oguni say that one who's mastered stillness could fool even Rah, convincing him that they were something immaterial, an observer that neither acts nor is acted upon. But the hour I've spent sitting here does nothing to comfort me, and I doubt Rah is so easily fooled. The knowledge that Annabeth's body lies on the altar at the center of the rotunda that joins my room with Iyanu's, Torrin's, and Sade's keeps my body rigid and my mind present. I imagine her pale skin turning gray and then blue as it decays in the space next door.

I know that the king will want an audience, I know that I should get moving, but my body wants no part of the directives my brain gives it. I imagine dying by the king's hand even though I know that he will do no such thing.

A swift beheading. It'll be over before I even know what's happening. The Waning, however, will be a slow, long death, but if I survive it, Sade, Torrin, and Iyanu surely will not. It will be my life or my sisters', and I intend to stay alive. But, if I should die, I need to see Ryland killed before it's all said and done.

Sade bursts through the door as I pull my gown over my body.

"Meera, hurry up," she whines. "You're going to make us late."

It's hard to imagine that she's nineteen, not nine, when she talks like that. She walks up to me and throws her hands over my shoulders. At five-five, we stand eye to eye, but Sade has bigger bones, which gives her a sturdier frame. Her hair is cropped close to her head, but it twists in neat, tight curls around her ears and the upper part of her forehead. Her black, almond-shaped eyes brighten her dark olive skin. All of her features seem crafted for the sole purpose of complementing one another.

"I'm almost done," I say.

My voice comes out like sandpaper rubbing against my vocal cords, even though I didn't make much of a sound as I cried through the night. I know that swollen eyes remain where my tears have gone and that even with the deep mahogany of my skin, the pinkish tint of swollen red blood vessels shows through my eye sockets.

If someone had seen me cry, they would have thought I was mad. The silent sobs that overtook me were cut through by traces of laughter. The bitterness of Annabeth's death made sickly sweet by the knowledge that I might complete my mission. When I return to the Oguni, they'll look at me as the savior who rid them of Ryland, and the monarchy by extension. I imagine my father's face. Stern, aged, betraying nothing in the ways of his thoughts. He won't show it, but I know that for the first time in my life, he'll be proud to call me his daughter.

"You look like shit, by the way," Sade jokes.

I swallow the lump in my throat before continuing. "I'll take that over whatever it is you look like," I counter.

Sade's eyes widen in mock offense before laughing the insult off. In truth, Sade looks great, like she didn't even turn once in her sleep, let alone have a sleepless night.

"Come on, let's get going," she says with a wave of her hand.

She doesn't bother to close the door as she leaves the room, and I wait a few moments before following her into the rotunda. Iyanu and Torrin emerge from their rooms on the northeast and northwest, respectively. I know that Torrin must have had a restless night, but she stands just as perfect and full of grace as ever. She holds two buckets of water, one for each hand. Her skin is the color of the moon, and the reddish tint on her cheeks is natural but could easily be mistaken for Redula powder. Torrin is twenty-three, one year older than Iyanu and me. She's the oldest among us now.

Iyanu stands a full head taller than Torrin, who is barely five-one. At five-eight, Iyanu is average height for a woman of noble birth. Her jaw is sharp, but the rest of her is all curves. Curvy nose, hips, breasts, and a slight bend at the stomach. Her curves are welcome among the nobles. Their kind view gauntness with distaste. It's rare for women from good families to go through the Waning, and it's rarer still for them to survive to become Galed. It was Iyanu who forced her father to volunteer her. She said Adara had come to her the afternoon when Roan, the woman who led the Galed before Annabeth, died. At that moment, she knew she would be devoted to serving the Goddess. No one except Iyanu knows whether this is true, but what an embarrassment it was for her family to have a daughter serve Adara when they trace their lineage back to Rah.

"Good morning, everyone," Sade chirps.

21

"Good morning again," Torrin says softly with a faint smile on her lips.

No one so much as glances at Annabeth's body, which lies covered in blood-stained sheets on the lazurite altar at the center of the room. Torrin's gaze points markedly away from it, while Iyanu's traces the jagged edges of the stone. Somehow, everyone knows precisely when to stop before their eyes land on the body lying in the crater at the top of the rock.

I've always loved that stone. The way its transparent dark edges gave way to sparkling blue specs reminds me of stars floating in our galaxy. Annabeth spent almost all of her waking hours working on it. Before it held Annabeth's body, the carved surface at the top of the rock was used to grind herbs, make ointments, and prepare medicines for the nobles. A bowl of palm nuts and cowrie shells sits on its surface. The nuts come from the palm trees found scattered across palace grounds and noble estates. The shells are mysterious things. They're buried all over Ile-Oma, surfacing whenever they see fit. Annabeth said that the shells came from living, breathing animals who made them for protection. If such an animal ever existed, it exists no more. The servants could just as easily prepare most of Annabeth's recipes with some instruction, but the plants used by the Galed withered in the hands of lay, and when they didn't, the medicines others made turned to poisons. There will be no medicine-making until a new leader is chosen. Though we are Galed, the rest of us have no talent for animating the flora, and we won't until one of us starts the transformation that marks us as next to lead.

The lazurite altar is an island separated from the rest of the rotunda by a circular trail of water, which fills a ring-like depression in the floor. There are no windows in the space, and the five doors that lead to each of our rooms are the only way to get into or out of it. The semi-sheer glass that covers the opening in the ceiling is the only way light gets through. It's deliberately placed to protect the low-light plants, which extend their stems and leaves past their pots, leaving no corner of the rotunda uncovered. When the moon is angled just right, light bounces off the lazulite altar for a precious few minutes, bathing the rotunda in an eerie blue light.

The only real piece of furniture in the rotunda is a canapé carved out of palm tree bark and padded with parchment leather cushions stuffed with fowl feathers. This, too, is entirely covered by the dark, leafy, meandering plants, which are so unlike their counterparts in the garden. Red, orange, blue, and yellow agate sitting stones dot the rotunda in no particular pattern. The stones are too heavy to move frequently, and in the two years I've been Galed, I've never seen anyone attempt to.

Torrin waters each plant.

"We'll leave as soon as I'm done," she says to no one in particular.

Torrin waters the plants that need it every morning, but I still get the sense that she is delaying the inevitable.

Iyanu breathes out a sigh of exhaustion. "How are you, Meera, and you, Sade?" She hesitates before meeting our eyes.

Maybe it's the way that Iyanu's voice cracks at the end. Whatever it is, it breaks something in me that I didn't know was capable of breaking. A sigh, more like a croak, leaves my lips as tears stream down my face. My breath feels hot as it leaves my mouth. It gets harder and harder to breathe, and I take each breath faster than the last.

Torrin stops watering the plants and straightens her form. She sets the bucket beside her and wipes her hands against her thighs before bringing them to her eyes. Torrin's cries are everything she's not. Loud, violent, and somewhat hysterical. Iyanu joins us in a silent cry of her own. The floor trembles with each hiccup Torrin makes, and the knives, bones, herbs, and minerals set on the altar beside Annabeth fall to the ground with a clatter.

"It's okay. It's going to be okay." Iyanu's voice is steady even as tears stream down her face.

"She shouldn't have died like that," Torrin says. "She deserved better."

"I just don't understand how she didn't see it coming," I add. "She would've known something like that was coming, right?"

"What if..." Torrin begins.

Sade cuts in. "We need to get going soon," Sade says matter-of-factly, moving to exit the rotunda through her room.

24

"Can't you even pretend to care?" I snipe. I regret the words as soon as they leave my mouth.

"I do care," she responds, meeting my gaze. "From here on out, we're on a countdown. Three of us will die in three months. I need to be in control of my emotions. I can't let them control me if I hope to have any chance of surviving."

Sade swallows a lump in her throat. "Let's get going then," she says when no one responds.

<hr />

The morning sun shines through the windows, illuminating the corridors as we walk down the smoothed stone path. Glass bouquets on either side of the passages shine hues of gold, silver, purple, and turquoise all at once. They send orbs of light all over, illuminating certain parts of the corridor more than others. Though the light shines through the thin glass, the sun's heat is absent. This is one of the few things King Ryland touts as an achievement of his reign. Thanks to the glass mixture commissioned by the king and pioneered by his scholars, palace residents can now enjoy the sunlight without the resulting heat.

The sun God is a God of logic, productivity, and advancement. The making of inventions cements the king's status as a ruler blessed by his essence. Of course, the king's mandate is strengthened only by his ability to innovate, not his willingness to apply those innovations to those who need them the most.

We are the first to arrive at the throne room, a balcony that juts out from the palace interior, covered by a quartz ceiling held in place by four quartz pillars at each corner. The king's throne, made solely of gold, sits in the middle of the room alongside a smaller throne made in its likeness but decorated with intricately placed gemstones. The balcony overlooks the estates to the left and right of the palace and the shore of Lake Sarran in the distance. It is rumored that directly beneath the balcony lies a sea of bodies fallen by Ryland's hands.

We take our places, kneeling in a line a few feet in front of the throne with our heads bowed, awaiting the king's arrival.

The palace poet arrives first. His skin creases into modest folds, and his bald head shimmers in the afternoon sun. He begins his recitation.

Rah, the primordial flame
Whose light was not started and can never be extinguished
Rah, the insatiable dragon
that devours all but hungers not
We bathe in your divine light
Rah, the life bringer
Whose seed is mightier than the desert storm
We worship at your children's feet
Lead us to our salvation

Two guards follow behind him. The first is a pale man with red freckles dotting his cheeks. Nicholas. His hair looks like he didn't bother to comb it. The second is Braun. They position themselves in front of us, one on either side of the two thrones in the center of the room.

King Ryland is the next to enter. At six-four, he's the tallest man I've ever seen. Possibly the tallest man in the whole of Ile-Oja. His frame is wide and sturdy. He seems to exude power from his very being. His beard is neatly trimmed and shaped, with gray flecks sprinkled in with his brown hairs. The gray hairs serve to highlight the gray of his eyes. He's inherited the honeyed complexion of his mother and his aunt, the duchess Reina, but not their freckles.

All the members of his family are dead. Their Majesties Grace and Floris Barracus had only one son, and upon their passing a decade ago, King Ryland inherited the throne with no challengers. Now, at forty, he, too, is without an heir.

I wonder what it must feel like to be blessed by the God that created the heavens and the earth, the God whose tears fall as gold drops, the God whose Voice splits mountains, a Voice you now possess, and yet, be unable to bear children. Of course, the king has never admitted to being impotent. Instead, his lack of heirs is blamed on Queen Antares, whose status has been so demoted that she has not been seen in official palace proceedings for over a year.

The first and only time I've ever seen her was at the last Waning ceremony. She wore a gold chain link gown over a red silk tunic, which dragged on the floor behind her. Like Ryland, freckles dotted her face, their deep brown color popping against

27

her tawny complexion. Her curls fell wildly atop her head, yet she managed to secure them with a simple diamond-encrusted golden tiara that fanned out above her head like the rays of the sun. She used a diamond-encrusted wooden cane to maintain her balance, though some say she never needed it.

Everyone knows Antares is not to blame for the king's lack of heirs. A truly desperate king will sire bastards if needed.

Ryland walks to the center of his throne. His eyes linger briefly at the empty one next to him before turning his attention to Braun.

"Who is this?" Ryland asks, pointing at Nicholas.

Nicholas answers for himself. "Nicholas, your Highness. Newly promoted to second rank." He answers.

"Very well," Ryland gestures towards the door.

Braun leaves briefly before returning, dragging an elderly man behind him. The man's face is hollow, his clothes are tattered, and fluid-filled blisters dot the skin of his forearms. His dry lips are cracked and oozing blood in several places, yet he still manages to draw them into a defiant smirk.

Braun throws the man to the ground, his body landing before the king's feet.

"Your Majesty," Braun says.

"This is the one," the king asks.

"Yes, sir."

"Read the charges."

"Of course, sir." Braun begins. "Here kneels Taron Rellor, accused of conspiracy to undermine the monarchy. On the evening of the forty-eighth day of the season of the moon, Terrell was captured during a standard raid of the cactus flower inn, a known hideout location for the Ogun resistance. After searching his body, my guards found a letter detailing the resistance's plans to topple the monarchy. The first step of the plan was to dispatch the women of the Galed in an attempt to release Adara's spirit. We believe that Terrel and the Ogun resistance are responsible for the death of Annabeth Wura at the hands of one Jordan Coure. The threads of betrayal run deep, Your Majesty. We believe that even the commissioner's daughter was one of them. No one can be trusted," Braun finishes.

The king remains stoic even after Braun's remarks. If there were ever a man whose thoughts were unknowable, it is this one.

The prisoner frowns but says nothing to dispute the allegations. He raises his head, staring the king down before Braun promptly shoves his head back down. The prisoner spits, missing Ryland's shoes by mere inches. Braun raises a heavy boot to the man's abdomen. The impact sends the man flying, heaving, and coughing when he lands on the ground.

"Braun," the king says.

"Yes, Your Majesty," Braun answers.

"You may proceed," he says.

Braun draws his sword, and in one fell swoop, his sword comes crashing down between the prisoner's head and shoulders. The head bounces awkwardly when it hits the ground, skittering across the floor before it rolls on its back, facing straight up. Braun takes the head and tosses it. It flies between the pillars and falls several hundred feet towards the ground. The sound of it hitting the ground never comes.

Iyanu's eyes harden for a brief second before her face goes back to being neutral. We've seen this happen too many times before. As king, Ryland owns all the wealth of the land, including the lives of his people. Everything is his to do as he pleases with.

"It is because of your kind that Rah turns his back on his people." The king turns to stare at Sade and me.

"After all I've done. All I continue to do. All Rah continues to do for you people. Perhaps Adara's madness spreads once more," the king says disappointedly. He tilts his head to the left and rests it on his palms. He breathes out an exaggerated sigh. "Who all knows about this?" he asks.

"No one, sir. Just those in this room, along with the guards on the raid," Braun says.

"Keep it that way," says Ryland. He turns his head to Nicholas before adding, "Nicholas is it?"

"Yes, Your Majesty," Nicholas responds.

"He makes a good second, doesn't he?" the king asks Braun.

"Yes, sir. I couldn't have asked for better. I've taught him all the intricacies of combat, leadership, and servitude to Your Majesty. I'm proud to call him one of my own."

King Ryland rises from his seat and stands by Braun's side. He puts one bulky arm over Braun's shoulder, making Braun buckle at his knees. Standing next to the hulking man, Braun looks like a small child.

"Tell me, Braun," the king continues, "how is it again that Annabeth died under your care?" Braun remains silent. The king tsks, shaking his head from left to right. "Under your command, my enemies grow stronger while my kingdom grows weaker."

"Your Majesty, we thought the commissioner was a faithful servant. You told us yourself. We stood outside, as is customary when honoring those who've served beside you all their lives. There was no way for us to know that he was part of the Ogun resistance. Your Highness, my guards and I will spend every second of every day weeding out any mole hiding within the borders of Ile-Oja." Braun's voice is higher than it was before. As he speaks, the king leads him towards the pillars on the far side of the room.

"Do you know what this could cost me?" the king asks. "The nobles grow restless in their quest to oust me and gain Rah's favor. The people are weak and influenced by the witchcraft of a fickle, juvenile Goddess. Now, in only the tenth year of my reign, they must submit their women for the Waning a second time."

"Look." The king points towards the sun.

Braun is slow to raise his head, but as he angles it upwards, the king fixes it, putting one hand beneath Bruan's jaw and the other on top of his head.

"Isn't it magnificent?" the king asks.

Braun says nothing as they stand there staring at the sun. Finally, tears start streaming down Braun's face.

"I can't see," Braun whispers.

"A pity," the king responds. He walks back towards his seat while Braun remains at the edge of the room. "You may leave now," he commands.

Even blind, Braun knows that he would fall to his death were he to take a step forward. He's been in this room enough times to memorize its simple layout, so he turns around and shifts to the side before walking back toward the palace's interior. As he walks past Nicholas, Nicholas lifts his arm, jabbing Braun in the abdomen. Braun loses his balance and takes three steps back. He falls to his death with a chilling scream that lingers.

The king yawns. "The time draws nearer now. You will meet with the tributes in a fortnight. You will prepare them to receive Adara's spirit during the Waning or die trying."

The mention of death causes the image of Annabeth's corpse to flash through my mind. I focus on the king's throat, silently willing the man to drop dead just like Jordan did. The effort earns me nothing but a trail of blood running down my right nostril. The air is dry. That's what I'll say if he asks.

The king's gaze lingers on each of us. His eyes take note of the blood smeared across the back of my palm. "In just three months, one of you will become the Mother of Witches and receive the honor of serving me as Adara's principal vessel," he continues.

Mother of Witches. Annabeth told me once that in the time of Rah's second and final descent, witch was an insult for powerful women. A term that marked her as one deserving of violence. In the time before that, when Adara roamed the Earth freely, witch was a woman both feared and adored. One who held the power of the gods in her palm and dictated the fate of the world with her tongue.

Nicholas shouts an order, and several guards appear at the doorway.

"Escort the king," he commands. The guards look around in confusion briefly before rushing to the king's side. If anyone wonders where Braun's gone, they keep it to themselves.

Several more guards appear and escort us out the door.

Ryland kneels on a wooden podium in the middle of the central plaza, prostrating in front of the most remarkable statue of Rah in the entire kingdom. The figure is made of solid gold.

33

It stands over twenty feet tall, an anthropomorphic form with the wings of an eagle at its back and the head of a vulture. The figure's chest is bare, and a tunic covers his groin. The king says his prayers, cupping his hands and bringing them over his eyes before drawing them downward and repeating the action twice. The sun sits at its highest point in the sky. This is when Rah is most likely to answer prayers.

Ryland turns from the statue, addressing the people sprawled before him. He wears an eagle-faced mask of red, blue, and gold. With the mask, he enters his role as an emissary between Rah and the people, giving people hope that Rah is listening. They marvel at his presence, each of them making their prayers, their hands rising and falling one after the other.

Sade, Iyanu, Torrin, and I kneel on the floor next to the podium. As vessels of the Goddess, Rah does not hear our prayers, but it doesn't stop Sade from trying.

The noblemen stand closest to the podium and to us, by extension—their gemstone jewelry twinkles in the sunlight. The Midzoners follow them, their attire less flashy but still neat and modest. If there are any Endzoners in the crowd, they're too far back for us to see.

"A witch has died," the king says. He speaks with the Voice. His Voice sounds like grains of sand picked up and pulled along the desert floor by the breeze. It is everywhere all at once, yet nowhere in particular. It is one of two gifts the sun God has bestowed upon his emissary. The gift of Rah's Voice means that without raising his voice, indeed, without even opening his mouth, those at the furthest corners of the crowd will hear the words of the king.

A few audience members gasp at the news, but the rest remain stoic. Some of the women in the crowd begin to cry. They already know what will happen next. They know what this might mean for them, and if not for them, what it might mean for their daughters or mothers.

"One hundred women will volunteer and gather at the palace gates by sunset," says the king. "Rah is a merciful god. Despite your transgressions, he loves you as his own because he created you to live in this world as his own. Remember this. Before Rah's reign, there was only chaos and suffering. Today, the fate of these women becomes uncertain, but before Rah's victory, Adara devoured women by the thousands. Remember this when you make your prayers and when you pledge your allegiances."

Ryland pauses.

"Rah sees all. He knows all. All who are found to be conspiring to undermine Rah's will or aligning with lesser gods will meet a swift and brutal end."

Chapter 3

In the evening, Sade, Torrin, Iyanu, and I gather at the rotunda that connects our rooms. Torrin removes her veil and strips down to her undergarments with a shimmy.

"Is it me, or is it getting hotter out there?" she says.

"Torrin." Sade shoots her a puzzled expression. "It is getting hotter out there."

"I know." Torrin smiles. "I was only joking."

Iyanu and I can't help but laugh.

"Very funny," Sade says, rolling her eyes.

"What do you think it was like," Torrin asks, "to live in the world before it was like this?"

Torrin is speaking to us, but she looks directly at Annabeth's corpse. If we were in the Endzone, Annabeth's body would have been laid out in the open for birds of prey to eat. Endzoners spring the trap to capture the birds, killing them for their meat.

It sounds brutal, but the desert sand prevents a body from ever truly decaying; it may be buried only to be revealed a few days later before being devoured by the birds anyways. Better to be there, to take advantage of the birds themselves, than not. Iyanu sits beside Torrin and grabs her hand before she answers Torrin's question.

"Can you imagine?" Iyanu sighs. "There was water on every corner of this planet. More water than anyone knew what to do with."

"That all changed because of her." Sade looks down at her hands, frowning. "We wouldn't have needed the water if it wasn't for her. It was the titan's foolishness to trust her in the first place."

Adara, bringer of death, also rules the bridge between life and death. While descendants of Rah ascend to his side, all other souls are kept in her realm. The details of life after death are lost to me, but the story of Adara's time on Earth is not.

They say Adara was a menace when she manifested on Earth half a millennium ago. The Goddess of Chaos grew frustrated with the rule of Rah's monarchs, so she possessed any person susceptible to her influence. Those possessed suffered brief bouts of insanity, many of them espousing treasonous beliefs about the monarchy before they dropped dead.

One in every seven women died, and a few men did as well. The entirety of Ile-Oja might have been destroyed had the Sun God not descended. Binding Adara's spirit in the bodies of the first Galed was the single act that saved the world. It's also why the people fear us. Why they look at us as if we could jump into their bodies and take possession of them ourselves.

"But we do need it. Her waters, that is," I remark. What can you do when the very thing that kills you is also what sustains you?

"Adara is merciful," Iyanu says. "I felt it when she first came to me, and I've felt it ever since she deemed me worthy of holding her spirit."

Sade scoffs. "Adara is wicked. But there is still hope." Sade shakes her head in affirmation. "Walking Rah's path faithfully will see us become titans once more."

That is the ultimate goal of the monarchy and of all those who serve Rah. The promise that with the king at the helm, directing scholarship and innovation, Rah's emissary on earth will deliver us back to titanhood, eliminating all death and suffering and completing Rah's triumph over Adara. But even if the rest of humanity were to gain enough of Rah's favor to return to titanhood, the sun God would never bestow such an honor on ones tainted by Adara. Besides, titanhood is a pipe dream. One meant to keep the people docile while the nobility plunder what little wealth the land holds for themselves.

"When Sarran disappears, I suppose we'll have to drink that hope and douse our crops with it," I counter. Hope won't feed you. It certainly won't quench your thirst.

Sade doesn't bother responding. Iyanu turns to look at Torrin before tracing her gaze to Annabeth's corpse.

"Well," Iyanu adds, "we have more pressing things to deal with right now."

"Yes, we do," Torrin says with a sigh.

Torrin walks towards the middle of the rotunda and places one cautious hand on Annabeth's wrapped body. She strokes the corpse through the sheets before gently unwrapping them to reveal her face.

"We will miss you dearly," she says as she kisses Annabeth's forehead.

"It's time then. We can't wait any longer."

Iyanu, Sade, and I join Torrin near Annabeth's body. Her skin is bluer than I've ever seen it. Iyanu takes Torrin's hand between hers. At this distance, I can see the creases of the paper-thin skin beneath Annabeth's eyelids. Her lips are pale, but her red hair is as vibrant as ever. Annabeth's spirit is stuck. It stays near her body in a state of confusion as Adara's essence slowly seeps out of her corpse. The plants can feel it. Their leaves point awkwardly but decisively towards her.

Here lies the body of the only woman who's ever been like a mother to me. Two years ago, on the eve of the last Waning, my blood coursed with the adrenaline that lingered from surviving when just over a hundred other women had not. My blood pumped with something else, too. Something powerful and dangerous. I didn't know what it was then, but I knew it cleared my head and sharpened my vision. That night, I waited in my room at the palace until I was sure that the others had already gone to sleep. I had no clue where the king's quarters were, but I snuck through the halls, determined to find it. I imagined what his face would look like as I drove the pointed end of my knife into his heart. I wondered if the mighty king would beg for mercy at my feet or if he'd die with the fire of defiance dancing in his eyes.

In the end, all I found was Annabeth waiting for me in the corridor at the end of the hallway that led to my quarters. She knew exactly what I was trying to do, no matter how hard I tried to play it off. Those thoughts never had a life outside of my head, yet she accused me as if I used my own mouth to tell her about them. Her knowing frightened me. If I couldn't get past Annabeth, how could I get past the king?

"I could smell the hate on you from a thousand miles away. You're not the first of the Galed to attempt something that stupid," she said. "Haste will only get you killed, Meera. Hone your patience, and sharpen it so that when you strike, the world will crumble at your feet."

We never spoke about that night again. But witnessing the countless deaths at Ryland's hand leaves no doubt in me that Annabeth saved my life when she stopped me.

Torrin picks up the knife on the altar with a shaky hand. She raises the knife over Annabeth's body and plunges it into her chest. Blood splatters over the altar and stains Torrin's undergarments. Bile rises up my throat, and I turn to vomit the contents of the meal I had earlier. Still whole pieces of spinach and peppers mixed in the mess of half-digested slime spewed across the floor.

"Get it together, Meera," Sade snaps.

"Do we all have to?" I ask, even though I know we do. When the high priestess dies, there's only one way to seal Adara's essence in the remaining Galed. The part of Adara that belonged to Annabeth will be split between us now. Partaking in Annabeth's flesh will make us stable enough to hold it, if only for now.

Torrin drags the knife down Annabeth's chest. She reaches her hands into the open wound and pries her chest open, revealing the organs within. Then she separates Annabeth's rib cage and pulls her heart out of her chest. A quiet, high-pitched sound escapes Torrin's lips as blood splatters across her face.

"It's still warm," she says.

Torrin uses the knife to cut four small pieces from the center of the organ and gives one to each of us.

"Just do it fast, and don't think too hard about it. Don't even chew. Just swallow," says Iyanu.

We put the pieces in our mouths and quickly swallow. I can't help but notice how it warms my tongue and leaves behind the ferrous taste of blood in my mouth. My face twists in disgust, but I manage to keep from barfing, maybe because there's nothing left for me to throw up.

"See, that wasn't so bad," says Torrin.

I open my mouth to agree, but something turns in my stomach. Then my senses blend into my sisters, and our core starts to warm. The heat intensifies until it spreads from our stomach

42

through our veins, down our legs, and up through our arms until it reaches our chest and head. Our brains feel like they're on fire, and our vision starts to blur. We can't think, we can't breathe, our body feels like it could explode from the heat. Right as I can't take it any longer, as I'm about to let out an anguished scream, the pain subsidizes. It disappears as fast and as mysteriously as it came.

"Whoa." Sade looks down at her hands. "Did you guys feel that?"

I glance up to see that the whites of Sade and Iyanu's eyes are slightly bluer than before. Meanwhile, Torrin's eyes are decisively blue, and her pearly skin glows more than I remember. The plant stems and leaves now fall naturally instead of pointing toward Annabeth's body, and we no longer feel any traces of Adara's essence in the air. My blood hums with the power that comes with being a fuller vessel. When Annabeth was alive, she was the only person who knew how to channel and direct that power. She knew how to siphon our portion for herself and use it for her medicine-making and who knows what else. Now, without her guidance or her knowledge, we'll have to figure it out for ourselves.

"We still need to send her off," Torrin says.

So, we begin our prayers.

Guide this soul with your calming winds
So she may be effortless and elegant like the breeze
Blessed are those who sing your name

43

For you alone guide our souls.

My heart feels lighter knowing Annabeth has been put to rest. Iyanu rests her hand on Torrin's shoulders.

"You did great," she says. Then she turns to look at Sade and me. "We all did."

Sade smiles as she stares down at her hands.

"What do you think we'll be able to do now?" she asks. She shoots her hands towards one of the root plants covering the rotunda floor. "Burn," she says. Nothing happens.

"Um... Sade." Torrin brings her hands towards her mouth to cover the beginnings of a smile. "I don't think that's how it works."

"Well then how does it work?"

"How am I supposed to know?" Torrin shrugs. "All I'm saying is it's counterintuitive to think that Adara's vessel might summon fire."

"Yeah, Sade," Iyanu teases. "Not the smartest move on your part."

"Sorry, Iyanu, we can't all afford the education that noble blood can buy. Maybe one day I can live up to your noble standards." Sade says this with nothing but sweetness, yet her words feel like poison.

Pain flashes across Iyanu's face briefly, before she settles into a neutral smile.

"There's no point to any of this power if we can't do anything with it. I'm tired of waiting for inspiration from the Goddess,"

Sade continues. "When I become Mother of Witches, things will change for the better."

I have to stop myself from gagging at that comment.

"And how exactly would things change?" I ask.

"With me advising the king, the kingdom might begin to heal from centuries of deterioration." I wonder whether Sade believes what she says or if she's deluding herself as a way to cope with the reality of our world.

Torrin and Iyanu give each other a quick look before deciding to change the subject.

"This isn't the time to be fighting amongst ourselves," says Iyanu. "Annabeth was murdered, and the perpetrators are coming for us next. We have to stay together now more than ever before, and we all need to maintain as much control as we possibly can."

Braun's words at the morning meal with the king ring through my head. *The first step of the plan was to dispatch the Galed in an attempt to release Adara's spirit. We believe that Terrel and the Ogun resistance are responsible for the death of Annabeth Wura.*

The resistance has been operating since the days of my father's youth, and their plans have gotten bolder as the years have gone by. But this might just be their most reckless plan yet. Since the binding took place half a millennium ago, generation after generation of the Galed have served to hold Adara's body within them, shielding the world from the madness she once wrought.

To attempt to plunge the world into such darkness again is unthinkable. Regardless of how bad the monarchy might be, Adara's wrath will be worse. *They're being stupid*, I tell myself. But I can't deny the thought buried beneath that one. *They no longer believe in me.*

Torrin frowns. "They've gone too far this time."

"How far into the palace do you think they've managed to infiltrate?" I ask.

Iyanu runs her hand over her voluminous, tightly coiled hair.

"Much further than probably anyone knows. We need to be cautious."

"How do they even know that killing us would bring her back?" Sade asks.

"They don't," Iyanu answers. "No one knows for sure. It could be that her spirit is too weak and killing us does nothing except release a sleuthing, decrepit ghost of a Goddess. Adara could vanish all together."

Sade crosses her arms over her chest. "We killed that girl, Jordan, with nothing but a word. We will be ready if they come for us."

"We did that without the slightest clue what we were doing or how we were doing it.

Like you said, Sade, there's no point if we're at the mercy of unpredictable surges of power brought about by the will of a Goddess. We need to figure out everything Annabeth knows about anything, and we need to figure it out quickly," Iyanu says.

"Annabeth was from the Wura family. Maybe she wrote some things down," I offer. Almost no Endzoners can read and write, and only a few Midzoners can, but Iyanu, who comes from noble blood, learned in her youth.

"I'll check her room and see if I can find anything there," Iyanu says.

Sade shoots her a skeptical glance before adding, "Together. We should check together," she glares. "You shouldn't get the upper hand just because you're a noble woman," she continues. "Everything you learn from anything Annabeth wrote needs to be shared with all of us while you learn about it."

Part of me believes that Sade would have burned everything Annabeth wrote in an instant if she could have. Why take the risk of letting someone else have the advantage?

"We can all get started on searching tomorrow morning." Iyanu turns toward Annabeth's body, chest plate opened and heart lying next to it. "For now, we need to give Annabeth a proper burial."

"Agreed," I reply.

Iyanu wraps Annabeth's body in the blood-stained bed sheets she died on and hoists her over her shoulders.

"I can take care of this myself," she says, "unless anyone else wants to join me."

Sade, distrusting of Iyanu, offers her company, and they proceed through Sade's room out to the palace halls.

In the rotunda, Torrin immediately tries to lighten the mood.

"Those two. Can you believe them?" she says with a nervous laugh. I turn to look at her.

"I'm sure Sade means well," she continues.

"No doubt," I answer sarcastically. "Iyanu is right though. We need to figure out how to use Adara's gifts to our advantage."

"It can't be that difficult." Torrin waves her hand over the vine crawling on the floor in front of her. Its stems wiggle before it perspires, releasing water from the invisible pores it uses to breathe. The leaves near the stems wrinkle, and the entire vine seems to slump.

"Torrin! How are you doing that?"

"I don't know, I just can. Here." She gestures towards another vine. "You try it."

I concentrate and silently will the new vine to do the same, but nothing happens.

"Oh, you're probably just tired," Torrin suggests. "It's been a long day."

"Right. Some rest will do me some good."

"Yes, well, goodnight then," Torrin adds with a strained smile.

"Goodnight."

We go our separate ways, Torrin casting a muted smile my way before disappearing into her room. I close the door to my room as well, pressing my back against it to nudge it shut. After counting five deep, slow breaths, I walk back into the rotunda situating myself in front of the labradorite altar. I trace my fingers over the smooth stone and will Annabeth to send me her strength and knowledge from beyond. With becoming a member of the Galed came the promise of the power of Goddess. Now is the time to claim that power as mine.

With hands outstretched, I summon the remnants of the energy from before and feel it tingling not at my fingertips, where I expect, but deep in my diaphragm. Focusing deeply, I let the power build. The air hums but just as I'm ready to channel my energy, to do something with it, the power eludes me, fading away like a whisper carried by the wind.

My hand comes crashing down on the bowl in front of me, smacking it to the floor. Its clangs echo through the room as the cowrie shells it was holding spill across the floor. *Useless.*

I reach for the dagger at the base of the altar.

"What are you doing?" Sade says, emerging from her room.

I drop my hand before it reaches the knife.

"Nothing," I answer.

Sade sits on a sitting stone and beckons me over to the one beside her.

"We've both come a very long way," she says with a smile, placing one hand over mine. Unlike Iyanu and Torrin, Sade and I are from the Endzone.

I met Sade for the first time when we were younger at her first labor assignment at the Fujisawa estate, a noble family much less favored than those whose estates stand closer to the palace. I had already been working for two years, but it was also my first week on the Fujisawa estate, having come from the Berkshire estate. The palace mandates that the nobles rotate their laborers randomly between them, lest the laborers gather, befriend each other, or form alliances. Wise to keep us divided during the day and leave us exhausted to the point of incapacitation by the time we return in the middle of the night.

Even then, as an eleven-year-old with little to sustain herself with, Sade always seemed sturdier than the rest of us. We pulled weeds that found their way onto the estate gardens with the other children. We came up with silly games to play as we worked. Sade's favorite was the Oracle game—a game where we dug holes and planted three seeds. The game was about predicting which of the three would sprout first just by looking at them and holding them in our hands. The person who guessed right won. I always won, and every time I won, Sade accused me of cheating. *How could I possibly cheat? It's not like I can bribe them into sprouting,* I'd say. I never told her that I simply noticed that the heavier seeds tended to be the most likely to sprout. Two years later, she was transferred, and we were separated for the first time since she started laboring. The next time I saw her was at the palace when we both volunteered for the Waning.

"I can't do anything with it," I say, referencing the power that's eluded me so far.

"I tried too, and I couldn't either," she says. "But no one deserves it more than we do. It's just a matter of time." Sade continues, "Rah did not create us to suffer, and I know in my heart that our suffering will soon come to an end. I can feel it."

"I hope you're right."

"I know I am." Sade rises to her feet. "Go get some sleep, Meera." She pulls me up into a brief hug. "I think we're both ready for this day to be over."

Chapter 4

Iyanu sits between Sade's legs, hissing as Sade brings a three-toothed comb to her scalp, creating a part through her tightly curled hair.

"Be gentler," she cries.

"No pain, no gain," Sade counters, chuckling. "Besides, I am being gentle. You're just not used to getting your hair done." Iyanu started growing her hair after she left the Idowu estates two years ago. Since then, it has grown an insane amount, transforming into a creature of its own.

Sade weaves a cornrow at the edge of Iyanu's head, right above her hair. The loose end of the braid falls forward, and Sade threads two cowrie shells to its end when she's done with the plait.

"How many more do I have left?" Iyanu asks.

Sade grabs the rest of Iyanu's unbraided hair in her hands, shifting it to the left and then the right.

"Maybe like four more," she says. So that means there are like ten more. Iyanu groans.

"Well, you could always go back to being buzzed," Sade suggests. "Torrin will love you either way."

"Never," Iyanu counters at the same time Torrin says, "it's true."

"Well, love, you'll just have to bear with it then," Torrin says, placing a kiss on Iyanu's cheek.

"Awww," Sade says, clasping her hands. "Absolutely disgusting."

"Jealousy looks bad on you, Sade," I offer.

She sticks her tongue out at me in response.

Iyanu and Torrin have been together since before the last Waning. The odds of them both volunteering for the ceremony and surviving to become Galed seem even lower than for Sade and me. When Iyanu was still at the Idowu estates, her father employed Torrin's mother. For what, neither Iyanu nor Torrin have ever said. They talk about growing up together often, though Iyanu's common refrain is that Torrin knew her before she even knew herself. When the Goddess appeared to Iyanu, Torrin knew she had no choice but to go as well.

The week after Braun's death has gone by quietly, and we've settled into our usual routine. A morning bath in our shared bathing room, morning meals prepared by the palace servants and delivered to our doors, short walks in the garden, and evening meals prepared and delivered the same way as the morning ones. A locket of Annabeth's hair, along with the golden ring she used to wear, sits on the altar where Iyanu's placed it. She attends to both items frequently, whispering prayers or speaking more generally to our remaining link to Annabeth.

Sade, Iyanu, and I haven't shown the slightest hint of new-found powers, and Torrin doesn't put her powers on display, so it's hard to tell if she still can. Neither Torrin nor I have told the others about her abilities. I've decided it's better not to share unless she does so first. It's a little too easy to forget that the Oguni have a death warrant against us when the days pass as peacefully as they do. Still, Iyanu maintains that we must stay vigilant.

The only source of activity within the palace grounds stems from the girls and women who've volunteered for the Waning. Ryland believes there are traitors amongst them; thus, the four of us have been kept from meeting them. So far, not a single girl has been identified as a member of the Ogun resistance. That is terrible news for Nicholas. I wonder how long it will take for someone to be scapegoated if he can't manage to produce any results. Even then, I doubt his time as captain will last much longer.

Ryland grows restless at the lack of results. His paranoia is heightened not just by the lowly women who now roam his palace as volunteers but also by the nobility, whom he suspects of treason. No noble has been allowed on the palace grounds since Annabeth's death. That is why I find myself anxious that today, the Galed have been ordered to accompany the palace guards for a visit to the Berkshire estate. As one of the king's advisors, Annabeth sometimes accompanied the king on outings to places kept hidden from the rest of us. Other times, we are permitted to leave the palace to help her guide the souls of departed nobles and high-ranking officials. One might think it strange that the nobles rely on us for such a thing. They deny that we, that Adara, have any power, even as they seek to use that power for their own gain. Rarely, we're invited to be viewed without our veils during gatherings held by the king, and even more rarely by those nobility who are closest to the king. But no Berkshire has died, and the king is not in a celebratory mood, so the circumstances surrounding today's visit are unclear.

Thirty minutes later, when Sade finished the fifth braid after the four she promised, we take our leave.

Nicholas waits for us at the palace stable, where an additional five hamels and six Endzoners wait beside him. The hamels all stand almost two feet taller than the tallest man. Hamel's are the only domesticated animals that have survived since the waters started retreating. They survive on barely any water, yet they run three times as fast as any human. Each hamel wears golden and silver neck bands stacked atop each other with matching earrings dangling from their ears—each band shimmers in the afternoon sun, the jewels splitting the light into vibrant and beautiful hues. A palace hamel probably wears enough precious metal and stone to feed a Midzone family for a year. An Endzoner could probably make it stretch three. Though the king owns all the wealth in the land, he makes it a point to display that wealth no matter the occasion. The hamels look over the four of us tepidly as they flare their lips and reveal their straight, square-shaped teeth.

As we approach, Nicholas reins in a hawing hamel, prodding the Endzoner beside him to coo at the animal. No, not an Endzoner. The men only dress as laborers. I recognize many of them as being part of the palace guard.

"What took you all so long?" Nicholas asks pointedly.

"We came as soon as the servant delivered your message to us," Iyanu says.

Torrin cocks her head up and whispers to me.

"He's in a bad mood because he can't figure out if anyone's with the resistance. It's not our fault you're bad at your job," she adds, giggling underneath her breadth.

Nicholas is not amused. "Speak without directive again, and I'll have your tongue."

Torrin bows.

I swing my leg over the tawny leather saddle, clutching the handle at the front. It's not easy to fall off a hamel, but that doesn't prevent my brain from racing through the numerous scenarios in which I manage to eat dirt. All it takes is one misstep.

We carry our procession away from the stables and maneuver our way through the palace gardens and past the servant girls that tend to it. It was a strange mandate, the one King Ryland made to ban men from serving on the palace grounds. Some said it was for fear of the collusion and resistance that men bring and that women, with their meekness, were safer servants.

As the hamel bobs along the shores of Lake Sarran, I surrender my body to its movements, letting it sway slightly forward and backward with each step. The lake is eerily still. Sometimes, I feel like I can hear it calling to me. As if it were singing a melody only I can hear. Though the Lake is still, there's a bustle of activity around it. Endzoners meander around carrying buckets filled with water to tend to the gardens of their respective nobles. Children as young as seven join their parents and grandparents, learning to tie cloth and place it upon their heads before balancing the buckets on their crown and bringing it back with them.

Young women float in small boats near the lake's edge, casting their fishing lines, hoping for some luck. Even so, they stay near the shores. Those that wander too far into the depths of the lake don't make it back. Only the Galed and the monarchs have ever been known to do so.

The noble residences are ordered so that the most favored of the families are given the lands closest to the palace. Starting from the left, the residences are the Hathaway family, the Idowu family, the Kim family, and finally, our destination, the

Berkshire family grounds. The Hathaway family estate is larger than the next two combined. It boasts twenty-six stone sculptures: ten of family members who achieved great feats during their lifetimes, five of Rah, and the remaining decorative pieces inscribed with the history of Ile-Oja and Rah's triumph over Adara. Their gardens are shaped in much the same way that the palace gardens are. Neatly cut geometric sectioning with exotic flowers and extravagant coloration. The Hathaway's value presentation above all things, so the Endzoners that labor for them are distinguished by their cropped hair, trimmed beards, and matching black uniforms. They remain just as starved and gaunt-looking as the rest, however.

The Idowu family residence is my favorite. Although smaller than the Hathaway's, it feels living and breathing rather than stoic. Their residence is distinguished by small, manufactured lakes embedded into a sprawling field of plant life that hasn't been shaped or sectioned in any particular way. They are much kinder to their laborers. As kind as one can be when they hold all the power and have no one to answer to when they misuse it. I wonder what it might have been like to be a member of that family. Iyanu never talks about it.

There are just three estates between the palace grounds and the Berkshire estate, but we wade through hundreds of laborers before arriving fifteen minutes later. Nicholas pulls the hamels into the Berkshire stables, whispering to the guards dressed as

Endzoners. They wander off, trying to blend in with the laborers on the grounds.

"I will ask Lord Berkshire a few questions regarding the resistance, after which I will dismiss you all to walk his gardens. Do not go beyond the gardens. Do not walk together. Go your separate ways," Nicholas says.

I doubt Nicholas is in a hurry to make the same mistake Braun did, and sending us off when there are so many Endzoners around is a clear and direct threat to our safety. There's no telling who might be part of the Ogun resistance. This is a set-up, then. The guards are dressed as laborers, so they can be there to capture anyone who poses a threat and bring them in for questioning.

A man opens the door when Nicholas knocks. He wears a beige-colored top that's cropped short near his bicep and reaches down just above his waist. It exposes the smooth skin of his midriff. He wears a pair of loose beige pants to match it. He's a sturdy man. A sign that he is favored amongst the nobility of this house. Most laborers would never get the chance to eat enough to look like that, no matter how much they worked. He was there the night Annabeth died. He saved the elderly man who fell, dragging him out of the way of our passing hamels on our back to the palace.

"Welcome to the Berkshire residences. Please wait here while I notify my lord of your arrival," he says with a low bow.

Nicholas sticks his foot between the door and the wall as the man attempts to close it.

"That won't be necessary," Nicholas says, pushing the door open. "We are here by order of the king."

"Aris!" Lazarus calls from a room deeper within the residences. "Stop being a brute and let them in, will you?"

The man, Aris, steps aside and swings his arms forward, beckoning us to enter. Though I've never seen the inside of the Berkshire residence, I recognize it from the stories Lazarus told me about his childhood. The set of five divans with velvet cushions overlaid with golden embroidery sit atop a hamel hair rug decorated with geometric patterns. The massive chandelier hanging over us with its warm golden candles lit with flames even during the day. The air smells of cinnamon and spice, and the ochre windows commissioned by the palace help to keep the inside of the house much cooler than the outside. A wall with five arches separates the living room from the other spaces in the home. Though I can't see them, I know one leads to a set of stairs that goes up to the grander living room, the other to a set of stairs that lead to the family bedrooms, two lead to workspaces, and the last is used as a gathering room where women entertain noble men.

"Aris, fetch us some tea." Lazarus turns to us. "Please have a seat."

Nicholas shakes his head. "That won't be necessary. We intend to keep this brief."

"So be it. Aris, you may join the others outside." Lazarus shoos Aris away as if he were a fly buzzing near him. "To what do we owe this honor from His Majesty? Why has he sent you and not Braun?"

"Braun had an unfortunate accident. I'm commanding the palace guards now. Where is Lord Berkshire?"

"I'm afraid my father has other commitments. You'll have to make do with me."

Nicholas gets straight to the point. "The king has gotten word that there may be resistance fighters amongst your laborers. What do you know of this?"

"It wouldn't surprise me. You can never trust a lot of dirty Endzoners." Even though I know Lazarus is just saying what he has to, the words *dirty Endzoners* slice through me like the polished edge of an obsidian blade. I know I shouldn't, but sometimes I wonder if he really does think of me that way. "Tell me which ones, and I'll bring them in for questioning," Lazarus continues.

"You mean you don't trust your laborers? Yet you have them here working for you. Are you all so incompetent as not to vet your laborers before bringing them in, or are you complicit in their rebellion?" Nicholas prods.

"Trust an Endzoner?" Lazarus asks. "A foolish thing to do don't you think?" Lazarus's eyes narrow. "Besides, what are you insinuating?" His lips pull themselves into a thin line, and his cheeks flush with annoyance. "My family has always been loyal to the king. We've served him tirelessly since the days before Rah's victory."

"Times have changed. The king is left to wonder if your loyalties have changed with it."

"You're correct. Times have changed, indeed. Sarran continues to retreat, and I wonder if it will live on when my great-grandchildren enter the world. That is why we stand with the king. We believe in King Ryland's divine mandate. Under his leadership, we stand a chance of not just surviving but evolving into something better. Humanity's time on Earth may end with Sarran, but under Ryland's leadership, we stand a chance of becoming something better."

"Leave us," Nicholas says.

We stand to leave. Lazarus turns to me for a brief second. I feel his eyes meeting mine, though I know he can't see them through my veil.

"Stay safe," Iyanu says as we walk out the door.

In the vegetable gardens, the laborers pull out weeds as they harvest bean, pea, melon, potato, and tomato crops. They turn over sections of the garden with shovels, laying tarp down over the dry land before planting new seeds in equally spaced quadrants and watering each section carefully and precisely with cups of water. The flower garden at the front of the Berkshire residence is used solely for aesthetic reasons, but the vegetable garden at the back is used for crops. The Berkshires are a prudent group. Unlike many of the nobles, they are meticulous about maximizing their food. Despite what Lazarus tells Nicholas, the Berkshires are preparing for the worst. The nobles don't just store food but weapons. Even the rich can't escape the end of the world, but that sure as hell won't keep them from trying.

As I round the gardens, I watch the laborers' faces. The palace guards stick out like a sore thumb. Too tall, too muscular, too heavy—definitely inexperienced when it comes to tending the earth. I'm turning around to make my fourth pass around the gardens when Aris steps into my line of sight.

"Meera, right?"

The last time I worked on the Berkshire estate, I was eleven. I search through my memories, thinking I might remember a younger version of the man standing in front of me, but I can recall no such thing. *Maybe he's a part of the resistance. Maybe he's singled me out to kill me.* The sun suddenly feels twice as bright as my heart pounds. I take quick glances around him and find some relief in the fact the two of the palace guards stand watching us.

"How do you know my name?"

"Lazarus has mentioned you a few times."

"But how did you know it was me?" My veil covers my face, so no one should be able to see me through it.

"You were the first one I asked, and you just confirmed it. No need to be afraid. You're not in any danger."

"What do you want then?"

Aris looks at me with some emotion I can't place. "I heard you used to work here for him, just like us. How does it feel living in that fancy palace now with all those servants at your beck and call?" He doesn't say the quiet part out loud, but I hear it anyway. *How does it feel being pampered while people waste away?*

"You know nothing about me. But by the look of it, you haven't done so bad for yourself either," I say, sizing him up.

"You have no idea what I've sacrificed to get to where I am."

"Nor you, I."

"Maybe not, but I know what your father sacrificed. He bragged to everyone he could after he found out you had survived the last Waning. Said things would change around here with you being Galed and all. Said you had what it took to get the job done."

"Is there a reason you're here, or shall I signal for the guards."

"Go ahead. I'll make sure to tell them everything I know."

"You'll be executed."

"Lucky me. Better a swift death than whatever fate you'd face." Even with all the hatred the king has for the Goddess within us, he would never kill a member of the Galed. Splitting Adara's essence between just three, none being Mother of Witches, could result in something untold—all that power condensed so tightly with no one able to channel it.

"What. Do. You. Want?" I ask again.

"I want you to answer my question. Are you still committed to the resistance?"

One of Nicholas's guards chooses that moment to walk towards us.

Aris fakes an exaggerated gasp. "But you have to be deathly hot under there! How do you do it!"

I do my best attempt at a light-hearted chuckle. "It's not so bad. The sunlight is kept from directly hitting my skin, and the veil actually reflects some of the light away. You get used to it after two years," I reply.

The guard hesitates before continuing onward, no doubt making note of the interaction.

"I am still committed. Things are not that simple. The king is not a weak man. He will be defeated by wit, not might. Is my father well?" I continue. "Did he order our deaths?"

Aris pauses before he answers. "He's dead. It was a few months ago. We have a new leader now."

Shame creeps up my throat until I can feel it burning in the back of my mouth. The truth is, since that night Annabeth caught me on my way to the king's quarters, I have never made another attempt at the king's life. Her knowledge had scared me. But the people I've witnessed the king slaughter for lesser offenses scared me more. Just as the Galed are no mere women, the king is no mere man, and I am no longer ignorant enough to believe that a sneaking girl would so easily claim his life. And now, my father has died before witnessing me become strong enough to do so.

I didn't know my father was leading the Oguni until I began laboring. I noticed the way the other laborers seemed to show him just a bit more deference than they did to each other. A brief nod here or a subtle glance there. Nothing so obvious that it would rouse the suspicion of the nobles. My father kept me in the dark about everything, including how my mother died. That all changed when he got word that one of the Galed fell ill. We waited for her death, and when it finally came, I volunteered for the ceremony. My father had never looked at me with as much pride as he did that day. I think about how desperate I was for his approval and how desperate he must have been for a resistance breakthrough. He was so desperate that he was willing to volunteer his only daughter for a ritual that spelled certain death for most.

We stand there in silence for a brief second before I let the news of my father's death wash over me. Suddenly, I'm overcome with rage.

"Even if I am a failure, at least I'm no murderer. How dare you order our deaths as if we were merely cattle for you to slaughter? It seems the resistance is content with being no better than the king. Dangerous and stupid."

"Not everyone on our side agrees, but the people trust Bear. Your father passed him the mantle, and no one has a better idea."

Another moment of silence.

"Tell Bear he's fighting with blindfolds on. Adara lives inside me, and even I don't know what she's capable of. A living member of the Galed is worth infinitely more than a dead one."

Aris nods but doesn't give anything in the way of a reply. "We'll be in contact, Meera," he says as he leaves.

He stops suddenly, twisting his head to meet my gaze. "Stay away from Lazarus," he adds as he walks away. I watch as he disappears behind the Berkshire mansion.

When Nicholas finally gathers us, I'm exhausted, and my bladder is ready to burst. My gown is damp, and the air trapped in my veil is starting to smell unpleasant. A pang of guilt hits me. Did my father spend his last days in the care of the Oguni, or did he drop dead while working on the Cho estates?

Nicholas calls out to two palace guards, who drop their facades to join him. "Prepare the hamels," he says to one of them. "Go get the others," he says to the guards.

I turn to Nicholas, "I need to make a stop inside the mansion." He glares in response.

The guard ordered to fetch Sade, Torrin, Iyanu, and the rest of the guards, comes to my aid. "For Rah's sake, Nicholas, the girl looks like she's about to have a seizure with how hard she's shaking. Let'er in to use the bathroom. She'd probably piss on the hamel before we make it back," he says.

Inside the house, Lazarus sits with his legs spread wide open on the divan facing the door. When I leave the bathroom, he's waiting in front of the door.

"Lazarus," I say cautiously.

He pulls me into his arms, fixing one hand above my waist. He uses the other to pull the cloth of my veil away from my face.

"I can't be here too long. Nicholas is waiting," I protest.

He draws his face closer to mine. His breath warms my chin, and his stubble feels rough against my skin.

"All right, all right," he says without pulling away. "It's been too long. I miss you, is all."

"It's only been a week." I try to make my voice sound dry, but I can't hide my amusement. I wrap my arms around his neck and pull him as close as possible. Lazarus brushes his lips against mine, smiling as he does so.

"My father died," I tell him.

At twenty-seven years old, Lazarus is just half a decade older than me, but he's never once treated me like a child. We met only a few months ago during a banquet held by the king. Annabeth compelled us to do petty tricks for the nobility in the audience. When we were dismissed for the night, Lazarus slipped a note into my hand as I walked past him. It was one of the few times I cursed myself for being unable to read. I kept it under my pillow that night, and I've kept it ever since.

The following week, we ran into each other again while I walked the gardens.

"You didn't come out to meet me," he said.

I was embarrassed then. I didn't know how to tell him that I couldn't read. Didn't he know that I was an Endzoner? And what use would an Endzoner have for reading?

Instead, I said, "my apologies, I was tired," even though I had no idea what was in the note. He didn't find out for another two months that I had never read the letter.

When he realized the problem, he chastised himself. "What was I thinking?"

He read the note to me that night.

You shine with the radiance of a thousand suns

You've already captured my heart

Meet me under the central palm.

I will wait for you till dawn.

Lazarus draws his face down, burrowing his chin into the curve of my neck. "I'm sorry," he whispers.

"It's all right," I answer as Sade enters the room.

Chapter 5

"What in Rah's name are you doing?" Sade asks.

The clamor of her voice chills my bones. I suppose someone was bound to find out, but I'd hoped it wouldn't be so soon. Though noblemen often keep mistresses, the pairing of a Galed with a nobleman could easily be considered a threat to the king—a valid claim to the throne as a direct descendant and a witch to help him take it. So we've kept it private as we could. But there's no denying it now that it's so painfully obvious. Even as Sade stands there, glaring daggers into our souls, my arms remain fixed around Lazarus's neck, our bodies so close together that a piece of parchment wouldn't be able to make its way between us.

Lazarus wraps his hands around my ribcage and gently lifts me to create distance between us. "It was my fault. She came out of the bathroom, and I couldn't help myself." Sade doesn't take her eyes off mine.

"Meera?" she asks, waiting for my response. Her eyes harden when it doesn't come.

"I can't believe you." Sade says. "I wouldn't pin you as the type to fuck someone just to try and get ahead. I mean, to think you used to have so much to say about the greedy nobles. Now you're in bed with one. I didn't think you had it in you," she says.

"We're not doing anything wrong," Lazarus says dryly.

"You won't mind then if I tell the guards of this or the king for that matter, then?"

"What exactly would you tell them? That we hugged? I think the king has more important matters to attend to than keeping track of the romances in his court." Even as I say this, I'm unsure of myself. The king has never been a predictable ruler. Sade walks away from the door to stand directly in front of me. She jabs the space between my two breasts with the tip of her index finger. Lazarus watches beside us but doesn't intervene. I look Sade straight in the face, refusing to give even an inch.

Nicholas is at the door in the next moment. "What's going on here?" he asks, eyeing Lazarus's grip on my forearm.

"Nothing," Lazarus says. The girls were just leaving. It seems the coming of the Waning is already taking a toll on them."

As we walk towards Nicholas and out of the door, Sade whispers to me, "This isn't over."

We pass by the familiar faces of the laborers working this morning on our way back to the palace. By the Kim estates, we come across an older woman working the newly exposed land created by Sarran's retreat. Her mahogany skin glistens as the sun's rays strike the water droplets on her body. Her matted hair falls straight down and stops at the curve of her shoulder. She dips her hand into a bucket full of white powder and sprinkles it on the land. The Endzoners used to get sick when working by the lake bed. It wasn't long before we realized the exposed earth was toxic and needed to be cleaned regularly if Endzoners were to survive working on it. The powder that neutralizes the toxicity of the soil is perhaps the only contribution the monarchy has ever made, directly or indirectly, to Endzoners.

Circular patches of scalp show through the woman's hair. Like most Endzoners, her frame is thin, and her bones jut out against the flesh of her skin. She stands awkwardly, knees bent inward, and elbows bent outward. Her pupils are cloudy from disease. When Nicholas's hamel passes in front of her, the weight of her body gives in beneath her, and her knees come crashing to the floor. Her head lies flush against the floor, angled to the side, so her cheeks press against the wet ground. Her eyes meet mine. I watch her pick herself up, her bones and limbs snapping in place with movements too fast to be natural.

"Hey! What are you doing over there!" Nicholas's voice doesn't sound like a shout. Instead, it spills out of the deepest corner of his throat, riding whatever semblance of a breeze there is towards its intended target.

But the woman doesn't notice. She angles her head while maintaining eye contact with me.

"Ase! Ase! Ase, is that you?" She laughs maniacally, her head swinging violently from side to side. "Can't be, can't be! You've been gone for too long. The lakes taken you."

She places one foot in front of the next and hesitates before stepping backward. She bends over so that her head is upside down, her forehead touching her knees. She grabs fistfuls of the remaining hair on her head and pulls until clumps come out in her hand. Then, again, her body snaps upright awkwardly. Determination, or madness, I'm not sure which, shines in her eyes as she walks quickly towards us.

"Stay right where you are," Nicholas calls out, unsheathing his sword from its holster.

"Ase! You've found me." Her voice is fervent. Her eyes weeping as she continues forward.

Nicholas warns, "I said stay where you are." Something changes in his voice now. I wonder if it reflects a change somewhere deep in his soul. It's like he's somehow turned off the part of him that's human, leaving a cold husk of a being to speak in his place.

She runs towards us, leaving footprints in the sand beneath her. Nicholas raises his sword, bringing it down and severing her head. She doesn't scream. She doesn't even flinch. She falls silently to the ground like a feather on a windless day.

Nicholas groans, "I'll need to explain this to whoever owns her."

"You didn't have to do that. She was just an old lady. She looked like she was sick." Torrin frowns deeply. You'd think she'd be used to it by now, but every death leaves as deep of a mark as the last.

I'm surprised when Nicholas's response is almost cordial.

"Can never be too sure with the threat hanging over your heads. You don't want to end up dead, and I don't want to end up like Braun."

Iyanu jumps in. "Did you find anything? she asks. "When you were speaking with Lazarus."

"The bastard didn't give a lick, not that I'd tell you lot if he did."

I'm grateful for this. In Ile-Oja, all it takes is the perception of guilt to warrant irreversible consequences. Lazarus doesn't know about my connections to the resistance, but that doesn't mean he's completely loyal to the king.

"Maybe you were questioning him about the wrong things," Sade says. I try to keep a straight face.

"What do you mean by that?" Nicholas replies.

"I'm just saying everyone has something to hide. Don't you agree, Meera?" she asks.

"I wouldn't know," I add. I hope my voice sounds steady, but I can barely hear it over the sound of blood pumping in my ears.

In the evening, a servant delivering my evening meal informs me of Nicholas's request for my presence down in the palace dungeon. The maid introduces herself as Bridget, second-year handmaid to the king himself. "And garden-hand hopeful," she adds.

When I asked her why she wanted to work in the garden of all palaces, with its brutal heat, she replied, "The pain of serving the king is worse than that of any sun."

Bridget is very pretty in a girlish way. Her golden hair is sun-streaked. It drops in ringlets across her face. Her lips are thin but somehow plump, and her cheeks seem to be in a perpetual state of blush. Her dull eyes, the same color as the lake, only make her prettier. She also talks a lot.

"My parents couldn't believe what I looked like when I came out of my mother," she exclaims. "That." She points at one of the copper hinges holding up glass bouquets on either side of the hall. "Plus this—" She points at me now. "—does not equal this." She finishes by pointing at herself. "If my features weren't an exact match for my father's, he might've thought Mom was having an affair!"

I smile, nod, and laugh when appropriate, though I'm only half listening.

The entrance to the dungeon is demarcated with a towering, solid doorway with bolted locks and not so much as a scratch on its surface. The door is adorned with two serpents. One golden, with the head of the other crushed beneath its fangs.

"This is where I take my leave. It was wonderful to meet you, Meera. I'm so sorry for your loss, by the way. Annabeth was a blessing to us all." Bridget bows slightly before walking away. Nicholas arrives shortly after that.

As the door to the dungeon opens, the smell of rotting flesh wafts forward, slamming into me. A cool breeze lifts the trim of my gown as I send a silent prayer up to the heavens, wincing at the thought that no one is listening. *Nicholas knows everything. He'll lock me in here and leave me to die. No, keep calm*. I made it twenty years in the slums and two years as a witch. I can survive whatever the next few moments bring.

There are no windows down here. The prisoners do not see the sun. I think it's a symbolic punishment meant to represent banishment from Rah's light. Or maybe it's a psychological punishment that drives one insane with the inability to perceive the passage of time accurately. Most cells lie empty anyways—a testament to the king's preference for murdering those who defy him. I only count two prisoners as I walk through the dimly lit enclave. Both turned towards the walls, bent down, and crouched into themselves, mumbling incoherently. I twiddle my index fingers reflexively, then drop my hands to my sides. It's better not to look nervous or, worse, guilty.

At the end of the dungeon lies a small chamber with a door-less entrance and a singular chair squarely in its center. The chair is so worn that it could collapse any second now. Affixed to its two armrests are a pair of iron cuffs matching those on the ends of its two front legs. To the right side of the chair is a small table decorated with an assortment of glass and iron knives, saws, and a pair of tongs.

"Sit." Nicholas directs me towards the chair.

I don a relaxed demeanor, doing my best to still the twitch forming in my arms.

"What's this all about, Nicholas?" I ask.

It's good that my voice doesn't betray my nerves. My father would be proud. He wouldn't have wanted me to die here because I gave in to my fear. I think about the pain I've endured until now. The sharp, throbbing pain that comes with intense hunger, the agony of a friend's passing, the seared skin, and battered hands from day after day of laboring. Pain that will prepare me for what I might experience here.

"No need to be worried. I'm just going to ask a few questions, and then you'll be free to go. Shouldn't take too long at all," Nicholas says.

"You could have asked me anything you wanted in the palace halls, or gardens, or anywhere else you wanted."

"We find that people are more truthful when we bring them down here. Can't imagine why." Nicholas picks up the knife and traces the cravings on its hilt.

"Ask away then."

"What did the boy laborer say to you?"

"Aris," I ask, inflecting the last syllable to sound surprised. This is about him?" He didn't say much, just asked about my life as a Galed."

"You spoke for quite some time."

"Like I said, he wanted to make small talk. He was curious about my lifestyle, and I told him some aspects of it."

"Small talk?" Nicholas drives the knife in his hands onto the wooden table he sits atop. "I'll ask you again. Why did he speak to you?"

He stands now and leans over me with his two hands gripping each armrest. His topaz eyes bore into mine. My mind swirls, trying to find an excuse that Nicholas will believe, but I turn blank. In the end, I decide to stick to my story.

"I already told you," I say with a slightly louder voice, hoping to convey some determination, "he wanted to know about the Galed."

"Meera, this might surprise you, but I take no joy in causing you or anyone else harm." Nicholas's eyes become distant. He looks away from me towards the wall, but his voice stays the same. He takes three steps toward the table and pulls the glass knife out of the table in one smooth motion.

"The choice is yours. I won't ask you again."

Nicholas walks toward me and leans over me once more. He traces the tip of the knife up and down my thigh, almost absent-mindedly.

"No?" he says.

He sighs shallowly, then plunges the knife deep into my right thigh. At first, it feels like nothing. I gasp, not because of any pain but in shock, despite the fact that I saw it coming. Then, a burning sensation swells and sizzles in my thighs before spreading to the rest of my body. I've never felt my body so deeply. I feel every muscle, every tendon, every ligament, and every bone near my thigh light up in a blaze of agony. I let out a piercing scream that I'm sure would shake the palace grounds if not for the dulling effect the stone walls have on the sound. Nicholas pulls the knife out of my thigh as smoothly as he pulls it out of the table. The tip of it is shattered. Tears stream down my face, and a thick, steady stream of mucus runs out of my nostrils before pooling around my upper lips.

"Nicholas," I plead, "how could I possibly know him?" My voice catches in my throat as I speak. It comes out in between hiccups of shallow breaths and sobs. "I asked him why he chose me, and he said he just came to the first of us he saw."

"That might have been the first true thing you said," Nicholas says approvingly.

I continue mixing half-truths with lies, hoping I still sound believable. "Maybe he wanted something more, but whatever it was, he didn't tell me about it." My gown darkens and clings to the blood pooling near my thighs. Nicholas hasn't bothered to strap me into the chair, but the thought of standing on my two feet sends such a tremor through my body that I think I'd rather die.

"Is that so?"

"Yes," I heave, then more gently, I add, "Please."

Nicholas grunts. "You can stop the waterworks. It's not like I would have killed you. The king would never allow that." Nicholas drops the knife, completely shattering it, before leaving the room. "You're free to go," he declares as he walks out.

I sit there motionless, except for the tremors that spread from my leg and rake through my body occasionally. My head spins, and my eyes droop involuntarily. The blood spilling from my thigh starts to pool around my legs, and I realize that if I stay here, the loss of blood will kill me. I throw myself to the floor, bracing my landing with my forearms. I place my forearm flesh against the ground and drag myself forward with a deep, heavy groan. Shards of glass lodge themselves into the skin of my palms—a trail of blood left behind where I once had been. Reaching forward, I propel myself with another long drag and heavy groan. Sweat pools in the creases of my forehead.

By the time I enter the prison halls, my cheeks are damp with the tears I no longer bother to hold back. My pain is so great that I don't think to allow the presence of the two prisoners to shame me. Strangely, the first door leading out of the dungeon has been left open, and the second opens with the slightest push. It seems out of character and slightly careless of Nicholas. When I make it out to the halls, the thought of crawling to my room drains whatever's left out of me. I'll rest first, then continue when I'm feeling better. I won't take too long. I let myself drift. Even though when I know I should keep moving, my eyes will no longer open, no matter how much I will them to.

When the weight of my eyelids softens enough for me to open them, Bridget stands wide-eyed, leaning over me. My firm but warm bed is beneath me, and Torrin, Iyanu, and Sade surround me.

"Oh, she's awake," Torrin exclaims.

"About time," Sade says with her arms crossed over her chest.

My body is drenched in liquid, either from the blood I've lost or the sweat streaming from my pores. I've been changed into a nightgown, and a thick, blood-stained sheet has been wrapped tightly around my left thigh.

"How did you guys find me?" I ask.

Torrin answers. "Bridget brought you here to us like this. Thank goodness she found you when she did. If you'd lost any more blood, you might have had some permanent damage."

I manage a whisper. "Thank you."

"Of course!" Bridget chirps. "With everything Annabeth's done for me, how could I not return the favor? You're just lucky something told me to stick around after dropping you off. Nicholas did this to you then?"

"Sade!" I hiss, sitting up too quickly, which sends a roaring pain through my thigh.

Hurt flashes through her eyes. *No, Sade didn't do this.* She wasn't anywhere near me or Aris. The palace guards are the ones who reported me. I'm even more anxious now that Nicholas suspects me. A word about me and Lazarus might be all it takes for Nicholas and the king to have a reason to get rid of me.

Bridget coughs before continuing, "I do have some bad news. There were quite a few pieces of glass lodged too deep into your thigh for me to remove. If they stay in there, they'll do much more damage. The injuries you've already sustained are extensive, and I'm afraid it'll take some time to recover."

I stare blankly at her, confused by her words. My ears hear what she's said, but my mind refuses to process it. *She doesn't know what she's talking about. I don't have time for recovering.*

Torrin comes to sit by my side. She takes my hands and raises them towards her forehead. With determination in her voice, she says, "Don't worry, we'll help you through the process."

The feeling that spreads through us is warm and airy. It leaves the sweet and spicy taste of cinnamon on our tongue and makes our eyes roll back. It's maybe the most pleasant thing we've ever felt. When I return to myself, the ache in my right leg is gone.

"Where did you guys go just then?" asks Bridget.

"Torrin? Was that you?" Iyanu asks.

"I guess it was," she answers doubtfully, like she can't believe what she's just done.

Iyanu unwraps the fabric on my leg. My skin is now completely healed. She runs her hand along the length of the healed skin and brushes off the small fragments of glass that have made their way to the surface.

"Miraculous," Bridget exclaims.

"Your gifts keep getting stronger," Iyanu says. "Have you done anything else like this?"

Sade glances between Iyanu and Torrin. "Wait. Has this been happening? And you knew about it?" She turns to me. "Did you know about this too!"

Iyanu answers first. "I've known that Torrin's abilities have been growing for a couple of days now, but I didn't know she was capable of anything like this."

"Neither did I," Torrin adds.

"So you all knew," Sade surmises, even though I never answered. "Keeping secrets, are we?" she says through a tightly wound smile.

"Sade, I —" Torrin begins before Sade interrupts.

"Save it." Sade clenches her fists once before releasing them.

She turns to walk out of the rotunda and through the door that leads to her room—the floor trembles with every step she takes.

Chapter 6

My locs hang beside me, their rounded ends resting on my thighs as I sit and stare at myself in the mirror. This one is rare. Invented during King Floris's reign, it involves a thin sheet of metal spread onto a glass sheet. Why the scholars under King Floris's reign invented such a thing, I'll never know. But the invention quickly replaced the copper and obsidian mirrors among the nobility.

There isn't much in my room—just the bed that lies in the corner, the chair I sit on, and the desk holding the mirror in front of me. I peer into it as I use a wooden comb to apply some eloh paste to the roots of my last part. Pleased with the results, I trace my lips with the point of my index finger, smearing them with the dark purple lip balm Lazarus gifted me a season ago. The pigment matches the thin, semi-sheer amethyst nightgown that ends above my knees, also given to me by Lazarus. He likes giving me things he says help me look "pretty." Blue and purple are his favorite tones to see me in. He says the colors mellow out the harsher hues of my skin.

Sade has been more distant since Torrin healed me. She no longer bothers to make a show of barging into our rooms in the morning or making small talk when we're in the rotunda together. Iyanu is concerned. Torrin even more so. I was so shell-shocked by my injury and Torrin healing me that I couldn't muster any words when Sade stormed out on us. Iyanu insists that Sade's temper will pass with time, as all things do. "It can be hard when you feel like the people you trust are hiding things from you," she says. I agree, but I've never seen Sade this upset, and it concerns me.

Lazarus brushes up behind me and places his hand on my shoulders. He bends down to place a kiss on my cheek. He's newly shaven and smells of the clay he applies to his face before sliding his razor across the skin. King Ryland has become less anxious in the last week, and following the execution of two alleged resistance members, he's started allowing noblemen back into the palace. But the king's mood seems too good to be a result of the execution of a few low-level resistance members. He's even ordered a celebratory ball to be held in the next week. Some of the palace maids have begun gossiping. They're spreading a rumor that the king might finally have an heir. Who the lucky woman bearing his child is would be anyone's guess. The queen would be the obvious choice if anyone had seen her within the last year.

"What are you thinking about?" Lazarus asks.

"Nothing," I say.

Lazarus moves his hand away from my shoulders and places it on my right hand. I hadn't realized I'd been rubbing my thigh, a habit I'd developed since Nicholas stabbed me two weeks ago.

"Why do you keep doing that?"

I start rubbing again, then stop almost immediately. I find myself a bit embarrassed to tell him, but he prods.

"Come on, Meera, you've been doing that since I got here."

"After we went to your estate, Nicholas brought me in for questioning. During his interrogation, he drove a knife into my thigh. Bridget thought it might never heal. I swear, I still feel it in there sometimes."

"Did Sade say something?"

"No. Nicholas questioned me about things she wouldn't know."

He reaches over me and slides my nightgown up, revealing the skin of my thighs.

"It wasn't about us then?"

"It wasn't."

"It doesn't look like anything happened there," he remarks. "Did you heal it? That's amazing! I didn't know you could do anything like that."

"Not me. Torrin did." I brace for the disappointment I know is coming.

"Still really amazing," he says. "Have you been doing things like that too?" He sounds like he's trying to tone down the excitement in his voice.

"Not that I know of. I'm just glad that I still have my legs, and I can stand on my own two feet." When he doesn't reply, I continue. "I'm so glad you're okay, Meera. Do you need anything? How have you been doing since? Has Nicholas done anything else? How about how are you handling your father's death!" I ask. Sometimes, I wonder if Lazarus hears what I say or if he hears only the things he wants to. Another day, I might have brushed it off, but today, I find myself more irritated than usual. I blink away the tears building in my lower eyelids.

"Don't be like that," Lazarus says. He slides the straps holding my gown down my shoulders and moves to place one kiss on my left shoulder where the straps once were. He brings his face upward, placing two kisses on my neck.

He looks into my eyes when he says, "I'm just curious about you, is all."

"The king no longer has Rah's favor. His rule imperils the entire kingdom. Endzoners, most of all. Things would be different with me on the throne. Your father might still be alive for one." He adds, "with you by my side, we can finally make that dream a reality."

"Here," he says as he pulls a gold chain with a sapphire pendant out of his pocket and clasps it around my neck. "I got this for you."

I temper the frown forming on my face, knowing that no amount of protest will get Lazarus to take the pendant back.

Lazarus and I bonded over many things in our first few days together, but a shared disdain for the monarchy brought us close enough to drop our guards. It probably came as no surprise to him that an Endzoner wasn't very fond of Ryland, but I never thought a nobleman would speak about their king in such a manner. We were on the same page about Ryland but not about everything. *Why don't you give more to your laborers?* I have no use for pendants, but the necklace hanging around my throat could feed an Endzone family for life. Lazarus is adamant that giving away any amount of his resources is only a temporary solution. For any Endzoners he might help, Ryland's rule creates two more. The best he can do, he says, is make their lives more bearable by being a compassionate lord. His kindness, his willingness to usurp Ryland, is what's paramount.

As direct descendants of Rah and distant relatives of Ryland, many of the nobles have a claim to the throne should Ryland be deposed. They stock their weapons in the event that such a day might come, but with no army to match that of the palace guards and no stomach to use the weapons themselves, they sit idle in their estate chambers. Lazarus says having me by his side is worth more than any army. He said that before he realized I hadn't shown any signs of manifesting Adara's gifts.

Even now, I know that when Lazarus says *by his side*, what he means is by his side until he's replaced Ryland on the throne. The nobles only marry each other, and having one of Adara's vessels on the throne beside him would jeopardize his already shaky mandate. My goal was never to be the wife by his side anyways. They say to keep your friends close and your enemies even closer. It's been almost two years since Lazarus dropped into my life, and all I've learned from him is that Ryland is as tight-lipped with his distant relatives as he is with any of his subjects. The nobles hold an unnatural fear of the man. Even though they share in his wealth, they throw themselves at him with the desperation of a starving Endzoner. The mixture of jealousy and hatred stinks the same no matter what class you belong to.

Lazarus turns me around. He kneels and places a few kisses on my thigh, right where Nicholas stabbed me, before sliding me off of the chair and onto his shoulders. He stands and maneuvers to the bed, even with the space between my legs blocking his vision. Lazarus has done it so often now that he knows what he's doing by heart. He lets me off his shoulders and onto the bed, climbs over me, and pins my hands above my head.

"Do you want it?" he asks.

I smile, even while replaying his words over and over again in my head. I let images of him turning his back on me as he mounts the golden throne, never to speak to me, never to even glance in my direction again. I tell myself that that is only one of several possibilities, and more of an impossibility. If the Oguni have it their way, Ryland will be dead, and no one will ever use that throne again.

I turn the corners of my lips upward stiffly. "Of course, I want it," I reply.

He draws me closer by my hips until I'm flush against his groin. I thrust my hips from underneath him, grinding against him. My hands make their way down towards his drawstrings, unwinding them and pulling his member out of his pants. I rub it gently, and he moans at the contact.

In one fell motion, he flips me over from my back onto my stomach and slips into me. He grabs a fist full of my hair and pushes my head further into my bed. I gasp at the fullness I feel with each stroke. Lazarus goes further and faster before peaking with a sigh. He collapses on top of me and stays there until my protests make him roll over onto his side. I take off my nightgown, which had remained on until now, and snuggle beside him, wishing to feel his bare skin on mine.

"What if Torrin is the only one to survive the Waning? What if I'm not here next year?"

"Don't talk like that." Lazarus shifts his weight. "Torrin's no better than you are but it wouldn't be a bad idea to get closer to her. You might need her."

I wonder if he says this to me or himself.

"I better be going," Lazarus continues. "And you have your gathering to get to. I'll see you soon, yeah."

"Yeah."

Torrin and Iyanu are already in the palace atrium when I arrive. Sade arrives shortly after, but she stands alone, a few feet separated from us. Obsidian columns of varying heights rise from the obsidian floor and frame the circular space.

The end of each column boasts sculptures of citrine stone. One is of the wings of an eagle, without its body. Several are of animals no one has laid eyes on for centuries. They are bigger, leaner, and bulge with power emanating from their forms. Their faces are pointed, and their teeth are sharp like knives.

The open roof brightens the space during the day, but at night, the moonlight makes the obsidian stones sparkle with a silvery glow. The roof also lets the cold in. The palace nights are even colder than nights spent in the Endzone, thanks to the lake, which chills the air at night as well as during the day when we welcome it. The cold here, just like the heat during the day, is nothing like what it is in the Endzone.

Our meeting with the volunteered women comes later than usual because of the time it took to vet the volunteers for potential traitors. Regardless, palace guards gather at either side of the atrium, watching over us. They're joined by palace maids who are busy polishing the columns with something slick and shiny.

The women filter in in clusters, undoubtedly already forming alliances and making pacts between themselves. The first three women seem no older than me. They are modest in appearance, wearing lightly embroidered skirts and plain blouses, but they seem well-kept, with hair and skin in decent condition. Probably Midzoners. All three have dark hair, dark eyes, and willowy frames. They are so similar that I suspect they might be related. A few dozen Endzone women stream in individually. The next group is a band of seven Endzoners. Half of them seem very young, between the ages of thirteen and sixteen; two are young women, while the others are elderly. They've likely joined forces, feeling too weak to make it alone but thinking they'd be better off together. During my time preparing for the Waning and the time before, there was at least one noblewoman who volunteered herself. This time, it seems like they've all decided against it.

All of the volunteered women maintain their distance. I don't blame them.

The four of us line up next to each other, while the volunteered women form a single file line next to us. Iyanu passes a steel blade to each of us, and we all make a small cut at the tip of our index finger.

As the women walk by us, Sade, Iyanu, and Torrin connect three lines on the women's foreheads, forming a triangle with their blood. I draw a line through it, completing Adara's sigil.

"You belong to the Goddess now," I say. "She will take you in life and death."

By the time the last woman has received her mark, the rest of the group has dispersed in the atrium. Sade saunters over to a younger girl while Iyanu and Torrin make their way towards the group of seven, leaving me to fend for myself in the sea of women. It is customary for the Galed to offer their gratitude to the women on behalf of the kingdom. I scan the crowd, looking for someone to approach, but the group of three women come to me of their own volition.

I plaster a smile on my face. "Thank you so much for your service to the crown. The entire kingdom depends on the sacrifice you have chosen to make. We are eternally grateful." These are the exact words Annabeth told me when she greeted me in this same atrium just two years ago.

The shorter one of the three scoffs at my remarks. "We're not here to sacrifice ourselves. We have no intention of dying during the ceremony," she says.

"What exactly does the whole thing entail anyway?"

Memories from the Waning flash through me. Being left near the edge of the lake, mist rising from its still surface in the dead of night. The compulsion that forced my limbs towards it until I was completely submerged in its waters. The creature swirling beneath me, pulling me down into an abyss and the island I somehow found myself on at the end of it.

I try to sound pleasant instead of condescending. I know what it's like to be in their shoes.

"You'll find out soon enough." Even if I feel for them, I'm not foolish enough to share any information with these women. I'll need every last bit of an advantage I can get if I'm to survive the Waning for a second time.

"You can't just leave us in the dark. Your guards spent the last month harassing and accusing us of treason of the highest order. We've given everything to be here and may just end up giving our lives. You just thanked us for our sacrifice. The least you could do is tell us what we're up against."

"I appreciate your curiosity about the Waning and your investment in it. The entire kingdom does as well." I bow softly before turning to leave, but the women persist.

"Hey!" yells another sister, "we're not done here!"

"You think we wanted to be here! We had no choice," says the third. She starts sobbing as she speaks. "Our father could no longer afford to keep all five of us. It was between us and his two sons. Guess who he chose?" she adds bitterly.

Strange. It's not uncommon for Midzoners to find themselves relegated to a life in the Endzone. Deaths are usually to blame. A palace guard dies, and suddenly, his widow can no longer support herself. Or a gem cutter or tailor becomes ill, no longer able to earn enough to provide for his family or pay the tax that ensures that family a spot in the Midzone. These Midzoners and their families go on to find themselves in the Endzone with everything they've managed to bring from their previous lives but no clue what they're in for. Most are pillaged of their items and left with nothing of value within their first season there. Many die, unable to shelter themselves through the freezing night.

I try to swallow my sympathy for the sisters. I remind myself that before now, they lived lives most Endzoners could only dream of. Their misfortune will end as suddenly as it came. It's nothing compared to a lifetime of such. Besides, regardless of what they say, they do have a choice. They chose to try their luck with the Waning rather than labor and scavenge in the Endzone. So why do I find myself doing the very thing I know I shouldn't?

"There's no way to prepare for it. The lake just swallows you whole, and if you're lucky, you'll find yourself alive at the end of it with no memory of how it all really happened. Your alliance won't help you. When it comes, it'll be between you and your Goddess." I walk away before they can think to probe deeper.

This time, I approach one of the girls who came individually. Her head is downturned, and she chews on her bottom lip while picking at the skin near her cuticles. We speak briefly without reflecting any of the hostilities of my prior interaction. All of the women I talk to afterward are just as demure.

The night passes by quickly after that. As the night ends, the women are ushered away by one of the palace servants, who has two guards following behind her. Sade, Torrin, Iyanu, and I make our way out, with Sade walking briskly in front of the group and me lagging behind. As I walk toward an onyx-carved creature, I notice one of the palace maids waiting behind it. My eyes wander away from her, but my attention is fixed on her movements. I keep my pace steady so as not to arouse any suspicion. She could be an ally just as easily as she could be an enemy. Torrin and Iyanu are close enough, I tell myself. They'll know if anything happens. She slinks from behind the statue as I walk past it and calls to me timidly.

"Meera!" She hurries over and grabs both of my hands before releasing them and leaving me with a piece of paper in my left hand.

I glance both ways, worried about who might have seen, but Torrin and Iyanu are a good ways ahead of me. Sade is out of sight, and the atrium is cleared of maids and guards. I fold my hands inside my sleeves to hide the note and continue on.

When I get to my room, I bring the letter out and stare at it blankly. I trace the symbols with my index finger, curious what the maid might have been trying to tell me. I stare as if the meaning will appear in my mind solely because I will it to. I put the note down, but for some reason, I can't take my eyes away from it.

The words start to shimmer, each letter glowing an iridescent blue before expanding and blurring into each other. The glow spreads across the paper before creeping outwards and downwards, morphing into a fine cold mist that wraps around my ankles and envelops the room.

The legs of my chair screech against the floor as I stand hastily. I walk forward blindly until I feel the sand beneath my feet wedging between my toes.

The moon is absent in the night sky. I know instinctively to keep walking forward until Lake Sarran comes into sight. My skin feels taut against my bones but numb on the exterior. I walk in a daze until I'm knee-deep in the lake. The water feels neither warm nor cold.

A thick, slimy arm wraps around my ankles, snapping me out of my trance and dragging me forcefully into the water below. I open my mouth to scream and feel the water rush into my lungs before a second arm wraps around my throat. I claw at the arms with my nails, wheezing for the breath I can't take.

I wake up with a jolt, clawing at my neck. The note sits on the table in front, now crumpled by the weight of my head resting on it overnight. A hiccup catches in my throat as tears stream down my face.

Chapter 7

Iyanu, Torrin, and I gather at the rotunda for morning tasks. Torrin waters the plants, and Iyanu crushes and mixes their trimmings, creating balms and medicines for the nobility. Sade's absence goes unmentioned, but Torrin seems to be in a great mood despite it. Her pearly skin is radiant even in the low light. Her dark hair shines elegantly, swaying back and forth on the tips of her shoulders. The stems and leaves vibrate as she nears them, as if they're singing to her. Iyanu doesn't take her eyes off her, pounding the pestle into the herb-filled mortar without glancing at her bowl or the plants before her.

"What did you think of the volunteers last night?" Torrin asks.

Iyanu scrunches her face but doesn't answer.

"They were nice enough. Did either of you talk to the three Midzone sisters?" I ask.

"I got stuck talking to the larger group," Torrin says.

"The sisters I spoke to," I begin. "They came from a well-off Midzone family. They said their father could no longer afford to keep his five children and that they had nowhere else to go."

Torrin shakes her head. "When did it get so bad in the Midzone?"

"Well, no matter how bad it is out there, the palace grounds flourish. And they'll continue to flourish so long as there's even one drop of water left in Lake Sarran and one servant who can be made to fetch it," Iyanu says.

A shiver runs up my spine as I think of Sarran's cool mists gathering at my ankles. "I dreamt of the lake last night. I dreamt of the Waning," I tell them.

"Strange, isn't it, how we can't remember the details of what happened that night. Every time I try to grasp the memory, it slips through my fingers." Torrin says.

Iyanu agrees. "I could never remember exactly what happened, even right after it was all over. It was like I was asleep and woke up after a couple of days, and everything that happened then was just a hazy dream. I can feel the memories buried deep inside me. I remember the pain and the fear, but nothing else."

"I think it's a blessing, really. I'd hate to relive those days if I didn't have to. I definitely wouldn't trade places with you." Torrin's voice is soft and kind, but the statement is matter-of-fact.

"Does anyone know where she is?" I ask.

"I tried looking for her in her room, but she wasn't there," Torrin answers. It's not like there are many places the Galed frequent. We don't stray far outside our rotunda and rooms, besides ceremonies and official visits. Where Sade could be is anyone's guess.

"She'll come around when she's ready," Iyanu says. Like Torrin, she always offers the best-case scenario to every situation. "For now, we must prepare for the king's banquet."

Later that evening, Bridget makes her way to each room to prepare us for the banquet. When she gets to my room, she drops the ceremonial robes in her arms and wraps them around me, squeezing me gently before lifting me and setting me back down.

"How's that leg treating you?" she says.

"It's fine," I answer tersely.

I wonder how Bridget can be so cheerful even in her circumstances. It's true that working as a palace maid is a coveted job most in demand by the Midzoners on the verge of becoming Endzoners. The ones not so unfortunate to end up in the Endzone but still lowly enough not to have the connections that would secure their life in the Midzone. Those who serve Ryland as handmaidens make it three years at most. It's a mortality rate worse than that seen anywhere in the kingdom except maybe in the mines.

"Why are you here? Shouldn't you be preparing the king for the banquet?" I ask.

"He's being dressed as we speak. Now, as for you."

Bridget walks over to the pile of robes on the floor and collects them one by one, hanging each on her forearm. She lays the garments neatly on my bed, then picks up a cream tunic, sliding my hands into it and securing it around my waist. She brings the gaping sleeves upward until they bunch at my shoulders, wrapping blue ribbons around my arms, from my bicep to my wrists. The last piece is a cowrie shell headpiece that dangles in front of my face, coming to a stop at my collar bones.

Bridget steps back to admire her work. She claps her hands together. "Perfect! Rah be praised. I was hoping I wouldn't have to make the tailors do any more alterations. I had to get Torrin's tunic cut and hemmed. It was much too long."

"Thank you," I say. "Do you have any idea why the king has called for a banquet? Did he let anything slip?"

"He hasn't said anything, but I know for sure that he'll announce he's sired a new heir. It's inevitable now that Annabeth is dead."

I raise my eyebrow. "What do you mean? What does Annabeth have to do with any of that?"

Bridget frowns. "You didn't know," she asks. "There's a reason the king has been taking on more and more women servants in the last decade. The palace was not always like this. During King Floris's reign and in all the time before, the servants were not only women. After it became clear that the queen could not give Ryland an heir, he started sleeping with the maids. When none of them fell pregnant, he brought more and more on. Eventually, he only started accepting women of childbearing age into the palace."

"That doesn't explain what Annabeth has to do with anything."

"Right," Bridget's voice drops as she continues, "the maids had a rumor going around that she was keeping him impotent somehow. Maybe by slipping him something or using the gifts of the Galed."

My eyes narrow as I stare sharply at her. "Rumors like those could get you killed," I chastise.

I'm irritated by the callousness of the accusation. The monarchy's cruelty knows no bounds, and any suspicions of disloyalty could have been fatal for Annabeth. Despite my annoyance, I find myself toying with the idea, and the possibility of its truth worries me. Annabeth's relationship with the king has always been obscure. If it weren't for the fact that she didn't turn me in the night I tried to murder Ryland, I might have thought she was just as devout as any of Rah's subjects.

Did Annabeth slip him something? An impotent king eventually dies without an heir, destroying the line of succession. There would be no one to blame but the gods. There would be politics, chaos, and, ultimately, bloodshed before a new king was crowned. It's in this chaos that a real threat to the monarchy emerges.

In the chaos lies the only opportunity for the Oguni to seize the throne—our only chance to destroy the monarchy and the system that keeps the nobility in control of Sarran. A wave of hope runs through me. The Oguni's objectives are clear, but what were Annabeth's? *What was her plan? Who were her allies? Did her plan work?*

"You know what they say." Bridget grins. "Every rumor has a kernel of truth to it." Bridget brings her hands together in a clap. "Well, I better get going then. See you in a few."

———◆———

Sade, Torrin, Iyanu, and I meet outside before proceeding to the banquet. It's strange seeing everyone outside of their usual white veils and gowns. Somehow, the color makes us seem more concrete, less like the weary ghosts of a Goddess past. On our way down the corridors, Iyanu tries to brighten the mood with a few jokes.

"I hope the king won't be boring us with a Rah-nt."

Torrin chuckles just a bit and pats Iyanu on the shoulder. "You're getting better at those," she chirps. I smile because I can't tell whether she's serious or not.

"See, even Meera smiled this time," Torrin adds.

Sade hisses, which makes me roll my eyes. Sade, so far, has not told anyone about my relationship with Lazarus. Part of me never believed she would. Even though we don't always get along, she's never done anything to directly hurt me.

There's a moment of silence between us before Torrin speaks again. "We know you must be feeling a lot of things right now," she says to Sade. "We can talk about it whenever you're ready." Iyanu and I nod in agreement.

We enter the banquet hall from the south, walking past the palace maids who stand in a line along the southern wall. They are dressed identically, each clad in calf-length cream linen gowns with their hair pulled upwards in neat buns. The hall has a plethora of windows, but they're more aesthetic than functional. The glass used to create them is geometrically patterned and colored, so that each face of each shape appears to change color depending on the angle from which the windows are viewed. Unlike many other windows in the palace, these windows block both the sunlight and the sun's warmth, leaving the hall cool and dimly lit by the candles on the tables. The ceiling is curved into a dome with a regular palace window at the top. The window barely lets any light in, however, because the sun isn't angled properly just yet. The floors are adorned with lush rugs, upon which sit rounded cushions set around low-lying tables. There are floor cushions placed randomly across the hall, as well as eating mats placed directly in front of them. At the center of the hall, there is a lack of furnishing, creating an opening in the space. In that opening lies a throne for the king. Sade, Torrin, Iyanu, and I sit on the carpet several paces in front of the king's seat.

The nobles start to enter from the north, one family at a time. Though no markers designate where each family should sit, they all know the arrangement to follow. The Kim family enters with their two young sons and two maids. The matriarch of the family, Eun-ji Kim, is dressed in a loose-fitting emerald green gown with long, gaping sleeves embroidered at the hem. Her hair is braided and pinned to form a circle above her head; the gown trails behind her, conjuring an image of abundance and durability. The patriarch also wears a loose-fitting gown in a more muted navy blue hue. He wears a leather belt across his chest and a pointed hat atop his head. The two boys are dressed similarly to their father, and the two maids wear cream gowns resembling those of the palace maids. The only thing to distinguish between the groups are the emerald-colored neckties the Kim maids have tied around their necks. The servants of the nobility take their places beside the palace maids at the southern wall.

More nobles follow, each with their families and their chosen set of servants. Finally, Lazarus and the rest of the Berkshires enter the room with none other than Aris. Like the other servants, he wears a blue necktie, distinguishing him as belonging to the Berkshires. Like many other noblewomen, Janice Berkshire is gilded from head to toe in gemstones. Her preferred stone for the night seems to be a mix of aquamarine and sapphire. They glisten even in the low light, and their color makes her blue eyes glow. Her dress is rather plain compared to her counterparts. She prefers to let her jewelry do the talking. She tilts her head and whispers something into Aris's ear before patting him on the arm. He leaves her side to take his place along the southern wall.

The Hathaways, Idowus, and Kims are closest to the center of the hall and, therefore, to us and the king. I can barely make out their words.

Lord Hathaway sounds almost amused as he speaks. "Could this be it then?" he asks. "Has Ryland finally sired an heir?"

"... impotent... line ends..." Lord Kim responds.

Lady Eun-ji Kim adds too loudly, "Rah forbid his cursed bloodline be continued," she scoffs. "What has he done for any of us? Lake Sarran continues to disappear, the Midzoners dwindle in number, and the Endzone rebels grow bolder by the day. How long before they grow bold enough to target us!"

"It's truly a shame. Even our servants grow lazier! The farmers complain of heat and thirst, so we send them home with less water as punishment. The miners can't even procure quality stone without falling sick or dying. The kingdom is truly in shambles," Lady Hathaway adds as she toys with her diamond-encrusted pendant.

Lord Kim says the unspeakable, "Perhaps Ryland's mandate is gone. Rah must have other plans for leadership. Lord Hathaway, you know you have my full support should you challenge for the throne,"

Lord Hathaway laughs. "And what will that support cost me?"

Before Lord Kim gets a chance to answer that question, the first rays of sunlight come streaming in through the window at the top of the dome, and two guards open the door on the eastern side of the room. I recognize one of them as Nicholas. The palace poet appears behind the door, followed by King Ryland himself. The palace trumpeters blow their horns, bellowing out a formidable tune that crescendos with each step the king takes. The entire hall moves to stand on its feet—everyone except for the servants who are already standing. The king is adorned with a red garment detailed with gold embroidery across every helm. His favored crown sits atop his head, reflecting the sunlight outwardly around the hall.

The guards remain in front of the door panes while the palace poet leads King Ryland to his seat at the center of the hall. They walk slowly, advancing until Ryland is seated with the poet by his side. The poet begins.

Rah, the God that eats serpents like the eagle devours the fowl
He who excretes gold through his pores
Pours honey down the throats of his followers
He who wears his enemies' intestines like chains around his neck.
Nothing escapes him,

For even in darkness, there is light

The nobles salute the king by cupping their fingers, bringing their hands over their eyelids, and motioning them down their faces.

Ryland beckons everyone to take a seat. "A glorious day this is," he says, using Rah's Voice so that everyone in the room hears even without him opening his mouth. King Ryland has no need to use his Voice. He does so to assert his dominance. The hall is large, but it's so quiet, I swear I could hear Sade's breath next to me if I listened hard enough.

"In the beginning, Rah created perfect beings using his divine light. He named these beings titans. The titans were mighty. They were immortal and had no need for food or water. Their intellect far surpassed that of any scholar known in the history of Ile-Oja." This must be an especially special evening if he's decided to recite the history we all know so well.

"Rah made these beings and saw that they were good. He walked among them during the day, and they knew that he was their father. At night, he left to replenish his light while the titans slumbered. The Earth was still a mountainous, magma-filled rock in those days. The world was just as it should be until one night, Adara approached the titans and enticed them with the promise to make them even more perfect. More like their beloved creator, Rah." The nobles hiss their disappointment.

109

"But there are none like Rah, and there will never be any like the supreme God. The titans were naive. They accepted Adara's blessing, not knowing that it was a curse. The titan's curse spread onto the land, transforming their species and the Earth in the process. They turned into the first of humanity's ancestors, becoming reliant on the newly flooded Earth to provide water to quench their thirst, food to bury their hunger, and shelter from the elements. Rah looked at his creations and saw they were no longer perfect, so he turned his back on them."

"Just half a millennium ago, Adara returned and made an offer to a woman. This time, Adara inhabited her body, driving her insane. Soon, Adara's spirit was spreading to others. Her plague left no family in Ile-Oja untouched. Women started dropping dead. Rah saw that this was bad, and he pitied his once-perfect creations. For the first time since the beginning, Rah descended from the heavens to help his creations. Rah fought to subdue Adara and won. He trapped her spirit in the bodies of five women who had been possessed, making sure her spirit would not be free to roam, consuming the lives of the innocent. Since then, the Waning ceremony has kept Adara's spirit trapped." The king gestures to us, and the nobles burst into applause at the last sentence. Even the Hathaways and Kims, who spoke brashly about their loss of faith in Ryland just moments ago, are jostling and hollering.

The king raises his Voice and shakes his head accusingly. "The historical record says that their battle was so calamitous, that

Rah's rage was so fierce that all the earth's lands were scorched, and almost all the waters evaporated as if they suffered the unintentional consequence of Rah's light. But Rah is a deliberate God. He does nothing without intention! He spurred the beginnings of Earth's transformation back to its perfected state—the state it was in before Adara's curse. Now, Rah asks that we do the same. I sit before you here today as Rah's chosen ruler to lead humanity back to the days of the titans. "Rejoice brethren! Our future starts today," he beams.

My attention snaps towards the east door as five guards appear near the entryway, pulling a large, charcoal-colored animal behind them. Each holds a thick, linked chain, which connects to a collar attached to the animal's neck in both hands. They drag the animal closer and closer to the doorway. My stomach churns with each step it takes. It feels wrong. Everything feels wrong. The animal is over ten feet tall, but it's hunched so far forward that its head appears just a few inches above the tallest guard's. Its horrifyingly human-looking eyes dart wildly across the room as it fights the guards, pulling it toward us. As it gets closer, I see that its skin is dull but very smooth. *Stop! Don't bring it any closer*! The room gasps in unison when the creature stills and raises its head. Its face is human. A human with large round eyes, a full mouth, and an upturned nose. A human that is identical to Queen Antares.

Chapter 8

I can feel Torrin's body shivering beside me. I hear her breath quicken, turning from its deep, easy draw to something desperate and shallow. Iyanu and Sade remain perfectly still, but it's all I can do to keep from bolting out the nearest door. This is wrong. I want to scream, but my voice catches in my throat. Could that thing really be a titan? Could it really be Queen Antares? What terrible things has Ryland done to turn her into this? I raise my head and bring my eyes toward it, although every inch of my body begs me not to do so. The guards continue to push the creature forward as the king beckons it to his side. As it draws nearer, Torrin can no longer contain herself. Her cowrie shell headpiece clinks together as she springs forward onto her feet. The sound makes Sade, Iyanu, and me turn, but neither the king nor the nobles notice. They remain fixated on the creature approaching. Iyanu grabs the edge of Torrin's tunic, attempting to pull her back down to her knees.

Torrin slaps Iyanu's hand away. "Don't touch me," she screams. Suddenly, everyone has their attention on her.

"Don't..." she says. Her voice is squeamish and shaky. "Don't bring that thing any closer," she says again. This time, her voice is deepened with authority, and it clamors through the room.

The air is heavy with the power she exudes. I want to jump on Torrin and force her back to her seat. The king will not tolerate anyone stealing this moment, especially not one of the Galed. The punishment for what Torrin's already done could be dire. Even as I move to stand, my knees remain glued to the floor. I can feel myself slipping inward, succumbing to Torrin's will. When Annabeth pulled us into herself, the process was instantaneous. One second, we were ourselves, and the next, we were all one being, lending our strength and the part of Adara within us to accomplish whatever was Annabeth's will. Now, with Torrin, the movement toward her feels shaky and incomplete. I can fight it, even though I've never been able to fight with Annabeth.

The guards drop the chains attached to the creature's collar in the commotion. Before anyone can stop it, the creature bursts into a run and heads straight towards us. My mouth opens unwillingly, and my vocal cords strain as Torrin bellows a piercing, terrifying scream. She hasn't completely pulled me into her, but she screams with all of her power and half of mine. The sound sends a tremor through the room—several of the wine glasses in the nobles' hands burst, including the one held by the king. Torrin's scream brings the creature to its knees, hands flying towards its ears—most of the nobles and guards

114

near the creature faint, including Lord Berkshire. Blood drips out of the noses of the guards that remain standing. Several of the noblemen and women, as well as their servants, burst into screams. They rush out of the hall using the southern and northern doorways.

Nicholas and his guards pull out their swords and run past the creature towards us.

"Charge the witch," he yells.

I try again to stand up, but it's useless. Iyanu and I might as well be frozen to the ground beneath us. As Nicholas and his guards get closer, Torrin waves her hand swiftly but with no haste. Her demeanor is chillingly calm. Even though there's noise from every corner of the room, the sound of bones snapping is unmistakable. Nicholas and the other guards fall to the floor, screaming and clutching their shins. King Ryland remains on his throne, taking everything in. It's hard for me to make out the emotions on his face, but I can't find even the slightest trace of fear as I look him over.

To my left, Sade shivers violently. In the next moment, she's bent at her waist, her hands balled into fists, which push against the ground to keep her upper body up. She brings one knee off the ground, then the next. Her hands remain balled at her side when she's finally upright.

Sade screams toward the approaching guards, but her scream is nothing like Torrin's. It's raw and bitter, but it holds none of the power. Still, the approaching guards stop abruptly, some of them dropping their weapons in surprise. They expected they'd be on the floor like the others before them. It occurs to me that this could be it. Torrin could massacre every guard in the palace in the state she's in now. What would she do if the king came after her? Would she be powerful enough to overtake him, too? We need to run. We need to get out of the palace immediately and find Lazarus in the hopes that he'll be able to provide us some refuge, if just for the night. We'd be off to find the Oguni by the next morning. It doesn't matter that they'd killed Annabeth or that they hoped that somehow killing us would release Adara's spirit back into the world. We'd need to convince them that we're more valuable to them alive. Even if they decide to have us executed, it's better a quick death than the life Ryland would subject us to.

As the guards resume their approach, Sade turns to Torrin and tries to tackle her to the ground. Torrin pushes Sade hard, and she flies a few feet and lands mere paces away from the nearest guard. The king speaks for the first time since Torrin rose to her feet.

"Arms down," he says, speaking in his normal voice.

He made the command fast enough to spare Sade from the sword that would have severed her body had he made the command a second later. All the guards halt again, gripping their swords but standing at attention. Unlike the king, fear masks every inch of their faces.

Sade rises to her feet, wiping the back of her palm against the top of her bruised and bleeding forehead. She stands with her legs wide, beckoning Torrin to do what exactly—I'm not sure. A look of remorse flashes across Torrin's face and her control over her power wavers for a brief moment. I know because, at that moment, I feel the tension leave my body, and I know that I could stand now if I chose to. Sade must have sensed it too, as she seizes the opportunity and strikes, using her gifts so that Torrin's hand bends suddenly and awkwardly. Her wrist snaps, and she's left gasping for breath on the floor. Iyanu rushes to Torrin's side, cradling her trembling form in her arms.

"Marvelous." The king applauds. I move towards Torrin and Iyanu when the king commands the palace guards. "Apprehend her and take her to the dungeons," he says.

The guards peel Iyanu away from Torrin. They grab Torrin by her misshapen wrists, undeterred by her whimpering pleas. Iyanu jumps at one of the guard's feet, but they dislodge her with a kick to the chin. I think to run after them as they march Torrin out of the southern door, even though I have no idea what to do when I reach them. I can't allow myself to think about what might happen to Torrin if I don't. I force my way through the crowd of bodies made up of nobles who are now beginning to wake up and the other set of guards who've come as reinforcements.

My brain churns, thrumming against my skull. I'll grab Torrin, and the rest will come to me later. A hand grabs me by the arm and pulls me into him. I claw at it mindlessly, trying to escape the man's grip, until I realize it's Aris.

"Let me go! They've taken Torrin." I'm yelling, kicking, and screaming now.

"Get a hold of yourself, Meera," he says, looking down at me sternly. I can see in his eyes that he thinks my father and the whole rebellion must have been foolish to put their faith in someone as weak as me.

"There's nothing you can do for her right now," he continues. "There's no use if you end up where she's going. They'll keep her alive at least until the next Waning, so use that time to come up with a better plan than getting locked in a dungeon."

"Why are you even still here! You were standing right by the exit! You should have left!"

"I needed to stay until I was sure Lord Berkshire was awake."

Aris drags me back into the banquet hall and points at Lord Berkshire, who's one of the few nobles who lie on the ground, unconscious. The creature stands just several paces in front of him, subdued by the guards who have regained the helms of the chains attached to its collar.

"Is he?"

"No, look more closely. His chest is still rising and falling."

Several of the noble families' servants have stayed behind, each associated with a nobleman or woman who has yet to make their way out of the banquet hall. They've been ordered to remain until they can guarantee the safety of their masters.

When I turn to ask Aris if this is the case, the clamor of the king's Voice rings in my head.

"Brethren, return at once." He's sent this command to everyone in attendance at the banquet hall. For everyone who is physically able, disobedience is not an option.

"Don't make a scene," Aris cautions. "I'll find you after the banquet is over."

As the palace healers rush the bodies of the injured out of the hall, the palace servants who are closest to the scene make quick work of scrubbing any traces of blood and grime from the floor. Some sweep away the broken glass splayed across the hall, while others rush in with new glasses of wine and goza pipes to replace the broken ones. Aris leaves my side and takes his place amongst the other noble families' servants along the southern wall. I, too, return to the opening in front of the king's throne. Sade and Iyanu are already kneeling with their heads bowed. Iyanu's face is stern, almost unreadable, but I can see her mind churning even with the hollowness of her eyes. Sade's face, on the other hand, seems soft. Almost victorious. She's happy that she was able to overpower Torrin. Bile rises in my throat.

One by one, the noble families return, this time with none of the pomp with which they made their initial entrances. They come in wearily, taking their seats in the same arrangement as before. When the last of the nobles return, the king speaks once more.

The king gestures towards the creature. "I said, rejoice, Brethren, for this is Rah's path. This—" He points to the beast by his side. "—is the first iteration of a titan. The creature has the strength of four men and feeds on nothing but the sun's rays. It is mortal, but it has little need for water or shelter from the elements." He pauses, but the rest of the hall remains silent.

"Your Majesty lets you bear witness to this miracle so that you might keep your faith in him and Rah. We are on a path towards salvation. Those who stray will burn in Rah's light while the rest of us grow stronger."

The nobles cheer wearily. Two palace maids walk in carrying the ceremonial meals for the monarchy. Roasted dessert fowl garnished with peppers and onions and framed with slices of orange and grapefruit and a cup of palm wine. They set them down in front of King Ryland with a bow, careful not to meet his eyes. I remember my mouth watering at the sight during my first few weeks as a member of the Galed. Imagine feasting on dessert fowl instead of lizard and scorpion meat. Other servants carry smaller plates with roasted peppers, okra, squashes, and root vegetables. They set these plates in front of each of Sade, Iyanu, and me, careful not to meet our gaze, even though they are not required to avert their eyes in deference.

The king uses the gift of his Voice to speak to all of the Galed, though he addresses only Sade. "Adara's spirit is a fickle one. She chooses one and claims the lives of the rest. It's clear the spirit has chosen you just as it chose Annabeth in her day."

Sade bows her head briefly to acknowledge the king's words. For half a millennium, the Waning ceremony has been done to choose the newest members of the Galed and to bind Adara's spirit within them. It's done only when a member of the Galed dies to keep the number of vessels at five. Every time a high priestess dies, the living members of the Galed partake in the ceremony, and despite having all survived it once, only one of the women survives it the second time. She becomes the high priestess and is joined by the four new women chosen by Adara's spirit. Because of this, the Galed are sometimes four and sometimes five, never more and never less.

More palace servants rush in, bearing platters of food for the nobility. Their platters overflow with nectarines and peaches, fruits of every shade and color. They eat rice with heavily spiced curries and have some fowl or fish to go with it. Despite the abundance and aroma of well-spiced food wafting through the air, no one so much as touches the food on their plate

"Eat," the king demands.

The nobles initially eat in silence, but soon, the banquet hall hums with whispers and hushed chatter. Lord Kim and Lord Hathaway continue their conversation.

Lord Kim hisses, "There's no need for an heir if one becomes immortal."

Chapter 9

It is the forty-second day of the season of the setting sun. The moon sits high in the sky, half of it shining brilliantly while the other half blurs into the night sky. On the ninetieth day, the moon will disappear entirely, and the Waning will be upon us. I haven't seen either Sade or Iyanu in the week following the banquet. Iyanu comes out only at strange hours of the night, and Sade maintains an unpredictable schedule. Both of them desperately try to avoid meeting each other in the rotunda. I know Iyanu tries to see the good in every person and every situation, but I don't know if she'll ever forgive Sade for what she's done.

It's no surprise that the king has given up on Lake Sarran. Sarran's retreat is accelerating. The palace aquametrists estimate that the lake might be completely dry in one hundred fifty years. At this rate, the king's great-grandchild, should he ever have any, would die of thirst despite being surrounded by wealth beyond belief.

The Galed are falling apart. Annabeth is dead, and Torrin is being held in the palace dungeon. The palace guards suspect me, and Sade grows more distant every day. This wouldn't be happening if Annabeth were still here.

I rise from my bed and make my way through the rotunda to the door that leads to her room. Annabeth had been Galed for over seven years. She's taken that time to make her room truly hers. Buckets sit in a corner near her desk, filled with bundles of indigo leaves and the stones atop them. Thirty-seven days after Annabeth's death, all of the water in the bucket has evaporated, but the still-damp leaves leave a musty, stale scent in the air. There's no doubt that they've started to accumulate a layer of mold.

Annabeth loved dying her clothes almost as much as she liked sewing them. Her once-white sheets, now dyed a deep purplish blue, are a testament to that. Annabeth confessed she felt guilty using so much water just for "fun." But she'd do it anyway.

"Pleasure is a form of resistance," she'd say.

Besides, the water used during the dyeing process doesn't need to go to waste. It's always collected and used to irrigate the expansive gardens adorning the palace grounds, something it would have been used for regardless.

I lie in Annabeth's bed, letting the covers envelop me, imagining it's Annabeth's embrace instead. I need her guidance more than ever. My body trembles as a bout of pain rakes up my spine.

I let out an unwilling gasp as my eyes fill with tears. But the pain isn't mine.

What are they doing to Torrin down there?

The pain subsides for now, and I pray that that means Torrin can heal herself just as effectively as she can others. I don't know why the pain hits me like it does when Sade and Iyanu aren't affected by it. It doesn't feel like it does in the brief moment of time when our spirits merge to create something bigger and we can feel each other. This is a one-way streak. And though I've felt glimpses of the other's feelings before, I've never felt anything like this.

The door to Annabeth's room cracks open. I sit up quickly, wiping the tears from my cheek and hoping that Sade, who's standing by the door, hasn't seen them.

"You can come in," I say.

Sade walks over and sits on the bed beside me without saying a word. Something in me is grateful to have her beside me. But some other part of me reels. Even when we haven't gotten along, we've never turned on one another. That unspoken rule has proved to be our greatest strength. How could Sade forget that? How could she betray Torrin?

"It all happened so quickly," she says. "I knew what I was doing, but it all happened so quickly that I didn't have time to think about it. That thing... it was unnatural," she continues. I nod my head in agreement. The creature *was* unnatural. Even now, the thought of it makes me recoil. What would I have done if I had been the one to stand instead of Sade? Could I have stopped Torrin? Or would both of us have been rounded up by the guards and taken to the dungeons together? Sade lifts her head to look me in the eyes. She's seeking my approval of her actions.

I say, "There's no telling what any of us would have done in that situation or even what we could have done. Torrin would never hurt anyone, but she was clearly out of control, and it could've ended horribly for her or the guests if someone didn't do something." I tell her this partly because it's true and partly because I know it's what she needs to hear.

"Right," Sade says, sounding unsure.

"We have to do something for her. We can't just leave her down there and let them continue doing whatever they're doing to her. We have to help her," I respond. Annabeth kept us all together. She treated each of us like we were her family. Now that she's gone, we have to keep the family together ourselves.

I'm surprised when Sade answers with more conviction this time. "You're right." A moment of silence passes, both of us unsure of what, if anything, could be done.

"What if you ask Lazarus?" Sade asks. "He might be able to help. The Berkshires might have curried some favor with the king. They might be able to leverage it for Torrin's release."

Even if they have, I can't say for sure that Lazarus would use it for me, let alone for Torrin. I decide to steer the conversation in a different direction.

"The creature... it looked like Queen Antares." I know what I saw, but this is the first time I've had the opportunity to confirm it with someone else.

"Could it really have been her?" Sade asks.

"Do you think Annabeth had anything to do with it?" I ask. The thought crosses my mind even if I'm unsure how she could be tied to all this. The extent of what Annabeth was capable of was a mystery even to the other members of the Galed. The king isn't known to have the gifts of transformation. His only gift is his Voice and the ability to call down the sun's rays. Yet it was there before our eyes, a never-before-seen creature bearing the queen's features. Annabeth's the only one I can think of who could have made something like that possible. I dismiss the idea anyway. She'd never do something like that.

"I don't know if she did, but I'm glad it's happening."

"You can't be serious, Sade," I say. "You saw that thing! That thing was..."

Sade cuts me off. "I know!" she says. "It was just the first trial. You can't expect it to be perfect on the first trial. You heard what the king said. The titans were immortal Meera. They don't need any food or water. Do you understand what that means, Meera? No water!" Sade huffs before continuing. "You remember what it was like living in the Endzone." She chokes as if just the memory of the kind of life we lived there could squeeze the air out of her. "Even your father would sneak canisters of water, and he was the best of us! It wouldn't matter if the nobles kept

127

us working on their estates or in their mines or wherever else. We'd go home every day free of hunger and thirst. We could finally have a life worth living." She says. "The trials will produce viable titans," she affirms. "We've always prayed that Rah make our existence on this earth more bearable. This could be the answer to our prayers."

I grab her arm and pull her down on the bed beside me, bringing her head towards my chest and twisting her dark, short curls around my fingers.

"I hope that it is," I answer. "I'll talk to Lazarus about Torrin. I'm sure he'll be able to do something." She nods, pressing her forehead into my chest. We lay down in silence until Sade's light snoring hums through the air. I fall asleep soon after, and when I wake up, Sade is no longer beside me.

———◆◇◆———

The next day, Lazarus knocks patiently on my door. I take a hard look at the note the palace maid gave me and decide to slip it underneath my bed. When I open the door, Lazarus confesses that he's been staying away from the palace, spooked by the creature at the banquet. The palace halls have been quieter these days, with few nobles appearing before the king.

"He can't possibly believe the nobles will submit themselves to become one of those *things*. The Kims are in disarray. The Tsosies are ready to threaten a full-on revolt, but of course, they're only saying that in private. A shame; Antares was one of their own yet they dare not speak against the crown." He paces back and forth, taking large steps to get from one side of my room to the other. His chin is covered with prickly new growth, and the skin beneath his eyes is gray with fatigue. Finally, he walks and sits on the chair by my desk, lowering his head in his hands while I remain on my bed. When I first got involved with Lazarus, I told myself I was using him. That one day, when it was finally the right time to dispose of Ryland, having Lazarus by my side would make the task easier. It's almost two years later, and this is the first time I've ever needed to ask him for something. And it's a favor to save my sister, not destroy the king.

"My father was this close to losing his life. He was right there, in between that thing and the girl. I swore that if it didn't kill her, she would have!" Lazarus runs a weary hand through his blonde hair.

"I'm glad your dad survived," I answer. I try my best to show Lazarus that I care about his father, but I don't want him to believe the worst about Torrin. "I'm glad everyone survived, but I don't think Torrin would have hurt anyone. You didn't feel what we felt. It spooked her, and she lashed out."

Lazarus looks at me. "Regardless..." He pauses. "Never mind," he says. "The king might just be mad, but if this experiment, this transformation, succeeds and he takes the step from human to titan, he'd rule forever."

Lord Kim's voice echoes in my mind: *no need for an heir if you become immortal.*

"Not only would he have the gift of immortality, but he'd also have the ability to bestow it on whoever he pleases. The nobles have stayed far away for now. But once they realize what this might mean, the palace will be filled to the brim with them. I've already convinced my father to visit the palace no later than the end of the week. We need to get ahead of this. Fast."

What Lazarus says doesn't surprise me. The nobles are and have always been in an endless state of jockeying against each other for power. To them, no advantage is too small, and an advantage like immortality is irresistible.

"If the king succeeds, the people will no longer need food or water. They could finally live lives worthy of living instead of living every day half-hoping it's their last," I say.

Lazarus chuckles. "Is that what you think will happen?" he asks incredulously. "Don't be stupid, Meera. Ryland doesn't give a shit about any of that. You know what he'll do? He won't let a single Endzoners become a titan. He'll let everyone die except for the ones he chooses to continue working as servants to the kingdom. Then he'll breed those that remain so that once they're dead and gone, their children can replace them. He'll do everything he can to stretch the water thin to keep them from going extinct, and once he can no longer do that, he'll finally turn them and find something else to hook them on to keep them subservient to him. Don't think for a second that this means anything for the Endzoners. He turned his own wife into a mindless beast for fucks sake."

I recoil at Lazarus's sharp words, even though I know there's truth in every one of them. I wanted to believe that the king's action represented a new hope for the kingdom, so I let Sade convince me that it was so.

I know better than to think that power in the wrong hands can be used for the right reasons.

"Meera." Lazarus softens his tone. "That's why I need you to help me. The kingdom can't thrive unless it has a new king. The Endzoners will never live a respectable life. I need you to survive the Waning to become strong enough to help me when the time comes." He walks over to my bed and kneels in front of me as he takes my hand in his.

I swallow the lump in my throat. "I want to help, I do. But I'm not strong enough by myself. Torrin...Torrin and Sade are the only ones who are strong enough to do it, and Sade has too much faith in Rah, in the king, to do anything like that. We have to help Torrin." My stomach twists in knots as I try to convince Lazarus. It doesn't matter that Torrin would never agree to be a pawn in Lazarus's make-believe coup. It doesn't matter that I doubt she'd even agree to play along. For Torrin, violence is a last resort, a means to eliminate direct threats to life, and nothing more. I push down the morsel of guilt that threatens to dissuade me. *I need to do this.*

"Besides, you'll want her on your side if she survives the Waning, and I don't."

Lazarus brushes off my comment. "You'll be alright," he says. "But, you make a good point. Breaking her out is too dangerous, but I'll see what I can do in terms of medicine and visitation."

I practically jump on his lamp, beaming. "Thank you! Thank you! Thank you!"

"Who's this girl, and what have you done with Meera?" he teases. "Seriously, I haven't seen you this happy in ages."

"I'll go get Sade and Iyanu. They need to know they can see Torrin, too." He makes a face at the mention of Sade. "Don't say anything about the throne," I warn. "Sade won't be receptive."

"Fine by me."

It takes me just two minutes to get Sade and Iyanu, with the latter protesting at my pulling her out of bed at such a late hour. Sade, on the other hand, well, I don't know if she ever sleeps. When we return, it's not just Lazarus standing at the center of my room, but Aris too. He stands firmly, his face stern and eyes peering intently. He seems to take up half of the space in the room and all of the air. Iyanu glances at Aris, then Lazarus, before looking back at me with horror. If she suspects anything, she says nothing about it.

"Be calm," Lazarus says. "I'm here to assist you with your friend, Torrin." Lazarus gestures to Aris. "This is my family's servant, Aris. You'll remember he welcomed you to my home a few weeks ago. He has an excellent knowledge of the many pathways and corridors in the palace, including those meant to be hidden from everyone except the king and those he bestows the knowledge upon. Aris has navigated these pathways successfully numerous times, and he can take you to see your friend using them. Once you are done speaking to her, he will return you to your rooms. He will do nothing less and nothing more than that."

I glance at Aris again, taking in the luster of his smooth, dark skin. The way his eyes take on the same dark, lustrous quality. He stays perfectly still during Lazarus's introduction. It's a sharp contrast to the thoughts racing through my mind. Aris is large—larger than most any servant I've seen. In fact, he's as large as many of the palace guards but without the stomach to boast. Why would he have any idea about the hidden pathways in the palace? I get the feeling that things aren't exactly as they seem with him and that maybe Lazarus's talk of overthrowing the king may not be just talk after all.

Aris crosses one bulky arm across the other. The black leather vest he wears strains from the flexion, hugging his skin more tightly.

"I'll take one of you at a time," he says.

Sade volunteers immediately. "I'll go first!" She can barely contain her excitement as she bounces with every word.

"Not today," Aris says. "I'll come back at dusk tomorrow and take each of you individually."

"Right, right. There's no need to be hasty." Lazarus interjects before Sade can respond. "Aris, you're free to leave."

Aris turns without a word, waiting briefly before leaving. Guards rarely patrol this part of the palace, however, and the only time servants come near it is when they're delivering food or messages.

Lazarus turns to Iyanu and Sade. "You're dismissed as well."

Sade scowls. Iyanu only looks slightly peeved. This is not the Berkshire estate, and no one in the palace is under any obligation to follow Lazarus's commands. Still, he does this out of habit, and a habit formed is difficult to break. Neither Sade nor Iyanu comment on the transgression. Though I have no doubt that Lazarus wouldn't change his mind, they know a snarky response here is not worth the risk of not being able to see Torrin.

"Of course," Iyanu answers. "Do greet my mom and dad for me when you see them next." Iyanu is a daughter of the Idowu family. Her comment serves to remind Lazarus of that. When Iyanu and Sade exit, I ask Lazarus about Aris and his role as a servant on the Berkshire estate.

"All the noble families have at least one of him," Lazarus explains. "It'd be suicide not to. Servants like him gather information on the palace and everything and everyone in it and on the other noble families. They keep tabs on the Midzoners who do business with our families, and they identify ventures that may be of interest and situations that might raise concerns for our standing with the palace. Information is power, Meera.

Aris is how the Berkshires get ours. Luckily for us, Aris shows great acumen in combat as well. Because of that, he can serve a dual purpose: to protect the family whenever necessary." He shakes his head gently. "He's good but not perfect. The king still managed to keep the details of his experiments from us after all."

"Why didn't you tell me?" I ask. Aris knew exactly who I was that day at the Berkshire estate. Panic begins to build within me. How much does Lazarus know about me or my ties to the resistance? Where do Aris's loyalties lie?

"There was no reason to, until now," he answers.

I wonder what else he's keeping from me.

Chapter 10

U nable to continue toeing the line between my dreams and reality, I rise the next morning with the half-moon still high in the sky. My mind buzzes with anxiety as I replay my interactions with Aris. I think about the first time I met him at the Berkshire estate when he told me he picked me out by random chance and how he stopped me from running after Torrin. *Is Aris a spy for the resistance? Is he a spy for the Berkshires? Could he be both, or maybe neither?*

In the rotunda, I grab a pair of shears from the altar, snipping blush-colored leaves from the stems of a moonshade. I place the snippings in the mortar, mixing them with carilea roots and grounding them together in smooth, circular motions with the pestle. Each thump bounces off the walls and echoes through the room, and I find myself entranced by the rhythm I create. Annabeth's ring shines in front of me. I find myself rubbing its smooth surface, sending her a prayer, and begging her to send me her strength and poise. I never thought I'd be mimicking Iyanu, but desperate times call for desperate measures.

When mixed in the right proportions, the compounds in these plants bind together, forming a substance that can travel through the bloodstream. No animation from the Galed needed. Anyone in the kingdom could make it if they knew how. Poisons are a lot easier than medicines. Annabeth called it the quake. "Just a nick with a blade soaked in this is all it takes." These were the moments when I listened to Annabeth the most intensely when she spoke of the many ways one might inflict death. I drank in her words more eagerly than any water, dreaming of when I would put it to use. I never imagined that my first victim would be an Oguni.

The quake starts with a tremble. A twitch of an eyelid, a slight shiver down the back. The sensation leaves for some time, only to come back stronger. In just half an hour, the person drops to the floor, convulsing so hard that the impact of their head thrashing against the ground ultimately kills them. When the symptoms of the poison started presenting themselves, people thought they could save the victims by tying them down, but stopping the external convulsions did nothing to quell the internal tremors. Even when restrained, the victims' brains would collide with their skulls, and their hearts beat out of rhythm, resulting in a quiet death.

I scrape the paste from the mortar with a dagger and dump its contents into the smallest of the three bowls on the altar. The only way to know if I prepared it right is to test it. That means I need to find something alive and make it dead. With guards patrolling every hall, my best bet is to blend in with the palace servants and hope to avoid Nicholas.

I walk into Annabeth's room and grab her indigo bed sheets, using the dagger and my hands to make rips and tears. When I'm satisfied with the results, I bring the sheet back into the rotunda and stain the fabric with soil and liquid from the roots and leaves of the renser plants, hoping to make the sheet look a bit more ragged. I tie the resulting garment across my chest, letting it fall over the rest of my body. I use one of the scraps I ripped off to secure the dagger and vial to the inside of my thigh. Hopefully, the guards won't notice that the garment still looks too new, that the tears too neat, or that the stains lie on the surface instead of merging with the fabric. In this, I should be able to pass for a garden-hand.

I turn just two corners before a guard stops me—one that I've never seen before. He has the kind of face that makes it hard to place his age. He could be nineteen years old just as easily as he could be forty. He's small in stature, with a moderate frame. His short, amber hair recedes on either side of his forehead, giving his hairline an arrow shape.

"What's your business?" He asks. His voice is raspy, his tone, reserved. He looks me over twice before raising his gaze to meet mine.

I stammer before answering. "I'm a palace maid."

He looks at me as if I've just said the stupidest thing he's ever heard.

"Yes," he replies. His tone betrays his annoyance. "What's your business?" He waits just an instant before continuing. "Answer now," he demands. He brings the tip of his sword out and presses it to the flesh of my breast.

Don't panic, I tell myself. "The king has requested my presence," I offer. The tenor of my voice makes me nervous, even to my own ears.

"No need to be coy about it," he says, averting his eyes. "You're not the first maid to grace the king's bed." He retracts his sword and stands at attention as I shuffle past him.

The dark stone floor in the atrium feels cool underneath my bare feet, and despite having seen this place for the second time in a month, the strange creatures carved into the citrine still send a shiver through me. They feel obscure yet familiar.

One of the four-legged creatures, with a sharp, pointed face and a slender yet muscled body, catches my eye. Something about it calls to me. As I stare at its form, a hummingbird lands on top of the creature's head. Its wings buzz wildly, and its small body whizzes when it changes direction. It pauses there, on top of the creature, for a second before descending towards me.

I snatch the bird out of the air, snapping its wings between my fingers. It makes a horrid screeching sound, but it doesn't so much as twitch. Its eyes remain steady as they bore into mine. My hands feel steady as they reach underneath my sheet dress, pulling the dagger and vial from the strip I tied around my thigh.

I dip the blade in the vial for extra measure. I drag the tip of the dagger across its neck, making the smallest nick. A singular drop of blood drips from the wound, tinting the iridescent purple feathers on the bird's neck a reddish hue. It takes all of ten seconds before the bird spasms. I breathe a sigh of relief. It worked. I crush the bird's head between my palm and the ground before I leave. The way its skull collapses in on itself is both surprising and terrifying. If what Lazarus told me is true, Aris will not die so easily. I stop myself from thinking about what this might mean.

In my room, I tear the indigo sheets off my body and quickly pull on my white gown and veil. I'm barely done dressing when Sade comes bursting in. Iyanu comes quickly after that, and surely enough, two faint knocks on my door alert us to Aris's presence on the other side.

Sade bounces gleefully as he enters the room. "Take me first," she beams. Iyanu stares daggers at her. Yep, she definitely hasn't forgiven Sade.

"I'm going first!" I interject before Aris has the chance to answer.

Everyone turns to look at me, and suddenly, the dagger feels cold pressed against my thigh. It would be too easy for Aris to pick us off individually, especially if we're not expecting it. If I don't go first, Sade and Iyanu could be killed.

Surprisingly, Sade doesn't fight back. "O.k.," she says nonchalantly.

"When should we come back?" Iyanu asks.

"We should be back within the hour," Aris answers.

Sade and Iyanu leave the room, leaving me alone with Aris. My heart starts racing. I wonder if he can tell that my guard is heightened. I decide to break the silence, hoping he hasn't yet sensed my apprehension.

"Are you sure you can get us to the cellars without incident?" I hope he'll interpret this as me not trusting his abilities instead of not trusting his intentions.

"I've done it often enough," he answers. "Lazarus took care of the guards down there. They won't be attending to Torrin for the next five hours," he continues. He raises his arms over his head, then brings them down, using his hands to smooth over his copper-colored hair. Aris opens the door and beckons me into the hallway.

"The guards keep to a schedule. We shouldn't be running into any of them before we get to the passages." When I move to walk past him, Aris catches my arm. He lifts a small piece of fabric from his hand and beckons me to turn around. I frown but don't respond.

"I'm going to blindfold you. It's just a precaution," he says.

I don't bother to hide my suspicion anymore. "A precaution against what?" I ask.

"Because if you're stupid enough to try running after Torrin with dozens of guards and the king himself present, then you just might be stupid enough to try getting her out of the cellars if you know how to get there," he answers. "Look," Aris says with a sigh. "It's just a precaution. Lazarus doesn't want you trying something you'll regret." I let him turn me around, keeping still as he reaches his arms in front of me and brings the fabric over my eyes. He ties a loose knot at the back of my head, his hands rustling my locs as he does so.

"Good?"

"It's fine," I answer.

Aris leads me through the halls with one hand on my arm the whole time. Even though I can't see, I make mental notes of our path. Take the first right when I step outside of my room. Take thirty steps, then another thirty. Take twenty steps, then turn right again. Eventually, Aris leads us down a walkway with bare, rough, unpaved stairs. I know this is a hidden path because all of the hallways and all of the staircases in the palace are polished smooth and draped with carpeting. The door closes behind us, and I sense the sunlight dimming through my blindfolds. Aris lights a torch, restoring a reddish hue to my vision. If Aris killed me here, no one would hear my screams. The thought alone is enough to send me into a panic. I pull the blindfold off and reach for the knife tied around my thighs, pointing it at Aris just as he turns and lunges towards me. Aris halts, giving me a pointed look before bringing his hands above his head.

"What are you doing with that?" he asks.

"Nothing. Unless you make me do something I don't want to."

143

"Go on," I prod. Aris turns his back and leads us down the corridor. My hands tighten around the grip of my knife. "You said it would only be an hour round trip, so we better be there in the next twenty minutes."

"Right," Aris says. We take a left turn, and then a right.

"Shit," I curse under my breath. Sometime between when we first entered the passageway and now, I forgot to keep memorizing the turns we took. Aris drops the torch in his hands, snuffing out what little light we had in the corridors. The hall turns pitch black before my eyes. Swinging my knife out in front of me, I take a few steps backward and brace myself. I might not be able to defend myself against Aris, but Rah be damned, I can make sure that he won't have the opportunity to harm Iyanu, Torrin, or Sade. I steady my breath and calm my heart rate. All I need to do is graze him.

I don't hear Aris's steps. I barely even sense his presence at all. In an instant, one of his hands has grabbed my arm, and the other knocks the knife out of my fingertips. Aris lifts me by the ribcage and shoves me against the wall. He pins my hands above my head and presses his body against mine, trapping me against the wall. I try to focus on the way the cobbled stone feels rough against my neck as he brings his lips to the side of my ear and whispers. His fingertips, the air in his breath, his thigh pressed against mine—it all feels dangerously warm.

"Do you have anything else up your sleeve?" His breath feels warm against my cheek. I raise my knee, trying to catch him between his legs, but he's fast. He moves his knee so that we collide kneecaps instead. I let out a loud whimper.

"Scream if you want," he says. "No one can hear you here."

Warmth rushes to my cheek, fueled both by my anger and my embarrassment.

"If you're going to kill me, just do it now," I seethe, even when I know I want nothing more than to live.

Aris bursts into laughter. "You think I'm here to kill you?" he asks, puzzled. "How do you think Lazarus would react if somehow, right after I was tasked to guide you to your friend, you disappeared." Aris shakes his head in disbelief. "I'm not so careless."

"Then what exactly is your plan? Who do you owe your allegiance to? Why did you lie about knowing who I was?"

He huffs, "I could ask you the same. You were sent here over a year ago, and you've turned up with nothing. Instead of playing your part, you're sleeping with a nobleman. I warned you about staying away from Lazarus. You have no idea what that man is capable of. What exactly is *your* plan?" he counters.

"Exactly," Aris says when I don't respond. He releases his grip on me, grabs the torch from the floor, and lights it. He doesn't bother with the blindfold anymore.

"Come on," he says.

We walk silently until Aris stops in front of a solid wall that spells a dead end. He turns to look me in the eye.

"You're not going to like what you see," he warns. I nod knowingly. If my time with Nicholas was any indicator of what goes on in these cellars, I know that Torrin will have been kept in horrid conditions.

"We won't stay too long, so the others can have time to visit before the guard's shift ends."

"The guard that Lazarus paid off?"

"Yes."

"Well, what are you waiting for?" I ask impatiently.

"One more thing. I want you to see something on our way back." He looks me over once but doesn't press when I don't reply.

Aris hands me the torch, places both palms on the stone wall, and pushes. He strains with the effort, and the veins running down the side of his forehead protrude. The wall moves slowly, swinging inward. The stench of rotting flesh and feces permeates the air. The corridors leading to the cellars were dark and gray. Lifeless. The cellars, however, are not just devoid of life but filled with death. The atmosphere is rancid. The weight of hundreds or perhaps thousands of souls who have suffered in the cruelest and most unusual ways presses down on me. The conditions only get worse the further into them you go.

Torrin's cell is only a few paces away from the door. I squint, trying to see her in the dim lighting. The cream tunic she had been wearing during the king's banquet is now muddied and opaque with a thin layer of something unknown coating its surface. Broken pieces of cowrie shells from her headpiece are sprawled over the floor. Her blue ribbons remain tied around her forearms, but they're tattered and hanging by mere threads. Something thick and pungent rises in the back of my throat. The taste of my spit feels bitter in my mouth. If the king had been down here with us, it would not have been Torrin he would need to worry about. Despite the state of her clothes, Torrin looks unharmed. She has no open wounds, cuts, or scarring to speak of. Her movements look pain-free, and besides her outward appearance, everything seems to be in order.

"Meera," Torrin calls. I run towards the cellar door and kneel in front of the gate, grabbing Torrin's hands and wrapping them in mine. Sparks run up my arms when we connect.

"I swear," I begin, "I will get you out of here."

Torrin nods emphatically. Tears run down her cheeks, leaving a trail of clean ivory skin in their wake. "And Iyanu and Sade?" She asks.

"They'll come with Aris after I leave. We don't have much time." Suddenly, the back of my throat starts to burn, and I choke. I say, "But you'll be out of here soon, and we'll all be back together."

"Of course," she replies, but I can tell she doesn't agree wholeheartedly. "Aris?" she asks.

"It's a long story."

"Is he a friend of Lazarus?"

"You know about Lazarus?"

147

She dismisses the question. "There's no time for us to discuss that now."

I swallow before asking, "What are they doing to you in here?"

Torrin gives me a knowing look. "Meera," she says with more force this time. She glances to the right, giving Aris a quick look before focusing back on me. "Something's coming, Meera," she says, hushed. "I can see it sometimes," she frowns. "When they... discipline me." Torrin shakes her head. "I don't get all of it, but I know you can feel it too." My mind drifts to my dreams where I'm in Lake Sarran, being dragged to the water's depths by a being I've never seen.

"The Waning?" I ask.

"No," Torrin hisses. "It's something different." Her lips press together, forming a straight line. "It'll come to you."

Aris takes a few steps towards us. His footsteps are barely audible, even in the stiff silence of the cellars. "We need to be going," he says matter-of-factly. Something in his voice sounds different to me now. Or maybe there's something different about the way my ears process his words. He sounds warmer. I turn back to Torrin, trying to get rid of the images of Aris pressed into earlier that are now running freely through my mind. Torrin raises an eyebrow but doesn't say anything to me.

Instead, she turns to Aris, "thank you for bringing Meera." Aris nods. Torrin pulls my head down, kissing my forehead gently. "I'll see you soon." My heart sinks even further into my stomach when the door to the cellar closes behind us.

"I need to show you something," says Aris.

"Right," I respond.

Aris sighs. "I understand if you can't today."

"Will it help Torrin?"

"What?" Aris asks.

"What you're showing me. Will it help Torrin?"

Aris pauses, considering what I've just asked. "It will help you. So if helping you helps Torrin, then yes."

Aris leads us on a path that's supposed to take us to the king's private study, which also serves as one of the largest libraries in the kingdom. He explains that the king and his priests gather there to discuss the experiments they conduct to create titans. Up until now, Aris had thought it was all theoretical.

After all, the king has always promised to bring Rah's favor and return the nobles to the glory of titanhood. He didn't quite understand all the jargon they were using, nor did he anticipate how far along in their experiments they had already gone. And how exactly was going to one of these meetings supposed to help me? He answered cryptically the first time I asked.

"Knowledge is power, and power is helpful." The second thing he said was more helpful. "I heard them talking about Annabeth once," he says. "Whatever they're doing, Annabeth played a part in it. And if Annabeth played a part in it, you or others might soon be called to take over from her. It could be your opportunity to get close to the king."

The mention of Annabeth makes me quicken my pace. I try not to jump to conclusions, thinking back to my conversations with Bridgette. Maybe these were the meetings that allowed Annabeth to get close enough to the king to slip him something that rendered him impotent. Annabeth may have been risking her life doing the work that I was meant to do. I've let myself get complacent over the two years, just hoping that something might change even though it never had, and it never would. My idleness is the reason Annabeth got killed. It's also why the king is even alive and well enough to act on his ill-fated dreams of immortality through titanhood. My days of sitting idle are over.

"You mentioned the resistance's new leader. Bear. Did you manage to convince him to stop targeting the Galed? Does he still think releasing Adara's spirit is the only way to change things for Endzoners?" Is he still trying to murder me and my sisters?

"He's put that plan on pause for now. He has his doubts, but I've managed to convince him of another way."

"And what way is that?"

"The women who've volunteered. About three dozen of them have ties to the resistance. Maybe one of you couldn't get the job done, but if we can get two or even three of you, that's a different story. Bear also knows that killing the king isn't enough. Not when there's a squadron of nobles ready to take his place. The resistance grows, but our numbers are no match for the kingsguard. They're hardly a match for the army a lower-born noble could buy. We need something deadlier than any man or any army. We need the Galed."

"How much bigger is it than when I was last there?"

Though it's not what I asked, Aris can tell I'm looking for any information I can get.

"It's changed a lot since you've been gone. We're three times as big, and Bear's a genius. We grow the food in just water now. It sounds crazy, but the plants are getting twice as big, twice as fast. Now he's thinking of a way to get more water. He thinks there might be some right underneath our feet. Meera. So much has changed. You'll see when you get there."

We climb a staircase that takes us to what again seems to be a solid wall.

"We're here," Aris remarks.

This time, he carefully removes four adjacent stones from the solid wall, revealing a glass-like material. When I peer through it, I can make out the four wide legs of a wooden table and the four legs of a wooden chair, which stand much closer together. Though we've climbed the stairs to get here, we're just at the ground level of the study.

"How can't they see us?" I ask.

"It's a special kind of glass. It only lets you see and hear through to the side with more light."

There are at least five people present. Three of them are priests, judging by the absence of footwear and the presence of sacrificial scarring near their ankles. One wears a pair of solid gold sandals with feet that dwarf those of the other four. That is the king. The last person is unknown to me. They are either a child or a woman, and the footwear seems to be that of a Midzoner. Hamel leather sandals. Nothing too fancy. What unnerves me is the color of the bottom of their garment—a pale white, just like the gowns the Galed wear.

Chapter 11

"**M**y king."

I wanted to believe that it was someone else. Anyone else. But the voice is undeniably Sade's. If the glass hadn't been a one-way portal, my gasp would have alerted anyone within one hundred paces of our presence on the other side of the wall. Aris shakes his arm free of mine. I hadn't even noticed how tightly I was clutching it.

"This is the first time I've seen her here," he says. Good, I think. I shouldn't jump to conclusions.

"Do you know why I've decided to bring you here, Sade?" the king asks. I don't hear the response, but I assume she's given some type of acknowledgment when he continues.

"My mother and father, Their Majesties Floris and Grace, ruled this kingdom justly. May they take their place among Rah's chosen. Still, no sovereign has the might to save a nation when the very planet it stands upon and the very gods that rule over it turn their backs."

"Of course, my king," Sade concurs.

"We're taught from the day we're born that there was no greater period on earth than the days of the titans. We all had Rah's favor after just receiving the blessing of becoming his creation. When I first began my rule, a return to the glory of titanhood was just a lip service I paid to the nobles—a witty motto meant to quell their overly restless minds. Now, that refrain is becoming a reality."

Sade doesn't answer.

"Do you know why I brought you here?" the king asks a second time.

"No," she says.

"I'm giving you the opportunity to help me make history, Sade. How would you like to be remembered as the person who helped bring humanity back into Rah's light? Who delivered us all from the weaknesses of our human flesh?" Sade is silent once again.

"There's great suffering in this kingdom. I know that that suffering is intensified on the margins." Aris and I scoff in unison, then give each other a look. What does the king know about suffering? "This could greatly alleviate that suffering for all the people. Don't you agree, Sade?"

"The titans. They don't need food or water." Sade says this as if she's assuring herself rather than asking the king.

"Yes. Even in these initial stages, our first successful trial drinks only a tenth of the water the average man needs."

"Why me?"

"I saw what you did during the banquet and was impressed by your strength and courage. I chose you because you are the only one strong enough to do what I'm asking. I know the Waning is fast approaching. Though your sisters will likely die when it comes, I expect you to survive to become the high priestess. Our work here is too precious to put on hold as we await the ceremony. You must begin your work now. The fate of the kingdom rests on your shoulders."

"What do you need me to do?" Sade says.

"During my readings, I kept coming across the same passage repeatedly. Adara presented herself to the titans and cursed them. Then, when Adara's madness possessed nearly one in every seven women, Rah descended once more and rid us of the demon. He banished Adara, trapping her essence in the bodies of five women. I knew this, yet I read it over and over again. Then it came to me. The curse, Sade, is that we are all made to harbor a little piece of Adara in us. It's not just the Galed, Sade. Even after Rah's efforts, Adara's spirit lingers like a parasite that lives within us. The parasite demands that we feed it and water it. It keeps our skin soft and our bones feeble. The only way to return to good health is to remove the parasite from our bodies."

The gold sandals on the king's feet chime against the stone floor as he moves closer to Sade.

"I need you to remove the parasite, Sade."

Sade starts to speak, but the king silences her.

"It took Annabeth and me years to get Antares right. It took the scholars several years before that to understand how the process might be done. When you remove Adara's essence from the host, I will fill the void left behind with Rah's light."

The priests scuffle around the study, walking towards the shelves and then coming back. The sound of books plopping onto the table fills the air.

"Annabeth kept a journal that might be of some assistance to you. Those that came before her kept some as well. They are all here for your reading."

"I can't read," Sade says plainly.

"Chandon here will assist you. He will not be able to read Annabeth's writings, nor will he be able to read the writings of those before her. They've written in a strange and inconsistent alphabet. Nonetheless, we've found that simply knowing how to read aids in helping your kind understand what the words mean. You will begin today."

I loosen my grip for the second time, realizing that I'd been clenching them so hard that the skin of my palms now burns from the marks left behind. How could Sade even think about becoming a pawn in the king's plan? Still, there is no saying no to the king. Sade and I must be strategic about going along with his wishes as we undermine them.

I turn from the glass pane.

"Where are you going," Aris asks.

"Back to my room."

"It's in the other direction," he says dryly. I turn around without a response. He sighs, then turns to follow me in return. "It's been a long day for you."

"It has," I answer. "You're going to tell Lazarus everything you saw?"

Aris shakes his head. "I'll tell him only what I need to."

"Good. Don't tell him about Sade yet." Aris raises an eyebrow but otherwise makes no indication that he's accepted or refused my request.

"We need to get those journals," he says.

My mind sifts through the potential information that could be in the journals of Galed past. Is there information about the Waning or Adara and what it means to be one of her vessels? I wonder how long the monarchy has been selecting a Galed of their choosing and grooming them into the person that would be most useful to them.

"I agree, but the king and scholars will notice their absence if they're stolen."

"That isn't a problem. We'll study them and leave them there. We'll go for as long and as often as needed until you understand what's in those journals." Aris doesn't look ahead, as he adds. "I'll teach you how to read so you have just as much of a chance as Sade."

"It's too risky." The study only has one entrance and one exit. There would be no escaping if we ever got caught. "Besides, there's no need for us to do that when Sade will tell us what she's learned." Aris raises a brow but says nothing.

I turn towards him. "How did you learn how to read?"

"What good is a spy if he can't gather information by all the means available for sharing it? The nobles read and write Meera. If I'm to be useful, I need to be able to report back to the Berkshires with what I've heard, seen, and read."

I think back to the note given to me by the woman. I wonder if she was a part of the resistance. But most Endzoners can't read or write, and they would have known that I would need the help of another to read it. "Did Bear or anyone else send me a letter through a maid?"

"No, did you receive one?" I hesitate to tell Aris this, but with all we've been through, it can't hurt to tell him one more thing.

"We greeted the women who volunteered themselves about a month ago, and as I was leaving, one of the palace maids gave me a note. I thought she might be a resistance spy, but now I'm unsure. I need to know what was written."

"Why didn't you have Lazarus read it for you?"

"Will you read it for me?" I ask again. Aris nods and carries on through the corridors, not bothering to press the issue. We emerge from the corridors into a brightly lit hallway. The change in darkness blinds me temporarily. When my eyes adjust to the light, I see that Aris is already several steps ahead. I race to catch up, but Aris turns to me with a frown, bringing his index finger to his lips, gesturing for me to be quiet. I soften my steps in response. It seems like every other corner we turn, we catch the back of a guard who's just leaving. Aris has this down to a science.

———◀○▶———

A sense of relief washes over me when we return to my room, and I collapse on my bed with a sigh. I unwrap the piece of fabric tied around my thigh, grab the knife in it, and throw it towards the corner of the room. It lands on the floor with a clink. I pull the thin piece of wrinkled paper from underneath my pillow and look it over. Aris stands in front of me, waiting for me to give it to him. He looks it over briefly, then brings the note down by his side.

"What does it say?" I ask impatiently.

Aris answers my question with one of his own. "All this time you've been here, Meera, what have you been doing? What did you learn from Annabeth, and why do you think Rah's chosen keeps Adara's vessels close? Tell me everything that's happened since you survived the Waning."

His questions catch me by surprise, although they shouldn't. This is an information exchange. Give something to get something.

I tell him about the night of the Waning, how I felt full, practically overflowing with power, and even though I didn't know what it was or how to use it, I slinked through the palace halls intending to end the king's life that night. "Annabeth stopped me," I explain. That night, my senses seemed heightened, but I know that not only were they heightened but enmeshed with my sisters'. After that night, Annabeth and I never spoke of what I was intending to do, and I never tried to end the king's life again. Instead, she gave us all upkeep tasks inside of our rotunda. Torrin fetches and waters the plants. Iyanu and Sade trim leaves and sometimes roots to prevent them from getting unsightly. We sharpen Annabeth's blades, sweep and mop our quarters, and attend ceremonies, banquets, or official visits per the king's request. The flora help Annabeth with making medicines, poisons, or whatever else she might need. She taught us some of them but not all."

"And the power? What is it?"

"I don't know. When Annabeth was around, it wasn't like this. We sometimes felt it. Like she was using whatever is in us to do something." Aris looks me in the eyes, prodding me to continue. "When we had an official visit to the departed commissioner's home, the day Annabeth died." I frown. "After his daughter stabbed her, I felt everyone else. It was like being in their bodies, experiencing what they were experiencing. It was impossible to tell what was coming from me and what wasn't. The others hadn't but I'd felt traces of something like it before, but nothing as intense as that night. Then, collectively, we poured Adara's essence out of us, and it felt like we were

160

bending reality to our will. We all wanted the girl to die. Then she choked and fell dead."

"And at the king's banquet," Aris asks. "Did you feel the others when Torrin shook the room and Sade stopped her?"

"Yes, a little. And sometimes I feel a bit of the pain Torrin gets in those dungeons, but it's nothing like what we experienced when Annabeth was here directing us. Nothing like this had ever happened before. Torrin couldn't heal herself or anybody else, for that matter. Sade couldn't snap bones on command. None of us could do anything that wasn't in conjunction with Annabeth. And now some of us can."

Aris's eyes never leave mine. "Why do you think that is?"

I scoff. "How am I supposed to know?" When Aris doesn't respond, I continue. "I think when Annabeth died, the portion of Adara's spirit she embodied was redistributed to us. Maybe Torrin or Sade got more of it."

"Maybe," Aris concedes. "Is it possible that Annabeth could have been tamping down Adara's power within you all?"

"I guess it's possible," I respond. "What does the note say?"

"The girl who gave it to you is pregnant," he says. "With the king's child."

Chapter 12

A knock at the door forces me to close my mouth and wipe the shock from my face. Iyanu waltzes in, striding tepidly but joyously. Aris's eyes linger on the space between the door to the rotunda and the wall as the door closes. They snap back to Iyanu when she speaks.

"I tried to get Sade, but she wasn't in her room," she says. "So, I guess it's my turn to visit Torrin next." I look at Aris at the mention of Sade's name but quickly look back towards Iyanu, hoping she didn't notice the exchange.

"That's weird," I respond, leaving it at that.

It feels strange telling half-truths to Iyanu. I've kept things from her before, and I've certainly kept things from the others, but nothing like this. I just need the chance to talk to Sade about it first and convince her that the king is not to be trusted. I don't know how Iyanu would react to the news. Iyanu's devotion to Adara is unquestionable, and after being born in a man's body and surviving an initiation that accepts only women, her resolve in Adara has only grown. She left a life of luxury and abundance that most people in the kingdom could only dream of so that she could fetch water, trim plants, do whatever Annabeth says, and be paraded around like the king's trophy—all at the beckoning of a Goddess who's appeared to her just once.

"How is she?" Iyanu shifts her weight from left to right as she asks this.

"She's doing better than I expected," I answer honestly. How Torrin is managing to do it is a mystery to me, but I'm glad that her strength has not been broken. Seeing Torrin in any worse of a state than she's in now would have shattered me. Iyanu runs her hands over her ferocious curls, smoothing them down only for them to spring back up as she passes over them.

"Ok, I'm ready," she says.

Aris walks past her towards the window, checking the stone-carved sundial in the center of the palace garden. He stands there waiting for a few minutes before he signals that he's ready as well. Before they leave, Iyanu pulls me in for a brief hug and gives me a weary smile as she walks out the door. I used to think Iyanu was the strongest of us after Annabeth died. I wonder how strong she actually is and how much of it is show for the rest of our sakes.

Iyanu and Aris return about an hour later, and Sade enters my room just a few minutes after they do.

"I can't believe I'm going last," she whines playfully. This bothers me. I hope her cheeriness is a veil for her fear and discomfort. I hope that she's shaken to the core at the king's request.

"The early bird gets the worm," Iyanu shrugs. "Where were you anyway?" Iyanu asks.

Sade doesn't miss a beat. "I was doing laundry."

If Iyanu thinks it strange that one would do laundry right before seeing a loved one who's been shackled and tortured for several days, she doesn't say it.

"It helps me stay calm," Sade adds.

Aris walks toward the window for the second time, gazing at the sundial. He beckons Sade when he's ready to leave.

As the door closes, Iyanu says, "We must get Torrin out of there." Her eyes light up, and the vein on the right side of her forehead becomes more prominent as she clenches her teeth.

"We will," I reply.

"You'll speak to Lazarus again."

"I will."

Her shoulders sag as if there's an invisible weight bearing down on them. Her hands shake as she runs her fingers through her hair a second time. She mutters something unintelligible before speaking again.

Her voice sounds hoarse when she says, "Meera."

Her lower eyelids glisten as the moisture pooling in them catches the afternoon sun. She takes two large strides towards me and gathers me in her arms. Her embrace feels hot and painful, like peeled skin after hours in the afternoon sun. My head presses against her chest, and both of my arms are sandwiched awkwardly between hers. The tears falling down her face drop onto the back of my neck, leaving a trail of moisture there. I feel my face getting hotter and my throat closing in on itself.

I try to reassure her. "Torrin doesn't look so bad."

"But what if they go too far, Meera? There's no coming back from..."

Death. There's no coming back from death. I shake my head, wrestling the thought out of my mind. The king would never allow that. If Torrin were to die, the part of Adara's spirit she harbors within her would be redistributed within Iyanu, Sade, and I, making each of us that much more powerful and dangerous. The Galed are sometimes five and sometimes four, but from what we've been taught, there have never been just three.

"The king won't allow that. It's too dangerous." I reassure Iyanu and myself as well. "We would never allow it. We're going to get her out."

"You're right." Iyanu's voice is low. It hums soothingly and melodically, carrying itself across the room like the wings of a hummingbird.

"Get some rest," I tell her.

"Yes," Iyanu nods, releasing me from her embrace. "I'm sure you need some as well."

As Iyanu leaves the room, I consider that murdering Torrin might be just what the king planned. If Adara's spirit was unequally distributed when Annabeth died, there's no reason it wouldn't be unequally distributed a second time around. A Sade with more power could be exactly what he needs to successfully create a titan.

That evening, a knock on my door rouses me out of my sleep. Aris doesn't wait to be invited in. Instead, he walks right past me without saying hello, closing the door behind him as he does. I've decided that Aris looks best at night. Something about the silver sheen of the moon's glow illuminates the blueness of his skin. His copper-toned hair makes him look not entirely of this world. Like he was sent here from a different planet or fallen to this world as punishment by the gods. I walk past him and sit on the edge of my bed. I have to beckon him towards the chair and desk at the corner of my room before he takes a seat as well. His dark leather pants crease awkwardly when he does, but his leather vest is better fitted and stays put. My mind suddenly wanders to what I'm wearing—my thin white nightgown with nothing underneath. I fight the urge to get back underneath my sheets or ask him to leave.

"Why are you here?" my voice sounds groggy. Not hostile, but also not very welcoming.

"We still have things to discuss," he answers.

That we do. The knowledge that the king might have an heir had been toiling around my mind for the better part of the day.

There's no way Ryland knows any of it. If he did, the girl would never have been given enough room to be at the atrium where she handed me the note. Even with a successor, King Ryland has the drive and the ego to believe that he should rule forever. Of course, he'd try to become a titan. But it's the child that weighs most heavily on my mind. The child, no matter how young, would always be a threat. Even if I killed Ryland and the resistance did away with the monarchy, the child could claim the throne as his birthright.

"Couldn't it wait until the morning?"

"I told Lazarus that the king and priests would meet this evening to talk about the titans a few days back. He expects me to be there right now. It's a good alibi."

It makes sense that the Berkshires try to keep a tight leash on Aris. They wouldn't want him coming and going as he pleased.

"I don't know what to think of the girl and her child. How do we know it belongs to King Ryland? It could just as easily belong to any of the guards, the priests, or the dozens of nobles that frequent the court," I muse.

"Have you ever known a guard or priest that's impregnated a palace maid? The king takes only female servants for a reason. He selects them for a reason. Even though he doesn't know the first thing about what it takes to survive as a maid in the palace. The guards know better than to go near them in that way. They have their fun outside if they must. If a child is born to anyone in the palace, it's to be the king's." Aris continues, "it's possible that it isn't the king's child, but we have to entertain the possibility that it is."

"She knew me by name, yet she didn't know I couldn't read. Why did she give me the note? It doesn't make any sense."

Aris concurs, asking some questions of his own. "If you were a palace maid, pregnant with the king's child, with no queen in sight, shouldn't that be the most joyous day of your life?"

"The maids had this rumor." I clear my throat before speaking again. "They thought Annabeth was doing something to the king that made him impotent." I wasn't impressed when Bridget first brought that information to me, but it can't be a coincidence that now that Annabeth is dead, one maid is suddenly pregnant with a child. "It was just a rumor, of course. But it seems like most of them were perfectly fine with thinking that was the case. Either they were too afraid to confront Annabeth and relay their concerns to the king, or whatever the king was doing to those girls was so horrible that the thought of bearing his child became untenable."

"It's possible," Aris says. "Maybe the right question is, what do you do if you're a king, unable to produce an heir for over a decade of your rule, and one of your palace maids has become pregnant with your child?"

"Another king might elevate her to some status. He might even marry her. But a king who turned his own wife into a monster?" And one that has likely turned others into something unspeakable in his attempts to create those monsters. I finish my sentence, "The king views them only as property. Being pregnant with his child makes her more expensive property. With no noble title and no one to defend her, the king will likely keep her hidden for the duration of her pregnancy and end her life shortly after she gives birth. She gave me the note because she wants me to save her."

"We have bigger problems than her right now." Aris anchors his elbows to the middle of his thighs and brings his head down so his chin meets his palms. He's thinking, and he doesn't like what's swirling around in his head.

"If the king is potent and trying, he will produce many more heirs."

"That's why we need Sade. Maybe she can help read what's in Annabeth's journal. She probably wrote about whatever she was using on the king. Maybe Sade can continue doing what Annabeth started."

Aris looks at me wearily but doesn't relay his concerns. He gazes at the floor between my feet, his elbows still on top of his thighs, palms still touching, and his chin still resting against his palms. His face travels up from my ankles to my shins before stopping and lingering right at the spot where my nightgown stops at my thighs. My stomach churns, and my cheeks feel heavy with the heat rising in them. It's anger, I tell myself. Why is he looking at me like that? I stand abruptly, feeling awkward with the silence hanging between us. Aris lifts his head to look me in the eyes. His left eyebrow arches. It feels like he's both

170

questioning me and challenging me. I force my legs to push me forward, unsure of my purpose for walking towards him. I stop when I'm only a few inches in front of him. I won't let Aris catch me flustered.

I try to make light of the situation by smiling the sultriest smile I can muster, placing one hand on my waist, and popping my hips.

"Why are you looking at me like that?" I ask gently.

Aris smiles a mischievous smile. His teeth are as white as eggshells against the darkness of his skin. He's threatened to expose my secrets to Ryland. He's had me cornered in a cellar that only he knew the way out of, and yet, I find myself more afraid of him than I've ever been.

"Like what?" he asks innocently.

My heart pounds against my ribcage. This is dangerous. The instant I think to step backward, Aris pulls me down onto his lap. There it is again. The scent he radiates overpowers my senses, making me dizzier and dizzier with each inhale.

"Don't be scared," he whispers. He grabs my waist, squeezing gently on both sides, sending electricity shooting up and down my spine. *I can't*! I repeatedly yell this in my head but make no attempts to stand or leave.

Aris pushes the strap of my nightgown and makes it fall by my bicep. He nestles his chin against the bridge of my neck and my shoulders, placing gentle kisses first on the top of my shoulders, then moving further and further up my neck. He nibbles softly on the outer ridges of my earlobe, sending another shock down my spine.

"Tell me you want this," he says.

I can't breathe. I can't even think right now. My mouth stays so firmly shut, I don't think a pair of pliers open them. Aris tilts his head back to face me again. He smiles, but it doesn't reach his eyes.

"Don't worry about it," he says. When I don't immediately stand up, Aris grabs me by the waist, hoisting me onto my feet. They feel weak and foreign beneath my body.

"Aris I..." I begin. But I have no words to say.

"Seriously, don't worry about it," he responds. "Let's save this for another night, yeah?" He breathes a sigh. I search for the right words but can't find them.

As Aris rises from his chair, three sharp knocks sound from my door. Lazarus. I look over at Aris, eyes wide with panic. He takes a couple of steps backward. The closet! No, Aris is too large to fit in there. I stare at the door to the rotunda. We've never brought anyone into the rotunda. Maybe it was an unspoken rule, but I've always considered it our sacred space, where we commune and heal. The thought of someone who isn't Galed seeing it unnerves me. I shove the feeling telling me not to allow anyone near the rotunda aside and run towards the rotunda door, opening it and beckoning Aris inside. He rushes in without a word.

When I open my room door, Lazarus stands there with his arms crossed.

"What took you so long?" he asks with a hint of annoyance.

"It's been a long day," I respond.

Lazarus's eyes soften, and he drops his hands to his side. "Right. I came to check up on you. See how you were doing after seeing your friend."

Shit, Aris must have known that Lazarus would be coming here tonight. That's why he was asking so many questions about the Galed and our abilities. That's why he was trying to peek through the door whenever Iyanu or Sade walked in from that side. Was he hoping I'd have no choice but to let him into the rotunda if Lazarus showed up while he was still here? *What is he doing in there?* I fume internally, trying to mask my anger and shame.

"Aris told me she wasn't in too bad a shape. The many perks of being Galed, I guess," he chuckles.

"So nice to be feared by half of the population, hated by the other half, and made to prance around like a prized pony whenever the king sees fit," I respond, my voice dripping with sarcasm.

Lazarus seems stunned. He didn't mean it like that, and I know it. "Sorry," I amend. "It really has been a long day," I offer with a shake of my head. Regardless of how I'm feeling, this is not the tone I need to take with Lazarus if he's going to consider helping Torrin escape from the cellars.

Lazarus sits on my bed and beckons me to sit by his side. I oblige, grabbing his arm and leaning into his side for support. I look up to meet his gaze, giving him a shaky smile, and then I take his hand in mine and stroke it gently.

Lazarus takes that as a cue. "You know what will make you feel better?" he asks with a silly laugh.

"Let me guess, it has something to do with what's in your pants."

"It might," he says in mock contemplation. "Want to find out?" he amends.

I laugh him off. I'm not in the mood and partly because the thought of Lazarus touching, nibbling, and kissing me in the same places Aris just did makes me rife with shame. *Stupid.* Aris may or may not owe his allegiance to the resistance. Just like the monarchy and the nobility, he might not care about anything or anyone except himself. Yet, one look from him was all it took to send me flying into his arms.

"Come on," Lazarus prods. He grabs me by my waist. His eyes are no longer fixed on mine. Instead, he stares unabashedly at my breasts. Lazarus tips his head down and places a gentle kiss on my collarbone, then another one in the space between the two of them. His lips feel cold and moist against mine. I shake my head in protest, but he pushes me back gently, so my back lies against the bed. In the next instant, he's on top of me, pressing his groin into mine.

"It'll make you feel better," he insists again. A muffled sound escapes my lips. My body burns, not with desire but with the aching of someone who's lost too much already and has everything else they have on the line.

"Can't you tell this isn't the time?" I half whisper, half yell. I don't know when the tears started falling from my eyes, but now it seems they won't stop—my body trembles with each breath.

Lazarus clicks his tongue, shifting his weight off mine, and rises back to his feet. "All right," he says coolly. He takes note of my tears, tilting his head in acknowledgment. "I'll come back when you're feeling better."

"Wait," I say before he can turn to take his leave. "I still need to talk to you about something."

Lazarus's jaw clenches. "What is it?" His tone is terse, and he angles his body slightly away from me.

I try my best to gather myself before continuing. "It's about Torrin. She's not just in good shape. She's in great shape. When Aris took us down to see her, I could feel the power radiating off of her. It was overwhelming even for me." Lazarus turns so that he's facing me more directly. His eyes brighten with curiosity. "I think, if she wanted to, she could break out of the cellars without even breaking a sweat." Lazarus lifts an eye in disbelief at my last assertion. Maybe I've gone too far. I have to temper the urge to lick my lips, so I don't look as nervous as I am.

"Why doesn't she just do it then?" he asks.

"She's a pacifist. She wouldn't even hurt a fly unless she didn't have a choice. She's not the type of person who could slaughter dozens of guards and live with herself afterwards. She needs a stealthier way of getting out, one that doesn't involve killing anyone."

Lazarus shrugs his shoulders. "A shame. I would have loved to see what she could do in the field. A pacifist is no use to a kingdom with a tyrannical king," Lazarus says flatly. I interject when he turns again, taking several steps towards the door.

"You're wrong!" I try to sound level-headed, not desperate. "She's a pacifist, but she's also seen firsthand the pain and destruction the king has wrought. She might be whole physically, but something has changed inside of her. Lazarus..." I say softly. "She wants to see the king in his grave. But only him. She won't participate in any bloodshed along the way."

Lazarus looks me over. It's hard to tell if he doubts what I'm saying or if he's considering what his options are. "Aris didn't report any of this to me." Fear rakes through me. Will Lazarus believe me and punish Aris for not including some crucial pieces of information?

"We asked Aris to stay a couple of paces back to let us have some privacy. I don't believe he heard anything we said."

"It is dark down there, isn't it?" If we had been in a more brightly lit room, that excuse would not have worked. It should come as no surprise that a spy who can read, access the palace like

176

the back of his hand, and somehow travel and get information back and forth to the resistance may also be able to read lips.

"Lazarus, if you got her out of there, she would help you depose the king," I say bluntly.

Lazarus takes a short pause before he speaks again. "It's not worth the risk to me," he concludes. "It's better to wait until after the Waning, with a new set of Galed who don't have the added liability of needing to be smuggled out of the palace. Getting her out, hosting her without incident, and getting her back to the king, and close enough that she can strike is too complicated."

"But she's already on your side," I protest, unable to keep from raising my voice.

"No matter," he says, unphased by my assertions. "The new members of the Galed will also be Endzoners. They will be just as eager to get some revenge on the monarchy if they feel like they have a chance at succeeding. Hopefully, they'll come with a useful set of gifts." Lazarus looks right through me as he says the last sentence.

They, Them. He doesn't bother speaking as if he expects me to make it. Though the odds are only one in four, I still expected Lazarus to bet on me. He pauses and looks me up and down, calculating.

"Or one who's willing to do what needs to be done for the sake of the kingdom," he continues. He stretches his arms upward and opens his mouth, letting out an exaggerated yawn. "If there's nothing more you want to speak about, I'll get going."

He turns to leave, not bothering to say goodbye.

Chapter 13

Aris must have sensed Lazarus's absence because he strolls back into my room through the rotunda door without any cues from me. He's bright-eyed and way too energized this late in the evening. A weariness settles deep into my bones again as I contemplate, for the millionth time since meeting him, what Aris's true motivations are. Whenever I think I know him, he does something to prove me wrong. I don't bother pretending I'm happy to see him, but I don't confront him on my suspicions that he came here tonight not to gather information on King Ryland but to gather information on me.

Aris speaks first, his voice light. "It's beautiful in there," he says with a smile.

"Thanks."

"How was the talk with Lazarus?"

"Bad." I clip my responses, unwilling to delve into the details.

At this point, I have no desire to give Aris any information he doesn't need to know. Knowledge is power, after all, and a power imbalance between us could spell the end of me. Aris walks to the corner of the room and sits on the chair next to my table. He seems more relaxed and less like a guest here now. It's Aris himself, not me, that brings up Torrin and the state she's in.

"It's strange, isn't it?" he begins, "how the scars of trauma never properly disappear from the human form. She looks completely fine, but still, I don't need to be connected to her through spirit to see and feel the horrors she's going through. I hope that her mind heals just as easily as her body."

I let out a low scowl, frowning at the floor. Snake. Aris crosses his hands over his chest, giving me a pointed look. His veins pop, pressing and wrapping against the flesh of his forearms.

"Is there something you'd like to say to me?" He says with a tone that's more curious than it is annoyed. Despite my suspicions, I need Aris now more than ever. Torrin will rot in the cellars unless I can convince him to do something.

I grit my teeth as I say, "We need to get Torrin out." Aris looks at me blankly.

Before he can respond, I continue. "You said yourself that the resistance needs more than just a small group of fighters if they're going to topple the monarchy. Torrin is capable of bringing down legions if she chooses to. She's no use to anyone if she's just wasting away down there. If you get her out, Iyanu and Sade will be indebted to you, too. Think of what could happen with all four of us and the resistance working together against the king." Aris squints slightly. "This is our chance," I say with more haste this time. "If you wait, if the Waning comes and there's a new set of Galed. There's no guarantee that all of them will cooperate. This is an opportunity to make us all indebted to you."

"I agree," Aris says. That's not the response I was expecting. "I know exactly what we could do if we had you all. Ryland's goal is to control just one of you and then use that one to control the rest. I bet you don't even know half of what you or your sisters are capable of. Bear could bring that out of you, and with some training from me, you guys would be real threats. I could get Torrin out, but if she's whisked out without a word or trace, there will be no doubt in Lazarus's mind that I was the one who did it. There aren't many other people with as much knowledge of the underground paths as me, and the rest of the noble families aren't dumb enough to attempt a rescue and risk the king's wrath without already having Torrin's allegiance."

If Lazarus suspects Aris of conspiring to rescue Torrin, not only will that be against Lazarus's direct orders, but it would also be a glaring indication that Aris serves as a member of the resistance. Any attempt to free Torrin has a cascading array of consequences for Aris. His only options would be to go into hiding within the resistance or risk getting killed.

"There are no good options then," I concede.

"No, but there's one very bad one," he responds. "Torrin needs to break herself out."

Aris delivers this plan with a smile, as if he's just said that there would be extra rations of water going out to the Endzoners this season instead of stating the impossible. "What I mean is, to everyone else, it needs to look like Torrin broke herself out, but that doesn't mean she can't have had some help doing it," he amends.

"What's your plan?" I ask, daring to hope.

"You, Iyanu, and Sade need to go to the cellars again through the paths. No guards are stationed in the passageways, so it should be easy to get to Torrin as long as you follow my instructions. I'll draw you a map and show you how to read it. Don't worry, maps are mostly symbols. Once there, you'll need to take out the guard stationed to watch Torrin and the other prisoners. You'll take his key and free Torrin."

"That's going to be difficult to pull off." The reality of what could go wrong starts to dawn on me. I anchor my fears. The potential consequences of inaction are unacceptable.

"That's the easy part." Aris's lips thin into a slight frown. "After you get Torrin out, you won't be able to come back up using the paths. That would raise too many questions about how Torrin discovered them and raise suspicions with the king about who else could be using them. Torrin will need to get out the same way she and all the other prisoners were brought in in the first place. Through the cellar entrance. There will be about a dozen guards stationed in the halls leading there. The guards make their rounds by themselves or in pairs. The three of you will need to help Torrin take them on one at a time."

"You expect us to take out a dozen and a half guards without getting caught or, better yet, without dying?" I ask in disbelief.

Aris shrugs. "I told you it was a bad plan. But if you all can do that, you'll prove your worth the risk the resistance is taking on you."

I shake my head, perplexed to even be considering something so stupid.

"I don't want to kill anyone," I say with a frown. I told Lazarus that Torrin had no taste for bloodshed, and though I have more of a stomach for such things, I'd rather not spill any if given the choice. Aris raises his brow as if answering the hypothetical question I raised in my mind. We both know I have no choice in the matter.

"No one has to die, but it would be better if they did. Simply knocking the guards unconscious means they'll know exactly who broke Torrin out of the cellars, and I doubt they'll keep their mouths shut about it when they wake up."

"We have some cultseed for that. I'll bring some with me, just in case. A couple drops into the mouth of an unconscious guard should wipe his memories starting two hours before."

"Cultseed? That's the purple one with the green veins, right?" he asks, referencing the plants in the rotunda.

"Yes," I reply tersely.

"That'll work. Now, on to the final part of the plan."

183

I twirl my hands in a circular motion, beckoning Aris to go on.

"At the entrance to the cellars, there's a hallway on the left side that leads to a dead end. In the middle of the hallway, on the right wall, is a stone with scratch marks. Remove the stone and use the hole as leverage to open the hidden door. It'll bring you back on the path to your rooms."

"What will Torrin do when she gets to the entrance?"

"I'll have someone waiting there for her, ready to take her back to the Deadends. I'll be as far away as possible when this all happens. Ryland is having a javelin contest for him and some of the other noblemen. He'll discuss the progress he's been making on his experiments and give them the opportunity to tear at each other for the chance to earn his favor. I'll be serving as one of two Berkshire servants for the occasion. The sports outing will be the best opportunity to get Torrin out. There'll be fewer guards in the palace than usual since they'll be serving as the king's entourage. This place will also be less busy with servants and attendants roaming the halls."

"It's a plan then. Three days from now, me, Iyanu, and Sade will free Torrin, and she'll be taken to the Deadends."

"You know, I admire you, but I can't quite figure you out." Aris switches the topic of conversation. "My whole life, I've been fighting to see this monarchy wiped from this Earth."

So have I.

Aris continues, "I'm grateful that, with your help, we might just realize that. But monarchy or not, the Waning comes and, with it, the deaths of at least two of your sisters and potentially you yourself. Even if Bear sees the resistance through, you probably won't be around to see what we build after. You're risking everything on Torrin's escape, but she might be dead in a few months anyway. Why not just wait out the rest of your days in peace?"

"Because my father gave me a mission and without Torrin, I won't be able to see it through," I say hoping to convince Aris of Torrin's value even though he's already acquiesced. Really it's because Torrin would do the same for me. She wouldn't even think about it. And before Torrin, Iyanu, and Sade (on her good days), I've never had that before.

Aris doesn't press for a better answer. "I'll need to run the plan by Bear and see what he has to say about it. I'll be back to let you know."

———— ◆◇◆ ————

That night, the desert winds stream through my window, chilling me to my bones. The cool is inviting. It serenades me into a restful sleep. Today, I dream of a shimmering landscape filled with life I've never encountered. My bare feet tread on the ground, covered by soft, lengthy, and pliable plants resembling the flattened stems of plants. The stalks glimmer in the morning sun as the water droplets gathering on their surface scatter the sun's rays.

Strange creatures roam the landscape, larger than the hamels and the animals carved into obsidian and citrine in the atrium of the palace. Unlike those creatures, these have flat faces and flat rows of teeth. They're almost human-like with their large, oval eyes. The animals are massive. They carry most of their weight on the abdomen, yet their legs remain thin and muscled. They have hoofed feet and brown hair framing their faces and bodies. Half of the species have large, arching horns. Dew gathers on their black, wrinkly snouts, and they look at me with soft, curious eyes. They continue roaming, stopping periodically to chew mouthfuls of the plants beneath their feet. A sense of relief washes over me. Yes, this is the world we should be living in.

Aris returns in the morning, briefly, to inform me that Bear approves of his decision and that the resistance is indeed willing to shelter Torrin.

"There are some conditions," he adds. Bear wants the pregnant maid taken to the Deadends along with Torrin. "We'll have some leverage that way," Aris says. "One of the Oguni will meet her in front of the cellar entrance and take her back to the Deadends." No guards bat an eye at the coming and going of palace maids, who are often sent on errands. The other condition of Bear's approval has solely to do with Aris. "I'll need to get those journals," he says—the details of when and exactly how he plans on doing so, he leaves out. Aris leaves as quickly as he comes. He makes no mention of last night, and neither do I. Whatever happened between us may well have happened a decade ago, with how far it seems like it's been pushed to the back of his mind.

I walk over to Iyanu's room, buzzing with fear and excitement about how reckless our "plan" is. When I get there, she's seated on her bed with her eyes closed and her arms clasped in front of her chest in prayer. She takes one look at me and smiles as if she already knows what I've come to tell her.

"I knew he'd come around," she says joyfully.

"Well, no. Not Lazarus. Aris has." When I tell Iyanu about Aris's plan, I watch her go through at least five stages of emotions. First, she's disbelieving and frustrated that Aris would even suggest such a thing. Then she's defeated, concurring that the plan is truly the only option. Eventually, she's beaming again.

I give Iyanu a knowing look. "Trust me, I know exactly how you feel."

"The Goddess doesn't send you what you want. She sends you what you need," she chuckles. Her laugh brings a smile to my face.

"It won't be easy, but if anyone can do it, it's us."

"Exactly."

Iyanu looks me up and down, faking an accusatory shake-down. "I always knew you were a resistance sympathizer. I just never knew how deep it went."

It's no secret that most Endzoners wouldn't lose a night's sleep over the king's death. Who and what they'd be replaced by is a different story. I could lie to Iyanu. I could tell her that Aris came to me with the plan and that I'd never worked with the resistance until they offered to help rescue Torrin. I know she wouldn't challenge me if I were to say those things to her, but I have no desire to. Annabeth lied to us. She kept things from us. She told us nothing about the king's experiments or her plans to render him impotent. She didn't tell us about the notebooks of Galed past. She didn't even tell or teach us about what we could do with this spirit that binds us together. Annabeth cared for us, and I have no doubt that she only wanted to protect us, but her secrets are the reason we're here today. Nothing good can come from hiding yourself from those you're bound to by spirit.

"You know, I've always wanted to join the resistance, ever since I was younger," Iyanu says. Smiling, she adds, "I figured the only thing my parents hated more than their son, who'd turned out to be their daughter, was those Oguni who always seemed to cut into their water supplies or food stocks without them knowing. What better way to piss them off, you know?" She laughs pleasantly. "I knew they'd have never taken me, though. I mean, I wouldn't have taken me either. Huge chance I could be playing both sides." And now the resistance doesn't just want Iyanu. They need her. Iyanu gets up, and despite the threat of failure looming over us, the atmosphere around her is lighter than I've seen in days. We can always depend on her to not just say she has faith in herself and the rest of us but to actually mean it.

I find myself unable to stop myself from telling Iyanu something I shouldn't. "My father led the resistance," I say.

Iyanu lets the words wash over her as solemnness displaces her once bright glow. "I'm sorry. Was he —"

I shake my head, waving the question away. "He wasn't killed. He died of natural causes." I breathe a sigh before continuing. "I knew that man for twenty-two years and never really felt like I knew him."

I tell Iyanu about the story my father used to tell me about my mother's death. She died after a sleeping pit collapsed on her just a few days after I was born. Too tired from her labor, she stayed in the pit with me while my father went out to work on the estates. When they returned, she had already been buried alive in the sand. It was a miracle that I survived. My father would say, *your mother died because of you. So now you must live a life big enough for the both of you.*

"He never passed up on a chance to remind me that I was to blame for her death," I say.

Iyanu frowns deeply. "Don't ever believe that. Not even for one second," she says. Iyanu clasps my hand in hers once again. "You're the last person to blame for her death and getting here, coming as far as you have despite the odds," she shakes her head. "You're amazing Meera. Promise me you won't forget that."

I nod my head in affirmation.

With a squeeze of my hand, she leaves the room, making her way toward the garden to fetch water for those plants in our rotunda.

The only person to speak to now is Sade, who is already waiting for me in my room when I return. She sits on my bed with her arms behind her, pushing her chest forward.

"What's going on with you?" I ask. *Why are you bouncing around like that?*

"I figured out how to do something else today!"

She's practically beaming as she jumps off the bed. She walks over to the desk in the corner of my room, where she's placed a pomegranate. She concentrated on it, and after a few seconds, the juice in the flesh of its skin seeps out and starts to bud on the waxy surface.

"This is only the beginning," she says. "When I get really good, I think I'll be able to make the water come out so fast that the seeds burst." A pang of jealousy runs through me.

I try to inject some truth into the words as I say them, "That's awesome. You're going to be able to do so much. But I need to talk to you."

I sit Sade down again before telling her what we need to do. "We'll need to help Torrin get out of those cellars ourselves." I begin. Sade's mouth twists in both directions as she turns to me and gives me a strange look. By the time I'm done explaining, Sade is openly shaking her head in disbelief.

"I understand exactly how you're feeling. I didn't think it was going to be possible either. But we have to do whatever we can. Torrin would do the same for us."

"I know that," she says tersely. "And your first instincts were correct. It isn't possible. The king might not have us killed, but he'll certainly have us thrown down there with her when we're caught. I don't think Torrin would want that for us either," she says pointedly. "The best we can do is try and get an audience with the king. We should plead with him on Torrin's behalf."

Sade's suggestion leaves me stunned.

"How often does the king release his prisoners?"

"How often do people try?" Sade counters. The conversation lulls to a standstill, both of us sitting there awkwardly racking our brains, trying to come up with the next thing to say.

"I know what you're doing with the king," I say gently, trying to make sure that my voice comes off as concerned rather than accusatory. "I know that you're trying to make a difference and that you think you'll be helping the kingdom by helping with his plans. But Sade, you can't trust him. He's lying to you. He's trying to use you."

Sade rolls her eyes, a sign that her anger is building and is soon to burst into the open. "Don't you think I know that? I don't care what his real plans are or whether he thinks he's using me. Have you ever considered that I could be using him? That I have my own plans? That the king is the pawn in the game that I'm playing?" Her voice gets louder, and her intonation becomes more forceful with each sentence.

I can't help but sound a bit frustrated when I say, "And what exactly is that game you're playing?"

She brushes me off. "You wouldn't understand. I know I have what it takes to save us, and I won't squander that on some half-thought-out escape plan." She crosses her arms before she continues. "It's you who needs to reconsider your plans." Sade glares at the sapphire pendant around my neck. She walks out, fist clenched, and gait purposeful.

She truly believes that she can be the savior for us all, but I'm not convinced that she can't even save herself.

Chapter 14

Iyanu and I meet on the morning of the fiftieth day of the season of the setting sun. Both of us wear fabric cut, thinned, and tied around ourselves to keep it from coming loose. Dawn is just breaking, and the sun's rays are not too harsh. The king and his entourage will be gone by now. Like most everyone, they prefer to do their sport before the sun's heat sets in.

I take stock of everything in our rotunda, studying each object like it's my first time seeing it. I notice the deep crimson of the sotist with its bulbous leaves and rounded leaf edges and the vendera with its dark green stems and thumb-sized leaves that refuse taming, snaking across the floor onto sitting stones and anything else present. I try to notice everything, and of course, the thing I notice most is Sade's absence. I break a dark purple stem from the cultseed, discarding the green and red leaves as I do so. At the altar, I grind up the branches into a paste, diluting it with water and adding a splash of citrus to activate the cultseed. Iyanu mumbles a prayer underneath her breath, asking the Goddess for grace and favor as we go through the day. Neither of us has spoken about how we plan to take down the guards without Sade, but neither of us dare suggest we turn back without at least trying. I transfer the paste into a small glass container and set it aside.

The map Aris drew for us is surprisingly intuitive. He's outlined the part of the tunnel we might encounter in blue and the path we're meant to take to get to the cellars in red. He's done the same for the path toward the entrance to the cellars and our path back toward our rooms.

Iyanu walks to my side, bringing her arm around my shoulder and peering over me to look at the map.

"We'll need to go soon," she says. Her voice is smooth, but it bears signs of tension.

"Let's not waste any time then," I answer.

As we turn to leave, Sade walks in, letting the door slam behind her.

"Where do you think you guys are going without me?" She brings a hand to her heart, feigning anger and offense, before a big smile stretches across her face.

"Sade!" Iyanu squeals. "We thought you weren't going." She's chuckling and laughing now.

"I couldn't let you guys get killed without me, now could I?" She jokes. "Besides, you guys need me to pull it off."

"Well, I never even doubted you for one second," I say, smiling. My cheeks burn with the strain of the smile plastered on them, and my heart warms at the sight of her. Sade can be unpredictable. She's hot, and she's cold and too annoying for her own good, but when it's mattered, she's always been there.

Sade takes the map from my hands, studying it carefully. She turns it around a few times, remarking, "How useful. Why haven't I ever seen one of these?"

"Because you haven't ever had anywhere important to go," I tease.

We're able to get through the brief section of palace hallways to get into the underground passages without encountering any guards. Aris's instructions are clear enough that our journey through the tunnels goes smoothly. It takes us just twenty minutes to reach the hidden door that will take us into the cellars where Torrin is being held. I hesitate, but only briefly. It takes both my and Iyanu's strength to move the imitation stone door, but when we enter through it, a guard is waiting right in front of us.

"What's this we got here?" he says. The man is clean-shaven with a dip at his chin and a smile that's too wide and too toothy. He brings his hand to the sword's hilt by his side but doesn't pull it out immediately. His face is rabid.

"Come to keep me company, have we?"

Iyanu, Sade, and I look at each other, betraying our uncertainty. But the guard has likely realized who we are and knows it would be unwise to strike us. He releases the hold he has on his sword, grabbing the rope on his other side instead.

"Come here now. I'll show you a good time before letting you join your friend."

Iyanu walks towards him, shaking as she does so. She holds her hands out, beckoning him to bind them together with the rope. The guard smirks, leaning in to do just that, but as he does, Iyanu balls up her fist, swings it, and connects it with the right side of the guard's face. He stumbles backward as blood starts pouring from his nose. He's shaken momentarily before regaining his composure and tackling Iyanu to the ground. He pins her to the floor with his weight, raising his fist and punching her squarely in the center of her face. Her nose shifts awkwardly to the side.

A scream escapes from my throat, part desperation and part battle cry, as I run towards them and kick the guard in the abdomen. My shin stings where I connected with his ribcage. The guard groans, toppling over, but when he rises, he does so with a smile. He enjoys this. He throws his sword to the side, beckoning us to come after him. We stay like that for what seems like an eternity, kicking, roiling, and rolling over the cellar floors. I sink my teeth into his forearms more than once, each bite resulting in a smack that bruises my cheek and leaves the inside of my mouth bleeding from the impact against my teeth. We scream for Sade more than once, but she remains plastered to the front of the door.

"That was fun, wasn't it, girls?" he says.

The guard takes two long strides towards me and grabs me by the throat, lifting me off the ground. Iyanu runs towards us, but she's pushed to the ground once she's within arm's length of the guards. I struggle against him, throwing my legs from side to side and gripping his arm in a bid to have him let go. His grasp gets tighter and tighter, squeezing my throat until I'm wheezing. My vision dims and fades to black. I think I hear Iyanu say something, but her words are muffled. Then I hear a faint popping sound followed by an excruciating scream that pierces the air. The guard releases his grip just enough that I'm able to shake his hands off and free myself.

He turns around, turning his back to me, Iyanu, and Sade, and hanging his head as he brings his hand over the right side of his face. When he looks up again, his hand still covers his right eye, but his face is twisted with rage. He's no longer having fun. The guard steps in Sade's direction before I hear another faint pop, muffled by a groan from the guard. The pops come again and again, the guard's left eye growing redder and his body convulsing with each one. Trails of blood spill from his eye, pooling at his lower eyelids and falling like a twisted display of tears. He covers both eyes, but the blood seeps in between his fingers, flowing down the back of his palms.

When the guard drops his hands, his eyes look like they've been replaced by bludgeoned blackberries. He takes labored breaths, walking blindly back and forth before releasing an anguished sound, sobbing, and collapsing. I kneel by his side and place his head on my lap. I remove the cultseed wrapped in the inner part of my garment, pour some into the palm of my hands, and tilt his head back to pour it into his mouth. A burst of pain explodes in my right hand as he lurches forward at the feel of my palm near his lips, chomping down on my index finger with his teeth. I pull my finger from between his clamped teeth, cursing as I do so. I throw his head out of my lap, and it hits the floor with a dull thud. The flesh of my finger is separated from the meat beneath it, allowing a viscous flow of blood to pour from the open wound.

The guard lies still on the floor as I cautiously pour more cultseed into his mouth for good measure. When he wakes up in a few hours, he'll have no memory of what happened in these cellars. Both his memories and his sight will be gone. I grab the keys to the cells from the guard's pocket.

When we get to Torrin, she's standing flush by the bars of her cell gates, waiting. She glows even in the dimness of the cellar halls. Although it's been weeks, she remains alert. She's buzzing with joy and excitement. Looking at her makes me aware of the blood pumping through my veins, pooling, and pulsating near my heart. Torrin wraps her slender, pale hands around the cellar bars.

"It's time," she says.

The three of us run to meet her by the cell gates. I grab the set of keys in my hand, fumbling once but regaining some strength in my arms. My anticipation builds with each key I try. By the third key, my emotions get the best of me, and the combination of my blood and tears soils the keys in my hand. Torrin reaches through the cell bars to help. She grabs one key, holding it up so the others dangle beside it.

"This one."

Iyanu is the first one to rush in after I open the cell gate. She lifts Torrin, spins her around, and sets her back to the ground. Torrin places both palms on either side of Iyanu's head and pulls her head down and their foreheads meet. With both eyes closed, they take in the smell and sound of each other's presence. It's here that I feel it again. That indescribable thing that binds the four of us, which makes one of us flow into the other, makes it hard to describe where one ends and the other begins. Are my tears truly mine? Is the heat and lump in my throat my own? We're relieved, we're elated, we're nervous, and we're guilty all at the same time. Iyanu chokes on her tears. She places a kiss on Torrin's forehead before finally releasing her.

Torrin walks to me next, grabbing my hands and pulling me into hers. She holds my head, as she did with Iyanu, bringing my forehead to hers. A smile spreads across her lips when they touch. I breathe in deep gulps of the air surrounding Torrin, savoring her scent. It must have only been a moment, but it felt like an eternity.

"I knew you guys could do it," she says.

I nod, unconvinced that I'd be able to say anything intelligible in my current state. It's no matter, though. Torrin understands exactly what I mean. When Torrin goes to Sade, Iyanu comes to stand by my side. Sade grabs her left hand with her right and shifts from one foot to the other. She meets Torrin mid-stride, sandwiching the smaller woman in between her arms. Torrin touches her head to Sade's, and they stay there, exchanging words neither Iyanu nor I can hear. They both come to me and Iyanu after they separate, with Sade standing to my left and Torrin standing to Iyanu's right.

"This is the hard part," I explain. "We can't go back out through the tunnels."

"So we don't expose your friend," Torrin adds knowingly, "or expose his knowledge of the palace grounds."

"Yes. A man will be at the entrance door waiting for you to arrive. Aris said he'd look like a Midzone merchant making a stink about hoping to get an audience with the king to discuss his taxes. He will be hard to miss," I tell her.

The cellars contain hundreds of individual cells, but less than one percent hold a single prisoner. The prisoners we encounter on our way out have their backs turned towards their cellar gate and to us by extension. They stare blankly at the wall, shaking and muttering. The sound is enraged and manic. They bang on the cellar door, cursing and shouting. I stare at the key in my hands, turning them slightly to look at them. Sade lowers my hand, shaking her head at the thought forming in my mind.

"We don't know what they did, and we have nowhere for them to go."

But anywhere must be better than here. We pause at the doorway leading out of the cellars and into the entrance halls, bracing ourselves for what's to come. Iyanu places a reassuring hand on my shoulder. Sade pushes the door open, revealing an empty entranceway.

"Strange," I say.

At each turn, my heart rate speeds up as my anxiety builds, but we've yet to encounter any guards. Somehow, this makes me more anxious rather than less.

"Maybe they've gone with the king," Iyanu offers. "To protect him at the javelin shoot."

There are always some guards who follow the king, though the king seldom needs any protection. Still, I can't imagine that the entourage at his side for a simple game with a few nobles is so large that it's entirely depleted the number of guards stationed at the cellars.

The map splits off into two paths as we near the doorway that leads out of the palace. One path has a few plants and some seating stones drawn at its end; the other has the sun and sand. We stop at the crossroads, staring at one another.

"Well, since there aren't any guards around, we might as well take you outside. We only have one map anyway." The latter point is moot, given Torrin's path is a straight shot from where we are now. Nonetheless, we agree with Iyanu and walk with Torrin to the palace entrance door, pausing again when we get there. Iyanu looks down at Torrin with an intensity I've never seen before. She holds onto Torrin's loose sleeve like the act alone will prevent Torrin from leaving.

Never one for goodbyes.

"We'll see you soon," Iyanu says.

Torrin smiles and nods her head. She pulls Iyanu in for a quick hug before turning to Sade and me and doing the same. As Torrin turns to walk out of the entrance door, my head snaps backward, jolted by a stomping sound coming from behind us. I cast a nervous look in that direction. The stomping quickens, forcing us to make a decision.

"We have to go," I say.

As we turn to race to the entrance door, it swings open of its own volition. Over two dozen guards in their black hamel leather uniforms, sword flesh against their sides, and eyes weary storm in through it. Behind us, the stomping sound has made a full approach, revealing another two dozen guards.

Nicholas emerges from the group, a bandage wrapped around his head and his shoulders. Not everyone can heal as fast as Torrin. Not even with the best medics in the kingdom. Nicholas shakes his head, signaling his disapproval. He looks annoyed not because we've done something wrong, but because it'll cost him his time and energy to fix it.

"Hands in the air," he commands.

We oblige, and the surrounding guards draw closer to us. They point swords at our sides, poking and prodding us to move towards the entrance door. The interior of the palace and the outside are two completely different worlds. Years of innovation have kept the palace temperate, cool even at times, but as we cross the threshold out into the world, the desert sun beams down on us, threatening to scorch the outermost layer of our skin. In the open, with no shade, eloh paste, or water, it would take a healthy person just three days to give in to the desert heat.

Outside, the emanating presence of King Ryland is as undeniable as the desert sun. He dwarfs the hamel he's sitting on and rises high above his dozen guards stationed near him and the noble lords from the Idowu, Berkshire, and Tanaka families and their servants who come in twos beside them. I look up briefly, daring to meet Lazarus's eyes. He looks away in a hurry, a deep frown marring his face. Aris is absent. Two other Berkshire servants flank Lord Berkshire instead. At least if I die, he won't be here to see it.

I notice the man meant to escort Torrin to the Deadends kneeling at the side of the king's guards. I can tell it's him because his eyes are blindfolded, his mouth is tied, and his hands are bound behind his back. He shakes from one side to the other, attempting to break free. A guard pushes him to the ground face first, then kicks him in the side, forcing him to roll back onto his back with a groan.

"The animal is making too much noise," Lord Idowu complains. The Oguni man might as well be a yelping dog. The king ignores his complaints, turning his head from the Lord and glancing at Iyanu, Sade, Torrin, and me instead.

"Come," he says.

Sade breaks away from the rest of us, the guards nearest her dropping their swords and parting to give her a path to the king. She rushes over to him and grabs his hand when she reaches him. He hoists her up unto the front of his hamel.

Ryland smiles. "You've done well, my girl."

Chapter 15

A tremor spreads through me, shaking me to the very core. I stare at Sade, who's now seated at the front of the king's hamel. I glance down at the blood on my hands, the tear in the flesh of my index finger, and the grime now coating the surface of my garment. I take one deep breath. The next is shallower. And the one after that, shallower still. Before I know it, I'm panting from the sun's heat, the mania in my head, and the anger in my heart. This is all a big mistake.

"Sade!" I cry.

My voice is equal parts accusation and anguish. Lazarus turns to look at me, shaking his head. His eyes are brutal and un-flinching. It's not a mask. I realize this is how he's always been. Indifferent to my fate.

The hum inside of me grows louder and more turbulent. To my side, Torrin is perfectly calm. She places one hand in the sleeve of the other, folding them both across her upper abdomen. I wouldn't think it possible, but Iyanu shakes even more violently than I do.

"I did what was best, Meera. King Ryland has promised to keep you all safe, fed, and well-rested in the cellars."

A groan escapes my lips. Tears of anger wet my cheek and blur my vision. Can you imagine that? There is no place for the Galed in the king's cellars. Of what's left of our lives, we'll live freely or die trying.

"How generous it is for the king to offer us a place in his cellars. There's no place else I'd rather live the rest of what's remaining of my life," Iyanu says bitterly, her voice dripping with sarcasm.

Lord Idowu takes one look at her but otherwise makes every effort to avoid her gaze. You can't help but get the sense that he's unaffected, relieved even, that his only daughter may not have a place in this world for much longer.

"There wouldn't be a rest of your life if it wasn't for me," Sade counters.

"Sade," I repeat, doing what I can to steady my voice, which has begun to sound strange even to my ears. "Get down." I plead. "Come stand by our side."

The king reins his hamel, turning it sideways in anticipation of his exit. He continues to look forward. Sade turns from us as well. A palace guard lifts the Oguni man from the floor by the rim of his shirt, dragging him by his hair towards the king. The lords, Idowu, Berkshire, and Tanaka, along with their servants, give one long bow to their monarch as he begins his exit. The king and the nobility set off in opposite directions while the palace guards close in on us. They maneuver themselves, forcing us to start stepping towards the cellar door.

My feet remain glued to the ground despite the sword that has now cut through the fabric at my waist and will begin to cut through flesh if any more pressure is applied. My vision narrows on Sade's retreating form, the palace guards, lords, and servants fading from the outskirts of my vision. They shout something at me, perhaps commanding me to move, but their voices ring hollow in my head.

"Sade, come back here!" I shout in an octave lower than any sound I've ever made.

Her shoulders hunch up, but she doesn't turn around. The king's hamel continues its purposeful gait forward.

Something slick, red-hot, and viscous bubbles underneath my skin, begging to be released. It coats my airways, threatening to choke me unless I breathe it out into the world.

"Sade!" I shout, though no sound escapes my lips. The shout is hypersonic, beyond sound, something that can be felt but not heard. It's over in a second, and yet it feels like time has slowed as I watch the force coming from me ripple the air like a pebble ripples the surface of a lake, pulsating in every direction until it meets its unassuming victims. Twelve of the guards in front of me fly backward as the force of the shout hits them, some colliding with the lords and servants who've started to leave, others colliding only with the scorching surface of the desert sand.

The guards behind me and to my left take one step backward. Big mistake.

Torrin removes her hands from the inside of her garment, and the earth trembles. In an instant, four guards surrounding her are brought to their knees, their legs snapped like broken twigs. Iyanu grabs the guard closest to her, catching him unaware, taking his sword, and throwing it to the ground. She bashes her head into his again and again, before he crumples.

My body tingles with the remnants of the power that flows inside me. Sade gets further still and the king doesn't bother look back despite the chaos that has erupted. How dare she not even think to turn back on her friends?

With my mouth dry and my face hot, I let out another excruciating scream, pouring my demands for Sade to return to us into something pure and primal. The remaining guards surrounding us collapse. Those further from us crouch to the ground with faces twisted in agony. The Lord's servants shield them with their bodies, though it's not enough, and both lord and servant succumb indiscriminately to the power emanating from me. Those guards and servants, still able to stand, get up quickly. Both Lazarus and Lord Berkshire have been encapsulated by a wall of servants who now pull out their daggers and measly knives. A laugh escapes me. I imagine I look truly horrid and undeniably maniacal when it does.

I hope Lazarus suffers. I hope they all do.

Some guards remain on the ground, either dead or unable to stand. The remaining ones, Nicholas among them, stand wide-legged and ready for their commander's wonder. Nicholas waves his sword in the air, slicing through the air from left to right, then right to left again. The display is meant to be menacing.

There was a time I truly would have been afraid, but the rage surging within me scuffs out any traces of the fear I might have felt. The power humming underneath my skin welcomes the battle. Nicholas yells for his soldiers to advance, but four fall upon taking their first steps towards us, crying in agony as they do.

I reach deep within myself, not relying on the power to bubble out of me but instead drawing it out by my will. I open my mouth, ready to send the wall of guards approaching us, stuttering backward. The action alone is enough to stop them in their tracks. A few stumble in their haste to abandon their approach. The guards trade nervous glances at each other and then at their commander. Nicholas shouts a command to advance once more, but only one guard follows the order. Even Nicholas himself remains rooted to the spot.

"I'll have this one," Iyanu says.

Torrin and I step backward, allowing the guard to reach us. Iyanu is swift. Faster than any eye can perceive. One moment, she's in front of us. In the next, she's taken several steps to meet the guard. She grabs the hand he has on the hilt of his sword, squeezing with a strength I'm sure she didn't possess until now. His hand bursts under the pressure, spewing human meat into the air. He looks up at Iyanu in horror as she raises her other hand, landing a blow to the center of his face. The guard stumbles backward, and one more hit to the same spot sends him tumbling to the ground.

In the distance, the king's hamel halts its approach towards the palace. The hamel, Sade, and the king turn towards us, watching the chaos unfolding outside the palace grounds. Some of the remaining guards, lords, and servants stand between us and them.

I won't let them leave. I don't know what I'll do when I get to them, but I will not allow them to hide behind the palace walls. I walk slowly towards the guards and lords in my path, pleased as the ones closest to us scatter in response to our approach. I pass Lazarus on my way. Where he once looked at me with pity, resigning me to my fate, he dares not glance in my direction now.

"Won't you look at me, Laz?" I taunt, letting the hatred in my heart seep into my words. My voice sings. It's heavy with the presence of something otherworldly. Lazarus flinches but otherwise doesn't respond. The servants on the opposite side of him rush to create a larger barrier between us. I fake an attack by opening my mouth and watching as some servants drop to the ground with their ears covered while others run, leaving the

Berkshires with no protection at all. Even the sound of my laugh feels strange and beautifully melodic.

"Don't forget everything I did for you," Lazarus protests. Lord Berkshires looks at the two of us, horrified by the implications of his son's words.

"You did nothing for me. All you've ever done was for yourself. You only sometimes pretended to do it in my name."

"All right then," he scoffs. "Kill me then," he shouts.

Maybe he thinks he's calling my bluff, but the way his eye twitches and his leg shakes assures me that I'm the one calling his. I reach a hand out towards him, and though he steps backward, I quickly enough to place it on his shoulder. His already pale face drains of whatever semblance of color was left in it. I pull him downwards towards me, savoring the terror wafting off him in waves. When we're finally face-to-face, I let my lips graze his before turning my head and whispering in his ears.

"It wouldn't be worth it." I take his sapphire pendant off my neck, dropping it at his feet.

I continue my gait towards Sade, who is attempting to get off of the king's hamel. Good. That will make things easier. With her body sprawled on the hamel's side, feet dangling, reaching for the ground, Ryland wraps one bulky hand around her waist and lifts her back onto hamelback. His Voice rings in our heads.

"Halt! Surrender yourselves," he commands. "I have given my word that you will remain safe in the cellars, but I will only ask once."

211

Behind him, a stream of guards begins pouring out of the palace gates once again, creating a formation of hardened bodies between us and Ryland. If I could get close enough, I could take him down, but I'd likely take Sade down with him. But if Torrin gets close enough, she could snap his neck—a clean and straightforward kill. The guards look to their peers lying on the battleground, undoubtedly feeling weary of their prospects on the field. It brings me no joy to fight them, and their presence only slows us down. A few of them become wide-eyed, some wafting their hands over their heads as a prayer to Rah to protect them.

They attack in sets rather than all at once now. The first dozen surge forward, but their approach is halted when three of the fastest collapse, thanks to Torrin. The other nine stay where they are a few paces further back, trading nervous looks between themselves. Their mates have fallen, and their commander refuses to lead the charge. It's the king who speaks this time.

"Advance!" He commands using the Voice that has no sound but rings soundly in our minds.

The guards look at each other once more, faces twisted in confusion now. They hesitate to step forward, and that hesitation costs them. The king bellows a terrible laugh.

"You're afraid of these children," he mocks the guards. "So, I've managed to pack my palace to the brim with cowards. Floris would be turning over in his tomb." He shakes his head, talking to no one in particular. The king's focus narrows to the nobles who have yet to find a way to leave the battlefield in the chaos. His lips wear thin, his expression angular and unforgiving.

"My guards betray me, and my brothers and sisters conspire on my downfall."

Lord Berkshire stands hastily. The graying monarch had been crouched on the floor until then, eyes closed and hands gripping the top of his head.

"My king!" he exclaims. "Who would dare plot against you?"

Unlike Lazarus, whose skin is gray and as devoid of color as it is texture, Lord Berkshire is tinted a splotchy red color, as if he refuses to use the eloh paste readily available to him and instead chooses to perpetually host a nasty sunburn. His face gets even redder as he addresses the king.

The king's hiss could be mistaken for that of a snake with all the venom behind it. He no longer bothers with the feigned pleasantries and polities favored by the nobility. "Do you take me for a fool, Cholan?"

Lord Berkshire recoils. His expression is a mixture of disbelief and regret.

"My king..." he murmurs, much too quietly for Ryland to hear at his distance.

"The silly little spies you have running around my palace. The talk of regicide, of a new king on the throne. The unfortunate excursion of the Galed into my cellars, sanctioned by your very son, Cholan. I've disregarded this nonsense for too long. If the nobility forgets my power, then surely the masses do as well."

It's Lord Tanaka who speaks up this time. "Only a buffoon would talk of such things! We owe our allegiance and, indeed, all we have, to your reign, Ryland!"

"Silence when your king is talking! You tremble at the presence of mere girls, cowering and whimpering at the sight of their shadows. You forget. I am the very light by which a shadow is cast." The king sighs, though the sound is not particularly tired or regretful.

"It wasn't my desire for the lot of you to be brought to justice this way. So...privately."

The king goes silent, and his body begins giving out a warm orange glow. The guards closest to him take a few steps forward, unsure what to do. The light changes from a warm orange to a deep red, a sight like the evening sun at the edge of a bloodied horizon.

The guards get the good sense to start running. As the first of them break into a sprint, the king lets out a narrow beam of light through his eyes, sweeping it across the palace field from east to west. The beam extends far but dissipates the further out it gets. The guards closest to Ryland disintegrate, their bodies ripping apart as the beam hits them. Their charring is quick and complete. They may as well have vanished from the face of the earth. It's the people further out who will leave evidence of the horrors that occurred today. The guards and servants further from the king are burned beyond the point of recognition. Their flesh melts off their bones, leaving the acrid scent of burnt flesh wafting around in the air and littering the floor with what were once people but are now bones with splotchy additions of charred skin.

The Lords and servants a bit further away meet a fate just as cruel. Lord Tanaka is hit with the beam first. He's far enough out that the radiance of it doesn't strip his bones of the skin surrounding it, but the beam manages to tear at his flesh anyway, giving him major burns across his abdomen that no man could ever recover from.

Lord Berkshire is next to be obliterated, suffering in much the same way Lord Tanaka did. Even at his distance, the beam emanating from Ryland pierces right through his abdomen, leaving the contents of his insides spilling out of him. I watch as Lazarus turns his back to run. The effort is in vain. His tan robe singed beyond recognition, and his once pale skin mirroring the blackness and redness of any ruby or obsidian gem. The skin flakes away easily with the wind, revealing bloodied, pulpy meat underneath. Lazarus falls forward, eyes wide with shock.

I watch intently as the beam races toward me, heating the air around me before it's even crossed my path. Somewhere deep within me, I know there is a panic, but for now, I cling to my sense of calm. In the few seconds before the beam finds me as its target, I inhale, reaching for the power that hums beneath my skin and directing it eastwardly. The air pulsates around me, quivering with the energy it now holds. The beam deflects before dissipating, leaving only a few hot threads of light that collide with my garment, burning holes into them or otherwise leaving angry marks where they meet my exposed skin. Iyanu, who stands a couple of paces behind me, is spared from the beam's heat as well, but it re-emerges, uncompromised, just a couple of steps to her left.

I continue watching the beam on its path, calculating the distance it moves between this breath and the next. A bit further out, Torrin stands with her front facing the beam, hands out-stretched, and face weary. The beam moves slowly yet quickly. My eyes are quick to take in the sight of it, and my brain quick to process the terror of it, but my feet remain slow, unable to take even two steps before the beam collides with her. In this moment, she's no different from the nobility or the dozens of guards fallen by Ryland. The beam chars her where it hits her chest, penetrating deeper to find skin and exposing a thin layer of fat before blistering her lungs. She gasps, bending forward in pain and crying out silently.

I force my feet to move more quickly, but in the time it takes me to think the thought and for my feet to comply with my wishes, the beam has come back around a second time, this time sweeping from west to east. Two more steps. Then, two more. But I'm not fast enough to get to Torrin before the beam does. It hits her crouching form for a second time, singeing her neck and face beyond recognition. She makes no sound this time. Her body doesn't convulse in pain. Instead, she falls forward stiffly. Her head bends awkwardly to the side when she hits the ground. The beam comes for me next, but I deflect just as I once did, saving myself and Iyanu, who has also begun to run toward Torrin.

As Torrin takes her last breath, lightning races up and down my spine, shocking me into straightening. My insides burn while tears blur my vision. Our mouths feel dry, but our throats feel wet, with a thick layer of mucus coating their walls. Every inhale we take smells of pure cinnamon, of cradleberrry. Of Torrin. We breathe some more, letting ourselves be filled to the brim by Torrin's spirit. Our anger is the only thing that matches our grief. Iyanu and I let out a deep howl at the same time. She runs to Torrin, but my feet remain glued to the ground. In the midst of our anguish is a certain anxiety, the type that makes a brain dart from one position to the next without ever fully considering where they are and where they might be going. Sade is still Galed, and her emotions pour into me as well, filling me with trepidation.

I'll rip her head off when I find her.

The power pours out of me now. The air rippling with every hiccup and every wail. The light beam reemerges, targeted now that Ryland has cleared out the human obstacles obstructing his access to us. My face dampens with the sweat pouring out of my pores, but the power pores out of me easily, and the worst of the beam dissipates like it once did.

Terror washes over me when I realize that Iyanu and Torrin are both too far from me. The beam will do what it did to Tor-

217

rin, to Iyanu. I'll have no sisters left living. My wails intensify, the hypersonic waves racing to intercept the light beam before it meets Iyanu. Iyanu doesn't even bother to reach her arms out or cover her face as the beam emerges behind her. As she huddles over Torrin, it hits her squarely on the shoulders, neck, and head, bathing her in its searing light. For a moment, the beam seems brighter than it was before hitting Iyanu, then dims again as Ryland releases it. Iyanu remains huddled, without a single burn mark on her skin, though the fabric hanging off her shoulders has turned to ashes. She doesn't even look up from Torrin to marvel at her own survival.

I cry deeply, mourning Torrin's death and thanking fate that it is not yet Iyanu's time to join her. Though my tears and screams come faster than they ever have, the frequency of the air rippling around me slows, imbued with less power than it once was. We can't keep this up forever. If we can't keep up with the king's power, there will be no one left of the Galed, and with Sade as Adara's sole vessel, who knows what type of horrors the king will perform? Instead of pouring the power out of myself, I will it into my lungs and take deeper breaths. I push the pulse into my legs and push myself towards Iyanu.

I grab her hand and attempt to pull her upright. But she remains as solid as stone, not budging an inch. "We need to go now," I protest. Trying again, in vain, to move her from her position, crouched over Torrin's corpse. Instead, Iyanu sits on the scorching sand, which is so hot it sends heat waves through

218

the air. She gathers our sister into her arms and rocks her back and forth as if she were cradling a newborn.

"Iyanu," I plead.

"We can't go anywhere without her." Even her voice remains solid despite the anguish smeared across her face.

"No, we can't," forcing my eyes to reabsorb the tears threatening to spill.

I bend over to pull Torrin out of Iyanu's arms, ignoring the way her once smooth skin feels hard, cold, and wet against mine. Iyanu stands on the other side of me, and we drape one of Torrin's arms over each of our shoulders, hoisting her up and beginning our march further away from the palace. We just need to make it far enough out that the beam is no longer hot and is easily dissipated. Each time the beam comes around, it comes weaker, and with a longer break in between, than the last time. Even Rah's chosen isn't an infinite well of power.

Iyanu and I drag our feet, hobbling and grunting with each step. Tendrils of power continue seeping out of my skin, but they do not harm my sisters. At every step, we encounter dead or partly dead guards who are wide-eyed but unseeing. We try to quicken our pace, hoping to evade the beam if it comes, but we struggle to carry even our own weight, let alone the weight of another. Lord Idowu is sprawled out, face down, on the desert floor, and his dead servants are neatly arranged in a semicircle in front of him. His gold and purple tunic and the servant's matching gray ones are now eroded by the blaze. Unlike the

Berkshire servants, his servants stayed to protect him. It still didn't do him any good.

Sharp pangs of pressure hit me between the eyes while blood pours out of my nose. A wetness in my ear forces me to stop and poke a curious finger into my ear canal. I pull it out and find that there is blood there, too. *We'll rest when we get far enough away from the palace. We just need to make it far enough.* I repeat this mantra in my head, but so far, the distance in front of us remains much larger than the distance we've covered. Never mind that we have nowhere to go or anyone to go to. Never mind that just a few healthy guards could track us down in the next half hour should we make it out of the palace grounds and reach the demarcating wall.

I curse as I stumble on a corpse, then curse some more when I find that it's a swollen and badly blistered hand wrapped around my ankle. My eyes travel down the length of the arm to find that it's Lazarus's head attached to its shoulder. He refuses to die.

"Meera," he groans. "Help me."

The right side of Lazarus's face is almost entirely without skin. The left side hisses and pusses, somehow looking worse than the right. A shiver rocks my body at the sight of him, my shoulders hunch, and the tears fall freely down my face. I wouldn't have wished this on him. On anyone.

My voice cracks when I answer him. "I can't."

I struggle to twist my ankle out of his grip, but he tightens it and tries to pull me in with a strength that emerges from somewhere deep within the soul when one is on the precipice of death. I shake my ankle vigorously, forcing him to let go. He screams something unrecognizable, ignoring the pain it must cause him.

"I can't," I repeat, forcing myself to look forward and vowing never to look back at the man I've left behind.

By the time we're a third of the way through the palace grounds, Ryland has regained enough strength to send out another beam. The light moves slowly, quite haphazardly now. It might not look like it to someone else, but there's a lag now that's palpable to me. This must be the last one, then. The air doesn't shudder at its approach. Heat waves don't blast off in either direction to foretell the beams coming. The beam is slower and cooler as well.

When I call my power to the surface, it answers in lags. What I pull out is still enough to dissipate most of the beam around Torrin and me, but Iyanu, who is on the other side, takes a bigger hit. Her skin, which was just impervious to the light, splotches a dark purple color where it hits her. Her face contorts in pain, but she continues walking, hauling Torrin and me along with her.

To the west, I make out a form moving swiftly. It races towards us and the beam by extension. Have the noble estates gotten wind of this, then? Will their spies start arriving by the numbers to extract their respective lords? I shake my head. Unlikely. That would mean someone on the battlefield survived in good enough health to relay the message to the noble estates. The figure slows only when it's within throwing distance of us.

He wears all black leather, and his face is covered with a mask, but he is no palace guard. When he lifts it, Aris's eyes stare back at mine. His eyes dart all over me and Iyanu, until, finally, they settle on Torrin.

"She's—"

He knows better than to complete the sentence. Aris grabs a hold of Torrin, taking her weight from me and Iyanu. With Torrin's weight lifted, Iyanu and I make better haste, jogging behind Aris to the edge of the battlegrounds. Aris's secured two hamels to a quartz statue of a re-enactment of the touch that secured the king's line as Rah's chosen and loosens the rope he's used to tie them. He drapes Torrin carefully across the front of one, so her weight is evenly distributed.

"How did you know?" I ask.

"I didn't," Aris answers. "Julius was supposed to come back, check in with me at a checkpoint before making his way to the Deadends. He never did." Julius must have been the man sent to retrieve Torrin from the cellar entrance.

"I'm sorry."

"No need to be," Aris replies, his eyes flickering to Torrin for an instant.

Iyanu climbs the hamel and sits behind Torrin without saying a word. This leaves me sitting in front of the other hamel, with Aris holding the reins behind me.

"They'll search the battlefield for your corpses, and when they don't find them there, they'll search the entire kingdom."

Aris sets the hamel into motion. "Lay low and do as I say until we reach the Deadends."

He takes us through the forest to an unguarded portion of the demarcating wall. We slip through tunnels dug underneath the wall and find ourselves in the Midzone.

Chapter 16

The sun sits low in the sky, not quite ready to dip down below the horizon. The Midzone streets are only warm, not yet bitingly cold. Each towering building here is made with rocks that resist the heat of the desert sun, and each building is positioned in such a way as to maximize any breeze billowing through them. This makes Midzone streets almost as cool as the palace and estate grounds during the day but even more devastatingly cold than the Endzone when the night comes.

Aris reigns our hamel in front of a Midzoner's home, and Iyanu stops by our side, Torrin's body bobbing awkwardly in front of her. If we had come directly from the palace, it might have taken us two hours to get here.

Once, Aris stopped to veil and re-clothe Torrin's body to not draw attention to her misshapen face. And twice, he repositioned her to make it look like she was holding herself up. Still, it was the circling back and re-routing we did that added another three hours to our journey.

The exterior of the Midzoner's house is made from plainly layered sandbrick, free of any adornments. The door is made from dried cactus husk, which was once yellow with a green tinge but browns shortly after the drying process. The house is maybe twice as big as a servant's quarter at the palace, where five servants may be expected to sleep. It lies on the bottom floor of the towering building, one of the least desirable spots. Although shaded during the day, the home bears the brunt of the wind the buildings create at night.

Aris says some loud and joyous thing to the man at the door, which results in them clapping each other on the back several times and pulling each other in several more. But their voices sound distant to me, and their joy seems even more so. It doesn't take long before the man's joy dissipates. A tense look is on his face as he glances behind Aris to find Iyanu and me staring back at him. His face shatters when he sees Torrin's unmoving body draped over on the hamel's side. He says something else now, shushed and angry, but opens the doors wider as he does, beckoning the three of us to come in with him.

Iyanu turns from the door instead, walking over to Torrin and carrying her in her arms. The man does not protest as she carries Torrin in through his door. He might have said something under his breath, but I did not hear it.

"Meera!" I jump at the sound of my name and turn slowly to face Aris.

I try to focus my attention on his face and not look at Iyanu and Torrin, both of whom are unmoving at this moment. Iyanu is so deep inside her inner world that she doesn't even remember to blink. Torrin's skin looks cold. It's burnt and blackened, charred and flaking, or rises in puss-filled domes. But the parts of her skin that are uninjured—those parts look too cold. Her skin wasn't always that cool, or at least it wasn't cool in that way.

Aris places his hands on both of my shoulders, squeezing gently and then with more pressure.

How long has he been squeezing this hard? Did I just notice?

A woman leads a child out of one of three rooms in the space. The child rubs his eyes, resisting the urge to fall back asleep. He yawns helplessly as his eyes lower. The woman bends and takes the child into her arms so the child's head rests at the back of her shoulders and her forearm supports the child's weight. She averts her eyes as she walks by, and the child's eyes close behind her, having eased back into his slumber. She closes the door as they disappear into another room.

I should have said something. Thank you, maybe? Or some comment about their graciousness in hosting us. Torrin would have said something. I look over at Iyanu and Torrin. Torrin's skin looks so cold. Was it always that cold?

Aris releases me, or he had released me at some point. He's already standing beside Iyanu by the time I notice. He ushers her into the room that once held the mother and child, and although I'm closer to the door, I wait until they've walked past me to follow them in.

Iyanu lays Torrin down gently on a narrow bed pushed against the corner of the creamy room. So gently that if Torrin were being laid to rest in a body of water, there wouldn't have been a single ripple as she touched its surface. Iyanu kneels on the ground, staring at what's left of Torrin's face. I imagine Iyanu moving a misplaced lock of hair, taking it from Torrin's cheek, and settling it behind her ear. But both skin and hair are missing from Torrin's scalp.

Torrin's cold because she's wet. Her blood, her water, and the viscous fluids inside her leak out and dampen the bed.

All three of us are unmoving now. Torrin, laying beautifully in the bed, Iyanu kneeling in front of her, and me, standing, watching them both.

Aris leaves us there for some time. I couldn't say for how long. But when he returns, he brings some food for us. Two bowls filled with something I don't recognize. It's Iyanu who rises, taking one of them from his hands. He places the other one on the ground. Iyanu cries silently as she eats, and I stand there watching, still. When she's done, she goes back to kneeling next to Torrin. She's not just kneeling! She's been praying all this time. How tedious it is to be alive. It is so tedious that even in death, one has to be pampered and cared for just to be ushered into the next world.

Iyanu comes and goes for a few minutes at a time, briefly leaving me alone with Torrin's corpse. I stare at it, or I never stopped staring at it, and I wonder, is Adara still there? Is Torrin still there? Does the Goddess' spirit mix with the host when she inhabits them, meshing and fusing until the two spirits are virtually indistinguishable? Then does she take what's left of you when she leaves your body, and will she deposit it with herself in the next? When Iyanu comes back, she arrives with a few extra sheets. She wraps Torrin around, cocooning her between the layers of fabric, but leaves her splayed out on the bed. Good. Torrin won't be so cold that way. She leaves and comes again with even more sheets, laying them on the ground and preparing herself for sleep. She doesn't say a word, but her shoulders rise and fall unevenly as she cries herself to sleep.

Aris enters the room again.

"Meera."

My head snaps towards him.

"You should eat something," he says, bringing the bowl of untouched foodstuff towards me. I must have shaken my head, or maybe he waited too long without an answer because he sets the bowl down again with a strained smile.

"Tomorrow then." Aris walks over to the side of the sheets Iyanu placed on the ground, smoothing the wrinkled fabric. "Don't stay up too late," he adds before he walks out the door. I can hear him faintly but clearly now. That's good.

———◆———

It's Aris again, walking into our room in the morning. Iyanu has yet to rise, but I knew the exact moment she woke up.

"Shit," Aris exclaims. He looks at me tearfully but I'm not the one whose corpse lies in a stranger's bed. He walks over to me, grabbing the lower half of my garment when he reaches me.

"You haven't moved all night, have you?" he asks.

No.

"You released on yourself," he continues. Oh.

Aris pulls me, and I try to resist, wishing to remain exactly where I am, watching over my sisters. But my body betrays me. My arms are too weak to slow Aris's momentum, and my legs feel strange beneath me. They creak with each step I take forward, protesting at the strangeness of the movement. Twice, Aris keeps me from collapsing, catching me before my body hits the floor.

When we get to the washroom, Aris works his hands around the fabric wrapped around my body, loosening it and leaving me bare. He gets a small bucket of cool water and dumps it in successive bursts over my head. The coolness of it shocks me. Aris plugs the tub hole and begins emptying buckets and buckets of water into it. After several rounds, the tub is full and ready for me to step inside of it.

What a waste of water. It might cost a typical Midzoner a week of pay, if not more, to fill this tub. The man won't be happy when he finds his reserves depleted. Still, I'm grateful for the cool kiss of water on my skin and the sensation of weightlessness that being submerged brings. Next, Aris grabs a washing cloth from the three stacked neatly on the corner.

"I'll get them a new one," he says.

He lathers the cloth and swipes it against my neck, wiping off the debris I didn't know was there. My skin stings where the soap meets open wounds.

Aris cleans my shoulders and my arms, circling my breasts, then pressing the cloth to them gently. He glides his hands past my stomach before turning me around to work on my back. He angles me so my back rests on the sloped surface of the tub, then lifts one leg and the other. He scrubs between my toes, ankles, and thighs, then stops.

"I'll let you take care of the other places you should take care of," he says. "I'll be back in five," he adds before he turns to leave.

Another time, I might have been embarrassed, but I don't have the energy to muster the emotion. Instead, I concentrate on nothing in particular.

I sink deeper and deeper into the water, letting my eyes close and feeling the coolness of the water on my skin more deeply. I find that my eyes are too heavy when I try to open them again, so I stay there, eyes closed in the tub. A tune plays in my head—one that's ethereal and familiar. But I know I've never heard it and that nothing like it has ever been heard on this earth.

When I open my eyes, I find myself transported to another land. The sun sits low on the horizon. It's so dim that it looks like a mere candle attempting to light the entire world. The land beneath my feet is not land but a never-ending plane of water stretching out in every direction. It holds me and refuses to let me fall into its depths, rippling without breaking with every step I take. The water's surface shines a blackish gold, reflecting its depth and the sun's rays. The moon, too, hangs overhead. It is so large that it seems to be the same size as the sun on the horizon despite being further up in the sky.

A woman approaches me. Her dark silhouette dims the already weak light of the sun. Her form sways from side to side, and she walks without seeming to walk but gets closer nonetheless. Her face is covered with a black mask depicting the face of one of the creatures in the palace atrium.

The creature has a smooth but sharp face and a lean and muscular body. Its eyes are pointed, like slits on its face, and its nose is an inverted triangle hanging just above its curved mouth. The woman wears a white silk gown that flows down to her feet. Her skin, too, is golden. When she speaks, she speaks with three voices at once. Her presence overwhelms me, causing the hair on my skin to rise.

"Welcome, sister."

"Welcome, child."

Three voices at once and two sentences at once, yet I know exactly what she's saying. Her form pulsates, phasing in and out of existence. Each vibration changes her slightly. She's shorter or taller now. Her once warm and golden skin seems pale, then paler still, then black as mine.

"Who are you? Where am I?"

"We're nowhere you'd understand, and I am too vast to comprehend. I believe your people call me Adara, but I am known in many places by many names. I am the beginning and the end. The darkness that creates and devours. The virgin, the mother, and the barren one. The sacred whore. I am the stillness from which chaos emerges."

She's speaking with Torrin's voice and with Annabeth's. The third voice is more of a distortion, something that can't be grasped fully without the aid of the other two. When she flashes in and out again, I realize that her skin, too, flashes between Torrin's and Annabeth's and sometimes looks like mine or Iyanu's. In the brief moments that she's not wearing anyone's skin, her form, again, is incomprehensible.

Thousands of questions swirl around in my head, one displacing the other, each begging to be the first to be asked. *What did you do with Annabeth and Torrin? How is there so much water in this realm but none in ours? Why are you here? Why did your petty warfare doom our ancestors and their descendants to life on a scorched planet?*

She answers each question without me asking, seemingly plucking each thought out of my head.

"I'm here because you called me here."

She cocks her head to the side at the thought in my head but doesn't reply. "This is not a realm that humans can inhabit, and these are not waters that humans might drink." I bend down, trying to force my hand into the water, but the tension at its surface is impenetrable.

"You'll return here at your death. You'll submerge yourself then," she offers.

"Why did you bring me here?" I ask again.

"You called me here," she says. "There's a deep ache in your soul, and the pain of betrayal lingers wearily in your heart."

I called her here? The last time a woman called Adara here, one in seven women died. And in the time before that, her presence introduced suffering and death into the world. Torrin and Annabeth are both gone because of the Goddess in front of me.

"I would not call you here," I whisper. "It's your fault. They died because of you. For centuries, we've died because of you. Why couldn't you just leave it alone?"

My anger does nothing to unsettle the Goddess.

"Those women called me into them just as you called me into you." She continues, "A possession, as you call it, is an invitation answered. Some delirium exists in the minds of those in the present, which leads them to glamorize the past. And history is told through the eyes of the victors. Those women called me to them like you've called me into you," she repeats. "Those women came to me in their desperation to fix the tribute system that kept them poor and their children destitute. You have called me into you because you are just as desperate as they were."

"And yet they lost," I sigh.

"I don't guarantee victory. Though my power aids you, your fate is decided by you alone."

What use is a Goddess or her power if it doesn't guarantee victory?

"What happened to Torrin and Annabeth?" I ask.

"One day you'll find out," she answers, then adds, "they aren't gone. They're just changed."

"What about the rain? Will it ever fall again?"

"When the first of the Galed extracted my essence from the world and drew it into themselves, it created a great wound in the world."

"The Oguni are right then. If Iyanu, Sade, and I die before the Waning ceremony takes place, then your spirit will be released, and the kingdom will be healed. The rain will fall once more."

The thought makes me shiver. Iyanu and I have already given too much to this kingdom, and now it demands we give it our lives.

The Goddess shakes her head, and though she does not frown, I know she is frowning. "If all of you die before the

Waning, my essence will gather still, moving in clumps from person to person, likely killing them, trying to find suitable hosts."

"But you said —"

She nods. "Have you ever let a pot of soil get too dry?" she asks.

"Yes," I answer, smiling at the thought of the only thing that could get even the slightest bit of a rise out of Torrin.

"Then you know that if you let a pot of soil sit out too long without being watered when you go to water it, the water glides right along the surface, streaming down the edges of the pot and refusing to soak into the soil. The world has been devoid of my essence for so long that it resists it," she says. "Meera," she continues, "the Galed are the bridge between myself and the world devoid of me. It is through you that I will begin to seep into the world again."

"How do we do that?"

"The Galed may be the bridge, but a bridge cannot function without a destination. The world can only be healed when I'm elevated as Rah is in the hearts and minds of the people. When they open themselves to me and allow me to flow freely through them to the world around them, it will right the heavens."

The monarchy mandates service to Rah. The king's position as his emissary makes Ryland's power and his ownership of the land and its people unquestionable. The people have two choices, serve the king and his God and hope to get just a sliver of his wealth, the minimum they need to survive. The other option is death. But the monarchy demeans Adara as the Goddess who cursed humanity, bringing death to the world in the first place. I know that here is no elevating Adara in the people's hearts as long as Ryland's line still sits on the throne. The Oguni must crush the monarchy thoroughly and ensure that no other human will ever sit on a throne in Ile-Oja again. But why should the people open their hearts to the Goddess who brought death to us all?

"When Rah created the titans, why —" I begin.

Adara's form flickers in and out of existence in the realm. Shaking the atmosphere as it does. The moon, which was just a crescent, has turned full as if weeks have passed, but the sun in the sky sits fixed like no time has passed at all. The world flickers again, and when I look down at my hands, I realize I'm flickering with it.

"Meera!" Somewhere in the distance, a voice calls me.

"Meera!"

I'm jolted out of the other realm, shocked back into the reality of the tub, and Aris, who has both hands on my shoulders, shakes me vigorously. My throat burns, filled with water. I heave violently, coughing up mouthfuls of the liquid.

"What do you think you're doing!" Aris shouts, wide-eyed and panicked. The coughs, which continue rocking my body, don't allow me to answer. "You were...you were drowning yourself, Meera." He says this faintly and more to himself than he does to me, as if he were scared to confirm his suspicions by voicing the allegation out loud.

I open my mouth to deny it, but Aris lifts me out of the cool water and brings my body to his. His bare skin squeezes my naked body gently, and he rests his head on top of mine.

"Don't ever do that again."

Chapter 17

In the room where Torrin lies, the smell of rotting flesh permeates the air. Iyanu rises from her kneeling position beside Torrin. She cries even harder than she has up till now, but her cries are interrupted with bouts of laughter.

"She came to me," Iyanu says. "I prayed, and she came."

"She came to me too," I say, surprised to hear the words coming out of my mouth.

Though I've always believed Iyanu about her experience with the Goddess, I always assumed that celestial visits were reserved only for those who were most devoted. Iyanu looks at me surprised, perhaps thinking the same, but quickly wipes the expression off of her face. We both turn to look at Torrin.

"We should send her off," she says.

We're far away from the altar made specially for this purpose, and there are no agate knives nearby. My mind wanders to all we left behind in the atrium. Will Sade continue the upkeep of the plants we keep there? Can one person alone fetch the water, trim the roots and stems, and maintain everything, or will she invite the palace servants into our holy place? I sigh. A simple glass knife will have to do for today.

I walk over to Torrin's body, carefully unwrapping the sheets Iyanu has placed around her body. I should have asked the Goddess why we had to do this of all things—needing to eat a part of the deceased flesh to cement the bond of Adara's transferred spirit. Why couldn't we just say a prayer or have a regular burial like the monarchs?

Voices from the dining area stream into the room. The man who is hosting us speaks bitterly.

"You need to get that body out of here. My son can't sleep at night," he fumes. "Now, you've done a lot for me over these last few years, but this is too much. Tell them to get that body out or leave."

Aris responds to him in a calm, hushed manner. He's too hushed for me to hear what he's saying, but he doesn't speak for long. The chatter comes to a halt when Iyanu opens the door. I follow behind her, willing my mouth to curve into a smile, but my efforts aren't rewarded. Though Iyanu looks stern, she manages to speak with some warmth.

"Can we borrow a knife?" Iyanu asks, straight to the point. The man blinks once and then again. These are the first words Iyanu has said to him in his home. He might have thought her deaf or mute up until now.

"Over here," he stammers as he pulls a short dagger from the crevice above his sun oven. "You can keep it," he adds, shoving it towards her and retreating sharply once the dagger is secure in her hands.

"Thank you," she says, turning and walking away.

"We'll be sure to clean it and return it when we're finished," I add.

"Don't," he says. He disappears behind the door leading to the other room. Aris follows and closes the door behind the two of them.

Iyanu presses the glass knife to Torrin's chest, applying a faint amount of pressure. Her skin gives way without resistance. Torrin's blood drips down her chest, trailing down her rib cage and falling onto the sheets below. The blood gathers, forming globs on the surface of the knife.

When Annabeth died, we were all frightened by the uncertainty and the potential for disaster that lay directly ahead. The Waning and the potential end of our lives seemed all-encompassing, pressing down on us from every angle, creating fear and tension. I couldn't have imagined that we would have already lost one of our own just a month before the ceremony and that we would have lost another to her delusions. But, both Iyanu and I are here, filled with something otherworldly, determined to face the path ahead.

Though Torrin's skin has turned ghastly, it seems like the decay has only settled skin deep. Her insides don't reek like I expect them to, nor do they ooze strange or nauseating fluids. Only the metallic smell of fresh blood wades through the air.

Iyanu reaches through the open skin, bypassing Torrin's rib cage, to reach her heart.

"Let's get this over with," she says.

Iyanu tears two pieces from the greater whole, passing one to me. We both swallow quickly and in unison.

Later that day, Aris helps us bury Torrin's body. Iyanu protests the decision to take her to a burial ground alone, but he's adamant that we're not to leave until he deems it safe. Aris gets word that the palace guards discovered Torrin's body just a day later.

<hr/>

The next few days go by in a blur. When Aris is around, he keeps a watchful eye on Iyanu and me, but he often leaves without notice at any and all times of the day and night. Once, he is gone for an entire day. He says he went to the Deadends to inform Bear of the change in plans. There won't be one but two Galed coming to join the resistance, and we are no longer four but three.

More guards than ever before have been called to the palace. The king has been sending them to scour the Midzone and the Endzone, hoping to catch traces of us. Aris creates distractions and plants false leads for the guards. Even the nobility has been hit hard by the chaos that unfolded on the palace grounds. The Tanaka's, Idowu's, and Berkshires have all been widowed. The

Berkshires and Idowus, in particular, with no sons to call heirs, have been stripped of their lands and titles. All their wealth will have been commandeered by the Ryland or disbursed sparingly to the nobles he deems loyal. Part of me wonders why Ryland hasn't used his Voice yet. He could easily speak to all the people in Ile-Oja, demanding the people turn us over or turn over those who might be harboring us. But such a move would make him look weak. It would make him look like he couldn't control a couple of girls, the same girls whom he used to parade around as a trophy and testament to Rah's victory over Adara's vessels and, by extension, the monarchy's victory over its people. Instead, he sends his guards out on a futile search.

"We can't stay here for much longer," Aris says, glancing at the door to our hosts' sleeping room.

It's been closed more than it's been open since we arrived, with the host coming out only briefly to prepare and bring food to his wife and child. "The guards have taken to going door to door. They'll be making their way toward this one soon. We can't be here when that happens."

"Why haven't we just left yet?" I ask, exasperated.

While we sit here doing nothing, the king gathers more of his army at the palace, continuing his experiments and using Sade to do his unnatural bidding. Even now, Adara's essence teems beneath my skin, begging to be let out at any opportunity. Will Sade be powerful enough to create the titans Ryland is hell-bent on bringing back?

"We can't keep sitting here and doing nothing. We need to figure out a way to fight back. You said Bear would help us!"

"Bear *will* help you. But he can't help you if you get killed trying to make it to the Deadends. We need to be smart. Not draw attention."

"*You've* been coming and going whenever you like."

"Yes. And I happen to be about the same height and size as Vern. People don't look twice when I enter or leave. Entering and leaving with two women who look nothing like Grace or their child, on the other hand—"

The door rattles as a fist strikes it twice from the outside. The noise drives Vern out of the room with his wife and child, a panicked look on his face. The child inside cries, having been awoken from his sleep. The gentle sounds of Grace's shushing contrast with the rough ones whispering outside.

"We're not expecting anyone," he says, answering Aris's questioning glance. It's too late for visitors. The sun set three hours ago.

Aris stands on his feet, prompting Iyanu and me to stand with him. He gestures frantically to the room with Grace and the child.

"Vern, you're here alone with your child," Aris half whispers, half yells. "Inside now," he says, ushering us to the door, coming inside with us, and pushing the still-yelling child towards his father before closing the door behind him.

Two more knocks sound through the air at the exact moment that the back of Grace's hand lands on Aris's cheek. She gasps at the moment of impact, as if surprised by the sudden outburst of violence.

Her hands cover her mouth, but she speaks through them nonetheless.

"Why would you do that?" she asks, referencing her child who is outside the room instead of in here, with his mother.

The sound of the door opening cuts off Aris's response. He looks at the three of us with pleading eyes and one finger held up to his mouth. Vern welcomes the guards in the same manner he welcomed Aris when we showed up at his doorstep about a week ago, laughing and clapping them on the back. There is none of the chaos I expect.

Aris brings his ear closer to the door, careful not to lean against it so the old thing doesn't creak. The door bursts wide open, revealing two lanky-built guards. Likely those called up from the reserve forces. Grace takes a few steps backward, retreating from them or maybe retreating from Iyanu, who openly glowers.

Foolish of Ryland to send them. And just two at that. I reach down inside myself, pleased not to have to reach so deeply this time. The power hums directly underneath my skin, practically begging to be let out, so I try to gather it to my throat, aiming to ready myself to use it.

Would the sand-brick walls hold up, or would the entire house collapse? The thought crosses my mind that I might not be able to spare Vern and his family if I were to release my power. Images of Lazarus's slain body flash across my field of vision the moment his arm outstretched, begging for me to take it and save him. His father, with his bulging stomach, sliced and spilling the contents of his guts out. The noble servants, with their skin blackened to a crisp, life departed from their static bodies. I stumble, and the movement catches the guards by surprise.

"Whoa there," the taller and lankier one says. "Calm your hamels. We don't mean any harm." He raises his arms above his head in mock surrender.

"We're just here to relay a message. A directive from the king," he continues. "Surrender peacefully and return to your rightful places at the palace, and the king will forgive any wrongdoing. He wishes to show you mercy, recognizing the hysteria brought about by the loss of your leader."

"Now, I'd say that's quite a generous offer," the other adds.

Iyanu spits directly at the man's shoes. The saliva lands an inch away from his polished boot.

"We won't be going anywhere," I answer. Ryland only needs to keep one of us alive to execute his plan. Nothing is preventing him from trying to execute us the moment Iyanu and I step foot in the palace. With Sade already more powerful than ever before, our deaths would only add to her power.

"Suit yourselves," the lankier one adds. The guards turn from us, returning to Vern. He reaches into the satchel by his side and pulls out two jugs full of water and five copper shillings.

"For the tip," he says, placing the jugs on the dining table and dropping the shillings in Vern's hands. The child watches shyly but gleefully behind his father's legs, pointing at the red and gold embellished uniforms the officers wear. The short guard bends down to ruffle the kid's hair. His mother flinches at the movement. The guard shoots her a blank stare before turning his attention back to the child.

"One day, you'll be big and strong like me. You'll make a mighty fine addition to the king's guard," he says before getting up and turning for the door. The door closes with a faint thud, the last sound we hear for the next few minutes as a deep silence descends over us.

"Let's go," Aris says, not bothering to hide any bit of distaste and irritation that's built up in him.

He pushes Vern to get to his mask and hamel leather attire. The bigger man stumbles aside, falling a chair in his wake. His child runs over to the mother, who scoops him up with both hands. She smooths his roughened hair, then turns her attention to Aris, who's already begun to stash his items in his bag.

"Don't you go stomping around in my home," the man yells. "You won't like what's coming to you if you try that again," Vern continues, hardening his tone. Aris stops packing to look Vern in the eye.

"And what exactly would that be?"

Vern walks up to him, pointing a finger to his chest. "I've housed and fed you and your lot for a godsdamn week."

"You were paid for your troubles, Vern." He says the name like it's venom on his tongue.

"The king paid more," Vern answers with a shrug. Aris grabs his satchel and pushes past Vern again.

"Let's go," Aris calls out to us, opening the door to the house.

"That's the problem with you Endzone lot. You never know what's good for you. It's called cunning, Aris. Moving up the ladder. How do you think I got myself out of that wretched place? I had the drive. I had the brains to cut deals when I needed to and take a payday however it would come. Now I live in a house, Aris, not some pathetic hole in the floor!"

"You need to go, Vern. Find somewhere safe to take your wife and children. I hope you've been cunning enough to find some good allies that you've stayed loyal to."

"Why? You coming after me now? Going to send the big bad resistance to kill me off?"

"I won't kill you, but Ryland might."

Vern scoffs at that.

Aris continues, "The only reason you're alive right now is because Meera and Iyanu were here." He waves his hands toward us. "A fight would have led to the guards' deaths and destroyed large swatches of this building and maybe this town. But they've delivered their message, and they know we'll be gone from here shortly. If you remain, Vern, they'll return, and they'll slaughter your family for hosting them." Aris shakes his head. "I hope you're ready."

"Fuck you, Aris," Vern responds. "You've never had no sense with you. Bullshitting ever since we were children."

Aris gives Iyanu and me a pointed look, jolting us both from the positions we've remained glued to. Neither Iyanu nor I brought anything but the clothes on our backs, so it's easy for us to walk right out the door when Aris does. He reaches for the hamels and reigns them in swiftly and angrily.

"Where are we going?" I ask.

"Where do you think?" he shouts. "The Deadends," he says, voice low but tone short and crisp.

I temper the urge to bicker with him, instead hoisting myself onto the hamel that's free. Iyanu hoists herself up onto the second one, and Aris comes to sit behind me on mine. He presses his groin against me, and the front of his knees pushes against the outer sides of my mid-thigh. The thought of him holding my naked body, bathing me, then soothing me after pulling me out of the water sends blood rushing to my cheeks. He reaches in front of me to grab hold of the reins, bringing his arms on either side of my waist and his face close to the back of my head. His warm breath on the side of my neck makes me jolt forward.

"What's wrong with you?" he asks.

"Nothing," I answer too quickly for my liking.

I jump off the hamel, wincing at the impact of my feet hit the ground.

"I'll go sit with Iyanu," I say, strolling away and climbing the other hamel.

My heart rate calms, and the goosebumps that I hadn't even realized had begun to form ease away in Iyanu's presence. I reach forward now, not to hold the reigns that are already securely held in Iyanu's arms, but to circle them around her waist and breathe her in. Much better. But I watch Aris even from here, noting the way the moon's rays bounce off of his body and that moonlight is the best light to see him in.

It was that time of the night. When the Midzoners bolt their doors and their singular rooftop window from the inside. Those who are wealthy enough lock the scrawny iron fences enclosing their compounds as well.

"We need to get ahead of the Endzoners returning from their assignments," Aris says, his voice leveled and calm now. "There could be guards or assassins mixed in the crowd. We don't want to lead someone back to the Deadends."

The hamel murres as Aris pulls its reins and rides off ahead of us. Iyanu and I follow closely, anticipation building in my chest as we make our way to the Deadends.

Chapter 18

It takes us three hours to travel to the Endzone, and I spend every minute looking over my shoulder. No guards have been sent after us, and the laborers who walk for miles on foot never had any real chance of catching up with us, so we made it without incident. In the Midzone, the buildings were made out of sand-brick piled atop one another perilously, with clusters of buildings giving way to narrow streets and unmarked corridors. At the edges of the Midzone, smaller, amateurishly made buildings dotted the desert landscape. These were the dwellings of people who had managed to procure sand-bricks for themselves but had no means to commission someone to lay it for them. Those dwellings soon gave way to the barrenness of the Endzone.

There are no buildings of any kind in the Endzone, just holes dug into the floor and reinforced with whatever could be found to keep the surrounding sand from collapsing in on the people and property inside them. The holes, or sleeping pits, are dug about six feet deep. They're ten square feet across—just the

251

right size for one person and one person's worth of stuff to fit into them. Any larger, and they became too unwieldy to manage. It was always a battle to keep the sand out. I wouldn't be able to count the number of times I heard of a wife or brother buried alive in their dwelling by a sudden shift of the sand. Saved if someone was close enough to notice. Buried alive and never to be dug out if not. That and the fact that Endzoners liked to keep family close were the reasons sleeping pits were usually clustered together.

Looking at the Endzone pits brings my father's words to mind. *Your mother died because of you. So now you must live a life big enough for the both of you.* A life big enough meant not learning to read or joining the resistance in any meaningful way, helping to coordinate attacks or plan strategy, or even working as a spy or foot soldier. He meant stand on the sidelines, do everything I ask of you without raising questions, and wait for the time to come when I can use you, even if it kills you. Aris tells me that he was the proudest anyone had ever seen him after he learned that I survived the Waning. "He said he always knew you had it in you," Aris said. I think he thought it was a ten percent chance of survival at best. And he was willing to take those odds.

I squeeze Iyanu tighter than I need to as we continue meandering between the sleeping pits. She squeezes me back reassuringly. We've slowed down a bit. Here, a misstep by a hamel could lead to serious injuries for humans and animals alike. Despite pushing to leave Vern's home for the better half of a week, I'm grateful that our speed has reduced slightly. The thought of facing the Oguni after failing my mission doesn't sound appealing. *What's done is done.* I chant that over and over in my head. Let it go. But I know that I haven't let it go and that I never will until Ryland is dead.

The Deadends is a pseudonym for Oguni outposts, moved every few years when I was a child. It was always accessed through one of the sleeping pits, but the exact pit was always subject to change. It wasn't difficult then to move the entire operation ever so often. With members numbering in the tens and not everyone showing up to gather consistently, it barely took a couple of weeks to dismantle the dried tree things used to reinforce the tunnels that led into a more spacious, under-ground gathering space, also reinforced with cactus wood to keep it from collapsing. No materials were ever thrown away. Every bit of everything was always gathered and used for the construction of a new site. My father used to tell me that the movement was necessary to deter enemies and throw off would-be spies. But in truth, the monarchy paid no mind to the fledgling movement just a few years ago.

Aris reins his hamel, bringing it to a screeching halt. In the distance, a boy walks with his hands placed firmly on his neck. He moves forward, then backward, swaying precariously. Aris considers the boy for one moment before leading us to him.

The boy is no more than fourteen years old. His wide eyes sink into his face, his lips chapped and cracking at every crease. He murmurs something to Aris, but he's inaudible. His body convulses once and then again. Aris opens his satchel, bringing out the jar of water he's packed for the journey. The boy looks ravenously at it, something crazed whirling in his eyes. When Aris tries to approach him, however, his face turns into a deep snarl, baring his teeth, and repeatedly launching himself a few inches forward before pulling back.

Aris, undeterred, steps forward and grabs the boy by his too-thin arm. The boy struggles, tears streaming down his face. He makes gut-wrenching, unintelligible pleas as he spasms. Aris brings him to the ground, laying him down on the sand. He goes without a fight. He tips his head up, and the boy knows instinctively to open his mouth. Aris pours a mouthful of water into the boy's mouth and waits for him to swallow before pouring again. The boy sobs between each gulp, but Aris says nothing, just dutiful pouring when the boy is ready again.

"That's enough for now. You don't want to drink more than you can take."

Aris returns to his satchel, bringing a piece of linen out and wrapping it around the boy. The thin fabric won't do much to keep the boy warm once the chill settles in, but it's better than nothing. He returns to his hamel and continues to lead the way.

"What was that?" I ask

"The first stages of madness, caused by the heat and cold."

My mind goes back to the woman I encountered on the shores of Lake Sarran with her inhuman strength and frenzied speech.

"I saw a woman by the shore of the lake. She was like that, too. She was stronger than she should have been and said some crazy things."

Aris looks ahead towards our destination. "The madness only started a few years ago, but it's becoming more and more common. Bear thinks the intense heat and cold is sending people into some sort of weather-induced madness. What you just saw was the latter stage. He's likely already been suffering for a few days now. The woman on the lake might have been further along. Sometimes they become extraordinarily strong and manic like that before they die."

"It's madness indeed," Iyanu says bitterly. "That we're taught that Adara brought a sort of madness to her hosts, and now madness returns in her absence."

Aris doesn't reply.

Soon, we're standing in front of the entrance to the Deadends. It's an obscure entrance. Just one normal-looking sleeping pit in a field of many with no markers or indications as to what's lying beneath it. Aris brings a rope out of his bag, digs lightly at the sand at the bottom of the pit, and reveals the wooden curve of a door handle. He attaches rope to the handle and hoists himself out of the pit, pulling the rope with him. Sand falls as the door lifts, transforming into a ramp leading to the entrance of a tunnel which will take us to the main meeting space.

We walk down the tunnels. Aris grabs a torch and lights a fire by striking it against the hard stone substance the walls are made of. It catches fire but only manages to illuminate a couple of feet in front of us. The tunnel leading into the meeting space slopes downward, and as we continue walking. The resistance has never met so far underground. We would have walked the entire length of the last outposts in just the time it's taken for us to make it a tenth of the way through the tunnels.

The tunnels split off into three. Aris leads us down the left-most path. After a few minutes of walking, the path splits into three separate routes again. He chooses the middle one this time.

"It's a labyrinth, then."

"We stay put now, so we need proper deterrents."

I'm willing to bet that there's a nasty surprise waiting for those who walk down the wrong path.

We make it to the gathering space, although I supposed it could be called a gathering arena with how large it is now. Firelights hang above us, burning with a plentiful supply of fuel, keeping them churning through the night. The warm light of the lanterns casts a dull glow on Aris's face, softening the angles of his cheek yet sharpening the angles in his jaw. Pillars jut out of the ground, holding up the ceiling up ahead. In the palace, the pillars were made of hard stone. Obsidian or quarts, sometimes rare gems like amethyst and citrine. They're carved to be perfectly cylindrical, molded by sculptors who carved intricate designs onto their sides before adorning them with statues on the top. These pillars, as well as the material used for the entire interior, feel hard but lightweight and porous. They are organically shaped, having wider ends but thinning out near their middle. Rather than being cylindrical, they look as if two pyramids had been stacked, tip to tip, atop each other.

There's a cubic depression in the ground with sharply sloped edges and a flat bottom. There are at least three rooms further away from us, the contents of which we're unable to see at this moment.

"Wow," Iyanu says. Her voice bounces off the walls of the empty enclosure. "I never imagined it would look like this," she continues. Neither did I.

Aris smiles a proud smile, as if he built the entire thing himself. "We've come a long way," he says, glancing in my direction.

Bear is doing things my father never did.

Chapter 19

A young woman streams out of one of the rooms. Her footsteps are tepid at first, but they become lighter and more steadfast as a flash of recognition crosses her face as she glances toward Aris and me. Her dark hair falls in ringlets around her heart-shaped face, and her chin sports a slight dip in the middle. Her eyes take on a honey-colored hue, shining bright with awareness. She's captivating. I've seen her before, but I struggle to place her in my memory. It's the slight bump of her stomach that gives her away.

"Aris!" she cheers, coming over and taking both of his hands in hers.

I smile tensely.

"Rin," he replies. She releases her grip on him, ruffling over to my side in the next instant and gathering me in her arms for a hug. The action catches me by surprise, and by the time I've decided to bring my arms up to join her, she's already let go of me.

"I'm Camrin," she says. "But you can call me Rin or Rinny if you like, although only my little brother calls me that, and I haven't seen him in years," she continues.

"Nice to meet you, Rin," Iyanu says, flashing her a smile.

"I just want to thank you, all of you so much for everything you've done for me," Rin goes on.

My discomfort grows as tears gather in her eyes, and her voice begins to break.

"I didn't know what was going to happen to me when I didn't hear anything back from you for so long, I thought..." She doesn't finish her sentence. "Well, that's all over now," she says, wiping the droplets that have fallen onto her cheeks and flashing a smile again.

Aris must have gotten her out without ever telling me. I remember asking, maybe even pleading with him, that he must, but I can't find any of the same enthusiasm I had for it that I did in the past. What if she's a spy? What if she's been sent here by Ryland to gather information on the Deadends and the Oguni? What if Ryland and his army descend upon us in the middle of the night or, better yet, at dawn when most of the laborers will be out of the Endzone, and there will be no one to witness our demise? I take two steps away from Rin.

"How far along are you," I ask. There's no reason she should be showing. Annabeth died just two months ago. There's no reason she should be showing at all. Unless that isn't the king's child, or if it is, Annabeth never had a hand in preventing him from siring children. Ryland would have noticed if the woman carrying his child vanished.

"I'm only about five weeks," she says. "But the child is growing very quickly."

If she's telling the truth, the child will be here in another two months. Three at most. The Galed do not have children. Or at least, there has never been a history of them having children. Maybe some did before they became Galed, but none have after the Waning. I'm glad that I will never be to blame for bringing children into this mad world. Is it typical for the king's children to be born at alarmingly fast rates? Is it to do with Rah's touch? I can't help the skepticism I feel, but I try my best not to make it evident.

"Strange," I begin. She cuts me off before I can continue.

"Strange indeed," she says with an awkward smile and a pleasing laugh.

If she's telling the truth, we'll know in a few weeks. If she's not telling the truth, we'll know in a few weeks, albeit under much more violent circumstances.

Rin talks about everything and nothing all at once. She talks about how Aris swept her off her feet in the middle of the night, how she almost screamed and woke up her flatmates in the servant quarters. She thought for sure she was done for when he put one giant hand over her mouth. She's going on about her family, the life she left behind in the Midzone to become a servant when the first of the Oguni stream into the Deadends.

261

The Oguni do not approach us. They stare at us as if sensing our inherent incongruity. There is nothing to mark us as Galed, and yet, they easily identify us as other.

"Should we go up to them?" Iyanu asks.

I shake my head silently, watching as more of them stream in. They keep their distance, gathering on the far side of the space where they huddle together, whisper, trade nervous glances, and occasionally burst into spirited chatter. I scan their faces, trying to see if there's anyone I might know. I recognize a few of them from my time on the estates, though all of them have been aged and weathered in the years since I've seen them. None of their names come to mind. When my father led the Oguni, he volunteered me on a suicide mission in hopes that I'd survive and live to kill the king. The resistance's hope lied with me, but I was never one of them. I was only their tool. I was never told too much, never knew of or was allowed in the Deadends outposts back when they moved from time to time, and I was certainly never consulted when it came to Oguni resistance tactics. Now, for the first time two years, I stand before the people who gambled with my life.

A man breaks from the crowd and approaches us. I recognize his heavy-set brows and the strange tilt of the corner of his eyes, which lie too far apart. The curl of his lips the way he switches his weight from one foot to the other. I haven't seen him in nearly eight years, but I know him instantly. Rohan, a distant uncle. The years have certainly not been kind to him.

My mind flashes to Ryland, with his sun-kissed skin. Power radiating from his every pore, resonating in every word the man has ever said. The king's power is equal parts performance and equal parts reality. It's hard to imagine that he and the man standing in front of me are nearly the same age. It's hard to imagine that a man at that age could pose the greatest threat I've ever known or look so frail that it's damn near miraculous that he's standing on his own two feet.

"What happened to you?" The words are out of my mouth before I can think them through.

The question sends a nerve in Rohan's forehead twitching—his face doing nothing to hide his displeasure.

"What happened to *you*?" he answers in response. "Your father gave you everything. He labored to feed you. He only asked for one thing in return. And you failed."

Rohan's tone is not angry, not even disappointed, just as matter of fact as if he were stating his name—a cool, calm, and collected rage much like my father's. I take in two deep breaths, trying to steady myself. Exhaustion finds me somewhere between the first and the next. It feels like the world's weight is bearing on me, and my shoulders slump in response. There was a time when I might have fought his cold flames with a fire of my own, but when I try to summon something, anything, I find my will has been extinguished.

My brain shuffles through the hundreds of things I could say. *Who sends their child on a murder mission?* But that sounds ungrateful. Who doesn't send them if they think that's their best shot at righting the wrongs in the world? Can you right large wrongs with smaller ones? What becomes acceptable, what are we willing to sacrifice, and what are we willing to turn a blind eye to in order to see the changes we want in this world? I wonder if my father really expected I could do it, or if he was just hoping my martyrdom would see him secure himself as a legend amongst his people. I can't pretend to have ever understood my father's thinking. He was already the Ologun, and where is there to go if you're already at the top?

Ultimately, my exhaustion deters me from saying any of those things. Instead, I tell him that he's right.

"I failed. But I'm still here, I'm still fighting, and I'll continue to fight until I succeed." I say.

I'm glad I don't betray any hints of doubt. If I'm honest, I haven't contemplated what's ahead. I don't know if I'll succeed or even live through it. *Open their hearts and their minds,* Adara said. But what if I can't do it before the Waning? What if I'm dead by then, and titans have spread like a disease across the Earth? How do I change the hearts of hundreds of thousands of people when I can't even sway the ones standing right in front of me?

Rohan fumes, his eyes hard and his jaw clenched. If he doesn't believe in me, he doesn't say so. The people gather behind and around us have begun to lose interest. Some continue watching us while others lounge on sitting stones, discussing things that are undoubtedly more important than the tension between an uncle and his niece. I take the time to really look at them. I realize my shame hadn't allowed me to glance in their general direction. Out of thirty, eight are women. Women. Not the daughters of Oguni, who were not quite old enough to fend for themselves or pose any danger to the cause. Real women who seem to be just as involved in the conversation.

Rohan takes one long step towards me, cutting the distance between us in half. In the same breath, Aris shifts to my side and drapes his hand over my shoulder. He doesn't pull me in. He rests it there to remind me and, more importantly, Rohan of his presence. Rohan scoffs at the move.

"Bear doesn't think we can win without Meera and Iyanu here. So here they are. Now, if you have a better plan, you can take that up with Bear."

Rohan takes Iyanu in for the first time now, having paid her no mind since he first walked up to us.

"Don't go acting tough here now, boy," Rohan says. "We all know what the Berkshire woman does to you."

I can feel the tremor in Aris's arm. Panic rises in me but cools just as fast as it comes. Aris will not strike him, but I can feel how badly he wants to.

"We all have things we need to sacrifice, moments we have to endure for the sake of the cause," Aris says bitterly. His smile is wicked. "Her head is on a pike now, courtesy of her beloved king."

Another man approaches from one of the three doors in the arena. He walks confidently towards us, the cane in his right hand leading. His skin is dark, his hair cropped, and strands smoothed, so they lay flat against his scalp. His hair is peppered, red, black, and gray, all fighting to dominate, none quite winning the battle—the crowd around him parts neatly as he walks through them. At just over five-three, his physical presence is unnoteworthy, yet the sway he has on the Oguni is undoubtable. This was not the man I pictured when I thought of the person who'd replace my father.

He nods at Rohan, then Aris, before smiling in acknowledgment at Iyanu and me.

"Welcome," he beams.

I can't imagine that this man called for the Oguni to kill us all in a bid to release the Adara. But it is. He killed Annabeth. But the way his eyes land on me, with nothing but cool tenacity, clams the rage burning in me. This is the man responsible for Annabeth's death, yes, but this is also a man who would do anything for his people and would never apologize for it.

Aris drops the arm he placed over my shoulder and smooths the folds in his shirt with his palms.

"It was a quiet journey. We made it back without any guards trailing us. There was a boy we met on our way. Sick with the madness, I left him with water and a cool cloth. He'll survive the night," Aris says.

"Rohan, you must be overjoyed to welcome your niece back home. I hope you've been giving our other guest a proper welcome as well." Bear says this with a smile so wide that his eyes have narrowed into thin slits, his eyeballs nearly invisible. Yet he also says this like the last thing he would believe in this world was that Rohan is happy to have me back or that he's given us any proper welcome.

Bear takes my hand with one of his, then takes Iyanu's in the other. He addresses his people, who all stop midway in their conversation to turn to him.

"Oguni!" He calls.

The people walk towards us at Bear's beckoning, the closest of them standing just a few feet away. Bear lifts mine and Iyanu's hands up above his head.

"Our salvation has come!" Bear's voice is powerful. It is not that of the king, whose voice can thunder in your mind without ever moving his mouth. But it is the voice of someone who knows how to command a room.

The crowd is silent. They do not chant or cheer. They watch. Bear might be powerful, but he is no king amongst his people. Bear lets go of our hands, letting them fall from their place above our heads. The action is sudden, leaving me struggling to catch my hand before it hits the side of my thigh.

"Meera and Iyanu provide us with something we've never had before. They offer us the strength of a Goddess. This is the opportunity we've been waiting for, and now it's come."

A chatter rises amongst the crowd.

"They don't —," Rohan begins.

A blade is thrown. It whips past me quickly, and I don't realize what has happened until it drops to the floor, having already found its mark. I turn sharply, my front torso moving quicker than my legs can. Iyanu stands behind me, mouth wide open, pressing her hand to her side. Slowly, carefully, she removes her hand from where the knife hit. A small tear in the fabric reveals her skin is unharmed. The obsidian blade didn't even leave a scratch.

A collective gasp emerges from the crowd.

The sounds of Rohan's laughter, a deep and guttural thing, slices the tension in the room in half. He walks towards Iyanu and me, grabbing our hands as Bear did, and lifts them over our heads with a grunt of satisfaction. One of the Oguni begins stomping, then another. Soon, the sounds of cheering resonate through the air, bouncing and synchronizing in a symphony.

"Oguni," Bear calls to his people.

"Oguni Ash'aka." In death, there is coolness. Or, the Oguni welcome the coolness of death.

Chapter 20

B ear gives the knife thrower the punishment of having to teach us how to defend ourselves with weapons instead of leaning solely on our gifts.

"The more tricks you have up your sleeves, the better off you'll be," Bear points his cane into the air, momentarily standing on his own two feet to emphasize his point.

Aris will act to supplement her teaching, imparting to us what he knows about stealth. All of that will have to wait until the Waning draws nearer, though. For now, Bear wants us to focus on other priorities.

Rin isn't the only thing Aris brought with him from the palace. He carries a stack of books with one hand and twirls a single book in the other. Setting the bulk of them down with a thump, he takes his place at the front of the room.

"I told you I'd teach you how to read, didn't I?" he says.

Even in the flickering light of the dimly lit room, his smile is blindingly bright. How he managed to retrieve the books from the palace, I never ask. Their presence here feels strangely comforting to me, like the words of Galed past somehow also contain their essence, and that essence seeps into the air, soothing me. Maybe it's knowing that if the journals are here, then they aren't with Sade, and maybe without them, Sade won't be able to do her part in Ryland's bidding.

Rin cringes as Aris haphazardly flings the binding of a petiole bark-lined book open. "Be careful," she chastises. "They're already falling apart."

The books come in many colors. They're made from many materials from different periods. One of them is bright and purple, with a velvety feel. Another is barely held together with flattened bark petioles and twine rope. Iyanu doesn't need any lessons in reading, so she's been placed in a separate room with a different set of journals. This way, she can get a head start on trying to figure out what they say.

"Where'd you even get these from," Rin asks, picking up a particularly worn book between her thumb and index finger and examining it from underneath.

Aris ignores the question. Instead, he picks up a dark, sooty writing stick and drags it across a piece of parchment, curving his fingers in a slow, smooth motion. He does this until the page is filled with many symbols of different kinds. He holds the page up to me and points to his creations.

"These are letters. They make sounds," he says.

My pride is not happy with him right now. I resist the urge to cross my hands over my chest and pointedly tell him I know what letters are because I know that's also where my knowledge ends. Aris goes through the exercise of sounding each and every letter in the order in which he's written them. He does it twice to help me remember.

"Now you do it," he says.

But I've forgotten every letter after the fourth. He goes through them again, then once more, as if he can tell that the sounds didn't quite settle into my head. I yawn when he's halfway through them the third time. Despite going to bed absolutely exhausted last night, I could not sleep. I stared hopelessly at the kerosene lantern-lit ceiling, willing my mind to drift off, but it never did. The little sleep I got was marred with dreams filled with ghosts, angry and out for vengeance. Lazarus, pulling my hair out, strand by strand, then my nails one by one, before moving on to my teeth, and Sade turning her back on us to run to King Ryland over and over again. I was glad to wake up, and I didn't try to go back to sleep again.

"Meera, pay attention," Aris demands, growing vexed at my lack of concentration.

"I am paying attention," I counter, even though I may as well have been sleeping with my eyes open. Aris casts me a wary look, and Rin smiles at the exchange.

"Let me try," she says.

Rin takes another piece of parchment from the pile, and instead of writing letters like Aris has done, she's made drawings of various things, small, side by side, in one neat line. I try to

271

follow the drawings, thinking they'd form a story when laid out beside each other like that, but the meaning is incoherent no matter how I try to interpret it.

"These things represent the sound of the letter next to them," she points to the first drawing, a silly caricature of Aris.

"Aris," she says. "The first sound represents the letter." With Rin's drawings next to each letter, I quickly memorized all the letters by associating them with something in the real world.

"Why didn't you do that in the first place?" I tease Aris. "Rin's a much better teacher than you," I continue.

"There are still plenty of things I could teach you," Aris flashes a devilish grin. Pleased with my progress, Aris dismisses me for the day while he goes out performing tasks for Bear. He leaves me with Rin and Iyanu, as well as the dozens of journals he's taken from the palace.

"You might as well have them. Take a look and see if anything comes to you. They aren't written in any alphabet I've ever seen. Maybe you won't need to fully learn how to read to know what they say."

Rin and I join Iyanu in the next room. She's lying with her head down, and one of the journals is cast aside to her left.

"I was always a shit student," she says with a laugh. "My head hurts just from looking at these. I'll never understand them."

Rin walks to her side and rubs her back in a silly and faux comforting way.

"It's okay," she coos. "We'll never understand them either."

Iyanu's eyes twinkle at her words, giggling at them like an inside joke was buried deep within them. I cough somewhat obnoxiously to remind them of my presence. I do not want Rin to get too close to Iyanu. We don't have the strength to withstand another betrayal.

"How's the baby doing?" I pry without shame.

"He's doing great. This morning, I felt him flutter inside of me. I think he's going to be a kicker."

"He," I ask.

"Oh, I just know it's a boy. All the kings' firstborn children have always been boys."

"Right," I answer.

"And how are *you* doing, Rinny?" Iyanu asks.

"Rah be blessed." Rin smiles tepidly after that, eyes fluttering between Iyanu and me, trying to gauge our reactions.

"The worst of it is over. I had the worst vomiting spells every morning and every night for the first two weeks. It was intense. I'd never felt anything like it, not even when I got sick with Sardia. It got better for like three days, and then it was gone just like that," she beams. "You never realize how wonderful it is to be healthy until you're sick beyond belief!"

Iyanu gives her a friendly nod and says, "Good that you're feeling well."

"Yeah, that's great," I mutter.

I walk towards the journals in Iyanu's pile, pulling out the one bound in indigo-dyed linen—the one Annabeth used to carry around. I let the book rest in the palm of my hand, feeling its weight bear down on me. It's light. I flip through its pages quickly and without looking at any of the words or symbols. Even though she carried it around for at least seven years, and maybe even before then, more than half of the book is empty. Annabeth was strange and mysterious, even to me. I had given up on ever understanding her ways or her motivations for doing what she did. But she left me something my mother never could have. Now, with her writings in my hand, maybe I'll finally start to understand her.

I take a seat on a sitting stone next to Iyanu and place the notebook on my lap. I trace the letters written in blue ink with my fingers, but they are unlike the ones Aris and Rin drew for me. Where those were mostly sharp and angular, only bending once, maybe twice in a few letters, these are all curves with very few lines. They have dots placed above them, in them, and under them. I pick up a different journal from the pile to see if the symbols are consistent between them. This alphabet is even stranger. There seem to be many repeating symbols, and every character is made up of at least seven intersecting lines. I set the book down, returning to Annabeth's indigo-dyed texts.

"Haven't you had enough reading for the day?" Rin teases. "We have equipment in the other room. I've been practicing while everyone's away."

I give Rin a blank look.

"Oh, don't worry! Exercise is good for the baby," she says.

I wave both her and Iyanu away with my hands.

"You guys go on without me. I'll come when I'm done."

Iyanu doesn't need to be told twice. She's already dragging Rin away by the time I finish my sentence.

With both of them gone, the room is quiet, and I can finally focus on Annabeth's writings. I trace the strange symbols with my fingers, willing them to reveal their secrets. This makes sense to me. I repeat over and over again, hoping that if my mind believes it to be true, my eyes will see something they can make sense of. The symbols swirl and shift under my gaze, one symbol spinning and turning into the next. They dance one by one, but the message is no clearer than when I started looking at them.

I raise the book in one hand and slam it to the ground in frustration, tears streaming from my eyes. What's the point of any of this?

"Are you okay?" Aris watches me from the back of a curved pillar. I quickly collect the book from the floor.

"I'm fine, just tired. You know how hard it is getting sleep in a new place."

Aris's eyebrows draw together with concern, but he doesn't challenge me. Instead, he drags a sandbag from the central corridor into the sitting room and plops it on the floor.

"Get some rest then," he says.

I start to argue, but my pounding skull tells me I might benefit from closing my eyes for a little while.

My rest is anything but restful. Every time I find myself falling asleep, my body convulses violently, jolting me back awake. I give up on getting some rest an hour in and decide to close my eyes and relax without falling asleep. But even with my eyes closed, I feel Aris's lingering gaze on me every few hours. I never hear his footsteps as he comes and goes, but I know in my gut when he's there.

I tell myself that I want to get up, that I've been wanting to get up for a while, but something about Aris returning again and again to watch me keeps me rooted in place. By the time I finally rise, the Oguni are streaming into the Deadends. Some of their faces I remember from last night, and others are new. Word must have spread, though, because the newcomers don't exchange looks or mutter under their breath. Most act as if our presence is completely expected. Some even smile in our direction.

Iyanu walks to them and talks to them like she's known them her whole life. She calls them by their names, clapping Soren by the back and asking after Kwame's sons. Aris joins her and Rin as well. I should join, too, but even after hours of doing nothing, I can't find the energy to do so. I make my way back to the room and lay down on the sandbag Aris brought for me. I shoot straight up when a man I don't recognize enters the room moments after me, panicking before I see Aris, Iyanu, and a few more Oguni walking purposefully behind him.

"You been lying there all day?" The man asks.

His voice is scratchy. He's older than Aris, but not as old as Bear or my father. He's average height for an Endzone male and average build, too. His skin is taught against his bones, besides the sliver of well-defined muscle between the two.

I frown at the man, not entirely understanding his question. What does he care if I've been lying down all day?

He looks at one of his friends, directing his next statement to the other man. "Piece of shit," he says loudly. He makes sure people next to him hear. "Sits here enjoying the cool. Hasn't raised a finger all day but can't even bother to say a word to us lay folks."

A wave of guilt surges in me, followed almost immediately by an upsurge of agitation. I didn't *choose* to go to the palace. I've always done what they wanted me to, from the time I was old enough to be useful on the estates to the time they decided that I was old enough to risk my life for a cause they never centered me in. How dare he? I've already sworn my life. What more do they want for me?

"I'm not here to chat, and I don't owe you anything," I say.

My words are sharp and crisp. They leave no room for argument, yet they earn frowns from the rest of the crowd. Even Aris and Iyanu look at me with something like concern in their eyes. The knife thrower raises her eyebrow in surprise, as if to say *this one has guts*. But I'm not feeling very gutsy. If it were up to me, the conversation would already be over right here, right now. I turn away from the provoking man and lie on my side, hoping

277

my pointed attempts to get him to take a hint work. It doesn't. He talks even more loudly, his words practically frothing as they come out of his mouth.

"Oh dear. I'm sorry. Best let our darling princess rest. Should I be calling you Lady Meera now? Do you have an estate you'd like me to work on miss? How about a foot rub or a nice cold bath? I know! Maybe we should crown you queen and sit you on the throne after Ryland is deposed. Looks like you already have plenty of experience sitting on your high hamel."

"That's enough, Shun," the man beside him chastises him. A brief scuffle ensues, with Shun attempting to break free of the man trying to wrestle him back to the other room. Shun pushes the man back before belting out the rest of his rant.

"Why should the gods favor you or the king?" he shouts. "You're not special! You're not worth any more than the rest of us!"

Two of the others help pull Shun out of the room, and the rest of the Oguni follow, leaving just Iyanu and Aris in the room with me.

"Get out," I tell them.

There isn't anything else to say. I don't want to discuss the man's words or anything else with either of them right now. I just want a moment of peace. But neither of them budge. It's Aris who speaks first.

"Bear needs to meet with all of us soon. I'll hold him off for a few minutes. Be ready when he gets here."

Iyanu leaves with Aris, giving me a few moments to myself. *Why should the gods favor you?* If this is what a god's favor looks like, then maybe we're all doomed.

Aris keeps true to his word, and a few moments later, he, Iyanu, Rin, and Bear have all gathered beside me. I've managed to wrestle myself off of the sandbag and pull it to the side before they return. I praise myself inwardly for having enough energy to prop myself up onto a sitting stone. Thirty-six hours now without sleep. My body will give out, sooner or later, whether it wants to or not.

"I'm sorry to be having this conversation with you all at this hour. I wanted to give you all at least one day of rest before we started making preparations, but we can't afford to wait any longer." Bear places one hand atop the other, resting both of them atop his cane, then resting the bottom of the chin on the entire ensemble. He's solemn but still manages to exude a calm and assured presence.

"We've heard from some of the spies in the Tanaka estates. The king's experiment continues, though not successfully. It looks like there are many more copies of books Aris stole than we realized."

"Of course, there are," Aris says, as if anyone could have easily come to that conclusion. "It mitigates the risk of theft. They might even have been trying to understand the text by writing in the script themselves."

Sade still has the books. She's still helping Ryland create titans. The thought hits me like a rock to the throat. My chest constricts. I knew this was possible, but I hoped Sade wouldn't have the means to continue betraying us if she wanted to. Didn't she see what the king did, and what he continues to do? How could she turn her back on us so absolutely?

I will my breathing to become normal. "At this rate, the best we can do is prepare for the ceremony. We'll need to continue gathering information on Ryland's experiments. With the Galed and a son of Rah by our side," he smiles at Rin, "it could be an option that might be worth exploring."

"You didn't see what they looked like," I say.

There is no way Bear would ever consider subjecting his people to one of those experiments if he had seen what happened to Antares.

"They turned Antares into a monster. I wouldn't help with something like that if my life depended on it," I conclude.

Bear isn't bothered by my defiance. "We'll cross that tunnel when we get there," he says dismissively. "We have more pressing issues now. The Waning is upon us," he says. It's just over three weeks away. "We need to decide now whether we'll attack before or after."

Aris raises a brow at the question. "We?" he asks. "Haven't you talked about this with the council?"

"I have. And we decided that the best people to know what the best course of action would be are the people who we're hinging our victory on."

"We can't afford to wait until after the Waning," Aris says tersely. "We'll have no guarantees that our tributes will survive, and no guarantee that either Meera or Iyanu will survive either. We'll have to start right where we began if that happens." Aris stands from his sitting stone. *Our tributes.* The thirty women Aris mentioned before.

Bear nods in agreement. "If we attack before we're prepared, we'll lose more people than we can bear. It could take us an entire lifetime to rebuild if that were to happen."

Aris sits back down, crossing his arms.

"Any progress on the journals?" Bear asks.

Iyanu and I shake our heads. "They're all written in strange texts," she says. "I thought I might have an easier time, but they've been spelled or enchanted. Looking at them too long causes an ache, and it feels like the longer you look, the more confusing they become."

Bear nods. "Something tells me that everything we need for victory lies somewhere in those texts. I want you two to keep trying. Look at them all day, every day, if you have to. There's a reason they've been left for you."

"We'll be ready before the Waning," I say with certainty, speaking for both Iyanu and me. "We can attack before then." I promised myself that the next time I tried to depose the king, I would be successful. I can't die before that time arrives.

Aris nods in agreement. "You should have seen them on the palace fields," he says. "The king had to stand a mile away." Aris omits the fact that if we had been standing any closer, we might have been incinerated ourselves. "We don't need an army to man the front lines. We don't need to fight an all-out war. We just need a distraction and a way to get them in front of Ryland before he figures out what's coming to him," he concludes.

"Are you sure about that, Meera?"

"Yes," I answer.

"What about you, Iyanu?" Bear says with a smile.

"I think we can do it," Iyanu replies.

"It's settled then. We'll begin preparations. Your combat training with Sasha will begin tomorrow. We'll have one chance. Just one chance. If we fail, we're finished."

We won't fail.

Chapter 21

My body refuses to surrender to sleep, and even when it does, nightmares from the carnage on the palace fields plague my memories. Twice, I dream of Jordan, the commissioner's daughter who killed Annabeth with nothing but a sharpened bird bone. In my dream, she plunges the creamy white blade into Annabeth's neck, and blood gushes out of a small hole in Annabeth's throat, spraying the entire room. Jordan bathes in the blood, wiping it on her face and all over her body. Lazarus joins in, his face liquified and dripping bits of skin and meat on the floor. He takes her hand, and they waltz all over Annabeth's corpse.

Iyanu feels me tussling on the sandbag beside her. She tries to put her arm over me to comfort me.

I scream at the contact. Her touch brings back all the memories. Sade, Lazarus, and Queen Antares flash through my eyes like I'm dreaming again, except my eyes are wide open. Her touch brings visions I've never seen before as well. Visions of Torrin, but she's nude and blushing, lying in bed, waiting. Visions of Lord Idowu in a royal blue armchair, face contorted in disgust as he peers down at me. Iyanu doesn't try to touch me again for the rest of the night.

In the morning, Bear pulls me away from the group. He instructs Iyanu to continue doing what she can with the journals and tells Rin not to exert herself too much.

He brings me with him through the tunnels leading out of the Deadends. "I want to show you something," he says. The last time one of the Oguni told me that, it didn't end well. We walk through the labyrinth of stone pathways, Bear directing our choices until we arrive at the surface, albeit through a different pithole than Aris brought us through.

"Multiple entrances mean multiple means of escape." I nod to signal that I've heard him.

The heat of the morning sun slams into me, sending a tingling sensation dancing across my exposed skin. My eyes strain themselves, adjusting to the light, having been used to the darkness of the Deadends. It takes me a few moments before I can see what's in front of me, and by then, Bear has already walked several paces ahead. His pants hang neatly off his frame. They fit just right at the waist, then hang down in a straight cut. His shirt is without wrinkles. He could be a Midzoner, but his hands are dryer and more calloused than the typical Midzoner, and if those didn't give him away, his weary eyes certainly do.

As we continue walking, Bear makes light conversation. He asks about the palace, about the time before I participated in the

Waning, about the Waning itself. He asks about Iyanu and how I've been feeling about Torrin and now Sade. I don't know if he asks to make small talk or if his questions are an attempt to gather some vital piece of information that he needs.

Still, I answer as honestly as I'm inclined to. *The palace is unimaginably large, unimaginably wasteful, and unimaginably lonely. I don't know half of what goes on inside those walls. My days were typical—the same as anyone else's. I slept in a pithole near my father. I woke before dawn to labor at my assigned estate. I played with my only friend at the time, and when my father asked me to volunteer myself, I did not protest.*

Bear doesn't say a single word as I speak. Not to ask follow-up questions or even to confirm that he's heard what I'm saying. He continues marching forward. And yet, I've never felt like someone was listening to me so intently.

I tell him about the life of the Galed.

"It's not much. We spend most of our time waiting on the plants we have in a rotunda that joins our rooms. Or we wait to be sent on assignments by the king. One of us, usually who survived the Waning last, leads the others as high priestess. At least for short periods of time, she can call Adara's essence from the rest of us into her."

Bear asks his first question, then.

"Have you tried it? Now that there's no leader."

I shake my head. "I wouldn't know where to start."

285

"The answer must be in those books." He turns to smile at me as he says this. It's warm and reassuring. He doesn't want me to feel like I'm failing. Bear turns ahead, marching forward once again, and I take that as my queue to continue.

"I don't remember much about the Waning. I remember the urge to dive into the lake. I remember a struggle happening. Maybe it was just a struggle with myself to keep from drowning in the water. In the end, there was an island in the middle of the lake. It's where Adara came down and was able to touch us. Then we found ourselves back on the shore, newly empowered, and with an envoy headed by the king to lead us back to the palace," I say.

"I've never seen an island in the middle of the lake," Bear says.

If I didn't have a hazy memory of there being one, I wouldn't have thought there was an island there, either. The mists that blanket Sarran make anything over a few hundred paces beyond its shores impossible to see. Even on days when the mist spreads thinly across the water's surface, there isn't a trace of the island in sight.

"Trust me, it's there," I answer. Bear thinks for a bit. His peppered mustache wrinkles as he says his next statement.

"Iyanu didn't tell me any of this."

"She doesn't remember. I barely remember. But I get bits and pieces through my dreams sometimes."

"Good. The more you remember, the better off you'll be when the time comes."

Bear leads us further into the Endzone which concerns me. The further out you go, the less of a cooling effect the lake has. Temperatures can become deadly if you're not careful. Endzoners have been known to walk off into the distance. Mostly adults who never intended to make it back in the first place, but sometimes children who wandered, got turned around, and could not navigate the barren lands. This happens during the day when the rest of the laborers are at their assigned estates, and there's no one to try and stop someone from wandering out.

"We're going too far out," I caution. "We didn't bring any water."

"We have water where we're going," Bear offers. He does that thing again, where he offers a big smile to reassure me. "Here's some eloh paste. Those years at the palace have made your skin soft." I take the paste gratefully. I won't admit it to him, but the tingling on my skin has started to turn into a pressing ache, and I fear going any further out. Spending more time in the heat would lead to first-degree burns.

"I heard what happened between you and Shun," Bear says.

I look him dead in the eyes.

"Who is that?" I ask, trying to play off his comment.

"The man from last night." My jaw locks, and I look away. I feel a lecture coming on.

"Oh," I offer, hoping Bear will get the hint. He does his signature smile again, but it brings me no comfort. Stop that,

I want to say to him, but I can't make the words come out of my mouth.

"Have you ever wondered why the council appointed me Ologun? You know there were many contenders. Shun was the favorite. He even asked his daughter to volunteer herself. Said she could do what you couldn't." Bear waves his hand, dismissing his comment. "She didn't even volunteer." Bear reads the expression on my face and answers the questions forming in my brain. "It wasn't her refusal to volunteer that ended his bid. Leaders often make promises that they can't keep and are rarely ever punished for it."

Bear continues, "He stopped laboring. Sat in the Deadends day and night, planning a way to win the council's support. It was a petty argument, really." He makes two tsk sounds by pressing his tongue to the back of his teeth. "Entirely avoidable. Shun insinuated that he was beyond laboring. That such work was beneath the Ologun."

"It is," I answer, confused.

"Maybe so, but the fastest way to lose respect as a leader is by insinuating that you're above the people you lead. Shun stood no chance after that blunder."

"He made them feel lowly. Weak," I respond.

"Exactly," Bear says. "Nothing makes people feel weaker than having someone else's stature used against them. Shun might have been fine if he hadn't voiced his opinions. They were not pleased. Discontent spreads as quickly as disease, and soon, everything Shun did was framed as an attempt to put himself above the rest."

A small smile spreads across my lips. Shun did this to himself. Good for him.

"You're quick-tempered and brash. You say things without thinking through them. Your emotions don't serve you. They get the better of you." That erases the smile right from my lips.

"No need to get upset," Bear continues. "You're young. I expect that of you."

"I didn't even say anything to him."

"It's what you didn't say," Bear counters. His cane pushes him forward with every step. The broad plane at its ends keeps it from pushing down into the sand. "Do you know why I go to the estates nearly every day, just as the others do? They don't need me there." Bear looks down at his leg, which bends awkwardly to one side. "I suspect they probably get more done without me there."

I suspect that's false.

"I go because that's what a leader does. They temper their tiredness, their fear, and their aches, and they walk alongside their people."

The rebuke feels heavy on my chest, and I sigh in discontent. "I haven't done anything to warrant what he said. I was holding my ground." The statement comes out like an admission of defeat.

"The best leaders are those who never asked to lead." He smiles that insufferable smile again. I swallow the lump in my throat. Blood thrashes around my cheek and my neck. "Instead of holding your ground, hold common ground. They see something in you, Meera. They want you by their side."

I'll try harder. I'll speak with the Oguni today, no matter how I feel.

As we walk deeper into the desert, a strange structure emerges from the mirage at the border between sand and sky. I might have thought it was an illusion, a trick of my mind, but I am not that dehydrated, and regardless of what Bear might believe, the palace has not made me soft.

"We're here," Bear says. The structure is much like the ones the lowliest of Midzoners reside in. But instead of sandbrick, the material is the same strange stone used to build the Deadends. Out here, in the light, I can see it shines a dull gray color. Not at all like the brilliant reds and oranges of our sand-based material. I lay my head on the rough, porous surface, feeling the cool stone beneath the tips of my fingers.

"What is this?" I ask.

"Caliche," Bear replies.

We enter through the thin curtain used as the only door to the structure, and we're greeted by blooming cactids and blossoming snakescales, named for how their iridescent and patterned flowers resemble the cobra's skin. The plants are all housed individually in nearly transparent glass containers. Many flowering plants are heavy with fruit, and the tubers, large and bulbous, seem ready to explode. Their roots, long, white, and gleaming, push up against the glass, fighting to consume every inch of space available to them. Each small glass container mimics the structure at large, filled to the brim and ready to burst open with plant life. A thick linen sheet on the roof is the only source of protection from the sunlight. It casts a warm and bright shadow over the teeming plants.

"I haven't seen yams this big. Not even on the Idowu estate," I exclaim. That these plants could survive or grow without the land is unthinkable.

"It's not much," Bear chuckles. "But one day it will be," he adds, letting his voice bear the weight of his conviction.

"Aris told me you were doing something like this. I didn't understand what he meant at the time."

"It's hard to believe they can survive like this," Bear says. "You'd never expect it, but these conditions are just right."

I reach my hand toward the snakeskin, bringing its stem to me and smelling the inside of the black and yellow streaked flowers. Their smell, just like lemons, always amazed me. How can two things seem like complete opposites when experienced with one sense and yet be indistinguishable when experienced in another?

"If you can do this on a large enough scale, you won't even need the estate soils!"

Bear chuckles. "We can already feed twenty people a year," Bear says. "We're still a long way out from achieving the scale we'll need, and doing so without drawing the eye of the aristocracy won't be easy. We'd need enough of these to make a small settlement if we want to feed the people that will need it."

He pulls out a small notepad from his back pocket and flips the pages until he finds what he's looking for.

"Quakeroot, purple quandary, Janus flower..." Bear lists most of the plants in the rotunda one by one. Aris needed to hide there to avoid Lazarus. He must have written down everything he saw and delivered it to Bear.

"We should have everything here," Bear concludes. He brings me to a section in the back of the structure where small cuttings stand with their roots submerged in water.

"Why did you bring all of these here? Why did you even..."

"Aris thought you might need them. He said you liked making potions. Most of them won't have sprouted many leaves by the time the Waning comes, and the ones where you need the flowers won't be much use at all, but you should be able to make a fair number of things using just what we have here. I'll show you how to care for these. Things are a little different for them than their counterparts in estate soil. You and Iyanu can tend to them while I'm at the estates."

"Thank you," I say, unable to muster any other words.

"I have one more thing to show you," Bear hands me a glass of water from the table, and we take one with us as we head back into the desert sun.

The thing he shows me is nothing at all. Just a place where the desert sand becomes a hard rolling rock underneath our feet. He bends down, picking up the raw material at our feet.

"This is why we've been able to come so far in the time you've been gone. The dessert seems like a hard, unwelcoming place, but I'm convinced that if we look far enough if we look hard enough, we'll find that it has everything we could ever imagine that we'd need."

"This is what you've made your structures out of?" I marvel at the rock.

"Caliche is a bit harder to build with. But it's lying here in droves, just waiting for us to harvest it. It's easy to crush, mix with water, and then mold into the desired shape for building." Bear looks out over the horizon. "I've only walked a mile out there," his eyes narrow. "From what I've seen, these deposits could go on for tens of miles, hundreds of miles even."

Nobody ventures this far out. There's no food or water here, and barring those who bring the necessary items with them, going out this far is almost surely a death sentence. The End-zoners that mine and the escorts that take them there, on the other hand, have to cross tens of miles to reach their mining destination. If they go that far, there's no way they haven't discovered these strange places where the desert sand turns into blankets of sheet rock.

"The king must know this is here. Why doesn't he use it?"

"Why would he? They have everything they need right at the edge of the lake. There's no reason for them to experiment or search for new material at the ends of a barren desert. They have the lake, and they hoard all its treasure because they believe it is the only treasure to be had. Little do they know, they leave the rest for us."

Even the deadest of things have some life to them, it seems. But I don't comment on the fact that Bear's caliche needs water to be useful. And that his plants live almost exclusively in water, even if they require no soil. There is no life without water. There is no life without Lake Sarran. There is no life without rain.

This is why Bear has been chosen to lead the Oguni. For as long as I can remember, the resistance has dreamt of toppling the monarchy and re-distributing the resources held by the king. But the thought usually centered on the king being deposed, and access to Lake Shore was opened to everyone. Bear is capable of planning and having a truly executable vision for what happens next. With the resources he needs at his beckoning, Bear's effect on the Endzone would be unimaginable.

Chapter 22

When the Oguni return that evening, I spot the knife thrower and walk to her with purpose. Iyanu and Rin stand together, giggling at each other like there's no one else around. It's like they've created an impenetrable atmosphere around them.

"Meera," I extend my hand to her, and she takes it, grasping my palm in a firm but painless hold. Her short, spiked hair and too-sharp teeth give her a manic look.

"It's nice to meet you," I add.

"Sasha," she replies. "You aren't too bad yourself." Her grin is wide and intensely infectious, even if the sharpness of her teeth is slightly off-putting. "I wasn't expecting your friend to survive my throw. Of course, I never miss a target. It's just my targets usually bleed to death," she says jokingly. I resist the urge to ask her who her targets have been, thinking it's probably best I don't know.

"How does the whole Galed thing work anyway?" She curves her palms and her fingertips, bringing them to her chin in a concentrated manner. The first time I left the palace, the first interaction I had after becoming Galed, a young man asked me the same question. I've been getting that question ever since, so I'm surprised that none of the Oguni have already asked me. I push away the pang of guilt that emerges. Maybe if I had actually tried to talk to them, then someone would have asked.

"I wish I knew," I respond with a shrug. I ponder my words for a brief moment, and I know that there's more I could tell her. I know much more than I ever did when I started, but it's a knowing that's in your body, not in your mind. I can feel Adara better. I'm better equipped to draw on her strength and use her power for my purposes. How there's a Goddess "living" inside me, what her aims are, if any, or why, and how she's chosen her vessels are beyond me. I draw the conversation away from where I sense it's heading. To regicide and the Waning.

"I'm sorry about not coming to speak to all of you sooner," I say.

Sasha looks taken aback, but realization quickly dawns on her.

"Oh, is this about Shun? You know how men get, always needing their egos fed. He felt really embarrassed about the whole situation afterward, but you won't hear that from him," she offers.

She beckons another woman over from a few paces next to us. The man she's speaking to comes along with her. I recognize him as the man who wrestled Shun out of the room the previous night.

"This is my sister, Jules, and her partner, Sangi." Both Jules and Sangi are extraordinarily friendly. Jules has a rich, dark complexion and pearly straight whites. Her eyes are sleek, the slits curving upwards at the end. She almost reminds me of Aris, but her hair is dark, glossy, and nearly jet black instead of the coppery red tresses that grow from Aris's head.

I glance to the side, watching Rin and Iyanu go deeper and deeper into their world of two, and a bad feeling creeps into me.

"Meera," Sasha calls my name, and I smile, realizing I had been zoned out for the last few seconds. More people join our group using their connections with one person or another to justify their presence. Soon, almost half of the Oguni present tonight have assembled around me. They want to know everything about the intricacies of palace life. Most of them have only ever seen the palace from a long ways out while laboring on the two nearest estates. None, except Aris, have ever been inside. I shyly tell them about everything—the silken garments provided for even the servants and maids. The balls and banquets with copious amounts of food—more than everyone in attendance could ever hope to eat, even if they were given a fortnight.

"I hear the king has a field lined with the bodies of those he's murdered," a woman shouts from the crowd. I shudder, thinking back to Braun and the countless others like him.

"I think he does," I answer sincerely. The woman wrinkles her nose in disgust. The Oguni are a death culture. Ash'aka. *We'll join at the cool Rivers of Death.* Death is not something to be feared but a welcome reprieve from a world of extreme heat and little in the way of food and water. The Oguni don't think twice about taking a life if they have to. The only guidance they live by is that every life given and taken must serve a purpose—a purpose they've deemed just.

To the Oguni, there is no worthier cause than the liberation of their people and the distribution of access to Sarran to all those who need it. They aren't disgusted that the king has a field full of those he's murdered. Sasha, or any one of the Oguni, may be able to fill a field of their own. The Oguni are disgusted because it's impossible for Ryland to kill with a purpose. There is no justification for murder when you already hold all the power.

Sangi's gaze hardens. "His time will come."

The others nod in silence. Even when I try to avoid talks of the upcoming battle, it still manages to weasel its way into every conversation.

Sasha breaks the quickly building tension with a playful slap on my back. I yelp in surprise and lurch forward, which earns a laugh from Shun and Jules.

"This was the perfect night to get your sorry ass out of bed," she says. I'm grateful for the topic change, and by how the mood in the room lifts, I can tell the others are grateful for it, too.

"We have two of our best fighters entering the ring tonight," The crowd breaks into cheers and chants. Sasha grabs me from behind, bringing her hands to either side of my shoulder and squeezing with excitement.

She makes a long, drawling whistle sound.

"It's been a long time since I've seen Aris walk into that ring."

She's nearly salivating with each word, looking into the distance at a marked-off section of the floor.

"Aris," I ask. I tell myself there's no need to be concerned. I am not concerned. "Who's the other fighter," I ask.

Sasha's grin becomes impossibly wide. She points her two thumbs back at herself. *This woman is crazy.* She's not much bigger than I am—a fraction of Aris's size. Maybe she'll use her knives, or maybe they'll restrain Aris somehow to keep him from being able to do too much damage. She clinches my shoulders even more tightly, squeezing and shaking me back and forth.

"No weapons, no interventions, and no holding back." Sasha is positively beaming.

Aris turns his attention to us, smiling wickedly as he approaches. The crowd's chants get louder, and Sasha finally releases her death grip on my shoulders. She stretches both hands in front of her, interlocks them, turns them so her palms face outward, and pops her knuckles. She rolls her head around slowly before turning to join Aris at the center of the ring. The crowd rushes them, sweeping me along to the edges of the ring.

"Sasha has been waiting for this for a while," Sangi says. "Since Aris went and became a double spy for the Berkshires, he hasn't had the time. He's the only one brave enough to go up against her." His words do nothing to reassure me.

"Don't worry," he adds.

The rest of the Oguni shout expletives at each other, cursing and placing bets on who they favor.

"Two days' worth of estate water pay on Aris," a high-pitched voice pierces through the crowd. The offer is countered by bets that are even more absurd. One man is willing to gamble away his entire store of dried food if Sasha doesn't win the battle tonight. All the while, Aris and Sasha get into positions, fists raised and hands spread apart.

"They're just joking," Jules says. "See. No one is taking down any bets, and no one will ever ask to collect on bets they win. No one could even tell you who's betting against who. It's a game. It's to hype themselves and Aris and Sasha up. Makes for a more interesting match."

Aris throws the first punch. Sasha dodges, curling her body sharply towards the left. Aris's fist seemed incredibly close to her face, but I can tell by the way Sasha smirks and brushes it off that she had anticipated the move from a thousand paces away. They continue like that briefly, Aris throwing a flurry of fists, left, right, left, then double right, and Sasha dodging each one with inhuman-like speed. If she had been Galed, I think she would have found that she could move so quickly that time would slow to a halt around her. Nothing, not even Ryland's rays, would be any match for that.

"Come on," someone in the crowd yells. Aris's next punch grazes Sasha on the side of her face, just missing her left eye. She stumbles, but regains her balance before Aris can land his next punch. Sweat beads on both of their foreheads, dripping down onto the caliche. Sasha's short and spiked hair now hangs limp, clinging to the side of her face.

"Why isn't she trying to hit him," I yell at Sangi, trying to make my voice heard above the dozens of others. What is she doing? You need to fight to win. It's Jules who answers.

"This is what she does. The fight pits Aris's strength against her speed. If he can land a blow before she tires him out, it's over for her. The more he fights, the slower he gets, but Sasha is an endurance animal. When he slows down enough for her to land hits, she will. Aris will be fine for her first two hits but not the next twenty."

"So Sasha needs to land twenty hits to Aris's one."

"Exactly."

I can just imagine Sasha saying something crazy like, 'I like those odds.'

Aris throws three more punches before dropping and sweeping his feet underneath Sasha. But again, she's anticipated it all and jumps up in time for her legs not to be tangled by his actions. This is where Sasha lands her first kick. Mid-air, while Aris's face is close to the ground, she extends her right leg and connects the ball of her feet with his nose. Aris catches her retreating foot right after the impact, and the crowd gasps. He attempts to hold on, but she uses gravity to aid her, bringing the foot down hard and fast so her heels connect with his thigh. He rolls away from her and then rises to his feet, assuming the position they started in, wide legs and arms high guarding his chest. Sasha mimics his stance.

A small trail of blood trickles down Aris's nose. In the dim light of the Deadends, the redness of his blood against the blue-blackness of his skin makes it look just like a stream of water pouring from his nose. He wipes the trail away, looking at his fingers for evidence of blood.

Aris smiles, his white teeth tinged orange by the light. "You're going to get it now," he says with a smirk. This earns thunderous approval from the crowd.

"I've been waiting for it all night," Sasha responds mockingly. This earns another round of cheers from the crowd and some jostling, which has me being pushed all over the place. More than once, someone almost pushes me into the ring. It doesn't matter who seems to be winning at any given point in time. The crowd is amped through it all.

Somehow, the crowd's joy and energy feed me. I haven't felt this great in a long time. Before long, I find myself shouting along with him.

"Get him, Sasha!" I yell at the top of my lungs, pumping my arms in the air.

Sangi and Jules cackle at my cheering, and someone grabs me by my shoulder, shaking lightly in camaraderie. Aris's heard me. He shoots me a pout before turning his attention back to Sasha.

In the instant it took him to turn his attention to and then away from me, Sasha has closed the gap between them by more than half. She brings her foot up and kicks Aris right underneath his chest. Unprepared for the impact, Aris stumbles backward and falls onto his back.

"Ah..." the crowd groans in disappointment. "It was a short one tonight," someone says, shaking their head. A short one? They've been going at it for over twenty minutes. It's a miracle that either of them is still standing. Aris quickly rises to his feet, seemingly unharmed except for the trail of blood that now runs down his other nostril. He walks up to Sasha, takes her hand in his, and raises it to the crowd, which is happy to cheer her on. She leads her own chant.

"Sasha, Sasha, Sasha," she begins, and the crowd is happy to oblige her.

Aris shakes his head even as he's grinning from ear to ear.

"Don't let this get to your head," he cautions.

The crowd disperses from the night, each person returning to their pit houses, leaving Aris, Rin, Iyanu, and I to sleep in the Deadends.

"Why don't they all sleep here?" I ask. "It's temperate, there's enough space, and there's no risk that the sand will ever cave in."

Aris looks around the place and nods in agreement. "There *is* enough space. That's not the problem. We can sleep here because no one expects us to be sleeping in a sleeping pit. If almost a hundred people disappeared one night and never reemerged until the next morning, and they did that every night, the other Endzoners might grow suspicious."

Right. The problem isn't the other Endzoners. The problem is the possibility of spies amongst the others. Spies who might discover the Oguni's identities.

Iyanu and Rin have finally decided to pay the rest of us some attention.

Iyanu jests, "I thought you were tougher than that, Aris." She tsks.

Rin interlocks her arm with Iyanu's and pulls gently. "Stop teasing him," she chastises.

Iyanu beams down at her, and I find myself smiling at both of them even though I still don't completely trust Rin. If she was going to rat us out to Ryland and if she was a palace spy in disguise, she wouldn't be this visibly pregnant, and her child wouldn't be growing at the pace that it seems to be. We've only been in the Deadends for a couple of days, and I swear I've seen her waistline grow at least two inches. A first-born son is not something Ryland would gamble with. But my joy at seeing Iyanu happy is displaced by a sudden sense of anger and grief. It should be Torrin here, standing by Iyanu's side.

Aris takes Iyanu's comments in stride. "Next time," he says.

At night, I close my eyes, willing myself to fall asleep. I think of every happy thing I can think of: Sasha's playfulness, the feel of cottonshoot on the tongue, the citrusy sweet scent of snakescales. The way Iyanu claps you on the back way too hard when she's excited, which is all the time. I end up falling into a state of half-sleep and half-wakefulness.

A dreaming awareness where I'm conscious of my surroundings, yet thoughts and images from my subconscious float into my mind and field of view. They turn my idealizing into demonic thoughts. Cottonshoot doesn't melt on the tongue, dissolving like a cloud on your palette. It bursts violently and unexpectedly, leaving me scarred and scared to take the next bite. But something compels me to do it again anyway.

I wake up from this non-sleep in a cold sweat, vowing to keep my eyes open instead of going back to it. I glance at Rin and Iyanu on the right. All the lanterns have been turned off except for the two above us. The curved outline of Iyanu's body obscures Rin sleeping beside her. I lay there, watching their chests rise and fall with each inhale and exhale.

Iyanu murmurs something incoherent now and then. I strain my ears to decipher her words. Eventually, I can no longer lie there. I roll myself out of my sandbag quietly and tip-toe away from the area where Iyanu, Rin, and I sleep. I'm just going to

305

see if Aris is also having a hard time sleeping. I try not to think too hard about the flaws in my logic.

Aris lies wide awake, his back pressed against his sandbag, arms crossed underneath his head, and legs stretched out in front of him. He turns and gives me a lazy smile as I approach, bringing himself to a seated position to make space for me.

I sit silently beside him, close enough that my thigh presses against him.

"Couldn't sleep?" he asks.

"Yeah," I answer.

Aris shifts his thighs from left to right, rocking mine in the process. "You and Sasha cheated today," he says. "I bet you guys planned that while you were talking," he chuckles.

"It's not my fault you can't keep your eyes off me." He stares straight into my eyes. I cough slightly, clearing my throat of the nothing stuck in it.

"Anyways," I continue, "I wanted to thank you for what you did while we were at Vern's place."

I think back to Aris's gentle touches, his steady hands dragging the wet washcloth across my bare body. Suddenly, I'm grateful for the dark room and for my dark complexion, neither of which betray the fact that I'm blushing.

"Anytime."

I can tell by the way he says it that he'd do it a million times over again. We sit in silence for a few more moments as I wait for Aris to make the first move. Finally, when I can't take it

306

anymore, I throw my arms around his neck expectantly. Aris responds instantly. He grabs a fistful of my hair with his left hand and tilts my head back. He looks into my eyes briefly, waiting for me to voice some hesitation before closing the distance between us. His lips are soft and warm against mine. He takes his time, licking, sucking, and nibbling on them hard enough that the action barely hurts. He pushes his tongue deeper into my mouth, and I surrender to him with a moan. I feel the corners of his mouth push up into a smile before he breaks the kiss abruptly.

"Shhh," he whispers—the stubble on his chin scratches against my ear. I swallow the knots forming in my throat right in time for Aris to pull me in for another kiss. This time, I remember to bring my hands over his shoulders and press my body against his, fighting to be close enough to blur the borders between us. Aris digs his fingertips underneath me and lifts me onto his lap. He presses my waist downward at the same time as he forces my weight downward, forcing me to grind against him. His member bulges through his pants, hot and quivering.

I break away from him long enough to pull his shirt over his head. The lantern by his side doesn't allow me to make out much of his shape. I drag my fingers across his chest, feeling the smoothness of his skin against my fingertips and the hardness of the muscle beneath. I take my time pulling them further down his abdomen, stopping to trace each ridge and valley. Grabbing the waistline in his pants, I pull the drawstring that keeps them taught against his frame, and they loosen with minimal effort. I reach my hand inside, tracing the skin in between his right thigh and avoiding the member that swings decisively to the left.

Aris lets out an agonizing groan. "Fuck, Meera."

"Shhh," I say, enjoying every moment of torturing him.

I tilt his head and peer into his face as I reach my right hand to wrap firmly around his penis. It twitches in my grip while Aris stifles another moan. I loosen my grip, tracing my fingers slowly and steadily around it at first, hoping to give the lightest and most tortuously pleasurable sensation I can. Aris is having no more of it, though. He guides my hand out of his pants and answers my gesture. Tugging at the hem of my shirt, he draws it over my head, exposing everything beneath. He grabs me by my rib cage, focusing his attention on my breasts.

"You're so beautiful," he says. I want to say something like *thank you*. Or even *I know*. Or maybe something more suave. But the sincerity in his voice turns me shy and fumbling once again.

"You've seen me before," I whisper.

"Not like this," he counters.

He grabs my breast, giving it a gentle squeeze with his hands, then bends his head to take the other one in his mouth. He sucks gently, then uses his tongue to caress my nipple with a flicking motion while pinching the other between his index and thumb. Something stifled, high-pitched, and utterly animal escapes me as I throw my head back in ecstasy.

"More," I plead.

Aris's mouth is too busy sucking, and nibbling, and licking to respond. A shiver runs through me with everything he does, my body defenseless against his touch—moisture pools between my thighs in anticipation of what's to come. As if he read my mind, Aris lifts me off his lap and turns me, laying me down on my back. He kneels, positioning himself between my open thighs, and brings them up so I can hook my legs over his shoulders. I'm equal parts anxious and excited. Lazarus flashes through my mind. He's the only person I've ever done any of this with.

Aris kisses his way down my thighs, burying his head in my crotch. I gasp. He smiles against my skin, interpreting it as a gasp of pleasure. *Don't think about him, don't think about him, don't think about him,* I chant in my head, but all that does is invite my mind to push images of Lazarus to the forefront of its workings. I think back to the first note he wrote me and to him reading the contents for me at our second meeting. I think of the many nights we lay in bed, cuddling and laughing together, his thin and lengthy frame huddled beside mine. I take a deep breath to steady myself for what I know is coming. Images of Lazarus's skin liquified, exposed cheekbones peeking through. Tendrils of charred black skin, mixing with blistering red skin, and the smooth pale skin that is his. I take another deep breath, and I let myself release one tear. If it were a choice between him and me, Lazarus would choose himself every time. There's no shame in me choosing to do the same. I didn't kill Lazarus. I simply witnessed his death.

"Are you okay?" Aris asks. His voice jolts me back into the present moment, dispelling all thoughts of the man that came before him.

"Fine," I say, trying to loosen up. "Just a little nervous," I add.

"Do you trust me?"

I don't think twice as I answer the question. "Yes."

Aris slips one thick finger into me, curving it and stroking. My arms reach out reflexively to the side, reaching to grab the sheets that aren't there. I whimper. He brings his head down again, this time with no lead-up. He positions his face right between me and begins stroking in one long movement, bringing the tip of his tongue from the edges of my crotch and pressing and flicking slightly at my clit. Pressure builds within me, threatening to burst at any moment. I find myself reaching for his head without pulling back. My breath comes out in short, labored moans.

"Just like that, please," I half beg, half command.

Aris is happy to comply, going at just the right pace to make my whole world crumble. Soon, the pressure in me has no more room to expand, and it bursts out with a roaring motion. My body shivers at the release, then slumps with exhaustion. Aris brings his head up, smiling triumphantly.

"Like that, did you?" He asks.

I nod, too exhausted to reply.

"Good," he says. He turns me over, bringing me on all fours, then guiding my back downwards. My ass sticks up, and my chest lies flat against the sandbag.

Aris releases a quiet moan as he enters me, cursing under his breath. The movement is smooth and slick. He glides in without the slightest bit of friction or resistance. I find myself whimpering at the sensation, not quite recovered from the pleasure that exploded in me just a few moments ago. Aris shifts his weight, moving as far back as he can without coming out, then using his torso to thrust himself back in. I throw my head back in pleasure, closing my eyes to feel him more deeply.

An image flashes across my eyes, but it's not one I recognize. I lay atop a silk mattress with red and gold sheets the only things in my field of view. The sheets are cool beneath my palms and my knees. My mouth is tied with a piece of cloth around them. I'm sweating profusely, biting down heavily on the cloth between my lips, when a thick leather whip comes crashing into my back. The pain is excruciating, and I gasp at its magnitude, but my body mixes the present with the memory that is not mine, filling me with a synchronous mix of pleasure and pain.

Aris thrusts faster and harder, grabbing my waist and pressing it against himself for more leverage. The movement thrusts me back into the mindscape in which the memory resides. It's the same scene, but somehow, I can tell that it's a different day. It seems now that the pain of the whip crashing into my back and lashing at my ass has subsided into a dull throb. The worst appears to be over in this part of the memory, and I sigh with relief. In the next breath, I hear a woman's high-pitched voice behind me. The sound of her cackling makes me sick. I feel her dainty, cold hands slide against my back. She brings her frame forward, so she's bent right beside me. Her silky blonde hair falls to her side. The strands brush against my cheek and pool on the sheets' fabric.

Suddenly, my heart is racing, and blood surges in me. I panic silently, but I remain hardened, not making a sound. I take this moment to observe the skin of my forearms and my hands pressed against the bed—a cool blackish blue darker and lovelier than my skin tone. Only Aris's is so pretty.

The woman anchors something behind her, presses into me, and enters with one clean stroke. No sound escapes me at the movement. I don't even flinch. This has happened a hundred times before. I've long since gathered that reacting makes it worse. I steel myself against what's happening. There are worse things in the world.

A figure scuffles to my left, watching as the woman thrusts into me. I try hard to look to the side, but in this memory, Aris refuses to bulge even one inch. If it weren't so automatic, I believe he would've refused to blink. But the figure shifts again, getting closer to have a better angle to witness what's going on. He walks towards the bed, his footsteps a gentle pitter patter to the jolting sound of flesh colliding with flesh. The woman behind me stops for a brief second to acknowledge the person who's now standing by both of our sides.

"Here," he says. "You can't let him enjoy it too much." The voice is unmistakably Lazarus's, and now I recognize that blonde, silky hair as his mother's. He steps aside, returning to the corner of the room in anticipation of what's to come, and it doesn't take long before a metal wire strikes the upper parts of my tender back. I cry in agony then, and the sensation jolts me back into the present.

"Stop," I cry.

I say the words with a soft whimper, and I'm briefly afraid Aris has not heard me, but Aris takes himself out of me with lightning quickness. He rolls over to my side, his eyes bulging with fear.

"What happened?" he says, panicked. "Did I hurt you?"

I want to laugh and cry at the irony of the question. Like any pain could compare to what I just witnessed him go through.

"I saw what happened," I say, trying my best to swallow the pain in my voice and forcing the tears threatening to spill from my eyes to stay pooled at my lower eyelids. "Lady Berkshire and Lazarus..." I continue. I only half win the battle with my emotions, managing to keep my voice steady but letting a few tears stream down my face.

"They..."

"Stop." Aris commands. Where his face was once wide with fear and concern for my well-being, it's now hard, stone-cold, and unmoving, just like it was while the Berkshires abused him. "Who told you that," he asks, thinly veiled anger seeping into his voice. "Whoever told you that is lying," he continues.

"I saw it," I begin, but Aris cuts me off, not wanting to hear any explanations.

"You saw it? You were in my head?" He scoffs in disbelief.

I want to tell him that it was a mistake. I didn't plan to do it; it just happened, but Aris is no longer interested in listening to a word I say.

"No, I wasn't—"

"I think it's time for you to go back now." He turns his back to me and lays on the sandbag, not even waiting for me to stand up or make my leave—pushing me out with his sheer willpower. The words curl up in my mouth. Years of living with my father have taught me when a situation is unsalvageable, at least unsalvageable, by the power of words alone. I know when a man has closed his heart to you so resolutely. That point when you go from being a person held close to his heart to an outsider looking in.

I pick up my pile of clothes on the floor and slip them on. I return to my sleeping bag without a word. The taste of salt coats my tongue as I let my tears fall freely, not for myself but for Aris.

Chapter 23

A ris avoids me for the next two weeks, refusing to speak to me one-on-one and talking to me only when necessary when we're in group settings. He's not openly hostile; instead, he acts like he can't be bothered with me anymore. I've tried talking to him countless times, and every time, he shut me down before I could get a full sentence out. If Iyanu or Rin notice the change in attitude, they've resolved to act like nothing is going on.

My sleep has been easier, coming in deep, long, uninterrupted stretches and only occasionally throwing me into the depths of a terrifying nightmare. I think Iyanu is what's triggering them, looking into her eyes, which shine brightly even in the dimness of the underground labyrinth that is the Deadends, and knowing that I'm the only one that can see the unbearable immensity of pain hidden beneath their surface. It's the wariness of her touch, the way her eyes linger on mine, searching for some connection there. It brings back memories of Torrin, Annabeth, and even Sade.

Iyanu tried to bring up the distance between us just once. It might have seemed to her that maybe I was distancing myself from Aris in the same way that I was distancing myself from her.

"You can talk to me about anything," she says, placing a gentle but firm hand on my shoulder.

I didn't even know Iyanu had a voice that could be that gentle. That she could caress your shoulder instead of slapping it a little too hard. The contact makes me flinch, and it sends the usual images scurrying through my brain. But soon, more delicate, intimate images appear. Things I shouldn't be seeing. The heavy fullness of Torrin's breast. The boot-shaped birthmark she spotted on the inside of her left thigh. I tell Iyanu I'm fine in a voice that's too high-pitched, full of embarrassment, and not at all convincing. Iyanu isn't the pushy type. She retreats, biding the time until she deems it appropriate to try again.

Our days in the Deadends are filled with routine, something I'm immensely grateful for. I had taken for granted how much having someplace to be, something to do, and a defined period in which to do had done for my sanity. My daily schedule, however dull and repetitive, gives me something to ground myself in. Something that would prevent me from spending my day ruminating. The mornings are spent with Rin, Aris, and myself, huddled together, Rin and Aris trying their best to impart the intricacies of literacy to me as best and as quickly as they can. The next hour is spent with the four of us, each with at least one of the Galed's books in our hand, trying our best to decipher any meaning from the strange texts. The meanings of the texts continue to evade us. Only Iyanu and I see the words shifting. We're the only ones that get the subsequent headaches that come with staring at them too long. Rin and Aris give up in the first few days of trying.

Bear makes good on his promise to teach us how to care for his hydroponic system. It's surprisingly manageable, only requiring us to replace the water every couple of days and swirl the contents of the glass jars ever so often to ensure the plants' roots get enough air. We go to check on them every other day, making sure none are suffering from diseases that would erode their yield.

My favorite time of the day is when we're training with Aris and Sasha. Both have their specialties: Aris is more interested in building our strength and stealth, and Sasha is more interested in building our agility and showing us where and how to hit to make the most impact. "Punch 'em right in the eye," she suggests. "If they got balls, don't think twice about kicking them," was another of her brilliant suggestions. "But your best and greatest weapon will always be the element of surprise. Hit them. Hard. When they don't know it's coming."

Our first sparring partners are sandbags that have been tied with ropes in strategic locations to make them look like abstract representations of human beings. Iyanu's fist moves swiftly with such power behind them that her fists break right through the bag, leaving a hole with sand pouring from it where she's hit. I punch, then punch again, and continue until my hands and wrists sting from the pain.

Aris takes my hand in his. "You need to ball up hard." He closes my hand and pushes my thumb into my fist to mimic the appropriate form. "If you don't maintain tension here, you'll do more damage to yourself than to anyone you hit." It's the first time he's touched me in weeks. He tosses my hand away like he's grabbed a snake when he realizes this.

Rin is excused from sparing, although Sasha is adamant that she start learning how to use a knife.

"You can never be too careful," she says.

In just two weeks, Rin's stomach has expanded to the point that she now looks like she's in her seventh month of pregnancy. She refuses to stand for more than ten minutes at a time, although she frequently needs to get up and pee. With no plumbing in the Deadends or anywhere in the Endzone for that matter, she empties her bladder into a pail kept separate from the general living area. Just a couple of weeks ago, she could make the journey out of the Deadends to a sanitary disposal site with Sasha or Iyanu escorting her. Now, Iyanu has taken to emptying the pail for her instead. Rin's emotions are all over the place. Once, Iyanu scolded me for laughing at her when she burst into tears because she couldn't scratch an itch on the inside of her left ankle. Everything, big or small, seemed to rouse big, fat, spattering tears out of her.

Watching Rin, unable to stand without the help of someone lifting her and unable to even walk the distance it takes to exit the Deadends, I feel bad for how I've been cold towards her, but more than that. It's relieving that I was wrong not to trust her. If Rin was a spy, well, she's certainly in no position to be of any use to the king now.

Rin's jet-black hair bounces and falls buoyantly around her face. The two sides of her chin come together at a sharp point that looks dainty and pretty. Her lips are small and pouty. She looks like she might simultaneously laugh or cry at any moment. Her eyes are the color of the midday sun. It's no wonder the king chose her. She's undoubtedly beautiful in a way that most people conceive of beauty.

Rin is a sight for sore eyes. But I wouldn't trade places with her if my life depended on it. The king chose her for the same reason he's chosen nearly all of the palace maids. Was the king as bad as Lazarus, as Lady Berkshire? I steer my brain away from that line of thinking before it can conjure images I won't be able to free my mind of. All the nobility do this then. They all use their power to enable their perversions.

Sweat drips down the side of my face, rolling down my forehead and dropping towards my chin before falling onto my garment. I crash beside Iyanu, exhausted from the exercise regimen Sasha's imposed.

I shake my head as she calls out, "Five minutes and then ten more reps."

I knew that woman was crazy. Bear is trying to decipher the notes himself, sitting to the side with his face buried in an earlier text. He reasons that maybe the first gives the most clues about how all the others were written.

The Deadends is dark and cool. The absence of the desert sun makes them almost as cool as the mansions the nobility live in. The heat is faint, the light is low, and the slightly addictive smell of lantern fuel permeates the air. Despite this, a heat wave rakes through me mere moments before Ryland's Voice penetrates my skull, bouncing around as it echoes inside my head. We all frown instinctively, and Rin bursts into an uncontrollable fit of tears. Iyanu grabs her hand, and their palms rest, locked together, atop her lap.

I've always wondered how far Rah's Voice goes. If I walked the entire length of the desert and got as far away from him as the Earth would allow, would I still hear him speak? I wonder, do the animals hear it too? What about if I perched on the surface of the moon? Would it reach me there, too? The thought hits me like a wind gust between the tallest buildings in the Midzone. Rah resides in all of humanity, just as Adara does. His Voice on earth exploits that.

I shoot fearful glances at Rin, anticipating what that might mean for her and the boy growing inside her. Ryland's Voice booms through the silence that's descended across the room. He's joyful and celebratory as he speaks.

"My people," he begins. "Today, Rah smiles favorably upon us." My heart jolts in my chest. Sade's cracked the notebooks! But the thought leaves as quickly as it comes. If that were true, if Sade had used the notebooks to create the first iteration of successful titans, one of the Oguni would know, and we would know by extension.

"It has taken five hundred years, but the day has come." His Voice cracks. The first I've ever heard. I do my best not to snort at the emotion he's trying to convey. Ryland has no heart. He has no tears to shed, and he possesses no emotions that could seize his throat in such a way.

"My son, Imoleaye, is conceived. His heart is strong, his frame, mighty."

Aris, Iyanu, Bear, and I collectively turn to Rin, who is heaving like she's just spent the day in full sun. Her face is red, and her cheeks and forehead are swollen. Something like recognition flashes across Bear's face. The king knows about his son. But how?

"Imoleaye, the first of his name, ushered into this new dawn where titans roam the Earth once more."

"Ile-Oja," he cheers. "I've kept this from you but can keep it to myself no longer. In mere weeks, after Adara's Waning, I will be reborn as a titan. We will all return to the ways Rah intended when he created us. Free of thirst, hunger, and disease. Free of death and the Goddess who wrought such evil upon us." The air thickens between Ryland's last statement and the next.

"Rejoice," he commands. "Your salvation has come."

Rin is shaking and heaving. Her wails puncture the air with short, piercing shrieks sandwiched between agonizing sobs. Her pain is palpable, and my heart clenches as I watch her shake.

"The baby's coming!" She's frantic—screaming, squeezing Iyanu's hand in a death grip, and demanding to be moved to a sandbag. Iyanu shoots to her feet while I grab some pieces of cloth and a pail of clean water. A million questions come and go in my brain. Is Rin really a spy, then? How did the king know about her pregnancy? He would have never let her escape with his child if he had known. One of the Oguni betrayed us then. Yet here we are, with no palace guards storming in or any hint or signs from the dozens of Oguni spies that there's even a contemplation of such by the monarchy. Something's not right. I push the thought away, wanting to be helpful to Rin in one of her most vulnerable moments. There couldn't be a worse time to ask questions about her intentions.

Iyanu lays Rin down on a sand bang, and I cover her forehead in the cloth I've dipped in water and wrung. Rin makes whimpering sounds, like an animal shot with an arrow, wounded and bleeding to death. Iyanu and I look at each other for a brief moment, both of us worried, neither of us knowing what to do here.

Bear is forced to take the lead. He snaps orders, commanding Aris to grab medicine packed tinctures. He holds Rin's hand, the one that Iyanu isn't holding, and whispers soothing words. But Rin is inconsolable.

"There's nothing to do but wait," Bear concedes.

And so we wait, our hearts breaking silently while Rin struggles and screeches.

After what feels like hours but was probably only fifteen minutes, Rin's cries subside. She can sit up with her own strength, and she's released her death grip on Iyanu.

"The pain stopped," she says, her face wet with sweat, snot, and tears. Mouth twisted in confusion.

Bear nods. "It's not uncommon for this to happen. Children will often test the waters before committing to entering this world. With how fast the child is growing, he'll be here any day. In your case, he could be here any minute."

But the child isn't here in an hour, and it's not here in two. So slowly, the air of caution and waiting in desperation lifts before subsiding entirely. Rin is fast asleep just a few hours after that.

Bear gathers the rest of us. His tone is hushed and very serious.

"Ryland knows we have his heir," Bear begins.

"What if he has another heir?" Aris intervenes. "Who's to say that Rin's child is Imoleaye?" Aris glances at me now, likely recalling the conversation I had with him about Annabeth. "There's nothing stopping him from siring legions if he wanted to at this point."

Bear smacks his lip and gives Aris a deft look. "Do normal children grow to full size in just under two months? Only his firstborn would do this."

Aris averts his eyes at the rebuke like a child being scolded by their parent. "Right," he affirms.

"The king may have other children, but this is his only heir," Bear says with a sigh.

The thought still puzzles me. Why hasn't he made better attempts to retrieve his child, and how does he even know this child exists? The Deadends are only known to the Oguni, and the Oguni are made to endure a terrible initiation ritual before they're fully welcomed into the resistance and told the organization's secrets. The king would not know about the Deadends unless an Oguni told him so. None of the Oguni who labor on the estate have reported any increase in activity from the palace guards—no searching of Midzone compounds, no interrogation of Endzone laborers.

Bear shakes his head, answering the question no one has spoken aloud.

"Rin hasn't betrayed us. She's been with at least one of us every day and every night. It's impossible."

"There's nothing to be done then. We will prepare as we have been and strike like we planned to," Aris says.

Bear shakes his head. "We can't do that anymore," Bear says plainly.

"What?" I half yell, interjecting. We have no choice but to strike. If Ryland isn't deposed, if the Waning happens and neither Iyanu nor I survive, the king's experiments will continue in earnest. Titans will roam the earth, and the people will suffer more than they've ever known suffering. I don't add that there will never be rain or that all traces of the Goddess that might bring it will disappear from this Earth, taking all with her. I don't dare mention that killing Ryland, that killing Imoleaye, might be the only way to save ourselves.

"That's not what I meant." Bear scrunches his eyebrows together and uses the tips of his index and middle fingers to smooth his mustache. "Ryland will be expecting us. He knows that the child is our leverage, so we're bound to leverage him sooner or later. He'll be waiting for us to come to him in arms or with some sort of proposal. Remember what Sasha taught you? Your greatest tool in any battle is the element of surprise."

"And we've lost that," I say defeatedly.

"Maybe we haven't lost it all just yet," Bear says. "Ryland must have known that if we were to attack, we'd do it before the Waning. We know for sure that the two of you will be able to lend us your talents. That explains the lack of guards roaming the streets or jostling the Mid and Endzoners searching for his heir. They're all at the palace. Ready to defend him should the moment arrive. What he won't be expecting is no attack or proposition at all. At least none before the Waning.

"Our only option is to put our plan in motion just an hour or two before the blood moon reaches its highest point in the sky. When Ryland thinks we've abandoned any hopes of confronting him with your aid. That's when we'll strike."

Tonight, neither Iyanu, Aris, Bear, nor I can find the time or the energy to welcome the Oguni that pour into the Deadends past dawn. It's all we can do to keep standing by the time the first of them streams in. I fall into a deep, dreamless sleep unplagued by memories of charred flesh or Annabeth. Not even Lazarus graces my dreamscape tonight. I would have slept through the entire night if not for Rin, who wakes occasionally with a startled scream and talks in her sleep through the night.

"Stop," she pleads. "Leave me alone." Her voice is soft and juvenile.

It comes out in sputters, then lulls. At first, I try to ignore the sounds, but even Iyanu, who sleeps like the dead, cannot sleep. She rises, then goes over to lie on the ground by Rin's side. I decide to join them, taking my place by Iyanu without a word and holding her as she holds Rin. I don't know how it happened, but the three of us manage to make it through the night wrapped in one another's embrace.

Chapter 24

The baby does not come. Rin is losing her mind. She spends all day heaving in pain, and when she's not doing that, she's mumbling nonsense. In Rin's brief moments of lucidity, she confesses, "I can hear the king."

I thought she'd gone mad the first time he said this.

"I can hear his Voice deep in my gut. He's speaking through the child. He's demanding I go to him through the child. He won't stop. I keep telling him to stop, but he can't hear me."

Rin is huddled in the corner, singing the same lullaby she's been singing since she woke up. It's Aris who's placed the tune as something he's heard in the noble houses. *The Children of Rah are Joyous and Golden*. It's a sordid tune.

Maybe it would have sounded lovely in the mouth of any other person—one who would have joyously welcomed a child. Aris and Bear trade glances with me, telepathically communicating their concern. Their wide eyes whisper, *what are we going to do?*

Iyanu gave up on trying to console Rin hours ago. She refuses to do anything but sit and sing, compulsively starting over again every time she nears the end of the song. This is the only thing, Rin says, that keeps the king's Voice at bay—distant enough so it isn't constantly echoing in her head.

Isn't it fitting that just as soon as her false labor pains end, a more horrifying pain takes its place? It seems foolish that I've never considered it before. If Adara claims to flow through all things, imbuing the very fabric of our reality with her essence, then the same must be true of Rah. And if Ryland serves as Rah's Voice on earth, he could exploit the link that tethers Rin to him—their son.

We stay like that for several hours, waiting in quiet terror until Rin finally gives in and falls into a troubled sleep. Iyanu comes to sit by me, and Aris and Bear leave to tend to matters outside of the Deadends. Iyanu pushes her hand through her hair. Her face has aged at least half a decade in just three days as Rin's condition takes its toll.

"It's happening again," Iyanu says. *Torrin.*

Though the words never come out of her mouth, I know exactly what she's thinking. That there's something wrong with her. That no matter what she tries, she's destined to lose the ones she loves. I grab her hand. Even when the urge to retreat overtakes me, I squeeze it harder. The familiar rush of memories and emotions fills me from within, but I'm determined. As each one flashes by, I look at the memories from Iyanu's perspective.

Feeling her joy, the warmth, and the light that flows through her when Adara appears to her for the first time. The way her heart swells each and every time Torrin is in the room, even when she can't see her. Just her voice, her scent, is enough. I let myself feel all of it. The burden lifted from her the first time she introduced herself, and not once did we question her place amongst us. Anchoring myself in these feelings makes the others easier to bear. I thought my heart broke when Torrin died. But if mine broke just once, Iyanu's shattered into a million pieces.

I look at her now as if I'm seeing her for the first time, and the magnitude of my stupidity hits me. How could I keep myself from this person who's done nothing but stand by my side from the very beginning? No one on this planet will ever know me the way Iyanu does. No one will ever understand the things we've been through, the things we're still being asked to do. No one cares for us like we care for each other. Iyanu begins to apologize.

"Sorry, I know you need some spa—" I pull her in for a hug before she can finish, letting my face melt into the stiffness of her shoulders.

"No, I'm sorry," I say.

Iyanu breaks down then, unloading the full force of her emotions onto me. I'm glad to be the rock for once. To let her lean on me instead of the other way around. I'll tell her about Aris and what I saw later, not now while she's like this. This is the first time I've seen a crack in her skin, and I intend to stay until it's mended. As her body heaves against mine, I draw her in closer, wishing I could protect her from what's to come. But there's nothing to do for Rin, whose demons lie inside her.

"I love you, Iyanu," I say. The words spill out of my mouth with ease. I've never said that to anyone before. Iyanu shakes her head vigorously, unable to stop her tears, and wails or answers. But she doesn't need to. Every day, she shows that she loves me, too.

When Iyanu's tears subside, she grabs a sandbag and uses it to get some much-needed rest.

———◇———

I try to read the journals again, using my alone time to concentrate on the strange texts. I sit with a different book each time. This one is bound with a velvet purple coating that is too bright and unlike any material I've seen before. Each character curves into the other, some punctuated by dots above and some with sharp horizontal lines striking through them. The script is beautiful, and I picked the book both for the strangeness of the binding material and for the aesthetics of the font. As I trace my hand across each letter, they move strangely, twisting and turning into something else the longer you stare at them.

However, the familiar throb of pressure in my head does not accompany the movement this time. I find myself grasping the meaning of the words one by one. Aris and Rin had still only managed to teach me the basics of literacy. Reading small words with intuitive spellings. It was exhilarating the first few times I got them, and I immediately understood why the skill would be useful to anyone who had it. This is a different feeling altogether. Less reading, which comes with a fair bit of deciphering for me. It's more of a knowing. A knowing that has no need for processing or deciphering before you can assign meaning.

The book's owner is Vera. She lived during the reign of Atol. She was a mother of two. One of whom died after working only a year at the mines, and the other whom she left behind with his father at the age of ten. Her book begins with an introduction page. *To my dearest sisters, I hope this book finds you well. May you see rain in your lifetime.*

Like Iyanu, Vera claims that Adara had spoken to her and chosen her specifically to partake in the Waning. She claims that the presence was so great that it imparted such strength over her mental faculties that she had no choice but to obey. She was as surprised as anyone when she survived along with four others.

Vera outlived her king and, indeed, lived through another Waning, which occurred just two short years later. By then, her writing had become more decisive. Sharp and observing.

It is unnatural to hold that much spirit within just a few, she muses. *Our only hope is to try and spread it far and wide. The binding of Adara's essence caused this great chasm in our world. Releasing it will be our salvation.* The next time she writes, her words are panicked and rushed, half-written like she was running out of time. *I forced it out of me. I took it all out of me and expelled it into the world. The force with which it returned to me sent me flying across the room. It was as if the whole world saw what it was and resoundingly rejected it.* Doing what she'd done, whatever she'd done to take the essence out of herself, even for a brief moment, made her desperately ill. She only lived for another year, judging by the date of the last entry. She spent most of that time bedridden, sliding into a dark depression.

The next book I pick up is by a woman named Bella. Judging by her writings, she was a scholar like none Ile-Oja had ever seen—a scholar of the Goddess. *When Adara inhabits a human, her essence takes on human qualities. In other words, when her power is channeled through someone, it is tainted by them. Adara's gifts come in many forms, many of which are shared by multiple Galed at once. Rare is the power of sonderance, the ability to identify so strongly with someone you find yourself unable to distinguish yourself from them. Rarer still is the power to call to those who've passed.*

To bring Adara back into the world, one must simultaneously become one with her and the entire Earth. It is said that the one who holds the key to achieving this is actually three. The creator, the destroyer, and the balance.

Bella goes on to recount the history of Ile-Oja. *Rah is a jealous God. The monarchs worshiped him faithfully, decreeing him to be the one true God of the kingdom for centuries. When the destitute women invited Adara into themselves and conspired to dethrone a line that had been so faithful, Rah interceded. He came down and touched King Varion, speaking through him to make the women a promise. Gather as much of Adara's essence from the world as possible and bind it to themselves. In exchange, the monarchy would no longer reign freely, being kept in check by a competing one composed of the people's representatives. So they did, but they could not gather the entirety of a Goddess into them, so instead, they cast the rest of her essence into the sea. A sea that became Sarran. Only traces of her reside elsewhere in our world now. Since then, the Galed must enter Sarran after every high priestess' death to renew their bond with the part of the Goddess that lies beneath the sea. Women who succeed continue to be Galed. Most women succeed just once, if at all. But the creator, the destroyer, and the balance cannot be killed by those depths.*

Rah did not keep his promise, as the monarchs have ruled alone ever since.

I grab Annabeth's book, eager to read what it says, to glimpse the life of the woman who knew so much about us but kept so much of herself hidden. Her opening page reads, *To my dearest sisters: I hope your eyes never grace these pages.*

Annabeth's gifts, from her writing, are twofold. She had a knack for separating truth from lies, which should come as no surprise to anyone who has ever known her. Her second gift was the same as Sade's, that is, the subtle or not-so-subtle manipulations of water. A burst of persimmon seed as a neat party trick, or the flooding of the lungs of your assailant and, in Sade's case, bursting the blood vessels in their eyes as a demonstration in fatality.

The passages confirm everything I already knew. Like Vera, Annabeth desperately tried to return the world to a balance she thought was lacking. In her words, the Earth had tilted off its axis, and the only way to bring the rain was to right it that tilt. She needed to find a way to set everything back into alignment. Unlike Vera, Annabeth seemed to have known that forcefully trying to remove Adara from herself would not work. Indeed, Annabeth had the knowledge of all those that came before her. She also knew that Antares was barren and didn't immediately consider the king might bear a child with her. Her plan, then, was to kill Ryland before he could sire an heir.

When Ryland cast his wife aside and began sleeping with the palace maids, Annabeth needed to act. She detailed getting close to Ryland, offering him what he'd never had—a spy with the gifts of the Galed. A person who could infiltrate noble houses and do his dirty work without leaving traces behind. The tasks were standard at first. She paid visits to noble houses usually, which to them seemed like they were being honored by the king. She used the time to question the laborers and Endzoners who always see and know more than the nobility ever gives them credit for. She did this until, finally, Ryland trusted her enough to not just let her be his spy but his confidant.

He told her of his worries about how the nobility grew restless. He thought that some of them would try and make an attempt on his life, but he wasn't bothered by the prospects of their success. After all, what were they next to the Voice of the supreme god? He knew that that didn't matter, though. A king needs his kingdom, and there is no king when the people refuse to bow to his reign. If the nobility won't follow him, why should anyone?

Annabeth slipped the quake into his drink three times during their initial meetings. It had no effect. She decided to taint the entire water supply brought into the palace with a contraceptive that prevented the maids from getting pregnant. That was what did it. A few more years without an heir, Ryland became obsessed with immortality. It was Annabeth's plotting that pushed him towards his experimentations. She lamented this fact over and over. She blamed herself for further disrupting the world instead of returning it to balance.

With the aid of his scholars, Ryland surmised that personhood could only exist because a person was jointly inhabited by both Rah and Adara, however meagerly, if they were not Galed and not the reigning king. When Rah created the titans, they were filled by him and only him. He thought the Galed had latent abilities to draw what little of Adara's essence remained in the things of this world into them, just as their progenitors bound the majority of that essence within them. If she drew this essence out of them and he imparted Rah's essence into them, they would transform into what the supreme God had originally intended.

Annabeth went along with the king's theories, initially believing them to be impossible at best. Though she knew expelling the essence from herself could be fatal, drawing it into herself was something she'd done repeatedly. At any time, a battle of wills may take place, she wrote. If the others don't know to fight back or indeed how to fight back, any of Adara's essence residing in them may be accessed and used to enhance the other's strength.

Ryland's experiments left a trail of bodies behind—a trail Annabeth had a hand in creating. It was the palace maids, gone, one by one. I didn't know why so few of them made it barely a year before they disappeared, but they didn't disappear. They were disappeared.

In her writing, Annabeth bemoans the position the king's put her in, but she rationalizes her way out of it. She writes that there is always loss on the path to liberation, and a life used for the greater good is better than a life simply lived, perished, and gone to waste. It reminds me of something Sade would say. Annabeth's journal gets sparser, with large gaps between the dates, until one day, she says the unthinkable happened. She had successfully pulled Adara's essence out of the hosts ages ago. The experiments were failing because of the king and his heavy hand. The maids were not being filled with Rah light. They were being burned by it from the inside out. Annabeth is frantic when Ryland learns to control himself and dose his victims appropriately. The king is so confident about the success of the new experiments that he chooses none other than his own wife as the first viable subject.

I close the journal, already knowing what happens next, choosing to leave the words on the last three pages unread.

Chapter 25

The Oguni return in the evening with hunched shoulders and crippled backs. The crowd has some familiar faces and some I've never seen before. I estimate there's been over two hundred people going in and out of the Deadends in just the two weeks we've been there. True Oguni numbers could be double that—easily four hundred.

A crowd of sixty people fills the space today, way more than the twenty or thirty I'm used to. Sasha, Bear, and Aris chat. Sangi and his wife, Jules, join them. Even Shun is joyous, practically basking in the cheery nature and welcoming energy Iyanu exudes. But there is tension in the air. The tension one feels when they don't know if the next day will be the last.

The Oguni never thought they'd see war in their lifetime. Of course, war was always the only viable option. It was just never the smart one until now. Much like the nobility, who depend on the lake drying slowly enough to sustain them for generations, the Oguni imagined that their numbers would remain small, growing slowly but surely until the time came when their small militia could overtake an unsuspecting army.

Two Galed, it seems, are as good as any army.

Bear's gruff laugh is punctured by an excruciating scream that sends shockwaves through the air. Everyone knows about Rin by now. It's been two more weeks, and the baby has not come. The Oguni's network may be extensive, but it's effective at moving information. People try not to let Rin's painstaking cries of pain get in the way of their festivities. This is the way the Oguni do it. Every battle is preceded by a send-off for those that will be lost.

A group of three men takes the stage. They've painted their faces with the blue pigment that results from the sieving of sand particles and their combination with certain rocks found across the desert grounds. Three thin blue lines start at the space underneath their chin and extend to their chests and arms, almost like veins.

The men line up close to each other, and their shoulders practically touch. They stomp their feet in unison, one foot after the other. They widen their eyes unnaturally and contort their face into expressions that unnerve me. Their tongues stick out periodically, slithering in and then slithering out, twisting and writhing. The second of the four steps forward and begins a chant. The others join in answering his call. The crowd doesn't join in. Their cue is yet to come.

When the leader is finally ready to move from the preparation scene to the war scene, the crowd turns to him, waiting for their cue to follow along. He brings his arm forward in one swell swoop, sweeping it over the crowd dramatically. The people step backward and eventually fall altogether, unable to withstand the metaphysical surge of energy he wafted over them. The Oguni will sweep their enemies away just like this.

When the men are done, another performer walks onto the stage. She holds a bignar, a two-stringed instrument made from the hollowed wood of a desert cactus. Her melody is soft and sweet, rising gently only to tumble. No words come from her mouth, but she hums and clicks her tongue periodically, creating a rhythm.

Sasha calls me in with her arms, beckoning me to join the rest of the group. Aris frowns slightly at my approach, but, to my surprise, he doesn't move to leave the group when he notices I'm coming to join them. Everyone besides Iyanu holds a small, shallow bowl of cool liquid in their hands. Sasha takes a swig of hers before she starts talking.

"Meera," her voice slurs as she drags out the 'e's in my name. "Tell this loser here you had nothing to do with me falling him on his ass."

I turn to Aris and smile. "I had nothing to do with Sasha falling you on your ass." I repeat the phrasing that Sasha uses for comedic effect.

The corners of Aris's lip tug up, but he fights a smile. Maybe he'll be ready to talk soon. I try not to let his half-smile make me too hopeful.

Sasha sets her bowl down on a stool with a clump. Sangi turns around at the sound and walks towards us with a tray filled with more bowls of miska, offering us one each. Iyanu takes one this time, but I shake my head at the offer. That is unacceptable, according to Sasha, who stares daggers into my eyes.

"Meera," she huffs. "For Rah's sake, take the bowl, loosen up. This could be the last day you ever have a chance to."

I frown at that and do as she says. I drank miska just once. It was the day before the last Waning had happened two years before. There was no send-off for me, as I wasn't officially a member of the Oguni. My father snuck me a bowl of the bitter and spiced drink on his way back and woke me in my sleeping pit to share it with me. The evening was complete with our own send-off ceremony, although he said no words that could be interpreted as a sending-off.

I eye the drink suspiciously, swishing it in my bowl before swallowing a mouthful.

"It's worse than I remember," I joke.

This earns a cheer from Sasha, who calls Sangi, urging him to bring another round of drinks. I imagine that when the ceremony was done before, everyone only took sips of the drink before it was gone. Now, Bear can grow at least a decent enough supply for the Oguni, which becomes more than enough when paired with the portise berries stolen from the noble estates. Iyanu follows my cue and takes a swallow herself. She lets the liquid settle on her tongue.

"Are these portises from the Remmer estates," she asks. "The nutty flavor is their marker. They've never told their secrets, but my mother thought they made the berries nutty by planting them on fields that had just been used to grow kola nuts. The kola nut roots put chemicals into the soil that change the flavor profile of the portises," Iyanu concludes.

Sasha looks at her with a blank face. Bear gives a look that matches Sasha, albeit less tight and less daunting.

Iyanu shies away, realizing she's just revealed herself.

"You're the one that left the Idowu estates, aren't you?"

Iyanu takes a swig from the earthenware bowl this time. Gulping it down, not bothering with really tasting it. Sasha breaks into a smile then.

"You've got balls, kid," she says.

The relief on Iyanu's face is palpable. Though the situation has blown over, I throw her a small smile to reassure her.

When Sangi arrives with the second round of drinks, I down the one in my hand and gingerly take the other. The drink burns in my stomach, filling me with warmth and a sudden desire to let loose. For the first time since I slept with him, I take a good, long look at Aris. He shifts from one foot to the other but refuses to acknowledge my staring. Instead, he turns to Bear and delivers some frustrating news.

"Some Endzoners are beginning to think that Ryland's play for titanhood might save them. I got some word that—"

Bear cuts Aris off before he finishes the sentence. "This is not the time to talk about that," Bear says gently with a slight smile. "This is a time for enjoying yourself."

Aris nods before leaving the group. I place one foot forward, trying to go after him, but the bignar player speeds up her tune, a man with a sand shaker joining her on the stage. Sasha grabs Iyanu and me, leading us towards the others. She grabs me by both hands, swinging me to the left, then turning me to the right. A line of other Oguni emerge on either side of us, imitating the same move. Sasha throws me to the next person, who gladly catches me and spins me around himself. A boisterous laugh emerges from my depths, and I commit to the moves, swinging my hips and rolling my chest with the beat.

I pick up a drink and take another gulp before throwing myself at the next dancer in the cue. Bear gives me a weary smile but joins me in the dance, nonetheless.

"I haven't had this much fun in ever," I shout out, causing him to grin and spin me with more vigor.

He skips around me and bows at the end of our turn, summarily bouncing me to the next person in the line. It's none other than Aris. His body stiffens as he looks me over. His eyes look anywhere but directly into mine.

"Aris," I plead.

344

I've been content to give him his space, but I'm not sure I can take it anymore. He's seen me at my worst. He doesn't need to hide himself from me.

"You've been drinking," Aris says dismissively.

He turns himself on with the heat, and I'm left standing there without him leading me into a turn of my own. I spin myself the next instant, and my eyes continue to roll in my head even when my body has stopped. Before I can answer him, Aris waves me over to the next person in line too quickly and not at all on beat.

The next man in line is Shun. The stench of miska rolls off of him in waves. His movements are slow and lazy, always seeming to be a half-beat slower than the tempo, and he is in no hurry to catch up with it. He gives me a wide, toothy smile and snakes his hand across my waist before pulling me closer.

"You and me—" He gestures between the two of us. "We had a misunderstanding," he says.

He eyes me once over, then does a double take. He wears the approval of what he sees on his face, not bothering to disguise the racy thoughts running through his head. Shun's lithe frame and broad shoulders might have made him a ladies' man when he was younger. He likely still is with women his age. The way he brushes his hand against my ribcage and the confident and lazy smile he throws my way are those of a man who's used to getting what he wants whenever he wants it. I find his confidence exhilarating. Something in me relishes the idea of playing the victim, falling right into his trap, only to reveal that I was in control all along.

So, I respond to his statement just as I know he'll want me to. I pout my lips and cross my arms, feigning offense at the words he said to me just a few short days ago.

"You didn't have to say those things. Do you really think that about me?" I ask.

I couldn't have cared less what he thought of me, and even now, I can't truthfully say that his opinions have any bearing on me. Bear was right when he said that a good leader shows they are one with their people. But it's also true that a good leader knows which voices to heed and which to safely disregard.

"Sweetheart," he says. I don't think I've ever been more disgusted with what's supposed to be a term of endearment. "Let me make it up to you."

I turn to Aris for dramatic effect, pausing wistfully before turning my attention back to Shun.

"Look," he continues, "I know you'll like me better than any of these other guys."

Shun pulls me aside, separating us from the dancing queue. He walks us to the side, sitting on a stone, and encouraging me to sit in front of him. I sit straight, arching my back slightly and pushing my chest forward.

Shun hands me another drink, which I gladly gulp down. The liquid burns as it glides down my throat. My limbs have already gone limp, and my entire body is relaxed. The world turns with no need for spins from me. I sway slightly back and forth in time with the beat of the sand drum and hum along to the singer's melody, even though I don't know the words. He places one hand on my knee, then leans forward to whisper into my ear.

"What do you say we get out of here?" he asks. I give him the most dumbfounded expression I can muster without bursting into a fit of laughter. Bear catches sight of us and leaves the queue as well, heading straight for Shun and me.

"With you?" I ask.

"Yeah, with me," he says.

"Why would I do that?" I ask with as much sincerity as I can muster.

The question takes him aback, and his once coy expression turns into a deep scowl. He looks ready for another verbal take-down, his ego bruised once more. I relish that this time, his anger was provoked, and his actions will be justified.

Excitement begins to swell in me at the prospect of him raising his voice. Anyone with eyes can see what Shun is trying to do by pulling me over to the side. I imagine him calling me all sorts of names. I can't stop myself. I'm already grinning when I imagine standing up and yelling back at him, screaming. It's amazing what just a little bit of miska will do. How easily it brings the things you really want to do out of you.

Bear has closed the distance between us before Shun can think of something else to say.

"Meera. Shun. Come join the rest of us."

Shun must have been glad for the interruption because he rises to his feet swiftly, purposefully leaving Bear and me behind. I laugh lazily as I rise, shooting Bear a beaming smile.

"Wow." He chuckles. "If all it took was a little miska to make you happy, I would have been pouring you a bowl every day since you arrived."

I bring my hand to my chest and open my mouth into a too-wide gasp, feigning a look of shock and offense.

"I'm always this happy."

"Seriously, Meera," Bear cautions. "You're drunk."

I wave Bear away, but he sits down instead.

"My leg's gotten about as much as it can take today," he says, setting his cane down beside him. "You go on and join the others."

Bear gives me a strange look as I leave. I've rejoined the dancing too late. As soon as I step in front of the only available dance partner, the bignar player concludes her tune. The two lines of dancers separate and merge into a disorganized crowd. The two musicians pack their instruments, and Sasha jumps onto the stage, earning instant cheers from the crowd.

Sasha widens her legs and arms and pumps the latter up and down to amp up the crowd. The sea of drunken Oguni are happy to comply, jumping, stomping, and cheering at her actions.

"Are you ready?" She screams at the top of her lungs.

The crowd's response is deafening.

"I can't hear you," she says.

They cheer more loudly than should ever be possible for such a small group of human beings. The cheers are so loud that I'm convinced that Rah up above might hear them. That he might swoop down at any moment and incinerate every one of us for daring to defy him.

Sasha lowers her hands and makes a calming motion to ease the crowd.

"Okay. Okay. I get it," she says, earning some laughs.

"It's not a proper Lakasha without a real battle. Now it is." Some people shake their heads, while others grunt in affirmation. "So, which two sorry souls are going to get up here and give us a show tonight!"

The crowd bursts into another fit of jousting and cheering.

One person begins chanting, "Aris! Sasha!" And soon, the crowd is cheering for the two of them to join each other on the stage. Sasha grins a ravenous thing, but Aris waves both her and the crowd off.

"Next time," he says.

Sasha taunts him. "Don't blame you, given what happened last time," she says. "All right, do we have any other contenders?"

I raise my hand, and Sasha's expression quickly turns from surprise to approval. I've noticed that about Sasha. She likes living life on the edge, never being too sure of what might happen next. The more you do things she might not expect you to do, the more she likes you.

"Get up here," she screams, much too excited.

The crowd starts cheering my name. "Meera, Meera." Everyone joins in, even Iyanu. Everyone besides Aris and Bear.

Bear gives me a disappointed look, shaking his head slightly from left to right. Maybe this might not have been my smartest idea. Bear doesn't need to say it, but I already know what he's thinking. Iyanu and I are the Oguni's greatest weapons. What if I get on the stage and I lose? How is anyone supposed to have confidence that we'll stand a chance against the king and his guards if I can't even beat a singular person, let alone one touched by our supreme deity?

"All right," Sasha cuts through the crowds, cheering. "Who's going to join her?"

Shun begins to raise his hand, but Aris grabs it, forcing it downward and shooting him daggers with his eyes. Shun forces his hand out of Aris's grip, but he doesn't try to raise it again. How unsurprising. Sasha sweeps her gaze across the crowd dramatically, searching for someone to single out.

"Come on, Chelsea, you haven't been up here in ages." Chelsea, a young blonde woman, grins at Sasha but shakes her head and refuses to get on the stage. The adrenaline coursing through me begins to subside, thinking I won't get the battle l wanted after all. But another woman raises her hand in

Chelsea's stead, approaching the stage even before Sasha calls on her.

"Perfect," Sasha squeals. She turns to the woman. "Bryce, don't go easy on her. You both have just a few weeks of training." A new recruit, then. Someone that I might beat. "You know the rules," Sasha continues. "No cheap shots, nothing fatal, avoid eyes, throats, and indecent body parts. First person on the floor loses."

"But you said anything goes," Bryce protests.

"Yeah," Sasha says, stupefied. "On the battlefield. This is fun and games."

"Right."

Sasha jumps off of the stage and lands squarely on her feet. "Begin!" she screams.

Bryce runs at me with everything she's got, fist in the air, ready to connect with anything in her way. I keep my hands down instead of bringing them up to protect my upper body.

At the last moment, I move to the left, completely evading Bryce's approach. The near miss exhilarates me. Bryce turns quickly as she passes me, not letting her back remain turned to me for more than a split second.

The sudden change in direction throws her off balance, and she stumbles backward before regaining her footing. I know that if Bryce had been a real fighter and had trained with Sasha for at least a year, I wouldn't have stood a chance at all. But Bryce is just as new and reckless as I am. This will make for a fun fight.

The crowd seems to agree with my reasoning as their cheers become louder. I could have had her in that split second if I was concentrating on the fight instead of relishing the opportunity to fight at all.

Someone in the crowd yells, "I'd bet three days' worth of Tanaka estate rations that Bryce'll get her by the third hit."

"Double that says that Bryce doesn't get her until the sixth."

Jules's husband joins in on the fun. "An entire month's worth of rations says Meera will have her pinned after ten minutes."

Bryce approaches cautiously this time, widening her stance and bringing her arms up defensively.

"That's my girl," Sasha yells from the crowd. I have no idea which one of us she's talking to.

I mimic Bryce's stance. "Show me what you've got," I tease.

This earns me a small smile. Bryce's lips tug about half a millimeter upwards. She bounces on her feet, but I remain planted, waiting for her approach. When she finally bursts forward, she does so with twice the speed of her initial attack.

Maybe it was the suddenness of it all. The unexpected switch between rocking back and forth in place to throwing her entire body with all of its force straight at me—but I'm underprepared for the motion, and Bryce lands a punch right in between my eyes. It lands with a plunk, and my neck strains with the effort it takes to keep my head from falling off my body. I know I'll feel that tomorrow. Bryce forgets to put her defenses back up. She stays too close to me, reveling in the fact that she got a hit. I feign

352

a punch that Bryce ducks to avoid. I sweep my left foot towards her, hitting her on the back of the shin. She stoops momentarily but straightens her stance before throwing a left hook, which I dodge. We break from each other now, tired, sweating, both eager to avoid getting hit again.

A trickle falls down my forehead, and I wipe it away with the back of my hand. Blood and sweat. Those are some sharp knuckles. Bryce smirks when she notices. I run full force at her, just as she did moments earlier, fully expecting her to use my momentum against me. If Sasha taught her anything, it'd be to evade and then disturb my trajectory somehow. The right push would see me splattered on the floor. I raise my fists, and when I'm right in front of her, she moves swiftly to the right, stretching her hands out to shove me. But I'm ready for the move. I grab her hands, pulling her with me for a brief moment, then turning my body weight sharply to throw her off balance and knock her to the ground.

Bryce lands right on her face, moaning on impact.

Someone in the crowd yells, "That's ten rations from you and twenty from you."

Bryce rises and stretches her hand out for a handshake. She raises my hand when it meets hers to cheers and applause from the crowd. The adrenaline coursing through me begins to settle down, a heavy fatigue replacing it. I will definitely feel all of this tomorrow. Right now, however, the extra miska I guzzled begins to catch up to me. A wave of nausea hits me, and I sway slightly at the queasiness.

"You okay?" Bryce asks.

"Yep," I answer.

I jump off the stage, intending to head straight for my sleeping bag, but Aris follows closely behind me. Two new people mount the stage, undeterred by the stains of blood and sweat we've left on its surface. The caliche is porous. The liquids seep right through it, and if not for the bright splotches of reddish discoloration, you would never know that any fighting at all took place on stage. I wonder how much sweat and blood has seeped into the pores of the caliche, never to be seen, let alone cleaned by anyone in the outside world again.

I halt, turning to look at Aris who's walked up behind me.

"That was stupid," Aris says. "You could have lost. Worse, you could have been badly injured. What if Bryce wasn't the one who volunteered? We only have two days left before we have to storm the palace. Everyone's life, the entire kingdom is depending on you, and you're still only thinking about yourself." We both know that Sasha wouldn't have let anyone on the stage who she thought might seriously harm me. Like she said, the stage is not a battlefield. It's a game.

"Unbelievable. The first time you talk to me in two weeks is to chastise me and throw insults my way." My voice gets higher with each sentence. "Look around, Aris. Everyone is thinking about themselves! That's what one does when their life might

354

end!" I walk the step between us, pointing my index finger. "You will not dictate to me how to live the bit of life I have left." I drop my finger in shock the next instant.

"I'm sorry," I say too quickly. "I'm drunk and the adrenaline," I amend.

He has a pained look in his eyes as he opens his mouth and then closes it again.

"You're right," he says. "I'm sorry, I shouldn't have said that."

"Can we talk about the other night?" I ask. I take a step in his direction, but he takes a step back.

"Aris," I plead, raising my voice and reaching for the hand by his side. He jerks away before my hand can make contact.

"Good night Meera," he says. "Get some rest, you'll need it."

I walk straight to my sandbag, refusing to cry or give into the desperation rising inside of me. The moment my head hits the surface of the smooth linen bag, the sand underneath gives way, cushioning my head on both sides. The world begins spinning almost immediately. It only gets worse when I close my eyes, and though I try desperately to keep them open, they droop involuntarily. Another wave of nausea overtakes me. My stomach heaves, trying desperately to expel the excess miska I've consumed, but the only thing that comes through is air.

A heavy pressure builds in my chest. I briefly consider pushing my finger down my throat, desperately trying to get any relief I can. Still, the sparring from just before has already started to take its effects, sending shocks of pain when I try to roll myself aside to get up. Barfing here, now, would mean sleeping next to my vomit. Why would I drink so much? I curse under my breath.

As I lay down, malaised, I feel a slight tingle building beneath my skin. Suddenly, I find myself concentrating intensely, reaching inside myself of Adara's essence, bending it to my will. The sudden focus is not mine. The essence I'm reaching for is not mine. The part of Adara housed within me is drawn out, mixing and colliding with Sade's. My anxiety grows tenfold, completely overwhelming the nausea and pain that had left me bedridden just moments before. I hold on to the power within me, giving my all to prevent Sade from taking what's mine. The sensation is like trying to climb a polished pole after greasing your fingers. The miska weakens me. The harder I try, the more the essence escapes me.

"Stop," I cry into the ether.

Sade finishes taking from me within the next few minutes. I dare not think about what she's done through me.

Chapter 26

Rin is in so much pain that Aris has to strap her hands and legs together to keep her from pulling her hair out. Iyanu tries to soothe her, but Rin shuns anyone who approaches. It's almost like she doesn't recognize her or that Iyanu's mere presence makes the pain tenfold. We pray, to whoever might answer, that the child is born quickly.

Bear dreams up concoctions to help ease her pain or at least induce her labor. Getting the mixtures down her throat has been just as challenging as getting them to work. She coughs them out, spits, and cries for us to stop. Bear tries just twice before her pleas get to him. Just two days after La'kasha, the mood has soured considerably.

It's not all Rin's fault. Today was bound to be somber. The sun shines through the horizon at only half its normal size. Its light is dimmed, and the early morning is relatively cool in the Endzone and positively chilly in the Midzone and near the noble estates. The moon is a black void in the sky that swallows the sun's light where it covers it. A third of the sun's light is completely lost. As the Waning approaches, both the sun and moon will rise higher into the sky, moving more and more into alignment until the moon swallows all the light the sun has to provide.

"You felt Sade that night," Iyanu says.

I'm almost surprised to hear her say the name. I guess by not talking about it, we both decided we could both pretend that it didn't happen. That when we storm the palace tonight, we would be confronting just the king and his guards, not someone we once thought of as a sister.

"Yeah," I answer. There's so much more I don't say. That I was too drunk to fight her or that I'm almost certain she was able to use me through her connection with me. That whatever Sade did last night, I had a hand in.

"I think she took from me," Iyanu confesses. I let out a sigh of relief.

"Me too," I say hastily.

Iyanu nods slowly. "We can't let that happen again."

"Iyanu, I need to tell you something," I begin. "When we hugged...I saw you with Torrin. I didn't mean to, but sometimes when I touch things, I see things."

"Of course, you didn't mean to," she says. "We're all still figuring it out. If you can—" She hesitates for a bit. "See things?" she concludes. "There's a reason the Goddess gave you that gift. Don't apologize for having it. Learn how to use it."

Chapter 27

Bear will stay with Rin. Her pain seems so great, and her stomach is larger than any pregnant person's we've seen before. We're convinced the child could come anytime, and someone needs to be here when it does.

The rest of us make our way through the Deadends and emerge from the tunnels. We're greeted by a darkened sky and bearable temperatures. Not long after, the Endzoners emerge from their sleeping pits, merging into a sea of people.

The walk to the estates is ten miles. Endzoners make this journey twice a day, every day, or at least every day they expect to collect a ration. Dressed in paltry clothing given to us by Oguni, we blend right in. None of the Endzoners recognize us. They certainly have never had the chance to see Iyanu, and even if they'd seen me while I lived amongst them, two years' worth of distance has erased any traces of recognition.

The winds pick up speed. In the noble estates, a cool breeze can sometimes be felt drafting from the edges of the sea. In the Midzone, intricate and purposeful arrangements of tall buildings amplify any wind that blows, turning it into a sizable gust. In the Endzone where there are no lakes or above-ground structures, wind of any kind is a blessing. A blessing that can quickly turn into a curse. Something odd happens on this day when the moon is pitch black. A normally windless kingdom suddenly turns into one with violent windstorms. The monarchy teaches that this is just the consequence of the Goddess of Chaos—a destroyer who has more powers to destroy on her day of sacrifice.

The strong breeze lifts my hair, loc by loc, raising and falling. Iyanu braces herself against the wind, bringing her forearms over her eyes to protect herself from the sand particles that jump up and crash into us. The Endzoners around us push forward despite this. I look around to see if I can spot any of the dozens of Oguni I've come to know, but the sand in the air makes it hard to see much more than those standing directly in front of me. A flash of light runs through the sky, followed by a thunderous sound. The monarchy teaches that this is a battle between Rah's peace and Adara's chaos. When the Waning happens, it'll come to an end.

We make it to the narrow ridges of road that allow us passage through the Midzone into the noble estates. Here, on these paths bordered by large buildings, the wind ceases to blow as strongly. The pelting of sand into our eyes, ears, and noses also stops. The floor is still filled with small amounts of sand and rock, but unlike the Endzone, the Midzoners have paved paths.

The wind is calm here, but it is positively monstrous everywhere else in the Midzone. Tall buildings purposefully constructed to magnify winds turn weak winds into cooling breezes and strong winds into forces strong enough to send people flying or entire buildings falling. No Midzoners will leave their home today. They can afford to take a day's rest, and they'd rather live to see another day.

Guards patrol the demarcating wall, opening the gates at designated checkpoints to allow the stream of laborers through. The laborers are checked twice during their daily commute. Once, when entering, to make sure they don't bring weapons to the nobilities' home, and once, when leaving, to make sure they don't bring out more rations than they're owed. Some guards take their patrol very seriously, while others are happy not to even look at the Endzoners as they walk past them.

A man is caught with a glass knife tied around his weight, concealed by his pants. The guard pulls him to the side, brings out a whip, and thrashes it against his back ten times before stopping. He directs the man to turn back and go home, depriving him of his rations today. The man continues to lie face down, unable to obey the command. The stream of people turns from one to two where he lies.

One freckle-faced, long-haired guard pats just the women down, taking his time to feel them out thoroughly. Neither the guards who work beside him nor the Endzoners near him confront him. Aris, Sasha, Iyanu, and I avoid him, walking towards a less 'thorough' guard instead. Aris looks down as he walks by, the bottom half of his face wrapped with some cloth to protect him from the dust and conceal his identity. Iyanu and I follow his lead, heads bowed and avoiding direct eye contact.

Petty, mid-range criminals usually have their sketches drawn and posted around the kingdom for easy identification. Awards are delivered to those who report any information that could lead to their capture. If the king is interested, the awards are usually so high that the person is found in a matter of days. No ransom has been offered for either me or Iyanu. We're pretty sure that besides the Oguni and the king's most trusted guards and advisors, no one even suspects that we're gone from the palace. Still, we can't be too careful. Sasha hums as she walks by. For all anyone knows, she's reporting to duty as usual.

As we cross the demarcating wall, my feet crunch on dried shrubs and dark brown grass drying from the lack of water. What used to be a marshland transformed into a Savannah. Ten minutes of walking finds us enveloped in a cool shadow cast by the Ceiba trees rising above us. In my father's youth, they pressed against the demarcation wall, sometimes casting their cool shadows on the Midzoners wealthy enough to live on the other side of the wall. The trees we encounter first are browning. The force of the wind on their canopy shakes hundreds of whittled leaves off of their surface, resulting in a sorry imitation of rainfall. If water in the form of rain brings life, the detritus falling from above is symbolic of death.

Lightning flashes across the sky. The cool light turns the red air purplish for a brief moment before the red cast overwhelms our vision again. As we go deeper into the estate paths, the vegetation gets denser around us, but the walking paths remain clear. More and more Endzoners split off from the larger group, moving towards their respective estates. We continue towards the Hathaway estates. The estate closest to the palace. Unlike the Berkshires and Tanakas, the Hathaways haven't been disloyal to the crown. Lord Hathaway's head remains squarely on his body, and his compound is still his to enjoy. Many Endzoners will arrive at empty estates where the lords are dead, and the families are disbanded.

A shiver runs through me as we walk onto the Hathaway estate. I turn to Iyanu, who turns to look at me at exactly the same time. Here, on the edge of Sarran, we already feel the strange pull that beckons us to enter its waters. The Hathaway estates are sprawling. It's almost an hour's walk from one corner to the next. This results in the highest concentration of Endzoners working the land.

Aris, Iyanu, Sasha, and I join the others. Towing the earth, spreading seeds, and harvesting vegetables. We keep clear of the Endzone enforcers who are tasked with making sure their people don't attempt to steal food or water from the estates. The Hathaways, like many of the nobles, have a love for citrus fruit. Their estates boast the largest variety and highest concentration of oranges, lemons, and grapefruits in the land. I grab a rake from the stores, joining those mowing the ground to make way for new plantings. Iyanu has joined the planters. She looks like she knows exactly what she's doing and has done this a million times, despite never having worked anything but a flower pot.

The enforcers watch resolutely, circling each laborer and then doubling back after they've completed a round. Often, they accuse laborers of stealing even when they haven't. Their rations do not depend on the accuracy of the accusations they make, just on their quantity and plausibility.

"You two over there," a young enforcer says. "Stop talking and get back to work."

His long chin is smooth, and his eyebrows sit like caterpillars on his forehead. A more seasoned enforcer would have taken their names down and marked them for lower rations later. Rations that will go to him instead. The enforcer is right nonetheless. All around us, Endzoners have been talking amongst themselves in faint whispers instead of silently carrying out their tasks. Communication, other than when absolutely necessary, is strictly forbidden.

The chatter grows louder despite the warning from the enforcer. Voices rise all around us. More enforcers join the younger one, demanding that the laborers end their talking with threats of lower rations. One laborer throws his plow to the floor, pushing the nearest enforcer to her. The other laborers take note.

"We demand an audience with the king," she says.

She looks to be a few years younger than I am. Younger than Sade even. The laborers around her shout with approval, and the enforcers scramble to return to their feet. The other enforcers scramble to get away from the Endzoners, raising the bells at their belts in unison.

The laborers rush each enforcer, snatching the bells from them and quieting their noise. The action comes too late, however. The sound of the bells would have already been heard in the estate house, and the palace guards stationed at the estate will be on their way. Some will come here directly, others will call for reinforcements—sweat beads down my neck from the heat. The laborers wait in silence, waiting for the guards to arrive.

The woman who spoke stands on one foot and raises the other to show her sole. A thin, obsidian knife adhered to the surface shines a dull purple in the dim afternoon sun. All around us, people follow her lead, pulling weapons out from underneath their feet, in between their thighs, and out of the tresses of their hair.

"There are more of us than there are of them," she shouts.

The people grunt their approval. I look around at their dirt-stained garments and their sunken faces. They've already walked three hours to get to the estates. They have no training. A palace guard with a sword would be able to take down fifty untrained laborers before he sustained any significant injuries. Thousands of palace guards could be deployed at any given moment.

The three guards from the Hathaway estates appear in under two minutes, dressed in hamel black and wielding their swords in their hands. They take one look at the enforcers on the ground, assessing the situation.

"Surrender your weapons," one of them demands. His voice is cool and steady, but there's a hint of uncertainty.

The young woman speaks again, her small obsidian knife raised, mirroring the guards' swords.

"We demand to speak with the king," she says again. Her voice is unshakeable. She's ready to die—not just once, but a million times for her cause.

"We shall starve no more," she says. Her voice comes out breathy but steady. "We've heard of the elixir King Ryland uses to turn his favored nobles into beings with no need for food or water."

The guard snares, baring a line of yellowed and crooked teeth, one missing from each row.

"Put your weapons down," he demands again, shaking his head like he's talking to a group of misbehaving children.

"There is no elixir," he says. "And even if there was, the king would never give it to the likes of you." He takes one step forward. "Now, I won't ask you again, girl."

"You lie," the woman says, her voice quivering.

"King Ryland spoke of the dawn of titans. We've all heard," she shouts to a chorus of Endzoners cheering her on. "If the king will not give it to us, we shall take it by force."

The guard looks around, assessing the other Endzoners who've also refused to drop their weapons. None of the palace reinforcements have arrived, and it's anyone's guess as to when they'll come. Failure to quell this uprising swiftly would result in certain punishment for the guard. He takes one more glance around and decides he likes his odds. It takes just two breaths for the guard to close the distance between himself and the woman. He raises the hilt of his sword and brings it down against the side of her head, knocking her down. She falls to the ground with a shriek, dropping the knife she held in her hands. The Endzoners surrounding her turn to each other.

Two of them break forward, attacking the guard at once. The guard sweeps his sword across them in one fell motion, slicing through their garments and skin indiscriminately. Blood sprays from their wounds, splattering across the woman's face and soaking the crimson-tinged vegetation. The woman sits wide-eyed, staring at the two bodies lying in front of her, frozen with shock. The guard's attack jolts the rest of the laborers into action, and they rush the two guards in unison.

I walk towards the scene, readying myself to release the power thrumming just underneath my skin but hesitating with so many Endzoners in my line of fire. Aris grabs my arm and starts pulling me away. I turn and watch as the corpses of three more Endzoners hit the ground. A stream of Endzoners burst forth from the estate home, carrying blood-soaked steel and obsidian blades. The blades are finely made. They're weapons from the Hathaway stock.

"We need to leave now," Aris says.

"Aren't you going to help them?" I ask.

"We *are* helping them," Aris answers, tugging me towards the palace path. I frown, and Aris adds, "I'd have to fight through them to even get to the guard, and by the time I've done that, someone else would have gotten to him."

On cue, the first guard hits the ground. The people around him don't let up. They continue to swarm him like bees to honey, stabbing, kicking, and tearing at his fallen body. His groans fade away, but the frenzy continues. I pull my eyes away from the crowd, joining Sasha and Iyanu, with Aris following closely behind me.

<hr />

The roads that lead to the palace are well-worn by hamel feet. The vegetation on them has been reduced to nothing, but all around their edges, wildflowers spring to life, adorning the streets with bright blues, yellows, and oranges, which turn to various hues of reddish to purplish in the crimson sunlight. We stay close to the roads, but we choose to traverse the forest instead.

Only five guards appear on the path instead of the dozens of guards the Hathaway guards would have hoped for. Sasha runs out into the open when she sees them. My hand twitches at my side, trying to reach out to grab her as she leaves, but she slips right through my fingers. Sasha falls in front of the five guards as they run by, forcing them to stop and acknowledge her. Iyanu tries to break towards Sasha, but Aris pushes her back. He shakes his head, silently telling her not to intervene.

Sasha brings herself to her knees. Her face is fear-stricken, and the way her bottom lip trembles makes her seem like she's on the verge of crying. One of the guards approaches her with his hand on the hilt of his sword.

She points toward the direction of the Hathaway estates, hands trembling as she says, "The people. They've..."

The guard moves closer to Sasha and releases the grip he has on his hilt. He towers over her, easily twice her size if they were both standing, but four times her size now that she's on her knees.

"Speak, woman," he commands.

Sasha moves quickly, and her form turns into a blur in front of my eyes. In an instant, she removes the sword from the guard's sheath and plunges it straight through the middle of his neck, sliding it out and bringing the blade up to prepare for the next guard. The other four don't hesitate to bring the swords up. They rush Sasha all at once, turning their backs on Aris and the rest of us. Aris throws a small knife that whizzes through the air, striking one of the guards in the back of his head, right where his head meets his neck. The guard falls forward, landing face-first.

One of the other guards turns around abruptly, squinting at the vegetation in the distance to make out where the knife came from. Aris sends another one his way, striking him inside his left eye. He doesn't drop dead but begins running towards us, blood dripping out of his eye socket. Aris throws three more knives, one hitting him on the left shoulder and the other two hitting him on different points of his forehead. The guard makes one last push forward, coming within five feet of where we're hidden before crumbling to the floor.

Sasha neutralizes the other two guards. She brings her sword down through one of the guard's hands, severing his hand from the rest of his arm before changing directions and slicing across his face. The other guard tries backing away, but Sasha plunges the tip of her sword straight through his back and doesn't bother pulling it out as he falls forward. The sword slides through him as it hits the ground along with his body, but it stays upright.

Sasha beckons us forward as she stands over the three corpses. She and Aris turn the guards around, reviewing their work. All the guards, except the one with a sword sticking out of his abdomen, have their uniforms mostly intact and free of dirt and debris.

Aris points to the guard with three knives in his head.

"You get that one," he says.

We strip the clothes off their corpses and drag their bodies out of the path and into the surrounding forests. Aris and Iyanu put on the garments of the two guards closest in size to them. The armor fits snugly over their bodies, and the suits seem like they were made for them. Despite wearing the armor of two of the smaller guards, Sasha and I look like we're swimming in the suits. They hang awkwardly off of us and bundle in places they shouldn't.

"It'll have to do," Sasha says with a frown, pulling the black mask over her face.

Chapter 28

Guards run through the palace grounds, scurrying towards the estates. A man, likely their new captain, stands at their center, commanding guards to go one way or another. Another man dispatches swords and armor by the dozens. It looks like the Endzoners on the Hathaway estates were not the only ones who demanded an audience with the king. The chaos unfolding at the palace suggests that almost every laborer on every noble estate has joined the uprising. The guards pay us no mind as we walk through the palace field with our newly scavenged uniforms.

"You!" someone shouts at Aris. "Didn't I send you to the Bronsteads'? What are you still doing here!" he shouts. A long, thick vein bulges out of the side of his neck and runs up his temples.

"Yes, sir," Aris shouts, and the man turns his attention towards the dozen other guards still waiting for their assignments. Rather than running back towards the estates, Aris pushes us towards the palace entrance.

"They'll have the most guards inside," he says. "To protect the king."

A group of four men joins us at the gate, merging with us as we walk through the palace doors.

"This is getting out of hand," one of them groans.

"All of them?" he questions. "At the same time?"

Another guard clicks his tongue.

"It's the witch Goddess," he says. "The people run a bit mad on her day. Things will calm down after she gets her sacrifice."

The first guard replies. "One of my cousins had his daughter volunteer for that. A pity," he concludes.

My lips stay glued together, hoping neither of the four guards probe Iyanu, Sasha, Aris, or me into the conversation. We don't need the attention.

We turn the palace corridors, strolling down long walkways adorned with embroidered rugs, glass flower bouquets, and precision-cut sandstone stacked one atop the other. Ever so often, we walk past a corridor with large windows, giving us a glimpse of the chaos outside. The rest of the palace guards look like disoriented ants scattered by the hands of a bored child. The chaos present down there stands in stark contrast with the calm that reigns inside the palace walls. The most chaotic thing in here is the way our footsteps echo to their own rhythm, out of sync and off-beat with each other. Aris turns to meet my eyes. We've diverged from the path to the king's quarters, but we dare not break from the four guards.

We turn one last corner and walk down the hall towards the only door in the entirety of a corridor. The queen's quarters have been empty for the better part of a decade. What are we doing here?

We file in through the open door one by one, taking our place next to the guards already stationed and spread across the dimly lit room. Long shadows cast by burning lanterns hang across the walls, blanketing the space in alternating patterns of light and darkness. The room boasts a cushioned chair embroidered in the customary red and gold décor of the crown, not to mention a hand-welted rug, sheer curtains, and a bed large enough for five people to sleep on. The bed only has one person lying on it though. Her body is almost completely hidden by a thin white sheet. Her front side is flush against the mattress. Five guards surround her, enclosing a few palace maids as they do. One holds a bowl of oil over her and fans the air above the bowl towards her.

Another two maids stand above her. One of them kneads the muscles on her upper back while the other massages the soles of her feet. She waves one slender arm towards the maid, fanning the earthly scent. The maid stops and walks towards a table beside her, giving me a better view of the form lying on her bed. Her hair is cut short, jet black, and loosely curled. Her skin is taut and smooth. It glistens with a layer of oil rubbed on its surface, even in this dimly lit room.

It's Sade lying on the bed, getting her shoulders rubbed, bathing in the aromas of finely curated oils. She's wrapped in silks while we wear the blood and sweat-stained garments of guards we had no choice but to kill.

"Would you prefer this one, my lady?" the maid asks, bringing another oil-filled bowl towards her and fanning the aroma in Sade's direction.

"I told you, you don't have to call me that," she replies.

"Of course, my lady," the maid replies.

Sade chuckles softly. "Yes, that one is perfect."

The maids continue to attend to her as Aris, Sasha, Iyanu, and I stand stoically along with the other guard. How long is this going to go on? Aris and Sasha show no signs of getting ready to draw their weapons, and we haven't even found Ryland. There is no way for us to leave our stations here as a group without drawing suspicions.

One of the guards standing by Sade's side motions to me to take his place, and I hurry to stand by his side. He makes a few gestures with his hands before leaving the door.

I watch as Sade's back rises and falls with each breath. I listen as she moans with delight as the maid kneads her tissues. I wonder if she can feel that it's me standing right next to her and if she has any suspicions that it's her sisters and not some random man who waits by her left.

"I've been needing this. Ryland has me working much too hard," Sade says to no one in particular.

376

If I killed her right now, the part of Adara's spirit bound in her would go to Iyanu and me. We'd have better odds of defeating Ryland. I let the thought filter through my mind, tossing and turning it around several times before I try to let it go. It stays stuck, however, and I'm left cycling between visions of plunging my sword into Sade's back and imagining the horror on Iyanu's face as I do so.

I glance over at Sasha and Aris, watching as they tilt their heads to the side and bring their chins up slightly, acknowledging the presence of one of the other guards. Like us, he's an Oguni in disguise. There'll be dozens in and around the palace now—assassins posing as would-be protectors. The Oguni will still be heavily outnumbered, but with so many guards deployed to the estates, the odds of victory look much more favorable.

Sade turns on her side, shifting so her foot, which dangles off the side of the bed, brushes the hand hanging limply at my side. A rush of images flickers through my mind. Sade in the king's quarters, a room twice as grand as the one he's in now. Ryland undressing her, caressing her. The images leave as fast as they come, but they also leave a bitter aftertaste in my mouth. Sade gasps as her skin brushes mine, a spark of electricity running through the both of us.

She scrambles out of her bed. Sasha, Aris, and the other Oguni pull out their swords, prompting the rest of the palace guards to do the same.

"Meera!" Sade hisses.

"Protect the lady!" a palace guard shouts.

Sade brings her hands up, and I instinctively reach deep inside myself, drawing Adara's essence to the surface of my skin and staving off the effects of Sade's attempt to disarm me. My wrists tremble with the effort. She would have broken them, shearing the water inside of my body with enough force to snap them in half.

While the guards hesitate to identify those working for the palace and the traitors in their midst, Aris and Sasha take down the two closest to them, and the third Oguni does the same. All three of them remove their masks in a hurry, and Iyanu and I follow suit, quickly establishing the side we're on. Sade looks frantically from me to Iyanu and draws her hands towards her. I run towards her, throwing my body at her and knocking us both down to the ground. I place three punches to her left eye before she shakes me off.

I grab her foot. It feels slick, and my fingers slide off because of the heavy layer of oil on her skin. Sade turns onto her back and kicks, releasing herself from my grasp. But I dive at her again, grabbing her leg this time. She kicks my face twice. A rush of blood streams out my nose, but I hold on.

"How could you?" I yell at her, tears streaming from my face.

Sade grimaces and kicks me off with her heel, but I crawl and jump at the base of her foot a third time.

"You're not leaving," I say.

One of the guards runs out of the door, and Aris runs after him. He's gone for just a few seconds before he returns, dragging the guard's body behind him. Another guard runs towards Iyanu. He raises his sword and strikes right beneath her navel.

His sword shatters from the impact, leaving him staring at the hilt, which is now without a blade. The remaining guards stare at Iyanu in shock, hesitating to approach her. Iyanu reaches out to the guard. Nearly as big as he is in size, she grabs him by his leather vest, pulls him in with one hand, and knocks him out with a blow to his head with her other hand.

"Shit," Aris curses. "The rest of them will be coming!"

"Meera, let's go," Sasha shouts. I break away from Sade as Iyanu rushes to my side. The other Oguni joins us as we run out of the door and down the corridor we came from.

"Where are we going?" I ask.

Aris only runs faster. "We need to get to the king's quarters before the rest of the guards do."

The sonorous ringing of bells thunders through the palace walls, bouncing off the walls of every empty corridor. The ringing pierces my eardrums, forcing me to bring both hands over my ears.

"Shit," Aris curses for the millionth time today.

Footsteps echo all around us, coming from every direction, guards all trying to reach the king's quarters before we do.

We push forward, running through corridors, until we meet a wall of guards encircling what can only be the king in the middle of their pod. Aris pulls the sword out of his hilt. Sasha does the same. Guards stream in behind us, trapping us between the king's entourage and themselves. Sade joins them shortly, pushing through their ranks to get to the front of the crowd. With at least twenty guards on one side of us and fifty and counting on the other, there's no way out for us. There's no way out that doesn't involve a score of dead bodies.

"Just put your weapons down, and we can talk about this," Sade says.

Aris and Sasha keep their swords raised. Against three or even twelve other guards, they would have fought without a thought.

One of the guards behind Sade raises his sword, bringing it down towards her back. Another pushes her out of the way, taking the brunt of the blow. His suit rips apart at its shoulders, blood pouring from the wound as he falls to the ground. The guard who struck him pulls off his mask, revealing a familiar face. All around him, the Oguni do the same, identifying themselves and drawing their swords against the guards surrounding them.

Two Oguni fall within the king's circle. But three more fall the guards beside them, wreaking havoc and forcing the ring to turn inwards on themselves to protect the king. Sade raises her arms, snapping the neck of an Oguni in the circle with the twist of her hand. Aris and Sasha rush in to join the fight.

"Sade," the king calls. His voice bellows across the room, even drowning out the sound of tearing flesh and glass and metal clashing against one another. Sade pushes through the deluge and disappears into the thinning ring of guards encircling Ryland.

A hot breeze rises in the room.

"Sasha, Aris!" I yell out.

By some miracle, my wide eyes tell them they need to come to me right fucking now. The king releases a blaze of fire like the sun itself, pouring out of his eyes, indiscriminately charring guards and Oguni alike. They cry out in pain, their flesh melting off their bones and falling into pools of liquid slush at their feet.

My stomach clenches, preparing to retch, but instead of vomit, I release the scream built up in me, neutralizing Ryland's blaze and sparing those guards and Oguni directly behind me. Everyone who makes up the king's circle, except for Sade, has fallen to the floor in an unrecognizable heap of blackened bodies.

Ryland emerges from the ashes of their corpses, golden, beautiful, and untouched.

He steps over the pile, careful not to step on the mush of melted flesh and bone before him with his gold-plated sandals. He might as well be stepping over hamel shit.

Beside us, an Oguni throws a knife at Ryland's temple. It whizzes past me, my eyes only registering it after it's traveled far beyond me. Ryland swats the knife away from himself like a man swatting a fly.

The king tsks, wearing a smile on his face. "How lovely of you two to join us, Iyanu, Meera."

Aris looks precariously down the corridor, waiting for more guards to stream down the hall, but they never come. Their numbers are far too thinned, spread across the many miles of estate lands. It would have taken many hours to reach the respective estates and twice as many hours to return to the palace.

My locs stick to the side of my face, sweat gluing them to my skin. My breath comes in pained heaves, dry air scratching the surface of my throat. My eyes water, but I refuse to shed any tears. I reach into myself again, preparing to end Ryland right here, knowing full well I'd likely be killing Sade, who stands directly behind him. My eyes drift to the bodies on the floor. Torrin's blackened, purpled, and nude skin flashes across my mind—the way her eyes refused to close, wide open but devoid of any life.

I open my mouth, ready to unleash the pain and sorrow inside me, but close it instead.

I feel a tug at my core. My eyes shoot to Sade, who's wincing in concentration. *She's trying to draw my essence out of me and into herself!* I grit my teeth against the intrusion, throwing up barriers in my heart and mind. Sade reaches her tentacles deeper, wrapping them around my core. They feel cold, dark, and sticky inside me.

"Stop," I grind out through gritted teeth. I use the connection she's already made and pull at the part of Adara within her with everything in me. Ryland steadies himself, preparing to release another ray of light. Aris and Sasha run towards Iyanu, but my feet are glued in place, fighting Sade's intrusion into my being. When the ray gets closer, the heat forces me to release my pull on Sade's spirit. I roar out the sonic waves held in my chest and disrupt the ray before it hits me. Sade digs into me again almost immediately, full force and unyielding. The light ray travels past me towards Iyanu at full speed. Iyanu's body deflects most of it, sparing herself and Aris.

Sasha screams as the ray passes. I resist the urge to turn towards her, focusing everything I have on Sade instead.

"SHIT, SHIT, SHIT! We need to go now!" Aris says.

Sasha's breath comes in strange, rhythmic, heaving sounds.

The sound of metal clanging against taught leather alerts me to the legion of guards running down the corridor, storming the palace. Ryland prepares another ray, but before Ryland can release his rays, one of the guards yells out in desperation.

"The people are storming the gates," he says.

The message shocks Ryland, whose rays flicker out before they've fully formed. Sade braces herself while the king makes a last-minute attempt to form a ray. The efforts are only partially successful; the hypersonic shout I release throws them both backward, their bodies colliding to the ground as they hit the wall behind them.

Sade crumples to the floor while Ryland gets back on his feet immediately. His expression is vicious. His eyes light up with fire and fury. His rays burst out of him, exploding with rage and indignation. The Oguni and palace guards are prepared this time, having learned from the fate of those who've found themselves in the king's line of fire before. They plant their shields in front of them, walling themselves off from the king. The rays hit the shields, blackening them but not breaking them and sparing the bodies of those behind them. It travels all along the line, meeting none of its intended targets.

As the ray passes, the guards and the Oguni spring back up, sparring once more. Aris uses the opportunity to hoist Sasha onto his shoulder. He runs down the corridor and out of Ryland's path.

"They've stormed the gates, my king," a guard yells again, hoping to cut through the chaos and the rage and reach the king.

Ryland pauses briefly, considering the statement. He briefly looks at Sade, who is slowly rising to her feet by his side.

"Release the titans," he commands.

Half of the guards begin running out of the corridor, almost in unison. Some look backward as they run, expecting a solar beam to sear the skin off their backs, but the beam never comes.

"We can't let them be released," Iyanu shouts.

"But Ryland!" I yell back.

"The people!" Iyanu yells back.

Iyanu pushes towards the running crowd, reaching out and dragging me in the same direction. The Oguni follow the guards, striking down whoever they can and lunging forward to reach those who've run further ahead. The guards must be stopped! I prepare a hypersonic wave but shut my mouth at the last moment. It's impossible to hit the guards without hitting the Oguni directly behind them as well.

Aris and Sasha come into view as we continue running. An Oguni fighter throws three knives at the back of a guard whose sword is drawn as he prepares to strike them. Aris sets Sasha off his shoulder, leaning her against the wall, and draws his sword in anticipation. Most of the other guards do not engage, and the Oguni immediately fight those who look in his vicinity. They rush past Aris and Sasha, determined to get to wherever they're going.

The guards slow down, turning a sharp corner into a corridor with no exit. One guard rushes towards the small window on the wall, and the other guards flank him as he reaches through the small opening with a knife in tow. He cuts at something and then quickly removes his hand. When he looks back at us, the blood has drained from his ghastly, angular face.

"Rah help us," he says.

The guards turn back toward us. They are trapped between us and the wall. The Oguni raise their swords, but a chill runs down my spine as a guard becomes hysterical.

"Advance," he says, frothing at the mouth. "We can't be here for what comes next!" The guards raise their shields and shove past the Oguni, rushing to get out of the battle instead of facing the Oguni head-on.

"Run!" I scream to the Oguni, who stand still with confusion before breaking into a sprint behind the guards.

My chest tightens as we turn the corridors so quickly that my shin scrapes the sharp edge of a corridor wall, tearing flesh and leaving a dull ache in the bone. Sweat drips down the side of my forehead. It pools awkwardly in the leather suit, dampening my collarbones, waist, and the insides of my thighs.

The palace entrance doors come into view, and with the, Aris and Sasha. The voices of Endzoners rise from the other side of the door. They bang on the thick wooden entrance, hinges and screws screeching with each blow. The guards turn their heads and peer down the corridor with trepidation. They turn back towards the door, releasing the locks and allowing a sea of Endzoners to pour into the corridors. The Endzoners' bodies mesh against each other, red twilight beaming through the space between them. Guards and Oguni alike push through as the crowd punches and hacks at us.

"Get out of here! All of you!" Aris commands, with Sasha hanging limply on top of his shoulders. He's barely audible over the chaos as we fight to enter the open palace fields. Aris heaves, falling to his knees but managing to keep Sasha from rolling off his shoulders. He struggles to get back on his feet. I wrap my hand around his waist, helping to carry his weight and Sasha's as he lags. Iyanu hoists him on the other side, and little by little, we follow the Oguni and guards, who distance themselves from us with each step.

Suddenly, Endzoners race past us. They scream as they run away from the palace grounds. I can't help but turn to look, even though every bone in my body begs me not to. At the palace entrance, three titans stand, their coal-like skin sizzling and sending heat waves blaring into the air around them. One of them roars something made of pure anguish as another grabs an Endzone woman. The woman yells something almost as anguished as the titan who grabs her. Her body snaps from the force of its grasp, her upper half becoming dismembered from the lower. The contents of her guts fall onto the titan's feet, the meat sizzling and smoking as it cooks on the surface of its skin. Her mouth hangs open in a permanent expression of shock.

Sasha drags her feet on the ground, demanding we let her down.

"I can't make it past the wall," she says, shaking his head.

"Just go without me. Don't worry, I'll catch up," she says, smiling through gritted teeth.

Aris grunts as he hulks the bulk of Sasha's weight back up so she's again planted on her feet.

"Don't be stupid," he says, straining with each word.

The titans moan an agonizing thing, charging forth in no particular direction, destroying anything in their path. They grab their victims and tear them apart. But it's their actions after that haunt me. The confusion that settles in their eyes, how they seem to relish in their destruction while simultaneously being disgusted by it.

A beam of light tears through the field. A fast twist and scream from me dissipates what's remaining of the weakened rays before it does any harm.

Sasha falls to the ground again, staining her dark skin with dirt kicked up from the feet of the hundreds of people who've run this path just before. "Go," she commands, tears falling from her eyes. The titans have cleared two-thirds of the distance between us and them, leaving a trail of dismembered corpses in their wake. Their faces come into sharp focus.

"Lazarus," Iyanu says, peering at the titan closest to us.

The lanky frame, the sunken cheeks, and the way his jaw jaunts out a little too sharply. I wipe the stinging in my eye with the back of my hand.

"Lazarus," I reply.

He locks eyes with us, searching for something in ours, before releasing a thunderous scream. He thrusts his lanky frame forward but moves no faster than walking speed. With what the titans lack in speed, they make up for it with strength and the sheer terror of their presence. As Lazarus approaches, Aris tries unsuccessfully to haul Sasha back up, but she stays planted on the ground, kicking and fighting whenever he tries to grab her.

"Sasha!" I scream. "We're not leaving you! Get up. We don't have the time for this!"

Another solar beam pierces the air, weakened significantly by the distance it takes to get to us. I let out a gentle wave, dissipating it with little energy. The beam strikes all three titans. None are affected by it. They don't even seem to register the scalding rays that sear the flesh of the corpse lying beside them.

My eyes dart to the sky, suddenly aware of the darkened sky. Lazarus halts his approach, and the other two titans stop abruptly. We all feel the shift in the air as the black moon completely overtakes the sun. The Waning is here.

My head snaps to Sarran. The red halo of sunlight bounces off its shiny black surface. The sea glows an ethereal hue. The mist rising from its waters promises to transport all those who enter into another realm. I look towards Iyanu, who's just as mesmerized as I am. My legs snap into place. At the palace doors, a deluge of volunteered women come running out into the field. Horrified, the first of them come to a screeching halt, some falling over as the women behind them collide with them. One of them is snatched by a titan. The rest rush towards the waters. The first of the pack dives into its depths, their bodies disappearing underneath the cool black expanse.

I look down at Sasha. "I'm sorry," I say. She nods in response.

Iyanu and I dart across the field, away from the titans and towards Sarran. Lazarus follows sluggishly, unable to move his new hulking form efficiently.

Chapter 29

The muddied sand bordering Sarran is thick and soft from the water of the high tide. My feet sink into the grainy coolness with each heavy step I take. The mist envelops me before the water does as I mindlessly push forward into the depths. Lazarus continues his pursuit, unrelenting as he walks towards the waters. His feet steam with each step, hissing and popping at the contact. By the time he's ankle deep, the steam rising from his skin has enveloped his hulking form, rendering him invisible and immobile.

The cool water caresses my skin, beckoning me to go deeper. I oblige, allowing myself to wallow forward until I'm neck deep in the water and bobbing up and down uncontrollably with every passing wave. A woman screeches too close to me. The sound is cut short by someone or something.

"Iyanu," I call out, to no response.

The water ripples with the movement of something large and powerful beneath its surface.

"Iyanu," I call out again, to no response.

The screams of two other women rattle the air, and before long, there's a chorus of them, one after the other. My ears become numb to them, and my mind and body are soothed by the calming waters. I tread deeper until my entire body is immersed, and I go deeper still until my lungs burn with the pressure of holding my breath.

A thick, bulky organ wraps itself around my ankle, crawling up and spiraling around my shins before anchoring itself at my thighs. I kick frantically, using my other leg to push the thing off as I paddle my hands furiously, trying to stay above the water. The thing wrapped around my leg only squeezes more tightly. It pulls me down into the water with such ferocity that water rushes into my nose, burning the back of my brain. I let out a blood-curdling scream, but no one hears me in the depths of the lake. The water rushes into my throat, forcing me to close my mouth. My ears ring, a sharp, pulsating pitch that shoots from one side of my brain to the other. The water burns hotter than any fire I've known. I let out another scream, desperate to set myself free, but the water just ripples around me, absorbing the bulk of the energy as the creature continues dragging me into the depths.

The edge of my vision starts to darken, but I will the light back in. I can't die like this.

My eyes flicker open as I dig into the creases of my leather suit. I pull a dagger out of my waist belt and slice blindly at my left thigh. Pain shoots through me with each cut, but I feel the blade cut through slick, tough flesh, completely unlike my own. A section of the creature's lengthy arm slides off the rest of its body, giving my upper thigh some freedom but leaving my lower leg entrenched in its grip. The creature hisses. I shouldn't be able to hear it this far down under, but the noise feels like it's coming from the inside of my skull. I slice and hack and repeat even as my chest feels like it's collapsing and the narrow disc in my vision has faded to blackness once more.

The thing retreats, leaving me floating in the water.

I kick one leg out, hoping to get close enough to the shoreline, praying that one of the Oguni will be there to rescue me, but the creature returns, wrapping itself around my leg and once again trapping me in its hold. It inches upwards little by little until it's wrapped itself around my waist, stomach, and upper chest. Its arm reaches upwards probingly. I open my mouth, trying to reach for Adara's essence once more, but my body is so weak. It's all I can do to pry my jaws away from each other. My mouth hangs slack, unable to produce the energy required to conjure a scream. The creature reaches its arm upwards, jamming the organ into my mouth. The lower section of my jaw pops out of place, but I feel no pain.

My vision turns in on itself until I'm watching myself floating in a sea of red with my arms bound tightly at my sides by a creature I cannot see. My hair floats around me, each loc turning and twisting according to its own will. My eyes are large; they sit heavily in their sockets, sunken with the weight of death. Faint trails of bright red blood pouring out of the cuts in my thighs and stomach are barely visible in the crimson waters.

This is it, isn't it? In the end, all I did was for nothing. There is no rain. The Oguni have no upper hand against the king. The nobility and the monarchy are stronger than ever, and they can add immortality and an army of titans to their many advantages. Maybe Iyanu is dead too. And what will happen to Sade? Sasha, Bear, Aris, everyone.

If I could go back, I'd hug Iyanu one more time. I'd tell Bear that I was sorry. That he shouldn't believe in me that much. That I'd only disappoint him in the end. Aris will never know that nothing he's ever done and nothing that's ever been done to him could ever make him lesser in my eyes. I didn't try hard enough to pull him aside and demand he hear me while I was alive.

And now those words will never be spoken. I think back to my father, whose only goal was to be respected. For people to look at him like he was the most important person in any room he walked into. I think he loved me, or maybe he didn't, or maybe he loved me just somewhat but not entirely, and certainly not how someone should be loved.

My spirit becomes red hot and scorching as it jets out of the waters. It speeds through the land, watching as the Oguni and Endzoners continue their fight against the nobility and palace guards. It watches as a Midzone family sits in their small parlor, enjoying a glass of water, playing chalo on a small stone board with small rocks for their pieces. They are indifferent to the plight of both Endzoners and nobles. It rushes through the Endzone where only a few Endzoners roam the barren grounds, and rushes past that until there are no human beings and no signs of life anywhere.

The dream visits me beyond my final moments. But instead of lying in an infinite field of tall, thin plants watching as giant animals roam and eat, I am the sky, light and beautiful. Unable to go this way or that way. Yielding as a cloud floats over me, underneath, through me with no will, desire, or mechanism to hold onto it.

And then I am the cloud, soft and mobile. Yielding to the movements of the wind around me, blowing me in this direction and then the next. I am just a singular speck of dust floating in the air before I'm the water that condenses over it. A drop of rain falling from the sky, falling according to the laws of the universe. The drops around me do the same, falling fast and sweetly. When I look around me, all I see are raindrops. Perfectly formed, perfectly sectioned, and perfectly perfect still from my vantage point even as we barrel towards the ground.

A blade plant springs backward as I strike its surface. It bends slightly and stays bent as the other raindrops do the same. In an instant, I am the grass itself, and then I am the earth from which it grows, but I remember the time when I was the rain, when I was the cloud, and when I was the sky. There is no desire to do, only the desire to be here in this moment, exactly as I am. It could have been a century I spent in that state, just as easily as it could have been a fraction of a second. Time has no meaning here. The illusion of it having faded death's door. Reality cradles me in its arms as my spirit rocks in and out, animating, experiencing, and then leaving the things of the other world.

The dream world fades, my spirit sinks out of the other dimension where rain falls indiscriminately, and animals roam the land freely and into the world I know, encompassing it in its entirety. There is a chasm in this world. A deep, nasty cut that oozes darkness. If I had eyes, I might cry at the severity of it, but I have no mouth, and no eyes and only the ability to be. So, I am the heat of the desert, the hunger in my people's stomachs, the pain of the death of a child, the greed in the hearts of the nobles, the fear of the end of the world, and the hope that it will continue anew.

Slowly, tentatively, my spirit separates itself from everything there is. It pulls itself out of the air, the rocks, the sky, and the water. Approaching my body until it's close enough to rejoin it. My spirit slams into my flesh, leaving me heaving in the flesh I've known all my life, but that, for just one second, feels like an ill-fitting meat suit meant for someone else. My body convulses with the newfound life it's been given. My jaw remains propped open by the arm of the creature. I peer at it curiously now, wondering why I haven't been able to see it before. The creature is much larger than I ever imagined. It's a hideous thing, long and bulbous, with a large head and no body to speak of. Its many arms jut out all across the waters, only one of which is wrapped around my body. Its skin is soft and slick, almost entirely transparent. It gives off a pulsating glow in the water—a dusty red, illuminating the deep, dark red of the waters at these depths. I remember Bella's words, *they could not gather the entirety of a Goddess into them, so instead, they cast the rest of her essence into the sea.*

I can breathe again. I take three greedy giant breaths before realizing it's unnecessary. No water rushes through my enclosed mouth, and though I'd never imagine that there was any air down here, my lungs manage to pull some in nonetheless. I begin to kick gently, trying to swim towards the surface of the water. The creature spins me around so my head is where my feet once were. It swivels its many limbs to propel us forward. As we move, the water gets lighter and lighter until, finally, we're at its surface, and the creature releases its hold on me.

Visions of Iyanu swimming in the crimson lake visit me. Her arms pump furiously, heading towards the island. Then it's Sade, whose form emerges, wet, and disheveled—her sturdy frame rocked by the terror that lies beneath the water's surface. I push my body through the water once more, marveling at the strength of my body as it glides effortlessly along the surface. The gashes on my thighs have closed themselves, and my lungs and throat no longer burn with pain.

My mind clears, and my senses sharpen the closer I get to Iyanu, Sade, and the island at the center of Lake Sarran. Sade gets there first. I feel it when her bare feet plant themselves into the soft ground. Her naked body emerges from the water, triumphantly reinvigorated by the overflow of Adara's essence bound within her.

It's that very same essence that sees me racing through the waters, shooting to Iyanu's side, and arriving at the edge of the island right as she does. The veins in her eyes look unnatural, like intensely blue trees rooting themselves on the surface of her eyeball. Her dark leather suit remains pristine, wet but without blemishes, gashes, or debris. She's beautiful in the blood-tinged sunlight.

As I plant one foot in front of the other, the ground mends to the shape of my foot, the sheer power of each step forcing the soil to either side. We feel the two others Adara has chosen on the island, too. We feel their joy, confusion, and power as it radiates from them and outward into the world. We feel it as Sade brings one hand up to hug one of the girls and drives the blade of a small knife right into her back, in the tender place between two rib cages where her heart resides. The woman is shocked. She coughs twice, blood spurting from her throat each time, warm and wet as it splatters on Sade's cheek. The woman crumples to the ground, all the essence she held shooting out of her and slamming into us with such force that we stumble on our feet.

Now, we hold more power than any human should be capable of. The air ripples with each breath we take, and the trees shiver from afar and tremble when we're near.

We feel it as Sade reaches through the woman's sternum, cracking the bones in her ribs and pulling her heart out of her chest. She takes her knife, eating just a bit of the flesh. The other woman is shocked at such cruelty. My heart tightens, and my throat closes in response to her fear. Iyanu looks at me wordlessly. She sprints towards Sade and the other woman, while I follow closely behind her. One gait is the equivalent of ten, and we reach Sade and the other woman, traveling half the length of the small island almost instantaneously. We're too late. Sade ends the second woman's life as easily as she ended the first.

"You're alive," Sade says.

A royal vessel emerges from Sarran's mists as Ryland and his crew creep towards us. Sade looks nervously at the boat rocking perilously on the water. Ryland has come to claim his prize. He's come so a newly empowered Sade can transform him into something more.

Ryland's eyes lock with mine. For the first time ever, I believe I see fear in his eyes. I look at Sade and Iyanu and immediately understand why. The air around us hums with light and power. Ryland readies his beam and releases it. Its light slices through the air and leaves a trail before slamming into my torso. The impact feels like a pinch. I take two steps forward to see the man better, and he takes two steps backward in retreat, as if I were right there on the boat with him.

Nakaluna, I call to the creature that resides in the deep, the final manifestation of Adara's essence on earth, the creature that holds the rest of her spirit.

"Don't," Sade cautions, but what's done is done.

Nakaluna plunges one strong arm straight through the bottom of Ryland's boat, severing the vessel into two.

"Stop!" Sade commands. My shoulder stings as Sade battles to sever my arm from my body, dislocating it by shearing the blood in my shoulder joint.

Ryland shoots beam after beam into the water, severing the creature's arm but destroying what's left of the vessel as well. Another arm shoots out of the water and ensnares Ryland as he summons another beam. The beam dissipates as it hits the water, the surface of which boils from the heat. But Nakaluna is relentless, throwing arm after arm at Ryland until the king is completely encased. She drags him with her to the bottom of the lake.

"Ryland!" Sade yells. "Meera!" Her face contorts in agony, and her shoulders heave.

"We won!" I shout. "Ryland is dead! There is no more monarchy. The nobles have been ousted. This is the end of Endzone suffering! We won," I shout.

I stand before her as she raises her hands, standing taller and straighter to look me in the eyes. She has defiance written all over her.

I grab the hand that now hangs at her side, squeezing it gently, rubbing my fingers over hers before letting go. I wrap my arms around her neck, drawing her closer to me, nestling the crook of her neck with my face. Sade's hands rise tentatively, embracing the air around me before allowing her hands nearer, pressing her body to mine.

"I needed him, Meera," Sade says, pausing at each word to rein back her tears and steady her voice.

I shake my head, letting my nose graze her shoulder with each movement back and forth. I listen deeply. The plants rustle in the wind. The water crashes gently into the steep, rocky shore of the island. Then I hear a heartbeat, small and faint, emanating not from mine nor Sade's chest but from her lower belly.

"You're," I begin. A thin blade, cold as ice, plunges into the space between my two ribs, puncturing my left lung. I open my mouth to speak, but blood is what pours from my throat.

Iyanu screams in the distance, and the sound rings in my brain.

"Pregnant," I finish.

Sade pulls the dagger out of my back, her tongue rolling over the flat edge of the bloodied blade. Sade drags my limp form towards the edge of the cliff, throwing me over, not taking her eyes off mine as I fall back down into Sarran.

My body hits the cool waters, the sea parting to cushion my fall, enveloping me in its healing waters. Iyanu throws the bodies of the two women off the cliff before jumping in after me. Moments later, she's swimming by my side. She grabs my shoulder with one arm and hooks her other arm around one of the women. I do the same with the other. Iyanu pulls us all towards the shore with ease, gliding across the waters like a bird gliding through the air.

The flesh of my back and my lungs piece together little by little, melding, and bringing me back towards wholeness. By the time we reach shore, the black moon has faded completely, leaving a bright, burning sun behind. Iyanu drags my body, along with the two corpses, out of the water and onto the shore.

I use my hand to shade my eyes from the brightness of the sunlight. A dark figure hovers over me.

"Take her inside," Bear says.

A man lifts me onto his shoulders and walks me towards an estate made of purple and gold chiseled stone. Bear follows closely behind us—the Oguni open carved palm doors to reveal an estate overrun with Oguni. The people clear a path for me, and the man drops me onto a cushion in the middle of the parlor.

"The Tanaka estates all the way around to the Mildred estates," Bear says. "The entirety of the eastern shore is ours."

"Aris, Sasha, Rin," I ask.

"Aris and Sasha are stationed on the Horus estates. Rin is… resting."

"The king is de—"

A Voice that is not a voice interrupts my sentence midway.

I feel the entirety of Ile-Oja as every person, every animal, and everything animated by the spirit of the gods, shivers with the knowledge of what this means.

Sade's Voice thunders in my head.

"The king is dead," she says. "His son, Imoleaye, will succeed him on his throne. Ryland's line continues, and Rah's blessings continue with it. You will bow to your queen if you hope to be saved."

"Where is Rin!" I shout.

Bear rakes one shaky hand through his peppered hair. "The baby didn't make it," he says. "She's upstairs. She hasn't come out of her room since we got here."

Sade's Voice rings once again. "Today, a band of traitors dared threaten the throne. I say to them, know that this is only the beginning," she says. "The end will see you all destroyed."

Chapter 30

Sade, the girl who became my best friend on the Fujisawa estates. The girl who used to sit down, braiding Iyanu's hair for long hours. The girl I thought was quick to anger but fiercely loyal. The girl I called my little sister. The sweetness of victory against Ryland turns sour. Just an hour ago, Ryland met his end. But now, I wonder if that end was just the beginning of something horrific.

"How could this happen?" Bear asks. He sits on a violet velvet cushion in the middle of the parlor, stroking his ginger-gray beard as he speaks. He leans awkwardly, his body sinking into the cushions just slightly. I know he's never experienced anything like this, but he makes a point of not fawning over the luxury afforded by even a medium-sized estate.

"There's a prophecy," I answer.

Bella's words play over in my head. *To bring Adara back into the world, one must simultaneously become one with her and the entire Earth. It is said that the one who holds the key to achieving this is actually three. The creator, the destroyer, and the balance.*

Most women will only survive the Waning once, if they survive at all. *But the creator, the destroyer, and the balance cannot be killed by those depths.*

"There's a prophecy about the three who hold the key to bringing rainfall. The creator, the destroyer, and the balance. The Waning can't kill them."

Bear nods. Iyanu does the same, both seemingly understanding the implications of what that means.

"Was there any mention of how?" Bear asks.

"No," I answer. "But Adara did mention something about bringing the people closer to her."

Bear raises an eyebrow but doesn't reply. The question of which of us is which remains unasked and unanswered. But the important bit is obvious. Sade's walking down a path of destruction.

"But she's speaking with Rah's Voice," Bear says.

Iyanu speaks. "It's the child inside of her. It's inherited Rah's gifts, and now, Sade's exploiting that."

A shiver runs through me. Titans can only be created by extracting Adara's essence and filling the vessel with Rah's light. With the child inside of her, could Sade do both all on her own?

The door to the parlor swings open, revealing two Oguni men and a man with bright red hair being dragged between them. When he raises his hung head, it's none other than ' smirking a cocky smile as he bleeds through the cuts in his black leather uniform. The men haul Nicholas forward and force him into a kneeling position in front of Bear and me. Nicholas uses the opportunity to spit near my feet, looking me in the eyes and delivering a bloody smile as he does so. The Oguni to his left slams a knee into his back and seems ready to do so a second time, but Bear raises his arm in time to stop the action.

Nicholas laughs. "You," he says, shaking his head. "Well..." He shrugs. "How unsurprising. Always the feeble-minded one weren't you," he says, pointing his chin towards Bear.

A small group of Oguni gather, intrigued by the commotion coming from the parlor. Some of them have raided the closets of the nobles who once lived in this estate while others still wear tattered clothing. Half of them glance at Bear, while the other half look towards me expectantly.

"Don't say anything you'll regret," I caution Nicholas.

"Or what?" Nicholas smirks. "Why don't you back off and let the men talk?" Nicholas points his chin towards Bear.

The Oguni with their attention on me turn towards Bear, waiting for his response. I breathe out a sigh, calming the anger that Nicholas's words stir in me. If he feels that way, it's only because I've given him reason to. I deserve that statement. Until now, it's been true.

"Go ahead," he says. "Our savior has already come," he finishes, referencing Sade or maybe her child.

"A puppet?" I ask. "Did you know, Nicholas, that we are made of, essentially, entirely water. It's everywhere, even in the places you least expect it."

Nicholas gives me another bloody smile, as if to say *do your worst*.

"Like for example," I continue, "there's just a little bit of water pooled on the inside of each of our ears." I reach for Adara's essence with softness and draw it out of me gently, melodically.

"It shakes just a bit when there's sound. It helps us hear. But, did you know that if I speak in just the right tone, the water there will hum? And that hum vibrates at just the right frequency to make your mind susceptible to my suggestions."

Nicholas's face goes blank as I speak.

"Do it," I command.

He reaches for the dagger at the side of the man who pulled him in, plunging it straight through the area where his throat meets his chest. A moment of lucidity flashes before Nicholas's eyes as my hold on him breaks. Fitting that my time with Nicholas should end just the way it started, with a blade to the throat.

Bear barely blinks, and Iyanu keeps her gaze focused on anything but the man whose blood is soiling the thick carpeting on the parlor floor. A few of the Oguni frown, and some who were openly staring just a minute ago can no longer meet my gaze. The Oguni are not averse to death, but every death must serve a purpose. They'll ask themselves if I needed to kill Nicholas. But it's because I did that they'll never question me or my power again.

"Sade will stop at nothing to get what she wants," I say, looking pointedly at Nicholas's still body on the floor. "We must be prepared to do whatever it takes to stop her."

The Oguni murmur in what I hope is agreement.

"With Ryland's child inside her, Sade is more powerful than ever. This is not the time to be complacent. Defeating Ryland and dismantling half the nobility—that was only the beginning. I know Sade better than anyone else, and Iyanu and I are the only ones who can stop her. But we can't do it alone. Titanhood isn't a blessing, it's a monstrosity. When the time comes, promise that you will stand by us."

Bear speaks up. "We trust you," he says, and the others grunt in agreement. I'm only half-pleased. I wish he said nothing at all and let the people speak for themselves.

I rise from my seat, taking Iyanu with me as I make my way towards the winding staircase that leads to the room Rin rests in. She lies there, body bare and still on the silky purple sheets. The last time I saw her, Rin did nothing but scream, but now, she's eerily silent. Her stomach still bulges from the child she grew inside it. A child she had to bury before it took its first breath. Iyanu sits beside her, stroking her cheek gently. When I reach out to hold Rin's hand, I brace myself in anticipation of the pain I know is coming. What I find is even more terrifying.

It is not a pain so deep that it knocks me off the bed or a chaos so debilitating that it scrambles my own mind. Rather, it's a vast coldness. It's an emptiness that makes me sweat and hold on tighter, even when every nerve in my body begs me to let go. And, I will not let go. I welcome the coolness. From here on out, I face every battle, even this one, head on. I know now that when Sade aligned herself with Ryland, she knew something that I didn't. Power isn't given, it's taken. And I intend on taking every last bit she's gathered for herself. That is the only way to right what's wrong with this world.

Epilogue

I yanu sits in the center of the parlor with me and the rest of the Oguni circling her. The air hums with energy, and trepidation builds. Iyanu has been having episodes. She's been speaking the words of the Galed of decades or even centuries past. Her eyes glow with the presence of something otherworldly. Her curls lift, though the air is stagnant. She throws her head backwards and starts speaking, her voice resonating throughout the space.

"In the beginning, there was not nothing but *something*. More precisely, there was *one* thing, and that one thing was Adara. She was the dark, cold, and expansive *one*. But the Goddess grew bored of with perfection of oneness. She contracted into a single point and burst forth into many things. All things were one with the *one,* some things were closer to the *one,* and some things were further, but the closest of all was the sun God, Rah, who was a shining light upon the universe.

Rah became preoccupied with the idea of separateness, even though he himself was a part of Adara. He devised a creation meant to exist outside of Adara's vastness and named them titans. The titans were clay vessels who were not empty of Adara's essences but deficient in it. They were filled with just a drop of the divine when they had the potential to hold a liter.

But like a ball rolls down a hill, Adara's essence expands to fill all voids, including the void contained within Rah's creations. The fuller vessels became known as humans. So, the coming of humans on this Earth was not a curse but an inevitability. It is simply the natural order of things."

Iyanu collapses as the spirit leaves her.

"That one was Bella," she says, heaving.

About the Author

Wunmi Aramiji is a scientist, artist and storyteller exploring the ways harmony emerges from, exists beside, and thrives within chaos. As both a scientist and an artist, Wunmi is driven by the desire to make sense (and nonsense) of the human experience. She is particularly passionate about centering the experiences of those on the fringes of society and sees community building and caretaking as essential to holistic being.

After graduating with a BS in Chemistry and a MS in Materials Science from Stanford, Wunmi spent almost two years as a research scientist studying works of art at the Metropolitan Museum of Art. During that time, she wrote her debut novel, *The Waning.* When she's not writing, Wunmi spends her time doing ceramics, pole dancing, and embroidering random articles of clothing for her friends.